"WAKE UP, SLEEPING BEAUTY."

Dimly, Melissa heard the words and struggled up through the layers of sleep. She had been dreaming of Dominic, and when she opened her eyes and saw his face just above hers, it almost seemed like part of her dream.

Dominic brought his mouth to hers.

Sweet fire exploded in Melissa's body at the touch of his hungry lips, and with no will of her own her arms went around his neck. His kiss deepened and Melissa had no thought to deny him . . . Even when his hands deftly undid her gown and she felt it slip down around her waist, she was unable to believe that this was anything but a dream. And since it was a dream . . . her questing fingers undid his shirt, touching his bare skin. It was exciting to feel the leap his heart gave as her hands wandered over him . . . to hear his low growl of delight . . .

"Don't!" he got out with effort. "Don't tease me—I am too ready for you as it is . . ."

Avon Books are available at special quantity discounts for bulk purchases for sales promotions, premiums, fund raising or educational use. Special books, or book excerpts, can also be created to fit specific needs.

For details write or telephone the office of the Director of Special Markets, Avon Books, Dept. FP, 105 Madison Avenue, New York, New York 10016, 212-481-5653.

Midnight Masquerade

Shirlee Busbee

AVON BOOKS  NEW YORK

AVON BOOKS
A division of
The Hearst Corporation
105 Madison Avenue
New York, New York 10016

Copyright © 1988 by Shirlee Busbee
Published by arrangement with the author
Library of Congress Catalog Card Number: 88-91494
ISBN: 0-380-75210-7

First Avon Books Printing: August 1988

AVON TRADEMARK REG. U.S. PAT. OFF. AND IN OTHER COUNTRIES, MARCA REGISTRADA, HECHO EN U.S.A.

Printed in the U.S.A.

K-R 10 9 8 7 6 5 4 3 2 1

For some of the sunshine in my life . . .

To GAYLA HAWKINS, for being my friend as well as my sister and for all the pleasure and laughter we share, for all the fun we've had and the few tears we've shed, but mostly for being the delight to me that you are.

To PETER HAWKINS, my *very* favorite brother-in-law, for having the excellent taste to have married my sister and for possessing the great wisdom *not* to take Howard seriously!

And, of course, without a doubt the most important person in my life, to HOWARD.

Part One

Masquerade

We cannot kindle when we will
The fire that in the heart resides.

Morality, Stanza I
—Matthew Arnold

Chapter One

THE WORN and shabby library at Willowglen was usually a place of refuge for Melissa Seymour, but not on this particular sunny morning in the spring of 1814. Instead of finding the solace and quiet that she so desperately needed before facing her irate uncle, she found herself right in the middle of just the sort of unpleasant scene she had hoped to avoid. But then she should have known that her uncle wouldn't let her escape so easily—when Josh Manchester made up his mind to say something, it was said!

Shooting him a quick glance as he stood across the room from her, his massively built body stiff with disapproval, his flushed features above the crisp white cravat clearly revealing his anger, she sighed. She liked Uncle Josh! She and her younger brother, Zachary, had always looked forward to Josh's visits and they both adored his wife, Aunt Sally, their dead father's only sister, but of late . . .

"Well, Lissa?" Josh demanded sternly. "What is this that I hear?" And not expecting or waiting for an answer, he plunged on. "You may imagine my disbelief this morning when one of my oldest and dearest friends—one of the richest and most respected planters in all of upper Louisiana—informed me that you had turned down his son, John." Frustration and honest bewilderment flickered in Josh's blue eyes, and in a voice mixed with resignation and vexation, he questioned, "I assume that there is some mistake? That you have not again whistled *another* excellent match down the wind?"

The subject of Melissa's marriage, or rather *lack* of marriage, was an old one. Once Josh had treated it lightly,

teasing her unmercifully, yet kindly about it. But not anymore, Melissa thought unhappily.

Even under the best of circumstances Josh would have
found her stubborn refusal to marry incomprehensible—
after all, wasn't marriage what all respectable women
craved? Wasn't it practically the only reason for their existence—that and bearing children and pleasing their husbands? Hadn't his own three daughters yearned for the day
they would marry? And hadn't they all dutifully and good-
naturedly married the men their indulgent father had
selected for them? So why wouldn't this beautiful and gay-
spirited niece of his do the same? Especially now, when
it would benefit them all. . . .

Melissa sighed again, wishing not for the first time that
her grandfather had not left that wretched, wretched trust
tied up in such a ridiculous manner. Or, she amended
fairly, if only this stupid war with England hadn't affected
Josh's investments in shipping so badly.

Mr. Madison's War, as the war between England and
the United States which had begun in 1812 was jeeringly
called, had by its very nature restricted traffic between the
two countries. Ostensibly the war was being fought over
the impressment of United States' seamen by the British
Navy, but the conquest of Canada by those Americans
eager for expansion had been a powerful motivator of the
war. The war was in its second year and was no more
popular now than it had been at its inception—the north-
eastern states flatly refusing to commit their militias, some
New Englanders openly trading with the British in Canada. There had been few victories to celebrate, and those
had been mainly at sea. Thomas Jefferson's comment that
the American attempt to seize British North America was
"a mere matter of marching" was being proved false time
and time again.

But Melissa really didn't waste much time thinking
about the folly of the War of 1812. There were more
pressing matters to occupy her, and at the moment it was
the unpleasant fact that her grandfather had seen fit, heaven
knew why, to tie up Sally's inheritance with her own and
Zachary's share of the trust.

When Melissa's grandfather, the late and much lamented Jeffery Seymour, had died some fifteen years ago, the handsome fortune he had placed in trust for Sally, Melissa and Zachary hadn't mattered very much to any of his heirs. Melissa and Zachary had been children, and Sally had been happily married to wealthy Josh Manchester, none of them had had any need *then* of the great sum of money that Jeffery had so prudently put aside for their futures.

But that had been fifteen years ago, and though Sally was still happily married to Josh, much had changed since that time, Melissa thought grimly. She was twenty-two years old now, and Zachary at nineteen was definitely no longer a child, although sometimes, his sister mused fondly, when his temper got away from him, he could indulge in what came perilously close to being a tantrum. But the greatest change of fortunes had occurred to Willowglen, the huge, lush plantation situated on a bluff above the Mississippi River near the small town of Baton Rouge in upper Louisiana and which had been settled by Melissa's great-grandfather in 1763.

Who could have guessed that her own dearly beloved father, Hugh, would prove to be such an imprudent, foolish wastrel? Melissa reflected sadly. So imprudent, in fact, that upon his death some eighteen months ago, instead of the flourishing, prosperous lands he had inherited from *his* father, Hugh's two children had found themselves the heirs of a rundown plantation piled with debts. Or who would ever have dreamed that staid and careful Josh would make some unwise business decisions of his own and that those, coupled with two years of bad crops, would put the Manchesters in a position where the money from the trust would suddenly look very attractive? *Too* attractive, as far as Melissa was concerned.

It wasn't, she admitted to herself, that she wouldn't have simply crowed with delight to have the trust ended; it was merely that she wasn't willing to pay the price. And, she reminded herself staunchly, the state of the Manchester finances was not *her* fault, nor did their temporary reverses in any way resemble the near ruin that faced her and Zachary. While Aunt Sally bemoaned the fact that the always elegant sitting room at the Manchester plantation, Oak

Hollow, could not be completely renovated before the November wedding of Daniel, the youngest son, Melissa and Zachary had to worry about making certain that the few faithful retainers they possessed had food and shelter. They continually feared that their animals would go hungry if the pitifully small amount of ground they had planted with crops did not survive. As for any luxury . . . Melissa smiled wryly. She and Zack counted themselves fortunate that they still had a home to call their own. Much of Hugh's mountain of debts had been settled, but the last few *un*paid creditors were growing weary with Melissa's sincere but woefully inadequate attempts to pay them.

She glanced down at the old faded gown she was wearing and, thinking of the smuggled trunk filled with silks and laces that Aunt Sally had received at great cost from New Orleans last month, she found it very hard indeed to believe that the Manchesters were in dire straits. It would do Aunt Sally good, she thought dryly, to practice a *little* economy.

As she continued to remain silent, Josh frowned and, his pleasant features harsh, he snapped, "Have you nothing to say? Don't you think that you owe me an explanation?"

An angry sparkle lit her golden-brown eyes, and Melissa bit back a furious retort before saying in a tight voice, "We have discussed the topic often enough, Uncle Josh, and I have told you time and time again—*I do not wish to marry!*" Hands clenched at her sides, she added sharply, "And certainly not merely to accommodate you and Aunt Sally!"

Josh had the grace to flush. He was not normally an unreasonable man, and "tyrant" was not a word generally applied to jovial Josh Manchester, but . . . He swallowed uncomfortably, not liking his position at all. He loved his niece, and nothing would have given him more pleasure than to forgo these increasingly acrimonious exchanges with Melissa. But all his life he had possessed money to spare, money he had lavished on his adoring wife and children, and now, at nearly sixty years of age, for the first time in his pampered life, he suddenly found himself no longer in that position. It pained him deeply to deny his wife her new sitting room; it embarrassed him that he could not instantly buy his second son the long-legged hunter which that young man had been pining for, and it distressed him that he could no longer carelessly bestow expensive gifts upon his married daughters. All of this, however, could be resolved at one fell swoop . . . *if* Melissa would only marry!

Almost resentfully, he glared across the room at her. She was a fetching young woman, of that there was no doubt, with her long, tawny hair curling attractively around her slim shoulders and her striking topaz eyes glittering brightly from under thick lashes. Astonishing black, slimly arched eyebrows intensified the impact of those jeweled eyes, and with her elegantly straight little nose and generous, finely shaped mouth, it was no wonder that, despite a crumbling, debt-ridden plantation, she was much sought after by the sons of the wealthiest families in the neighborhood. Of course, Josh had to admit that the fortune that would be hers when she married was a compelling magnet. But even without her fortune she was undeniably lovely.

Tall and slim, Melissa moved with a natural lithe grace; and when she smiled, when those great eyes of hers danced with laughter and that deliciously kissable mouth curved in amusement, it was not surprising that many a male heart beat faster. Golden, gay and valiant, that described Melissa, and even Josh would be the first to admit that Melissa in a high-spirited, teasing mood was very nearly irresistible.

She was not, however, in a teasing mood at the moment, and the fierce look she bent upon Josh made him decidedly nervous. With his own placid daughters, he had always known what to expect and how to react, but with Melissa . . . He sighed heavily. It was all her father's fault, he decided blackly, and not for the first time. If Hugh had raised her properly after her mother's death when Melissa was ten, none of this would be happening right now. Melissa would have known what was expected of her and she would have behaved in a dutiful manner. If Hugh had not let her grow up undisciplined, like some wild gypsy wench . . . If Hugh had not taken such delight in his daughter's unconventional and wayward antics . . . If Hugh had curbed some of those high spirits and forward manners . . .

The list of faults to be laid at Hugh's door was endless, and Josh grew depressed. Whether he approved or not, Melissa was Melissa, and with a lowering feeling, he knew that it was too late to teach her to be a *proper* lady. But on one point he was adamant: she must be made to understand that it was her honorable duty to marry. That not only would he and Sally benefit from this act, but so would she and Zachary. Besides, he decided with an unusual spurt of malice, if she didn't marry soon, she would be labeled a spinster! All of *his* daughters had married before they reached twenty, and no *normal* female could possibly wish to remain unmarried at twenty-two!

Preparing to launch a new attack, Josh had just started to speak when suddenly the library door flew open with great force, slamming loudly against the wall. Spinning around in surprise, Josh felt his spirits sink when his gaze fell upon the young man who stood in the doorway glowering thunderously at him. Zachary!

The resemblance between brother and sister was obvious; except for the springy black hair on his head, Zachary's features were simply a very masculine version of Melissa's. At nineteen, he already looked a man, his shoulders broad, the bronzed forearms showing below the rolled-up sleeves of his white shirt well muscled; but the set of his hard jaw and the angry gleam in his golden-brown eyes made Josh groan inwardly. Zachary was obviously determined to rescue his sister from what he thought was further intimidation and browbeating.

There was something very raw and earthy about Zachary Seymour as he stood there in the doorway, his tall body poised for action. The rolled-up sleeves bespoke a man who worked, as did the tanned skin of his face, forearms and neck. His well-worn brown breeches clung to his muscular thighs like a second skin, and from the few pieces of straw and hay which persisted in clinging to his breeches and boots, it was apparent he had come directly from the stables.

Scowling darkly, his voice ringing with scorn, Zachary

snarled, "If you've come to berate Lissa for not marrying that jackanapes John Newcomb, I'll tell you fair, Uncle Josh, you can just take yourself to Bedlam! I'll not have you bullying my sister!"

Somewhat nettled by the unpleasant picture Zachary had conjured up by his words, Josh replied testily, "I have *never* bullied your sister!"

An imp of mischief in her eyes, Melissa murmured sweetly, "Nagged, perhaps, Uncle?"

Like a bull caught between two sleek leopards, Josh glared from one Seymour to the other. Huffily, he exclaimed, "I can see that there is no talking to either of you in this mood. I shall come back tomorrow, and we shall then see if we can discuss this like reasonable adults!"

Zachary gave a rude crack of laughter, and with regret and amusement warring in her breast, Melissa watched her uncle turn on his heel and stalk with offended dignity from the room. She detested these battles of will with her uncle, her genuine affection for him making it extremely difficult for her to continue to defy him. Especially when, in so many ways, what he wanted her to do was in her own best interest!

Flinging himself into a patched leather chair, one long leg swinging over the arm, Zachary muttered, "Why couldn't Grandfather have left Sally's money to her outright? Or better yet, at least have the blasted trust end when you were twenty-one?"

"Because," his doting sister said dryly, "he didn't want it dispersed until *you* are twenty-one!"

Zack shot her a teasing look. "Or until *you* marry, my dear."

Melissa pulled a face. "I know, and the devil of it is, if Josh hadn't had such a run of bad luck and Father hadn't been such an awful planter, it wouldn't have mattered if we waited until you were twenty-one."

They both looked bleak. Two years wasn't an enormous amount of time to wait for the money that would be theirs, but when one wondered daily how much longer there would be a roof over one's head, it suddenly became a *very* long time.

In a small voice, Melissa asked, "Do you think I ought to marry John Newcomb?"

"That cawker? Good Lord, no!" Zachary burst out. "If you don't wish to marry the fellow, I see no reason why you should . . . besides, I can't abide him—he's hamfisted at the reins!"

Melissa smiled slightly. Dear Zack! No matter what she did, he was always on her side. But sometimes she wondered if, deep in his heart, he didn't wish she *would* marry. Certainly, she thought dispiritedly, it would make life so much easier for all of them.

For just a moment she let her mind wander, thinking of all the things that could be accomplished with the money from the trust. Uncle Josh and Aunt Sally would no longer look so reproachfully at her. The remaining creditors could be paid and she and Zachary could go to sleep at night, knowing that Willowglen was safe. The servants could have decent food and clothing; repairs could be made to the house and outbuildings; the tattered interior of the house could be completely refurbished, and the stables . . .

She turned away from Zachary and glanced out the long window behind her. From here she could just barely glimpse the stables from among the massive spreading oak trees that dotted the large, ragged expanse of grass that lay between the main house and the stables area. If the trust were ended, new stables could be built, new paddocks erected, and Folly . . . The powerful bay stallion, Folly, would finally have the setting that Melissa and Zachary felt was his due. After all, wasn't Folly practically the only thing that stood between them and utter defeat? Hadn't the young stallion's impressive winnings at various sporting events in Virginia and Maryland the previous year kept Willowglen from being sold beneath the anvil? Just last month, hadn't he won them a large sum of money in New Orleans? And within the next few weeks weren't they once again traveling to Virginia, where they hoped Folly would win them even more money? Wasn't his incredible speed and spirit already causing comment and interest among the best breeders of horses in America?

A half-rueful, half-bitter smile curved Melissa's mouth

as she remembered that fateful trip to England which had seen Folly's conception. In the spring of 1809, against the advice of those wiser than he, Hugh had gone to England to purchase horses, taking six of his finest brood mares with him to be bred by a famous stallion. He had been pursuing his fanciful dream of recouping the family fortune—the fortune *he* had depleted—by raising and breeding a most superior line of racehorses at Willowglen. And of course, like most of Hugh's plans, it had gone awry.

The gaming hells of London had caught his lively attention and he had whiled away his time in England, losing what little capital he still possessed. When he returned to Louisiana, not only did he not have the select English brood mares he had intended to buy, but of his own mares taken there to be bred, only one remained, Melissa's mare, Moondust, who thankfully had been bred to the St. Leger winner of 1795, Hambletonian, a grandson of the revered Eclipse and one of the outstanding stallions of the day.

Melissa and Zachary had shared their father's impractical dream and had waited anxiously at Willowglen, eager to see the new stock, pleased to think that some of their very own mares would have been bred to one of the most renowned English Thoroughbreds. It had been a bitter blow to discover that all of their hopes were now tied up in the foal which grew within Moondust. Fortunately, almost from birth Folly had displayed the speed and stamina of his famous ancestors, and Hugh's dream had suddenly begun to seem not so impossible.

A shadow of regret crossed Melissa's expressive face and she sighed. Hearing that faint sound, Zachary asked softly, "What is it, Lissa? What makes you so unhappy? Surely not this latest dust up with Uncle Josh?"

Melissa pulled a face and swung around to look at him. "No, it's not Uncle Josh, although I don't like arguing with him. I was just thinking of Father and wishing that he could have lived to see Folly's successes. He would have been so elated to have backed a winner at last."

Far less sentimental than his sister, Zachary replied sardonically, "Just be thankful that he gave our pitifully few horses and cattle to you and that we didn't have to suffer the ignominy of watching our only real hope to salvage Willowglen auctioned off with everything else!''

Giving him a considering glance, Melissa asked, ''Does it bother you? Do you think that Folly and the others should have been yours along with the land?''

''Are you mad?'' Zachary demanded incredulously. ''If Hugh hadn't had that attorney draw up those papers leaving all the livestock to you, we wouldn't be sitting here right now. Making certain that the animals were your private property before he died was the only way he could ensure that they wouldn't get sold to cover his debts—and I am damned grateful for it!'' Zachary flashed her an endearingly lopsided smile. ''For once in his life, our father knew exactly what he was doing—Willowglen is my inheritance, and Folly and the other animals are yours—but he also knew that it wouldn't occur to either one of us *not* to share our fortunes—whatever they might be!''

When Melissa remained silent, Zachary's smile faded and, leaping to his feet, he crossed the room to stand in front of her. Grasping her slim shoulders in his strong hands, he gave her a little shake and muttered fiercely, ''Lissa! You can't believe that I begrudge you the damned horses and cattle! Haven't we always shared everything?'' As if suddenly struck by a thought, he asked huskily, ''Is that it? You don't want to share your inheritance with me anymore? You want to leave Willowglen?'' His mouth twisted. ''I would understand if you did! God knows that there's precious little here for you.''

Appalled that he should even think such a thing, Melissa paled and she hugged him impetuously. ''Oh, Zack, never that!'' she exclaimed vehemently. ''Don't say such things! We swore that together we would make Hugh's dream come true, and we *will!*''

Vastly comforted by his sister's words, Zachary relaxed and, pushing her away gently, smiled wryly. ''We will— *if* our creditors don't win in the end.''

Her chin rising purposefully, Melissa replied grimly, ''They won't! All but a very few have been paid, and of those who remain, I've put enough on their accounts to hold them for a while longer.''

''Including the Englishman?'' Zack asked dryly.

Melissa flushed and slowly shook her head. "No! You know we don't have that kind of money. We're fortunate that he has not pressed us. *Especially* since Hugh's note is so long overdue!"

In addition to Folly, there was one more legacy from that disastrous trip to England that Hugh had made—a voucher he had signed for gambling debts that was in excess of twenty-five thousand dollars! His children had not learned about this until several months after his death, and with all the other troubles that beset them, it had been a severe blow—Zachary taking it even harder than Melissa.

The fact that it was Melissa who was supporting him with her horse's earnings at race meets and that it was her frugal planning that was keeping Willowglen from the creditors was an extremely touchy point with Zachary. He hated it! Ashamed of himself for even bringing up the subject, he turned away from her. His young face tight with embarrassment and frustration, he said savagely, "If only there were some way of breaking that damned trust before you lose everything trying to save this blasted place for me!"

Well aware of his bruised pride—there was always a furious argument whenever she put what little extra money there was into small improvements to the plantation— Melissa hid a smile. Calmly she said, "Well, I suppose we could just let it be sold . . . which would really be a shame, considering that Willowglen would make a wonderful stud farm. Besides, I thought we were saving it for *us.*" Innocently she added, "Wasn't that the understanding? That we would use Folly's winnings to keep us going until the trust ended? That we are partners and that we *share* our few resources?"

Zachary gave a reluctant laugh. "Oh, Lissa! You always make it sound so sensible! As if someday I can repay you and that we really will succeed in making Willowglen profitable again."

"Do you doubt it?" Melissa asked softly. "Haven't we managed so far?"

"So we have," Zachary admitted a little shamefacedly. "It's just that I don't like to think of you forsaking your own future for me, or"—his face darkened—"think of you having to put up with Uncle Josh and Aunt Sally trying to marry you off to anything in breeches!''

Her eyes dancing with laughter, she replied, ''Not *any*-thing, Zack! The man they want me to marry must be a wealthy landowner, of the right background and family, someone *they* can be proud of.''

Suddenly curious, Zachary asked, ''Have you ever wanted to marry anyone? I mean, I can understand you turning down John Newcomb, but there are several other gentlemen in the neighborhood who I know wouldn't be averse to receiving a bit of encouragement from you.''

Melissa made an impatient sound. ''It's so hard to explain—I don't even understand it myself. I suppose it's just that I've never met anyone yet who makes me feel like Aunt Sally does about Uncle Josh. They *adore* each other! He would do anything for her and she would be willing to die for him! I want that sort of love, not some tepid emotion that wears itself out in a few months or years and leaves me married to a man who has a mistress tidily tucked away in town, while I content myself with bearing a child every year and exchanging pickling recipes with Aunt Sally!'' Suddenly embarrassed by the intensity of her words, Melissa flushed slightly and muttered, ''I know it all sounds rather silly to you, but you did ask!''

Zachary flung an affectionate arm around her shoulders and grinned down at her. ''Well, I just hope that when you do finally succumb, you have the good sense to fall in love with someone who will benefit us! A wealthy man would be very nice indeed!'' At the militant sparkle that sprang into Melissa's eyes and the expression of outrage that crossed her features, Zachary's grin widened. ''There, now! That took that unhappy look off your face! Come along, sweet sister, we have work to do, and if we don't want your growing bevy of rejected suitors mooning about the place, we're going to have to do something about your appearance—even I will agree that you're a tempting handful.''

Her spirits lightened by Zachary's teasing, Melissa left the room with him, a smile on her face. But later, as she groomed and brushed Folly's already satin coat, the events of the morning came back to devil her.

Laying her head against Folly's strong neck, her fingers idly playing with his luxurious black mane, she asked aloud, "Am I being a fool? Silly to yearn for a true and lasting love?"

Folly seemed to guess that she was troubled and he nickered softly, turning his elegant head to brush her shoulder. Melissa grinned at his actions, for a moment her self-searching thoughts vanishing.

She stepped back from the stallion, admiring his tall, powerful body. He was a beautiful animal, from the well-shaped, intelligent head to the long, almost delicate legs. Bay in color, his coat shone like polished mahogany, the black legs, mane and tail contrasting nicely with the reddish shade of his body. As if sensing her approval, Folly arched his neck, almost preening before her.

Melissa laughed. "Showoff!" she scolded gently, and as if agreeing with her, Folly tossed his head spiritedly.

There was a great bond between Melissa and the stallion. She had been present at his birth, had seen his first wobbly attempts to stand, and it had been she who had begun his earliest training, teaching him to lead and stand and obey simple commands. He would eagerly accept her slightest order, but with others, although he would instantly obey—he was too much of a gentleman not to—there was not the same slavish desire to please that he showed with Melissa. She returned his devotion, sometimes wondering if she didn't love her horse more than she did some humans. Certainly she found him far more entertaining than the suitors for her hand!

Lightly stroking Folly, she frowned. There were times that she feared she was not normal! Why else did she prefer a horse's company to that of a man? Why else had she never felt anything but the lightest of emotions when John Newcomb and some of the other young men in the neighborhood had passionately expressed their undying love? Why else had her heart never beaten faster at the sight of one particular man? her pulse never raced at the touch of a man's hand on her arm?

Her head once more resting on Folly's warm neck, she made a face as she thought of the young men who had attempted to court her. Mostly all she had felt were annoyance and impatience with them and, remembering conversations with her married cousins as they had recounted the thrills of courtship, the dreamy looks as they had told of stolen embraces and the smugly happy expressions when they had returned from their honeymoons, Melissa sighed. Would she ever experience those feelings? Would she ever look at any man with some feeling stronger than mere liking?

Sometimes she doubted it. It wasn't, she admitted slowly, that she didn't want to feel as her cousins apparently did; it was just that so far she hadn't met any gentleman who aroused anything but the mildest of emotions. She had genuinely liked John Newcomb; she had even found his polite courtship enjoyable. And while it had been pleasant when his hands seemed to linger on hers longer than necessary as he had helped her from her horse or carriage, she had never felt any reason to encourage an intimacy beyond that which was proper. With none of her suitors had she experienced a burning desire to escape the eyes of her elders to share the rapturous kisses her cousins assured her were a sign of true love.

Perhaps, she mused unhappily, if Willowglen were safe . . . If there wasn't so much that had to be done before she could turn her thoughts to more frivolous pastimes . . . But did she really want a husband? Did she want a man to have control over her, for her life and her body to no longer be her own?

Hugh had given her an inordinate amount of freedom, and even if their ages were reversed, it would never occur to Zachary to curtail her activities, to tell her what to do, to *compel* her to do his wishes. But a husband . . . She swallowed painfully. A husband had rights. Not only to her person, but to all of her possessions. Once she married, what freedom she had would disappear—her life would no longer be hers to command, she would *belong* to him. It wasn't an unpleasant idea, she admitted ruefully, belonging to someone . . . provided that person also belonged to *her!*

She smiled faintly. Would she ever find someone she could love like that? Someone who would love her to distraction? Someone she would belong to and who would belong to her? A man who would make her long to lose herself in his arms? Who would awaken her to passion and desire?

Well, she finally thought grimly, she hadn't met him yet, and until she found him, she had no intention of getting married! Definitely, she wasn't going to let Uncle Josh and Aunt Sally force her into a marriage with a man she didn't love, just so they could gain possession of Sally's share of the trust! And if she never met a man she wanted to marry? Would it be so very bad? Melissa rather thought not—she was happy with her life the way it was! As for love, she was beginning to think that it was a much overrated emotion! And a marriage without it would be purgatory on earth!

Chapter Two

DOMINIC Slade, visiting with his brother Morgan at the gracious Château Saint-André some miles south of New Orleans, would have agreed wholeheartedly with Melissa's assessment of love. And "overrated" would have been by far the kindest thing he would have had to say about it! As for marriage—ha! It was a trap *he'd* not fall into—no matter *how* attractively baited it might be.

It wasn't that Dominic was against marriage; it was just *his* marriage that he was violently opposed to! And at the age of thirty-two, he had grown very adept at recognizing that certain gleam in the eyes of matchmaking mamas and their eager daughters. But it wasn't only matchmaking mamas who had tried their hands at capturing the attention of the fascinating and, some would say, far-too-handsome-for-his-own-good Dominic Slade. Within his own family, the female portion of it, at least, had upon occasion approached him with that look on their faces which made him suddenly extremely wary of the young lady being introduced to him.

That Morgan, his much admired older brother, would try such a trick was tantamount to betrayal of the most depraved kind. And just as soon as the company that had dined that evening at Château Saint-André had departed and Dominic was able to gain a few moments alone with Morgan, he immediately tackled him with his suspicions.

His cool gray eyes full of mockery, his long-lipped mouth curved in an ironic smile, Dominic drawled, "Matchmaking, Morgan? Or did I mistake your manner with Miss Leigh tonight when you pressed me into turning the pages of her music for her?''

The two men were in Morgan's comfortable office in one of the two new wings which had been added to the house since Morgan's marriage to Leonie Saint-André some nine years previously, and Morgan had been in the act of pouring them each a snifter of brandy when Dominic had spoken. A wry grimace crossed Morgan's dark face, and sending his brother a faintly guilty smile, he murmured, ''And I thought I was being so clever!'' Handing Dominic a snifter, he added lightly, ''I told Leonie that you would know instantly what I was about, but she was positive that you would never suspect *me* of promoting the match.''

Taking the snifter, Dominic said resignedly, ''I should have known that her fine hand was involved somewhere! Just because she's so besottedly happy being married to you is no reason to assume that everyone wishes for marriage.'' With more force than necessary, he growled, ''If I *wanted* a wife, I'm perfectly capable of finding one of my own!''

''No doubt,'' Morgan replied affably. With a glint of humor in his blue eyes, he continued. ''But you haven't found one yet, have you?''

''My God!'' Dominic burst out, half amused, half vexed. ''I do not believe my ears! Don't tell me that you have gone over to the side of the enemy? Will I no longer be safe in your home?''

Morgan laughed. ''Don't start packing immediately. I promised Leonie that I would do my best to make you understand the error of your ways, but I have no intention of throwing you to the wolves. And you should take Leonie's interest as a compliment—she is concerned over the, er, ladies in your life. She thinks it is time that you stopped racketing about and settled down. A wife, she has informed me most solemnly, is the only thing that will make you truly happy.''

''I wasn't aware,'' Dominic replied dryly, ''that I was *un*happy.'' And spreading his hands wide in a deprecating gesture, he asked mockingly, ''Do I look unhappy?''

No, his brother did not look unhappy in the least, Morgan decided with amusement. Dominic's muscular legs, snugly encased in a pair of skin-tight black kerseymere breeches, were stretched out comfortably in front of him; his broad shoulders, covered in a superbly cut coat of dark blue cloth, rested negligently against the smooth leather of the chair, and the face rising above the fine cambric ruffles of his shirt revealed only lively good humor. In fact, Dominic looked very pleased with his life as he lounged there in the big wing-backed chair, clearly enjoying the bouquet of his brandy as he gently wafted the snifter beneath his nose.

It was difficult for Morgan to view Dominic through the eyes of a woman, but even he, allowing for a certain amount of brotherly pride, had to conclude that Dominic had grown up to be a very handsome-featured young man. And when one added a tall, loose-limbed body to that handsome face, a careless charm to the already winning personality and an indecently large fortune, it really wasn't surprising that Dominic was much sought after by the ladies. Nor that it drove the women of his family half mad when he showed no inclination to change his single state.

The Slade family was a wealthy one whose various estates spread from Bonheur, near Natchez, Mississippi, down the river to below New Orleans where Morgan lived on the plantation where his wife had been born. It was also a large family. In addition to Morgan and Dominic, there was a forty-year-old brother, Robert, who was just two years younger than Morgan; an elder sister living in Tennessee, and the youngest siblings, the twins, twenty-five-year-old Alexandre and Cassandre. They were all very fond of one another and all were married with the exception of Dominic and Alexandre. As Alexandre was still considered a mere youth by his family, the fact that he wasn't married didn't seem to arouse the same passion that Dominic's lack of marriage did.

Morgan could well understand Dominic's aversion to marriage—hadn't he felt the same way until Leonie had burst into his life? Of course, he amended fairly, he'd had reason to view marriage with a jaundiced eye; his first wife had deserted him for another man, taking their child with her, only for the three of them to be killed by bandits on the Natchez Trace. It had taken Morgan a long time to recover from such a blow, and it was only after Leonie had entered his life that he came to realize that all women were not liars and cheats.

But Dominic had no bitter experience to make him so prejudiced against women. . . . It wasn't women, Morgan conceded ruefully, staring at his brother's dark, lean face, that Dominic objected to—it was marriage! Dominic certainly *liked* women. A smile quirked Morgan's chiseled mouth. Leonie would have added tartly, "All the *wrong* kind!" And Morgan supposed that from a respectable woman's point of view, the various highfliers and soiled doves who had willingly availed themselves of Dominic's protection over the past several years were decidedly the wrong sort of women.

Breaking into Morgan's musings, Dominic said suddenly, "I'll tell you what it is Leonie wants to make positive that I marry only someone who she likes and approves of! Look how she maneuvered Robert into marrying Yvette!"

While not denying Leonie's propensity for matchmaking, Morgan did say with suspect meekness, "Well, yes, but you must admit that Robert needed very little, er, maneuvering. He fell in love with Yvette practically on sight, and it was only Yvette's elusiveness that prevented them from being married for so long."

Thinking back to those days, remembering how Robert had mooned over Leonie's companion, Yvette, Dominic had to reluctantly agree with Morgan's assessment. Robert *had* been in love with Yvette right from the beginning, despite the unpleasant situation that had surrounded them all that summer of 1805. Hell, Dominic confessed to himself, *he* had even been a little in love with the breathtakingly beautiful Yvette; and recalling some of the other events of that time, he grinned. Morgan had certainly not been so enamored of the married state then as he was now, and he had furiously denied ever having laid eyes on Leonie Saint-André when she had suddenly appeared in Natchez and stated vehemently that Morgan had married her six years previously in New Orleans and that Justin, her son, was Morgan's child!

His gray eyes filled with mocking laughter, Dominic teased, "I remember once when you were not so complaisant about marriage. . . ."

Morgan grinned back at him, and the resemblance between the two brothers was suddenly very marked. The Slade siblings bore a striking resemblance to one another; all had the same thick black hair, strongly marked eyebrows, deep-set eyes and very firm and unyielding chins which they had inherited from their father, Mathew. Their dark coloring came from their spirited Creole mother, Noelle, and it was from her, too, that they had inherited their quick tempers and family pride.

The grin which Dominic's comment had aroused still upon his lips, Morgan murmured, "Well, yes, but it is your marriage we are talking about."

"Oh, Lord! Must we?" Dominic groaned theatrically. "Why," he asked with annoyance, "is everyone suddenly so determined to see me married?"

"I don't know that they are determined so much as they feel that it is such a waste of good husband material for you to remain single," Morgan replied sardonically. On a more serious note, he added, "However, I do wonder, if for no other reason than producing an heir of your own, that you don't marry."

"You *have* gone over to the side of the enemy!" Dominic exclaimed with mock wrath, the gray eyes glinting.

Smothering back a laugh at Dominic's reaction, Morgan shook his head and said quickly, "No, I haven't, and I swear I'll not bring up the painful subject again. Leonie will just have to be content when I tell her that you are set upon becoming a lonely old bachelor."

"*Lonely!*" Dominic retorted derisively. "With that pack of brats that you and Leonie seem intent to thrust upon an unsuspecting world? And what about Robert and Yvette? How many do they have now? Five? Six? And what about the others? I have a *legion* of nieces and nephews—I'm sure that when the time comes, I'll be able to name at least *one* of the brats as my heir!" Grinning, he continued audaciously. "You can tell Leonie that although I have every intention of turning into a disgustingly fat old man surrounded by a covey of lovely, adoring, ah, *ladies*, I will do what is proper and leave all my earthly belongings to one of her children. And now,'' Dominic asked with feigned plaintiveness, "could we please dispense with the subject? It does weary me so.''

Not one to belabor the point, Morgan easily turned the conversation into other channels, and the two brothers spent an enjoyable hour or so talking casually about the things that interested them—the fine bear that Dominic had killed only last week; the exquisite pair of French dueling pistols that Morgan had just purchased the previous day; and, of course, the more usual things of crops and horses. . . .

"Are you serious about setting up your own stud farm, Dom?" Morgan asked as their talk wandered around to what was still one of Dominic's paramount pursuits.

"Hmm . . . yes, I think that I shall,'' Dominic replied, setting down his empty snifter on a small table nearby. Sending Morgan a faintly cynical smile, he went on. "You see, I *have* been thinking about my future and I agree in part with Leonie when she says it is time that I settle down. And if I am to do this, I must have something to amuse me. Horses have always done so, and selecting prime horseflesh is something that, you will admit, I am rather good at doing.'' A flicker of annoyance crossed his attractive features. "If it weren't for this damn war of Mr. Madison's, I would return to England and cast about for a really good, reputable stallion to bring over here, but as it is . . .''

For many Americans the war seemed very far away, which in fact it was—fought primarily along the border between the United States and Canada and on the high seas; for the most part it had little impact on the majority of their lives. It was only when some unpleasant aspect of the hostilities intruded into their day-to-day living that people remembered the war, and then there was more anger expressed about the President, James Madison, and the Congress than about the British!

With far more seriousness than he had shown all evening, Dominic asked abruptly, "Do you think that anything will come of the British proposal for direct negotiations?''

Morgan shrugged. "Madison accepted the offer, so it's possible, but I don't see a great deal happening before next year. We would be wise to come to terms soon, though. Since Napoleon's defeat last year at Leipzig, it is only a matter of time until Wellington and the other British allies completely annihilate the French—and then we will be in trouble! With the war in Europe at an end, England will be able to bring all of her might against us, and I wouldn't want to make a wager on the outcome."

Dominic nodded gloomily. The war between the United States and Great Britain was particularly unpleasant for him; he had friends on both sides of the conflicting forces and he disliked excessively the notion of having to choose between them.

There was no question on which side he would fight if it became necessary. He had been in England when word of the American declaration of war had arrived in London in the summer of 1812, and he had not hesitated a moment before finding a ship and sailing for home. The Slade family had strong ties to England—the Baron of Trevelyan was their father's older brother, and nearly all the younger Slades had at one time or another spent time with their uncle. Of all of them, Dominic had stayed in England the longest; he had made London and its environs his home for nearly three years, only the outbreak of war ending his pleasant sojourn there.

Dominic had not been unhappy to leave. For some time before the news of war had arrived, he had been conscious of a strange restlessness and had found himself growing bored with the constant round of balls and routs, of deep gaming at Boodles and Brooks, of drinking "blue ruin" until dawn and generally concerning himself with nothing more important than the cut of his coat, the spiritedness of his horse or the charms to be enjoyed in the arms of his latest mistress. It had all been very agreeable, and the danger and excitement of a duel, which, with his Slade pride and ready temper, had occurred more than once during his stay in England, had only added a bit of spice to the even tenor of his days.

It was not Dominic's nature to be idle—he was filled with a restless vitality—but as one of the younger sons of the family, he had no need to shoulder the day-to-day responsibilities of running the great plantation, Bonheur. Even the necessity for him to strike out on his own had not been essential. When Dominic had turned twenty-one, Mathew, as he had done with his two elder sons, had given him a tidy sum of capital and several hundred acres of prime land in the area of what had then been West Florida and what was now the West Feliciana parish of upper Louisiana. Dominic had spent his money wisely and he seemed to possess the gift of prospering effortlessly—his crops were abundant, his cattle and horses prolific breeders, and his shrewd investments made him an impressive profit. In the ten years or so that had elapsed since Mathew had given him his start, Dominic had more than trebled his initial holdings.

Fate had been extremely kind to Dominic Slade. It had endowed him with a tall, lithe body, a strikingly handsome face and a mocking charm. When those attributes were added to his background and fortune, it was not astonishing that there had been little that Dominic had ever wanted that had been denied him. He was the darling of his parents, the despairing delight of his sisters and sisters-in-law and a genial, welcome companion to his brothers and friends. He was not precisely spoiled, but he possessed a not *un*natural arrogance, and he was certainly used to getting his own way and expecting events to turn out exactly as he wanted.

Upon his return from England nearly two years ago, his life had continued just as he had presumed it would: his family and friends had been gratifyingly happy to see him, his businessman had shown him the continuing growth of his investments and his overseer had presented him with the plantation account books, revealing that the land had yielded a rich harvest of crops over the years. For a while he had been content; it had been very pleasant to be back home, back in the bosom of his family, and to renew old acquaintances, but of late . . .

Of late, Dominic was once again aware of a lack in his life. Of something that was missing . . . He was conscious of a strange restlessness within himself, a growing dissatisfaction with his extremely comfortable existence. A cynical expression crossed his face. Leonie, he was quite positive, would put it down to his unmarried state, but if there was one thing Dominic knew he did *not* need or want, it was a wife! He had finally decided that it was simply because his life was without purpose, that he had no great consuming interest, and in order to change that, he had hit upon his current scheme of raising horses—not just *any* horses, only the *most* select!

Rising to his feet, he poured himself another brandy and, after doing the same for Morgan, sat down again, saying, "Well, I, for one, am not going to worry over this bloody war until it comes knocking on my door. Now tell me about that bay stallion, which you said impressed Jason so much."

Before Morgan could reply, the carved door to his study was opened, and Leonie walked into the room, her green silk skirts rustling gaily about her ankles. *"Mon amour,"* she murmured teasingly, "do you intend to spend the entire night locked up in here?"

Morgan's face softened as it always did when Leonie was near him and, putting down his snifter, he rose, saying lightly, "Absolutely not!" With a glint in his dark blue eyes, he added huskily, "Especially not if you require my attention."

"Morgan!" she exclaimed with a giggle, her sea-green eyes reflecting a similar glint. With mock demureness, she added, "What will your little brother think of us?"

At thirty-one, Leonie had changed little over the years. Her tawny hair, worn now in an elegant chignon at the base of her neck, was just as bright as it had been when Morgan had first seen her; the mischievous sparkle in those almond-shaped eyes was still very much evident, and it was only her fuller curves that showed the passage of time. She was a small woman, finely boned, but after four children and nearly ten years of marriage to Morgan, her slender shape had a lush richness to it that had not been there when she and Morgan had first fallen in love.

That they had remained very much in love was obvious from the glances they exchanged and the sweet content-ment that seemed to surround them. There was never any doubt that, after a tempestuous beginning, Morgan and Leonie had found a deep and lasting happiness.

A grin on his face, Dominic got up from his chair and said, "I do believe it is time that I retired and, er, left you two to your amusements."

Leonie gave him a slightly annoyed glance. "I think I am angry with you, *mon ami*. Did you ask Mademoiselle Leigh to go riding with you tomorrow morning?"

Putting a brotherly arm about her waist, Dominic dropped a light kiss on her hair. "Sweetheart, I know that you have my best interests at heart, but I really had no desire to further my acquaintance with Mademoiselle Leigh."

"But, Dominic!" Leonie cried. "She is *so* beautiful. And she is kind and gentle. And her father is *very* rich." A little frown creased her forehead as she asked, "Didn't you like her at all?"

His gray eyes glittering with mockery, Dominic murmured, "Oh, indeed I did! But you see, I don't think she would accept the offer I would send her way."

"I think you are wrong," Leonie began seriously, only to stop abruptly when she saw the amusement dancing in Dominic's eyes. "Ah, bah!" she said. "You mean you would offer her only your protection, not your hand!"

"Precisely, my dear," Dominic returned with maddening cordiality.

Leonie ignored the smothered laugh that came from Morgan. Her gaze narrowed, and with hands on hips, she muttered, "Someday, Dominic, it is my sincerest wish that you fall in love with a young lady who will drive you half mad and lead you a merry chase. I hope she will spurn your advances and puncture, at least for a little while, your infuriating complacency!" Shaking her finger at him, a mixture of amusement and earnestness in her voice, she ended, "You mark my words, *mon ami,* someday it *will* happen, just you wait."

Laughing, Dominic pushed her away from him. "Cursing me, Leonie? Now think how terrible you will feel when my heart is broken!"

"It will be good for you," Leonie returned sweetly.

Looking across at his brother, Dominic complained,

"You don't beat her often enough, Morgan. Hasn't anyone ever told you that a woman needs a firm hand—especially a woman with a sharp tongue!"

Morgan smiled and, pulling an indignant Leonie against his tall body, remarked, "I have my own methods of controlling her, and if you don't want to be embarrassed I suggest you leave, because I have every intention of kissing my wife soundly."

Dominic looked at the pair of them, Leonie's head leaning against Morgan's broad shoulder, and he grinned. "Shameless! And you a respectable married couple!" A smile still curving his lips, he left the room, carefully shutting the door behind him. As he walked down the broad hall that led to the main part of the house, he was suddenly conscious of an odd feeling of envy. It must be a glorious thing to share the sort of love that existed between Leonie and Morgan. Then he shook himself. Good God! What was he thinking!

The next morning, his fleeting moment of envy—if that was what it had been—was gone, and he strolled outside to the gallery that ran across the front of the house. Despite the early hour, Morgan was already there, apparently lingering over one last cup of chicory-flavored coffee before beginning his day as a busy planter.

The white-railed gallery was a pleasant place and the family spent a great deal of time here. There was a round black iron table and several chairs with gaily covered scarlet cushions scattered about. From this vantage point the wide, rolling Mississippi River was barely discernible above the treetops, but the lush emerald lawns with the moss-hung oaks and white-flowering magnolia trees made a delightful view.

After exchanging greetings, Dominic helped himself to a cup of coffee from the large silver pot that sat in the center of the table. There were some still-warm cross buns on a plate nearby, and picking one up, Dominic remarked with a gleam in his eyes, "And did you teach Leonie her much needed lesson?"

"That," Morgan replied dryly, "is none of your business."

Dominic grinned, not the least abashed by Morgan's

answer; it was precisely what he had expected him to say. There was an amiable silence between the two men for several moments as Dominic ate his bun and drank his coffee, but setting down his empty china cup, he suddenly said, "About that bay stallion we were talking of last night . . . What exactly was Jason's opinion?"

"Just that the horse was one of the most beautiful and fleetest animals he'd ever seen."

Dominic whistled. "It must be some horse to gain that sort of praise from Jason."

"It is," Morgan answered. "The stallion effortlessly ran into the ground one of Jason's most promising young colts." A reflective smile curved his mouth. "He was *not* pleased! Jason Savage does not like to lose!"

Both of the Slades were well acquainted with the man of whom they spoke. Jason's brother-in-law, Adam St. Clair, was Dominic's close crony in Natchez, and Jason had been Morgan's friend since the two older men had met as schoolboys while attending Harrow in England. Dominic had grown up knowing Jason, and he could well imagine Jason's dislike of losing. Dominic suspected it happened only with *great* rarity!

A look of deep interest on his lean face, Dominic asked, "Do you know anything else about the horse? Such as who the stallion belongs to and where the animal can be found?"

Morgan sent Dominic a considering glance. "Are you thinking of buying the horse?"

Dominic shrugged. "I might be—if he lives up to what I've heard."

"He will, believe me," Morgan replied. "I was there at the race meet and I saw the animal. If you're serious about breeding horses, he would certainly make an excellent stud for your stables."

"Which brings me to why I'm here—besides wanting to see you and Leonie and your pack of brats," Dominic said easily, but there was a bit of uncertainty in his gray eyes. At Morgan's questioning look, he said rather in a rush, "Would you be willing to sell me the house at Thousand Oaks and possibly some of the surrounding area? I'll give you a good price for it."

Morgan stiffened, a shuttered expression closing down over his chiseled features. Thousand Oaks was the plantation his father had given him when he had married his first wife, Stephanie. It was situated halfway between Natchez and Baton Rouge, in the virgin, verdant wilderness along the Mississippi River. Morgan had intended that one day Thousand Oaks would be as elegant and gracious as Bonheur. With that objective as his goal, he had spent long, arduous months overseeing the building of the house and outbuildings, watching the land being cleared for cotton fields, dreaming of the day he would bring his wife and young son to their own home. . . . And while he had been busy at Thousand Oaks, his beloved wife had been busy falling in love with another man.

Morgan's memories of Thousand Oaks were tainted, and in all the long years since Stephanie's death and that of his first-born son, Phillipe, he had never set foot on the place. He had installed a competent housekeeper and her husband in the house and had left a few field workers there simply to maintain the land that had been cleared at such backbreaking cost. He never thought of the estate, and his family was always very careful not to mention it . . . until now.

He glanced across at Dominic and, seeing the concern and anxiety in his brother's eyes, he let out a sigh. "Don't look so worried—I am not about to have a case of the vapors simply at the mention of Thousand Oaks!" He smiled crookedly. "I'll not sell it to you, though—you may have the damn place and with my blessing!"

"Ah, no," Dominic answered firmly. "You are going to sell it to me, and at a price that will not offend my pride."

They were still amiably haggling over the price when the "pack of brats," as Dominic affectionately called them, suddenly exploded onto the gallery, Leonie laughingly following in their wake.

The eldest of Morgan's sons was Justin, who bore a remarkable resemblance to his father, only the sea-green eyes that he had inherited from his mother differing from Morgan's sapphire-blue ones. Eagerly he took the chair next to Dominic and immediately launched into a conversation about the panther he had seen last night along one of the bayous that crisscrossed the lands of Château Saint-André.

Eight-year-old Suzette was also obviously Morgan's daughter, even down to the brightness of her vivid blue eyes and her curly black hair. But there was something . . . something about the shape of her nose and mouth that made Dominic think of Leonie. Suzette was also shy, painfully so, and although it was apparent that she wanted very much to approach Dominic just as Justin had, she held back, standing close to her mother, her fascinated gaze on Dominic's dark face.

Five-year-old Christine, with her honey-blond curls and laughing, sea-green eyes, had no such scruples, and with a shriek of delight she launched herself onto Uncle Dominic's knee. Nor was four-year-old Marcus the least bit in awe of his favorite relative. His chubby little legs moving as fast as they could, he followed Christine's actions and flung himself in Dominic's direction, his dark hair still tousled from sleep, his blue eyes dancing with merriment.

It was glaringly apparent that for all his comments about the "pack of brats," Dominic was extremely fond of his nieces and nephews and that they returned his affection fully. Deftly, he stopped Marcus from playing with the folds of his immaculately white cravat; convinced Christine that she did *not* want to clutch at his jacket in that fashion; continued his conversation with Justin and even took the time to send a teasing wink in Suzette's direction.

Watching his easy, affectionate manner with the children, Leonie sighed. He would make such a wonderful father! She started to say something, but she caught Morgan's eye upon her and the almost imperceptible shake of his head caused her to press her lips firmly together. Bah! What did Morgan know? she thought rebelliously. Dominic was throwing his life away on gaming and women, and if she didn't care for him so much, it wouldn't bother her in the least. But he would make some woman an exceptional husband . . . if only he could be made to give up his rakish ways!

No more was said about Dominic's rakish ways or the possibility of his marriage during the remainder of his visit

at Château Saint-André. He spent an enjoyable month with
Morgan and the family and before he departed, he and
Morgan had finally, after a great deal of argument, come
to terms about the sale of Thousand Oaks.

He had also been able to speak with Jason Savage and
to discover that the stallion, Folly, was situated somewhere north of Baton Rouge. The owner's name was not
known to Jason, but he was certain that Dominic would
discover it with little difficulty—a horse of that caliber
would not go unnoticed!

On his last evening at Château Saint-André, Dominic
and Morgan were once again enjoying a snifter of brandy,
this time on the front gallery of the house, moonlight shining with a silver glow through the towering oaks. His
booted feet propped carelessly on the white railing, Dominic said quietly, ''I hope that your memories of Thousand
Oaks will not stop you from coming to visit me periodi-
cally.''

Morgan smiled faintly. ''No, they won't. What happened was a long time ago, and since Leonie came into
my life, I find that nothing but her happiness matters to
me anymore.'' His face momentarily sad, Morgan added,
''My only regret is Phillipe's death. I sometimes look at
Justin and wonder what Phillipe would have looked like
at that age. . . . As for Stephanie, her betrayal hurt me
badly at the time, but time does heal one's wounds.''

For just a second Dominic recalled the look on his
brother's face when he had returned from the Natchez
Trace, bringing back with him the news of his wife's death
and that of his young son. It had been a terrible time for
the entire Slade family, and they had done their best to
alleviate some of Morgan's bitter grief, but the memories
of those days had left their mark on all of them. Dominic,
with his hero-worship love for his older brother, had been
particularly affected by the tragedy. His features hard as
he remembered Morgan's pain and his own unhappiness
some three years ago in London, when he had *thought* he
had been in love with the lovely Deborah, he suddenly
muttered grimly, ''Women are delightful creatures—it's
when you love them that they become dangerous!''

Chapter Three

WHILE Dominic was having his conversation with Morgan near New Orleans, at Willowglen Melissa was lying awake in her bed wondering how she was going to rid herself of the unwanted attention of the persistent John Newcomb. It had been a blessing to leave Willowglen for the race meet in Virginia at the end of April, for no other reason than she escaped from his mooning presence. But once she had returned home again barely two weeks ago, the first visitor to the plantation had been John.

She sighed. He was such a nice young man, but she didn't love him! she didn't want to hurt his feelings more than necessary, but she had to hit upon some scheme to discourage him—and any future suitors. She was not a vain young woman, yet she could not help but be aware that her physical attributes had much to do with her seeming irresistibility to the gentlemen. If only, she mused wryly, she had been born with a squint and a bean-pole frame! Suddenly an idea occurred to her, and with a mischievous grin on her face, she lay there considering it. Maybe, just maybe, there was a way to rectify that situation!

The next morning, oblivious to the warm May sunshine pouring into her bedroom from the open window, Melissa stood alone in the middle of the room. Scowling fiercely, she glared at her image in the age-spotted cheval glass. Not quite pleased with the picture that met her eyes, she deliberately pursed her full, delightfully shaped mouth into a tight, disapproving line. There! That was what she wanted! Swallowing back the bubble of laughter which threatened to escape, she gave herself one final glance. She looked, she thought with satisfaction, absolutely horrid!

Dancing from the room, she went in search of Zachary. Finding him sprawled comfortably on the faded chintz sofa in the sunny morning room at the rear of the house, she pirouetted gaily in front of him.

"Well," she demanded lightly, "what do you think? Do I look dreadful enough?" As he remained silent, his incredulous gaze locked on her slim form, a little frown of concern crossed her face. "Zack! Say something! I've done all that I can think of, and if it isn't enough, I'm at my wit's end!"

"Enough?" Zachary managed to get out in a strangled tone. "My dear, you have surpassed yourself! You look . . ." Words seemed to fail him, and the laughter he had been choking back finally got the better of him. Manfully he tried to control himself and once again he began, "You look positively . . ."

"Ghastly?" Melissa suggested hopefully as Zachary struggled for words to describe the vision his sister presented.

"Ghastly" was perhaps too strong a word to describe how Melissa looked at the moment, but certainly she bore no resemblance to the attractive young lady who had faced her uncle in the library some six weeks previously. Except for the gleam of laughter in the golden-brown eyes, no one would have immediately recognized her as Josh Manchester's lovely niece. Gone was her thick, curling mane of hair, and in its place was a prim, tidy bun securely fastened to the back of her head. The honey-colored curls were so tightly scraped away from her face that her slightly cat-shaped eyes had a decided slant. The severe hairstyle threw her delicate features into sharp relief, actually bringing attention to them, but Melissa had countered that effect by putting on a pair of old-fashioned, wire-rimmed spectacles she had found in one of her father's trunks in the attic.

The spectacles had been a godsend. Not only did they distract the gaze from the sweet line of her jaw and mouth, but they also caused Melissa to squint as she tried to peer through the small, square-shaped lenses. The squint, the spectacles and the bun had definitely changed her appearance, and for the final touch, she had managed to find some of the dowdiest gowns imaginable from the horde of odds and ends stored in the attic. The gown she was wearing at present fitted badly, sagging at her small, firm bosom and slim waist, very effectively disguising the undeniable charms of the slender body it covered. The gray-green material gave her usually golden-hued skin an unhealthy pallor, and when she pursed her lips . . . When she pursed her lips, the picture of a sour-faced, frowsy old maid was complete.

Unfortunately, she could not hold her mouth in that uncomfortable position for very long, and when she laughed, as she did now, when her generously curved mouth softened and amusement danced in her thickly lashed eyes, the image she wanted was very nearly destroyed. But all in all, she was satisfied, certain that her appearance, coupled with the state of the Seymour affairs, would disenchant even the most persistent suitor.

"Well?" she demanded again. "Do you think this will deter John Newcomb from mooning about the place?"

"Lord, yes!" Zachary returned unflatteringly. "He'll take one look and that will be the end of him!" Mischief glittering in his eyes, he added, "But the one I'm most anxious to watch when he sees your, ah, new appearance is Uncle Josh!"

Melissa nodded happily. "I know—he's going to have an attack of apoplexy. But at least I think this will stop him from hounding me to reconsider John's proposal."

"I sincerely hope so!" Zachary replied piously. "The arguments you and Josh have had since you refused Newcomb are worse than any I can remember. The way you two have been snapping and snarling at each other since we returned from Virginia, it's a wonder that they don't hear you in Baton Rouge!"

"I haven't noticed," his sister said dryly, "that you have been particularly quiet either these past weeks. And I think the exchange you had yesterday was far worse than the one you had the first time he tackled me about refusing to marry John. *Then* you only referred to him badgering me, but yesterday—yesterday *you* were the one who shouted him down and thundered at him to leave your house!''

Zachary looked embarrassed. ''I can't bear having him talk to you in that fashion,'' he answered defensively. ''You have every right to refuse to marry John Newcomb or anyone else if you want to, and I'll not have Josh forcing you to do anything you don't want—no matter how much he threatens and blusters.'' A flicker of anxiety in his eyes, he added quietly, ''He couldn't really take me away from Willowglen, could he? I mean, he's not really my guardian, is he?''

Any amusement she might have felt about the situation vanished, and with just a touch of worry in her own voice she admitted, ''I don't know. I know that Father's will says that Josh and I *share* your guardianship, but I don't know what would happen if Josh demanded that you live with him and under his control. I would fight him, of course, but . . .''

For a moment they both looked unbearably disheartened, each of them aware that as far as Zachary's guardianship was concerned, Josh held the upper hand. After all, the local judge was a great crony of his, and when the conditions at Willowglen were compared with the comforts and elegance of Oak Hollow . . .

Melissa swallowed painfully. Uncle Josh had been so good to them in so many ways. All through childhood, it had been Uncle Josh and Aunt Sally who had remembered birthdays when Hugh had been too absentminded to recall when his children had been born; it had been bluff, jovial Uncle Josh who had placed Melissa on her first pony; Uncle Josh who had come and entertained Zachary many an afternoon after he had broken his leg when he was thirteen. Uncle Josh had been the rock that she and Zachary had clung to when Hugh had first died, and it had been Uncle Josh who had tried to shield them from the true extent of the disaster Hugh had made of running Willowglen.

Josh Manchester was a good man, and Melissa knew that he deeply loved her and Zachary and only wanted what he thought was best for them. Which made continuing to resist him extremely painful and difficult. If only he were a wicked man, Melissa thought unhappily, then it would make her task far easier. But every time she defied him, every time they had one of those terrible arguments about her refusal to marry John Newcomb, she was guilt-stricken. She didn't want to hurt her uncle and she was beginning to wish passionately that she *could* fall in love with John Newcomb or some other eligible young man simply to please her uncle, but she could not! Even loving Josh and hating to distress him, she was *not* going to be pushed into a marriage she didn't want.

But if he played his final card . . . if he gave her a choice between marriage and losing the guardianship of Zachary . . . Her throat felt tight and she was aware of the prickle of tears at the corners of her eyes. It was a measure of the man that all these months he had never once mentioned the guardianship . . . until yesterday.

Remembering the uncomfortable expression on Josh's heavy features during their latest confrontation, Melissa felt herself torn in two. He had not liked threatening her about taking Zachary away from her care, that she knew. It was obvious that it pained him; obvious too that he did not like the strained, unpleasant situation that had developed between the Manchesters and the Seymours since April any more than did she and Zack. But it was also obvious that he still sincerely believed that Melissa's marriage was the only way out of his current embarrassing lack of funds . . . and he had pointed out *again* that the Manchesters weren't the only ones who would benefit from the ending of Jeffery Seymour's trust.

It wasn't, Melissa reminded herself dolefully, as if Josh wanted her to do something dreadful and vile. All he wanted was for her to marry a kind, pleasant, wellborn, wealthy young man. What, she asked herself in despair, was wrong with that?

A strong sensation of guilt suddenly swept over her. Was she just being selfish and pigheaded, as he had accused her? Perhaps she *should* marry John and end all of this unpleasantness and constant arguing. But I don't *love* John! her heart protested silently.

Melissa's enjoyment in her disguise vanished, and somewhat dispiritedly she turned away from Zachary's concerned face. Was she really being self-centered and selfish? She didn't think so; the Manchesters, for all of Josh's moanings and complaints, were not in dire straits. *Everyone* had a bad year now and then. And Melissa supposed that therein lay her reluctance to throw herself away for the sake of her family. If the Manchesters were in a desperate way, in danger of losing their plantation and everything that Josh had worked for, she knew that she would not hesitate. She would marry John Newcomb in a flash and try very hard to be a good wife. Unfortunately for her, by the next year or even next month, if one of Josh's ships should slip past the British barricade of the coasts, things for the Manchesters would be just as they had always been—and her great sacrifice would have been for nothing. Besides, everyone knew her cousin Royce was independently wealthy and that he would not allow his father to come to grief. If Josh would swallow his pride and ask his oldest son for help . . .

Zachary's arm about her waist jerked her from her unhappy musings. Giving her a comforting hug, he said morosely, "I just wish that Uncle Josh was a real monster—then all of this would be so much easier. I dislike fighting with him excessively, but I will *not* have him badgering you!" His young face reflective, he muttered, "The odd thing is that in five years' time, we will all laugh at this situation and Josh will take as much delight in recounting our antics as they infuriate him now."

A watery little smile on her face, Melissa nodded. Taking a deep breath, she said staunchly, "We shall just have to convince ourselves that what we are doing is in his best interests! Life has been too easy for our good uncle and he needs a challenge."

His mood lightening instantly, Zack grinned at her. "And that, my dear, there is no denying you are proving to be!"

Melissa giggled and gave Zack a pinch in the ribs. "You haven't been exactly docile either, you know."

A slightly superior smile on his handsome mouth, Zack looked down at her. "I know, and if we are to get over the heavy ground lightly, we must view this entire state of affairs as one great jest—one that we will all enjoy . . ." His mouth twisted. ". . . eventually!"

There was a chuckle from the doorway and a gruff voice with a decided French accent demanded, "And which jest is that, *mes enfants?* The one where the young monsieur put cold pudding in my best pair of boots, or the one where a certain mademoiselle poured pepper in my coffee?"

"Etienne!" Melissa and Zachary chorused together in delight as they spun around to regard with affection and amusement the small, elegant Frenchman who entered the room.

Excitement gleaming in her eyes, Melissa said breathlessly, "You've returned! Were you successful? Did you bring them back with you? Where are they?"

Etienne held up a restraining hand. "One question at a time, *s'il vous plait, petite.*" Suddenly aware of Melissa's appearance, Etienne's jaw went slack in astonishment. *"Mon Dieu!* What has been happening while I have been away? Why is it that you look so . . . so . . ." His black eyes narrowed. "Ah. Of course. It is your *oncle* who causes you to look like a hag, *oui?"*

"Oui!" Melissa answered fervently, a smile curving her lip at Etienne's quick comprehension. But then little escaped the sharp eye of Etienne.

Etienne Martion had been a part of Melissa's life for as long as she could remember, and if Josh had helped her onto her first pony, it had been Etienne who had picked her up the first time she had fallen off and had firmly put her back on again. And again and again, until there was no horse in the stables that she could not ride.

Small in stature, finely boned, Etienne had the lightest hands of any horseman Melissa had ever known, and yet there was strength in that wiry body and those slim wrists—she had watched him time and again bring the powerful Folly effortlessly under control. Etienne's age and background were a mystery to the two young Seymours, and Melissa sometimes wondered if even her father had known very much of Etienne's ancestry before he had appeared one day at Willowglen some forty years ago. He had been a young man then, and by his speech and mannerisms it was obvious that he had come from a good family. He also knew a great deal about horses. Because of this, Jeffery Seymour had hired him to oversee his stables, and Hugh had relied heavily upon Etienne's advice when it came to the buying and breeding of horses.

Etienne looked to be any age between fifty and seventy, and Melissa and Zachary had decided that he must be in the region of sixty-five, but it was difficult to tell. His hair was thick and black with no hint of gray, and Melissa rather thought that he was a little vain about it—he grew quite outraged when she teased him about seeing a gray strand near his temple. The swarthy skin of his complexion gave no real clue to his age, and his intelligent black eyes gleamed with youthful humor and vitality. Certainly *he* never gave any clue, and from his actions and conversation, Melissa and Zachary treated him as their contemporary rather than their elder.

But in matters to do with the stables Melissa deferred to him without question, and when he had suggested during the Virginia trip that instead of using all of Folly's winnings to pay off more debt they use a part of it to purchase a few young brood mares, Melissa had not hesitated to follow his advice. Consequently, they had all traveled to Virginia to Tree Hill plantation near Richmond, one of the increasingly well-known race tracks in America. After watching Folly once again beat every horse placed against him, Etienne had remained behind while Melissa and the others had returned to Willowglen.

Melissa and Zachary had been home for nearly two weeks now and had been eagerly awaiting Etienne's return. As the days passed, Melissa had experienced a strong sense of déjà vu; once before she had waited at Willowglen for someone she loved to return to start their stables. Anxiety darkened her eyes as she remembered the disaster of Hugh's trip to England. "You do," she asked carefully, "have good news for us."

Etienne's smile softened. "*Petite*, I would not fail you." Shaking an admonishing finger at her, he added sternly, "Not all men are like your father, and you should learn to trust."

Melissa grimaced and shrugged her shoulders. It was an

old argument between them, one she did not wish to pursue today. Absently removing her spectacles and laying them on a table nearby, she teased, "Don't try to change the subject! When, dear monsieur, may we see how you have spent our money? You did spend it wisely, I hope."

Etienne gave his rich chuckle. "You are a shrew, *mon coeur,* but an adorable one at that, so come along now and see what awaits you at the stables."

No more was needed to be said. Melissa and Zachary, followed more leisurely by Etienne, flew from the room and raced away in the direction of the stables. They darted inside, eager for their first sight of what they hoped fervently was the beginning of their excellent horse farm. But there were no signs of the new mares.

Puzzled, they waited for Etienne to join them. "Where are they?" Zachary asked curiously. "Didn't you bring them with you?"

Etienne smiled ruefully. "It seems that one of the ladies was very, ah, desirous of meeting her new husband, and in the confusion, I'm afraid they all ended up in the paddock with Folly—much to his pleasure, I might add. I'm surprised you didn't hear him trumpeting his satisfaction up at the house!"

Laughing and talking all at once, the three of them turned and walked quickly the short distance to the large paddock that lay beyond the stables. Leaning against the freshly whitewashed rail fence, they stared at the five horses lazily cropping the profuse growth of green grass.

Folly was easy to pick out amongst the newcomers, his great size—he stood sixteen hands high—and his powerfully sleek muscles in pleasing contrast to the slimmer, more delicately formed mares. For once, though, the stallion did not absorb all of Melissa's interest as she carefully scrutinized the four mares who shared the paddock with him. There were several moments of silence as her gaze wandered over the new animals, two chestnuts, a bay and a black. All of them showed their Arabian blood, the small, finely shaped heads and the long, almost incredibly slim legs a clear indication of their background. And, Melissa admitted thankfully, they were undeniably gorgeous, precisely what she and Zack had wanted.

Letting her breath out in a shaky sigh of relief, she spun to look at Etienne, who lounged at her side. "Oh, Etienne, they are everything we could have wished for! How did you find them—and how did you manage to purchase four horses with the amount I gave you? The most we had hoped you could buy was two."

His expression sly, Etienne replied, *"Petite,* you forget that I am a Frenchman, and a Frenchman is noted for his thrift. I merely cast about for an imprudent planter who happened to own blooded stock, and *voilà!* I was able to strike an excellent bargain for one of the chestnuts and the bay. The other two I had to pay considerably more for, but I think that I have done very well!" Smiling benignly, he added, "I am quite wonderful, am I not?"

As it was well known to them that modesty was a virtue that Etienne did not possess, neither Melissa nor Zachary was the least disturbed by his statement. He *was* quite wonderful as far as they were concerned! They all stood there for some time watching the horses and talking quietly amongst themselves, and later, when they began to walk toward the house, there was an air of contentment about the oddly assorted trio, Melissa and Zachary towering above the gesticulating, dapper little Frenchman.

The feeling of contentment stayed with Melissa for the rest of the day, and it was only on Wednesday, when she put on another of the ill-fitting and unattractive gowns she had found in the attic, that she experienced a lowering of her spirits. She tried to convince herself it was only a natural reaction after the excitement of yesterday and that no young woman would enjoy making herself look a dowdy, but she knew that there was more to it than just an ugly gown and a return to normal events.

And yet, she admitted later that day as she sat on a pile of hay near the entrance to the stables, there was much that she had to be satisfied about right now. Folly's latest winnings from the races at Tree Hill had not only enabled her to give the money to Etienne to purchase some new stock, but she had been able to spend a small amount on Willowglen, and more importantly, pay off all but one of Hugh's remaining debts.

Being Melissa, the money she spent on Willowglen had naturally gone into the stables area. Not only had the fences of Folly's paddock been repaired and whitewashed, but so had the fences of two other paddocks and the main large stable itself. The stalls and tack room, as well, had been put in as good a condition as she could afford. And though the area was still slightly shabby, at least now, she told herself encouragingly, if a prospective breeder came to inspect their premises, they need not feel *too* ashamed.

If there was an improved appearance in the vicinity of the main stable, it was the only place on Willowglen that was not in pressing need of money and repair. Things had somewhat improved financially these past weeks, but the future was still not very rosy, she thought heavily as she idly picked up a piece of straw and began to chew on it reflectively.

The fact that there was now only one person owed money was definitely heartening. Unfortunately, the last of Hugh's debts was by far the single largest amount owed, and in many respects it was the most troubling. Primarily, the debts had been centered in the Baton Rouge area; a few had even been in New Orleans. But it was that trip of his to England in 1809 that had come back to haunt his children, and Melissa rather suspected that her father had, as he had done with so many unpleasant things, merely pretended that it did not exist. The holder of Hugh's voucher did not, however, subscribe to such tactics, and during the past several years he had written some very polite letters requesting payment of the twenty-five thousand American dollars owed him. Letters that Hugh had seen fit to ignore, which Melissa thought, with unfilial disrespect, was just like Hugh! She and Zachary had been appalled and frightened, their only consolation the knowledge that Mr. Robert Weatherby, the holder of the damning voucher, was safely far away in England—they would not be dunned for payment until at least the current war ended.

Or so they had thought. Despite the war, Melissa had immediately written to London, informing Mr. Weatherby of her father's death and requesting time in which to make restitution. She had been stunned when, some six months later, a letter from Mr. Weatherby's man of business, Mr. Honeywell, had arrived and imparted the unwelcome information that Mr. Robert Weatherby was dead and that his heir, Mr. Julius Latimer, was not in England at present. Mr. Latimer's sympathies with the American cause had led him to visit that country and he was currently domiciled for the duration of the war, somewhere in the northern section of the United States. Mr. Latimer had taken the voucher with him, intending to personally collect the debt, which was *long* overdue. Mr. Honeywell would forward her letter to Mr. Latimer, but, considering the war . . .

That had been last fall, and Melissa and Zachary had lived in dread since then that someday Mr. Julius Latimer would appear on their doorstep demanding payment—payment which was rightfully his. And just prior to the Virginia trip, that was precisely what had occurred. Fortunately, it had not been as bad as they had feared—at least that was what Melissa had thought in the beginning.

Mr. Latimer was all that was kindness and politeness, a true English gentleman. He was also, she was startled to discover, a much younger man than she would have suspected, being just over thirty years of age. He was very good-looking, a golden-haired Adonis, one of the gushing young ladies of the neighborhood had exclaimed after meeting him. Melissa hadn't cared particularly for his sister, who was traveling with him, but overall, she rather liked the Latimers and had been grateful when Julius had confided to her that he was more than willing to wait for payment.

A most charming smile on his perfectly chiseled mouth, he had murmured warmly, at their first meeting, "After all, dear Miss Seymour, my uncle had already waited several years, and as far as I am concerned, you may have all the time you need."

She had been so relieved that he had not instantly begun proceedings to have Willowglen sold that she had not looked for any deeper meaning to his words. But the last week or so, she had discovered that she was increasingly uneasy in his presence and that she didn't quite like the way his eyes lingered on her mouth and bosom or the certain way he smiled and repeatedly assured her, ". . . not to worry over the voucher—I'm positive that we can decide upon some method of payment which will please us both." There was nothing overtly sinister about his statement, but there was something about the way he said it . . .

Melissa shook herself. She was being a ninnyhammer! Looking for trouble where there was none, and heaven knew, she had enough to worry about without deliberately creating more for herself. Her mouth set in a stubborn line, she forced herself to think of other things.

Despite the strides forward they had taken since April, Melissa knew that what they had accomplished was paltry when compared with what must still be done before Willowglen could become profitable again. Folly's winnings always seemed to disappear at an alarming rate, and as yet, nothing but the barest minimum had been spent toward rectifying the effects of decay and mismanagement caused by Hugh's careless and eccentric behavior.

Melissa didn't let herself dwell on failure very often, but today for some reason she was unable to lift her flagging spirits. The jubilance that had been hers yesterday upon Etienne's return had faded, and she was dismally aware that the situation hadn't really changed that much: Willowglen was still dilapidated and in desperate need of money, men and repair; their only source of revenue was Folly's winnings, and Melissa lived in constant fear that something dreadful might happen to the stallion, that some terrible injury would occur which would end his racing days, if not his life. And, of course, there was the unpleasant situation existing between her and Uncle Josh.

She gave a heavy sigh. Would the day ever come that she was not besieged by so many worries? At the moment, she didn't think so; there were far too many hurdles ahead for her and Zachary, and one of them might spell disaster.

"I might have known this was where I would find you!" A sharp voice cut into her melancholy thoughts. "Young lady, you're supposed to be helping Martha with the hoeing, not lolling about the stables this way!"

Not a bit discomforted by the stringent tone and words, Melissa grinned up at the speaker. "Yes, ma'am," she said meekly, her eyes resting fondly on the tiny, gray-haired lady standing before her.

Neither the grin nor the obvious affection in Melissa's clear gaze seemed to affect the woman, but there was just the tiniest hint of amusement in her hazel eyes as she said, "And don't think that you can fool me by that soft-as-butter answer. I've known you since the moment you were born and I'm not about to be taken in by your antics! You and that hell-born brother of yours don't fool me in the least."

While Etienne held sway over all matters to do with the stables, it was this little Englishwoman who ruled the household and all its environs. Frances Osborne had been a novice lady's maid, not yet twenty, when she had accompanied her mistress, Melissa's mother, from England many years before, to settle in America. But in time her role had changed, the death of her mistress suddenly putting her in the position of nanny to the two young children as well as housekeeper for the widowed Hugh. And in spite of the uncertain conditions in which she found herself, she had never considered deserting either her charges or Willowglen. As she had told Melissa on more than one occasion, "Your dear sainted mother wouldn't have it! I loved my mistress, Anne, and I love you and your brother, and it will be over my dead body that I leave you!"

Frances had proved as good as her word, and Melissa was extremely grateful to have her competent hands on the reins of the household. For all her tiny size, she was a despotic, if loving, ruler and no one ever questioned her precepts—except Etienne. There had been a continuous running battle between the Frenchman and the tart-tongued Englishwoman for years, and Melissa sometimes wondered if they didn't enjoy their arguments far more than either would ever admit. They were both, however, violently jealous of the other's influence on what they clearly considered their charges, but since Hugh's death, an uneasy peace existed between them. Etienne grudgingly admitted that Melissa should not spend quite so much time in the stables, and Frances reluctantly agreed to act as chaperone when Melissa accompanied Etienne and Zachary to the various race meets. The truce was a fragile one, and each was quick to resist what they perceived as encroachment upon their own territory, so Melissa was just a little surprised that Frances had sought her out here, where it was, unquestionably, Etienne's domain.

Rising up gracefully from where she had been musing on her pile of hay, she teased, "I suppose we had better hurry away before Etienne discovers your presence in his beloved stable."

Frances sniffed haughtily. "I can assure you that what that strutting little coxcomb thinks doesn't matter to me at all!"

Relishing the scene that would have erupted if the "strutting little coxcomb" had heard Frances' provocative words, Melissa smothered a laugh and, putting her arm through Frances', quickly hustled the older woman away. It was a lovely May morning and they lingered over their walk to the house, idly discussing what plans Frances had in store for the day. The plans were rather mundane, and Melissa pushed aside the unworthy wish that Frances had had something more exciting in mind than seeing that the garden patch was kept weed-free and that the faded carpets of the main salon were taken outside and beaten soundly.

Martha was already hard at work in the garden that lay just beyond the kitchen, and after exchanging greetings with the black girl, Melissa found a hoe and attacked the persistent weeds with vigor. Watching her brisk actions, Martha finally exclaimed, "Miss, you gonna drop over dead if you doan stop workin' so hard in dis heah heat!"

Melissa grinned at her. Martha was a big, strapping girl of eighteen, her round face seemingly always to have a smile on it. Martha and her family were the only slaves who had not been sold when Hugh died. In addition to Martha, there were her parents, Martin and Ada, an older brother, Stanley, and a sister, Sarah, and two younger brothers, Joseph and Harlan, who ranged in age from sixteen to twelve. Ada had been the cook for the Seymours ever since Melissa could remember, and Martin had been her father's head groom. The entire family was hardworking and industrious, and Melissa and Zachary were exceedingly grateful for that fact.

The two women worked in companionable silence until

Ada called them for the midday meal. Melissa gladly put away her hoe and eagerly hastened to the house.

Zachary was already in the dining room when she arrived, sitting in his usual place at the head of the table. They greeted each other as Melissa sat down, and after she had taken a long swallow of lemonade from her tall glass, she said with open pleasure, "That was delicious! Especially since I have spent the morning hoeing and was about to perish from thirst." For a second, she scowled. "I *hate* hoeing!"

"Well, don't expect me to sympathize," Zachary replied unfeelingly. "I spent the entire morning mucking out the brood mare stalls, and believe me, I would have immediately traded the air inside those stalls for what you had to breathe!"

A wry grimace crossed Melissa's face and, thinking of how fortunate they were to have a stable to clean and a garden to hoe, she muttered, "What ungrateful wretches we are! At least Willowglen is still ours." Deliberately, she did not look at the huge water stain on the ceiling above her head and kept her gaze from the old, sun-rotted draperies that hung at the window. "And," she continued in a bracing tone of voice, "we have Folly!"

But she might not have been quite so pleased if she had known that at that very moment, one Dominic Slade had just arrived in Baton Rouge for the express purpose of buying a particular bay stallion.

Chapter Four

ARRIVING in the small town of Baton Rouge, which was pleasantly situated on a bluff on the left bank of the wide Mississippi River, Dominic found himself a room at an unusually clean and comfortable tavern and proceeded to inquire about the whereabouts and owner of Folly. The proprietor of the tavern, Jeremy Denham, was quite helpful, nodding his balding head in understanding.

"Josh Manchester is the man you want to see," said Jeremy as he placed a large tankard of foaming ale before Dominic. "He would have the handling of the family affairs. You'll find him at Oak Hollow, about three miles up the River Road north of town."

Dominic was both pleased and surprised at the information. Odd, though, he thought idly, that Royce had never mentioned that his father raised horses. But then, wasting little time, Dominic promptly wrote a note, explaining his reason for being in the area and requesting a meeting with Mr. Manchester. Mr. Denham's youngest son, Tom, was pressed into service to see that it was hand-delivered that very evening.

Mr. Manchester's immediate and encouraging return note was all that Dominic could have wished for, and he retired that night with the pleasurable thought that on the morrow he would see for himself this animal that had aroused much praise from knowledgeable horsemen. From Mr. Manchester's reply, Dominic was certain that by to-morrow night he would be the proud owner of Folly. . . .

Joshua knew very well that no such thing would happen—the most obvious reason being the fact that Folly was not his to sell. And although he might have been named joint guardian of Zachary, he had no illusions about the extent of authority he had over Melissa—under no circumstances would she allow him to order her to sell Folly. So why was Josh misleading Dominic?

The Slade name was not unknown to Josh; his son Royce frequently mentioned Dominic's name, and Josh himself had, years ago, visited the elder Slades at Bonheur. He was well acquainted with the extent of their wealth and their eminently respectable background. The fact that Mathew's older brother was an English baron had not escaped his attention, nor that Noelle Slade had been a member of one of the rich and powerful Creole families in New Orleans. And even though he did not know Dominic personally, what he had heard of Mr. Dominic Slade would have interested *anyone* casting about for an addition to one's family: he was young, reputably handsome, wealthy, charming and, most interesting from Josh's point of view, he was *un*married! Josh had nearly wept with joy when he realized the full import of Dominic's presence in Baton Rouge—since Melissa had turned her nose up at every eligible beau in the neighborhood, perhaps Mr. Dominic Slade would pique her interest!

With this idea in mind, Josh had decided instantly that a little subterfuge on his part might not come amiss; after all, if he told Mr. Slade that his niece, Melissa, was the owner of the horse, he knew very well what would happen. Mr. Slade would ride out to Willowglen, see Melissa, who would, Josh was quite positive, never realize the prize before her and would quite, *quite* vehemently inform Mr. Slade to go about his business, that Folly was not for sale! And that, Josh had thought sadly, would be that!

However . . . if he were able to *prepare* Mr. Slade for what Josh was certain would be an uncomfortable meeting with Melissa, then things might not turn out so disastrously. Given a little time, Josh believed that he could change the course of events. Pacing the elegant confines of his book-lined study, he spent considerable time working out a feasible plan to ensure that when Melissa and Dominic met, Dominic's interest in his niece was sure to be aroused.

He saw no difficulty in delaying that first meeting—there were all sorts of ways of postponing it—and he would use the time to good advantage. First he could look over young Slade for himself and decide if that gentleman really did live up to what he had heard about him. If Dominic proved not to be the paragon he was touted to be, then Josh would simply send him on his way. But assuming that Slade would be everything that was desirable in a future in-law, Josh would proceed to invite him to stay a few days at Oak Hollow. Royce was sure to second the notion once he learned his friend was in the neighborhood. Mr. Slade would see for himself that the Manchesters were every bit as aristocratic as his own family, that their house was just as elegant and immaculately appointed as Bonheur, that there were hundreds of fertile acres owned by the family and that their background and assets were very similar to his own.

For a moment Josh stopped his pacing and stared unseeingly at the gleaming top of his fine mahogany desk. The first part of his plan should be simple enough to accomplish, and even introducing Melissa's name into the conversation should present no trouble. During Mr. Slade's visit, he could casually mention his niece—her loveliness, her lively spiritedness, her gallant struggle to maintain Willowglen. A frown creased Josh's broad forehead. He would have to be careful in that area. Mustn't let young Slade think Melissa was destitute or that she was desperate for a rich husband. No. He would have to walk a very fine line there, giving Slade some warning of what he would find at Willowglen and yet making light of it. He could, he thought slowly, let slip some remark in passing about the rejected John Newcomb, letting Mr. Slade know that the deplorable state of affairs at Willowglen was not viewed as a detriment by other eligible men. Of course, he would have to make it clear that none of Willowglen's problems were of Melissa's making, but he would have to skirt around Hugh's wastrel habits.

Josh sighed. It was going to be extremely tricky, and for just a second he wondered why he had ever considered trying his hand at matchmaking. Then, thinking of the trust, of the uncomfortable interview he had had with his banker just last week, he stiffened his massive shoulders and continued with his plotting.

Josh foresaw no immediate obstacles in his handling of Dominic Slade and was confident that once he had dropped his hints and gotten Mr. Slade in the right frame of mind, Melissa's beauty would do the rest. Mr. Slade would take one look at her glowing features and succumb just like all the others.

Deliberately Josh had made himself not think of Melissa's probable reaction to all of his plans, but he knew the time had come that he must consider what to do about her stubborn, willful and utterly incomprehensible refusal to act like any other normal young lady and fall in love and marry. His expression gloomy, he idly poured himself a stout drink of Monongahela rye.

There was no use trying to reason with her—she was unreasonable! There was no use trying to explain all the advantages for all of them—he'd been doing that! And damned unpleasant it had all been!

Taking a quick drink of his rye, he once more began his pacing, his mind busy with ways of turning Melissa up sweet. There didn't seem to be anything that he could immediately think of. If he even mentioned Mr. Slade's name, Melissa would instantly be on her guard. All in all, he concluded heavily, any attempt on his part to present Mr. Slade in an agreeable light would be viewed with the deepest suspicion by his too-sharp-by-half niece.

His face suddenly brightened. Perhaps that was his mistake; perhaps he *shouldn't* mention Mr. Slade's many attributes. Instead, he should warn Melissa away from Mr. Slade. Warn her to be careful around the fellow, let her think that he didn't quite approve of this young man from Natchez. Act as if he found him a bit of a bounder. Praising prospective suitors had never worked, so it was possible the opposite tack would provide results.

Quite pleased with himself, certain he had hit upon the right scheme, Joshua left his study and went in search of Sally. He found his wife of thirty-five years in the small parlor, sitting comfortably on a rosewood sofa covered in a luxurious silk damask. She had been absently leafing through a collection of fashion plates her seamstress had left off earlier. At her husband's entrance, she glanced up and smiled. "Ah, there you are, my dear. I wondered when you would join me."

There was little resemblance between the two young Seymours and their paternal aunt. Sally Manchester, at fifty-four years of age, had no signs of their vibrant coloring, nor had she ever been tall. She was simply a still-pretty, plump little hen of a woman. Zachary would have added sotto voce, "Hen-witted too!" That might have been the case, but not even her worst enemy would have denied her generous nature and sweet personality.

Despite five children, there were still obvious signs of the beauty she had been in her youth. Her eyes were large and well shaped, their color a clear, pale blue, and her faintly lined creamy skin still had the softness of a rose petal. She wore her silver-dusted brown hair parted down the middle with girlish clusters of curls dangling near her ears. A cameo brooch rested amongst the ruffles of lace at her throat, and the deep blue of her silk gown intensified the color of her eyes. Joshua thought she looked adorable.

Sitting down beside her, he grasped one of her soft white hands in his and said happily, "Sally, I think that this young Slade fellow may be just the man to snare our Lissa's heart." He paused, adding thoughtfully, "Provided *we* like the look of him! When he comes to call tomorrow, I want you to invite him to visit with us for a few days." He hesitated a moment. Even loving Sally as he did, Josh was not blind to her lack of intellect and he wondered how much of his scheme to tell her. He finally decided to say as little as possible, already regretting having even mentioned Slade's name in connection with Melissa.

Looking at Sally keenly, he eventually admonished, "Um, it would be better if you didn't say anything about Melissa to young Slade. Mustn't let him think we are out to snare a rich husband for our niece. Just do the pretty and ask him to stay."

Sally appeared puzzled. "But don't we want Melissa to marry? And if he's a nice gentleman, won't he do?"

"Well, yes, but he doesn't have to know that!" Josh answered a bit testily. "It won't do to have him get the wind up and shear off. We want to play these cards close to our chests.''

"Oh! Does Mr. Slade like to play cards?'' Sally asked somewhat doubtfully. "It seems a rather silly way to fix a young woman's interests.''

Giving her an affectionate little pat on the cheek, Josh said gently, "Don't worry about it, my dear. Just be the wonderful hostess you have always been and make Mr. Slade feel right at home.''

And so the next morning, when Dominic came to ca'l at the appointed hour, he was greeted by an effusively genial Josh Manchester. He would have spun and run if he had realized just why Mr. Manchester seemed so very pleased to meet him.

Even at their first handshake, Josh was favorably impressed with the tall young man before him, liking the firm clasp and the clear, direct gaze of the smiling gray eyes. Dominic's appearance was everything Josh could have wished for—the freshly laundered cravat beautifully and neatly arranged at the neck; the coat of blue superfine fitting the broad shoulders impeccably; the buff pantaloons resting snugly against the long, shapely thighs and the Hessian boots so highly shined that Josh was positive he could see his reflection in them. Dominic's waistcoat also met with his approval, being a discreetly light-colored material, unlike the gaudily embroidered ones that appealed so strongly to his youngest son. Obviously, young Mr. Slade was a man of fashion in the manner of the English Beau Brummell, and Josh felt confident that not even Melissa could have faulted young Slade's sartorial elegance.

Nor, he thought smugly as he ushered Dominic through the wide, tastefully decorated hallway to his study, would Melissa, or any other young lady for that matter, be totally immune to Dominic's dark, handsome features. After several moments of polite conversation over cups of freshly brewed coffee, it was apparent that everything he had heard of the gentleman lounging negligently across from him was true. Dominic Slade was, indeed, handsome, charming and wellborn. A sigh of near bliss escaped Josh. Now to convince Melissa of that fact.

The first part of Josh's plan unfolded with miraculous

ease, Dominic innocently accepting Josh's rambling excuses of why it was not convenient for him to look over Folly today.

Dominic smiled faintly. "It doesn't really matter, sir. I am in no hurry. I intend to remain some days in the area and I'm sure that we can decide upon a date later in the week or even the next that will suit both of us."

Josh beamed at him, almost rubbing his hands together in glee. Restraining himself with an effort, he warmly invited Dominic to join him and the family for a light repast. Dominic smiled and said ruefully, "I feel that I have been here this past hour or so under false pretenses—I am well acquainted with your son Royce. We met in England some years ago and have kept up a halfhearted correspondence since then. I had every intention of seeing him while I was in the area, and your gracious invitation enables me to combine business with pleasure."

If it were possible, Josh's delight with the current state of affairs grew. He was nearly dancing with pleasure a few minutes later as he ushered Dominic down the large main hallway in search of Royce.

Royce was extremely pleased to see a friend from his days in London. For several minutes he and Dominic bantered back and forth, bringing each other up-to-date with various happenings since they had last met and also chiding the other for not having written more frequently, as they had promised faithfully to do before Royce had left London. Seeing the easy friendship between the two men, Josh couldn't have been better pleased. His heart, however, did jump uncomfortably when Royce suddenly asked casually, "But tell me, what brings you here to Oak Hollow?" Grinning, he added, "Since it obviously wasn't the wish for my company."

"Folly," Dominic replied lightly. "Why else would I tear myself away from the illicit delights to be found in Natchez or New Orleans?"

A frown creased his handsome features as Royce asked, "Folly? Melissa's—"

That was as far as he got before his father interrupted hastily. "What does it matter? Your friend is here now, and I do think that I just heard your mother calling us to

join her in the dining room. Do come along, Royce—you
and Dominic can talk later.''

Royce sent his father a considering glance, but seeing
the oddly pleading expression in his eyes, he shrugged and
without comment followed his lead. Putting his hand under Dominic's elbow, he said mildly, ''Come, let us find
my mother and I shall introduce you to her.''

Except for that one nervous moment, the next few hours
passed in a manner that Josh could only call fortuitous.
Dominic was a charming and affable guest, his graceful
compliments to Sally Manchester causing her to blush with
pleasure, and the invitation for Dominic to stay with them
at Oak Hollow was issued warmly and naturally.

Dominic hesitated to accept, but Royce instantly sec-
onded his mother's request, saying lazily, ''Do stay, Dom.
There is much that we have to reminisce over, and I'm
certain that you will find the accommodations here much
more to your liking than those in town.''

Shrugging his shoulders in good-natured defeat, Dominic demurred no longer and cheerfully accepted their offer
of hospitality. ''I'll ride to Baton Rouge with you to get
your belongings,'' Royce said, ''but before we leave, I
would like to have a word with my father,'' he added,
shooting a sharp look at Josh.

A few minutes later, alone in his study with his eldest
son, Josh somewhat warily faced Royce, who was leaning
casually against the doorjamb, his arms loosely folded
across his chest, the expression on his handsome face doing nothing to allay Josh's nervousness. For just a second
Josh considered bluffing his way out of the situation, but
then he sighed. Royce was *very* good at calling a bluff.

Royce Manchester greatly resembled his cousins Melissa and Zachary—it was freely acknowledged that he
was the very image of his late grandfather Jeffery Seymour at the same age. Curly, thick tawny hair clung to
his well-shaped head, and he possessed the same black,
well-defined eyebrows and topaz eyes which Melissa and
Zachary had both inherited. He was a tall man, broad-
shouldered and lean-hipped and just a bit of a rogue. He
was also extremely (''uncomfortably,'' Josh would have
piously averred) astute, and little escaped his notice.

Fixing his fidgeting parent with a keen glance, Royce demanded, "What exactly was the meaning of that little scene earlier?"

Josh cleared his throat awkwardly and muttered, "Dominic believes that we . . . that I own Folly. He doesn't know about Melissa, and I thought—" He stopped abruptly, pitifully aware of the frailty of his plan.

He didn't need to explain himself to Royce, though, sudden comprehension dawning on that young man. A sardonic gleam in his golden-brown eyes, Royce said, "So you thought that you would try to sweeten him up before he met my intrepid cousin." Shaking his head disgustedly, he added, "You'll catch cold at that! Dominic is too wily an opponent for you. The moment he hears of Melissa he'll know precisely what you are about—believe me, he is *very* knowing when it comes to spotting matchmakers."

Not willing to argue with Royce on that point, Josh merely asked, "You won't tell him? You'll let him go on believing that Folly belongs to me?"

There was a thoughtful pause; then Royce said in a measured tone, "I will not tell him . . . unless he asks me directly." A smile curving his well-shaped mouth, Royce confessed, "Who knows, your little plan might bear fruit, and it will definitely be amusing to watch Dominic spar with Melissa. I'm positive that he has never met a young woman quite like her and I'm equally confident that she has never come up against any man as devilishly charming as Dominic Slade."

Although Royce's reaction was not precisely what Josh would have preferred, he did breathe easier once Royce and Dominic had departed for town. He also didn't waste a moment before setting out for Willowglen—with the first part of his plan under way, it was time to set the second phase in motion.

Not to his surprise, upon arriving at the main house, he was informed by Frances Osborne that Melissa was busy down at the stables. Whistling happily to himself, Josh strolled off in that direction. For the moment, the reasons behind the necessity to see Melissa married as soon as possible had faded from his mind, and he was thoroughly enjoying his attempt at matchmaking.

It took a second for his eyes to adjust from the bright light outside to the pleasant shadows of the interior of the stables, but once they did, he instantly spotted Melissa. Her back was to him and she was busily raking out one of the stalls.

Idly he noted the old, shabby gown and the prim little bun at the back of her head, but assumed that both dress and hairstyle were the result of the chores that presently occupied her. It was only when he called her name and she spun around to face him that he realized his error. In stunned dismay he gawked at her staid appearance, his happy mood vanishing immediately as the full effect of the ugly spectacles, ill-fitting gown and severe coiffure finally penetrated. Not even an uncle's fondness could ignore the fact that she looked . . . well . . . drab! And it didn't take a great deal of intelligence for Josh to know why she had altered her appearance in this fashion—she was obviously determined to repel any further advances made by the male sex. Uncertain how to meet this unexpected turn of events, Josh stared at her in gloomy silence.

Seeing his dejection, but never guessing the reason for it, Melissa almost felt sorry for her uncle. *Almost.* She had steeled herself to be met with a great deal of angry exasperation, and Josh's expression of utter astonishment and discouragement left her torn between amusement and compunction. It was obvious that her changed appearance was having precisely the effect she wanted, but the fact that Josh was not shouting and blustering made her a little uneasy. An angry and irascible Josh she could deal with firmly, but not a Josh who looked so very defeated; her face softened, a tentative smile curving her mouth.

That smile changed her entire face, making one hypnotically aware of the pleasing shape of her lips and the gentle curve of her jaw. The change was remarkable, and despite the scraped-back hair and ugly spectacles, an enticing glimpse of her natural loveliness was glaringly apparent and, in that instant, Josh wasn't quite so discouraged. Who knows, he told himself stoutly, Dominic Slade might enjoy discovering the beauty which lurked beneath the spinsterish exterior. Uncomfortably conscious that he was probably deluding himself, but determined to press on with his plans, Josh hectically sought some way to turn Melissa's latest act of defiance to an advantage. Struck by a sudden inspiration, he finally said slowly, "Ah. I see that you have already been warned."

Dumbfounded, Melissa stared at him. "Warned?" she repeated weakly, wondering frantically why, beyond his first obvious astonishment, her appearance didn't seem to bother him in the least. "Warned about what?"

Warming to his theme, almost enjoying the situation, Josh answered smoothly, "Why, about Dominic Slade."

Melissa gave her uncle a keen glance. He didn't *look* foxed, but then she wasn't that familiar with the behavior of a gentleman who had imbibed too freely. But something odd was going on, and not knowing what else to do, she asked cautiously, "Dominic Slade? What about him?"

Josh feigned an expression of surprise. "You mean you haven't heard yet? I thought that you must have—surely it was because you knew that he was in the neighborhood that you have dressed yourself in such an unbecoming fashion?"

Mystified, but gamely trying to make some sense of his words, Melissa shrugged and replied airily, "Oh! *That* Dominic Slade." Feeling a perfect fool, yet unwilling to let Josh know how baffled she was, she added mendaciously, "Someone did mention his presence in the area, and I thought it best if I . . ." She let the sentence trail off, not wishing to reveal that she had absolutely no idea of what he was talking about. Sending him an uncertain smile, she asked, "You approve?"

"Oh, yes, my dear! I can't tell you how happy I am that you used your good common sense and took immediate steps to protect yourself from the possibility of the rogue's unwanted attentions. You were very wise to disguise your undeniable charms this way." Giving a hearty chuckle, he continued blandly. "Few men if any would make advances to a woman who looks as you do now! Certainly not Dominic Slade! Only the prettiest fillies will do for him!"

Slightly nettled by Josh's comments, even though the opinion expressed was precisely what she had been striving for, Melissa said stiffly, "That may be, but perhaps the 'prettiest fillies' won't be the least interested in Mr. Slade!''

"You're wrong there, m'dear!" Josh replied pityingly. "He's a handsome devil, I'll tell you plain. What's more, with his family background—he's one of the Slades from Natchez, a very wealthy and respected family—there will be few of our neighborhood ladies who won't find him utterly irresistible.'' Slyly he added, "I had the pleasure of meeting him today and I can assure you that he is indeed *very* handsome!''

Melissa's upper lip curled scornfully. "And I suppose he thinks rather highly of himself!''

"Oh, no! Not at all! He's a charming fellow, quite unassuming. One would never guess, except from his beautiful manners and impeccable attire, that he comes from such a prominent family.''

Thoroughly baffled now—Dominic Slade sounded just like the sort of gentleman her uncle had been trying to get her to marry for years—Melissa frowned. What was Josh playing at? And why? Some of her confusion showed in her expression as she asked warily, "If he is such a paragon, why should you be happy that I am dressed to repel his advances? I would have thought that you would have ridden over here pell-mell to insist that I rig myself out to catch his attention, not the other way around!''

Josh appeared scandalized. "Oh, but he would never do for *you,* child! He is far too sophisticated and worldly. Besides,'' he murmured pensively, "I really don't know that he would make a very good husband . . . it is said that he is rather fond of a . . . ah, certain type of woman. And, of course, there is his gambling.'' Josh shook his head with regret. "No, no, he isn't the type of man we would want you to marry, and I'm very pleased that you were so quick to realize it and have taken steps to make certain that you do not attract his roving gaze.''

Conflicting emotions raging in her breast, Melissa was aware of an unworthy impulse to stamp her foot with vexation. How dare Uncle Josh decide that Mr. Slade wasn't the man for her! How dare he so high-handedly dismiss Dominic Slade as too sophisticated and worldly for her! She might like Mr. Slade very much once she met him, and it was humiliating for Josh to cavalierly reject her chances of attracting the attention of such a handsome, wealthy, charming man.

Suddenly realizing where her rebellious thoughts were taking her, Melissa narrowed her gaze and shot a closer look at her uncle. Was this a clever little plot on his part? Was he deliberately misleading her, hoping that she could be tricked into liking Mr. Slade?

Josh met her suspicious look, not by so much as a batted eyelash allowing his innocent expression to change. But Melissa's unblinking stare was a trifle unnerving and, rushing into speech, he said the one thing that could divert her attention. "Have you seen young Newcomb of late? I understand that he is still willing to marry you."

At his words, all speculation about Josh's possible duplicity fled. With a wrathful glint in her fine eyes, Melissa snapped, "Willing? I would say more like languishing! It is to escape his attentions—and Mr. Slade's as well," she added hastily, "that I have disguised myself in this fashion." Sending her uncle a half-angry, half-vexed look, she went on almost imploringly. "Will you please stop trying to get me married? I know your need is urgent, but so is ours, and if I will not marry to make our own situation more comfortable, why do you think I shall do so to change yours? I will *not* marry John Newcomb! And I would greatly appreciate it if you would cease your meddling in my affairs!"

Patting her arm gently, Josh said soothingly, "There, there, my dear. I had not realized that my actions have caused you so much distress. You must believe me when I say that I will no longer make any attempt to convince John Newcomb to continue in his suit."

Melissa stared dumbly at her uncle for a moment. Then, hardly believing what he had said, she prodded, "Will you promise?"

Giving her a benign smile, he said with perfect truth, "You have my word on it!" And dropping a fond salute on her cheek, he bade her a pleasant farewell.

Melissa watched him go in dazed astonishment, hardly able to comprehend the ease with which he had given her his promise. He must have been foxed! she finally decided. But later she discussed the conversation with Etienne and Zachary, who both were of the opinion that he could not possibly have been drunk.

"It was too early in the morning," Zachary said with all the superior knowledge of a nineteen-year-old male.

Etienne shrugged. "It was early, *oui,* but the time of day has nothing to do with it. Your *oncle* would never come to you in such a fashion—his manners are far too nice."

Reluctantly, Melissa agreed with Etienne's reading of the situation. Josh *was* a stickler when it came to what was due the ladies of the family, and he would no sooner appear naked in front of her than he would appear drunk.

"Then what do you make of his remarks about this Dominic Slade?" Melissa asked with a frown. "Don't you think it was sort of odd? Doesn't Mr. Slade sound *precisely* like the sort of gentleman Josh has been trying to throw my way ever since I turned seventeen?" Her scowl deepening, she went on. "It was almost as if he didn't want me to like Mr. Slade, yet he made very certain that I knew that the man was handsome and wealthy and came from an impeccable background. Could Uncle Josh have been rather devious?"

At Zachary's expression of confusion, Melissa explained somewhat incoherently, "Oh, you know what I mean! By appearing *not* to want me to like Mr. Slade, he was actually hoping that I would act perversely and like the man simply because I would think that it would annoy him, when exactly the opposite would be true."

Zachary blinked at her. After a discreet pause, he offered cautiously, "Er . . . do you think that Uncle Josh is *that* clever?"

Melissa sighed. "I don't know—he could be. Perhaps I'm just unduly suspicious of his sudden change of heart."

"I think, *mes enfants,* that you are worrying too much about nothing," Etienne said calmly. "And whatever his motives, be glad that, for the moment, you are not at dagger's drawing with him! As for Mr. Dominic Slade . . ." His dark eyes twinkling, he teased, "Who knows, *ma belle,* he might prove to be the answer to all of our prayers!"

Chapter Five

DOMINIC wouldn't know about being the answer to anyone else's hopes; he only knew that after ten days at Oak Hollow, though quite pleasant, his own hopes of owning or even of *seeing* the stallion Folly were rapidly vanishing. Whenever he tried to bring the conversation around to the horse, Royce proved to be surprisingly adept at changing the topic, and as for Josh Manchester . . .

Standing at the window of his handsomely appointed bedroom at Oak Hollow, Dominic scowled down at the rolling expanse of green lawn that stretched out beneath his gaze. Mr. Josh Manchester was proving to be singularly elusive whenever the subject of Folly was broached. Oh, he was a very cordial and accommodating host, and it was very enjoyable to spend time with Royce, but after all, Dominic *was* here as a prospective buyer. As yet, however, there had been no further discussion about the stallion. He hadn't even been able to arrange to view the wretched animal, and his patience, not one of his virtues to begin with, was wearing thin. He was also, he thought with annoyance, growing damned weary of hearing about Josh's blasted niece, Melissa Seymour. If he heard Josh tell him one more time how lovely and spirited she was, how sweetly independent, how gallantly she was helping her young brother restore their temporary reverses, Dominic knew he would be driven to violence. She was so gallant, in fact, that she had, at great sacrifice to herself, turned down more than one tempting offer of matrimony. Oh, there was little doubt that Dominic would find it a great treat to meet her, Josh had stated positively. Why, they had so much in common, he had averred on more than one occasion—she was a neck-or-nothing horse-woman and very knowledgeable when it came to the breeding and raising of prime horseflesh.

A cynical little smile curving his mouth, Dominic decided that Miss Melissa Seymour must be an opinionated, bracket-faced, overbearing female! Why else was this paragon of virtue and beauty still unmarried? Josh could say what he wanted, but Dominic was quite certain that Miss Melissa was just the sort of female he couldn't abide, horsey and domineering—and worse, the unpleasant notion that Josh was not so subtly attempting to arouse his interest in her had begun to uneasily cross Dominic's mind with increasing frequency.

Royce had remained carefully noncommittal on the subject of Miss Seymour, and that too aroused Dominic's suspicions—especially when he had the distinct impression that Royce was finding something *very* amusing. That alone, he thought with a narrowed gaze, should be a warning to him. Royce had a damned strange sense of humor at times and he was perfectly capable of taking sardonic enjoyment in watching the frantic efforts of male acquaintances as they violently fended off grimly determined matchmaking mamas—or *uncles,* as the case might be!

Dominic suddenly grinned to himself. Well, he had done the same thing; he and Royce had even wagered on a similar situation, and if their positions were reversed . . . Chuckling to himself, he turned around and headed for the door.

Once he was in the spacious hallway, though, his grin disappeared; and with an ominous tightening of his square jaw, he went in search of his host. He was *not,* he decided in that instant, going to be fobbed off a minute longer. He would see the horse and make his offer and that would be that! To Miss Seymour he gave no further thought.

He found Josh seated comfortably in the library, and with no preamble, Dominic said quietly, "I think it would be a good idea if I saw Folly today. I cannot trespass longer on your generous hospitality." Taking his gold watch from his vest pocket, he glanced down at it and murmured, "Shall we plan to leave the house for the stables in, say, half an hour?"

Caught utterly by surprise, Josh could think of no ready excuse. Gamely he attempted to forestall the awful moment when he must confess his duplicity, and he blustered, he stammered and he stalled, but to no avail. Dominic remained politely unwavering in his intention, and finally, Josh somewhat shamefacedly confessed the truth.

There was silence as Dominic, astounded, took in the full import of Josh's words. Uncertain whether to swear or laugh, Dominic asked eventually, "Are you telling me that you don't own Folly? That this niece of yours, Melissa Seymour, is the actual owner and that for the past ten days, delightful though they have been, you have kept me here under false pretenses?"

Embarrassed and extremely uncomfortable, Josh moved restlessly in his chair. Reluctantly he admitted that this was indeed the case. He glanced nervously across at the unsmiling young man in front of him, suddenly wishing fervently that he had never embarked upon this once seemingly clever scheme.

"I see," Dominic said flatly, the expression on his dark face hard to decipher. Neutrally, he asked, "Would you mind telling me why you went to all this subterfuge? Why you didn't tell me the truth when I first arrived at your house?"

Josh cleared his throat anxiously, wondering bleakly why he had not thought of what would happen when the truth about the real ownership of Folly came out. Desperately seeking some way to excuse his actions, some way to redeem himself and yet not divulge the scheme nearest to his heart, he came up with the germ of an idea. Embellishing his hastily created tale as he told it, he said with more confidence than he felt, "I thought it best. I wanted to make certain that you were a proper gentleman before you met my niece. I *am*, after all, her brother's guardian and I feel great responsibility for Melissa." Encouraged by the lack of obvious signs of anger on Dominic's part, he added with a complete disregard of the truth, "Since their father's death, *both* my niece and nephew look upon me as a trusted adviser and protector of their interests.'' Beginning to believe his own words, he ended self-righteously, ''It is my *duty* to shield them from those who would take advantage of them.''

Thoughtfully Dominic regarded Josh. There was something about Josh's explanation that didn't quite ring true but, considering the circumstances, it appeared plausible— if unpalatable! Dominic's credibility had never been questioned before and he was nonplussed to think that all this time Josh had been judging him. His pride was just a little wrung to think that *anyone* would dare to speculate about his suitability!

Amusement warring with chagrin in his breast, Dominic asked dryly, ''And have you satisfied yourself that I am not about to take advantage of your niece?''

''Oh, yes!'' Josh quickly answered and, realizing that he might have offended, added hurriedly, ''There was never any *real* question about you, you understand . . . it was just that . . .'' He paused. Then, seeking to distance himself from this uneasy situation, he blundered on. ''Melissa needed to be reassured.'' An unpleasant thought suddenly occurred to Josh and he muttered, ''Er, I should warn you that she is not in favor of selling the horse. She has some nonsensical notion to establish her own stud farm.'' Spreading his hands deprecatingly, he added, ''I have told her it is ridiculous, but as I have mentioned to you, she can be, um, stubborn when the mood strikes her.''

''If she doesn't want to sell the animal, my time here has been wasted!'' Dominic said with exasperation. ''Why didn't you tell me that the horse was not for sale?''

''Ah, well,'' Josh floundered, not about to reveal his fond hopes of seeing Melissa make an excellent match with Dominic. And still not willing to give up entirely on his original scheme—especially since the worst moment seemed to be behind him—he said craftily, ''The animal *might* be purchased if my niece could be convinced that you will be a responsible owner and will not mistreat the horse.''

''I only want to buy Folly, not marry him!'' Dominic retorted acidly, his temper flaring. But Josh's statement was encouraging, and, reluctant to abandon his plans without at least seeing the horse, he finally said, "If what you say is true, with your permission I shall ride over to Willowglen and meet with your niece myself. Since she appears to be overly fond of the horse, perhaps I can convince her that I mean the animal only good will!"

Josh beamed at him, greatly relieved to have the unpleasantness disposed of so easily. "Excellent!" he said happily. "And of course you have my permission! Why, you are already like one of the family!"

Dominic cocked a derisive eyebrow at him, his suspicions fully aroused. Having Josh Manchester as an in-law was the *last* thing he wanted!

Taking his leave from the older man, Dominic met Royce in the main hallway. Sending his friend a darkling look, Dominic growled, "I'm on my way to see Folly, *Miss Seymour's* horse. You, I'll talk to when I get back!"

"Ah, found out, did you?" Royce asked with interest. "I wondered how much longer it would take you."

A reluctant laugh broke from Dominic. "Damn you, Royce! You could have warned me!"

Royce chuckled. "Yes, but it wouldn't have been half so amusing."

A wry smile on his mouth, Dominic walked to the stables of Oak Hollow and very shortly thereafter, with directions from the head groom firmly in his mind, he was riding toward Willowglen. His thoughts were not kind as he rode along, and ironically, it was not Josh who aroused his ire but Miss Seymour! Inexplicably, he had convinced himself that it was at Miss Seymour's request that Josh had embarked upon the silly little charade that had had him wasting his time at Oak Hollow. He felt a fool and he was more than a little annoyed about the entire situation. If it weren't for the fact that the very delay and Miss Seymour's apparent reluctance to meet him had stirred a stubborn determination on his part, he would have departed immediately from Oak Hollow and given Folly no further serious thought. But as it was, against his will, he *was* curious about Miss Seymour and, of course, there was the stallion. . . .

His first sight of Willowglen was not encouraging. With a sardonic twist to his mobile mouth, he decided that Josh had greatly exaggerated the *temporary* reverses. To his expert eye, it was obvious that the condition of the main house was not due to some recent lack of funds but had been of a long-standing duration. The gracious lines of the wide and low, once-handsome two-storied house were still apparent, and the setting amongst the moss-draped oaks, giant mimosa trees and large crape myrtles was undeniably attractive, but it was glaringly apparent that it had been several years since any money had been spent on the up-keep of the house and grounds. The paint was blistered and peeling, the years of the hot Louisiana sun having inflicted great damage, and there were several unsightly gaps in the graceful though rusting wrought-iron railing which adorned the gallery that ran the entire length of the front of the house. The expanse of lawn which wandered through the various trees that surrounded the house was shaggy and choked with weeds, and there was a general air of neglect about the whole area. No, Dominic told himself grimly, this was no temporary reversal of fortune, and he wondered how much more Josh had misled him about Miss Seymour and her brother.

When his knock upon the pair of double doors at the front of the house was not answered, he made his way with a sigh around to the rear of the house. Not only, he reflected dismally, did the Seymour place appear unkempt, but it seemed that they also did not keep a proper amount of servants either!

At the back of the house, he cast a jaundiced eye over the untidy kitchen garden and the few scrawny hens in a sagging pen nearby. Seeing the small brick building which was set some distance from the main house, he approached it with a quickening step. Surely someone would be in the kitchen!

Someone was. This time his knock upon a door was answered by Ada, her hands covered with flour and an expression of impatience on her shiny black face. She was not particularly welcoming, and a brief conversation elicited the information that Miss Seymour was not there (where she should have been, Ada informed him roundly, helping with the baking) but that she could be found at the stables. His reservations increasing with every moment,

Dominic slowly walked in the direction indicated by Ada, but his interest in meeting the eccentric Miss Seymour was definitely piqued—*none* of the ladies he knew would ever be found in either the kitchen or the stables!

Miss Seymour, presently hard at work raking and shoveling out one of the large box stalls which had been recently built to house the new mares, was *not* thinking about Mr. Dominic Slade in the least! But that wasn't to say that her interest in that gentleman hadn't been piqued too. During the days that Dominic had spent at Oak Hollow, Josh had been able to ride over to Willowglen only twice and he had been very careful not to overplay his cards with regard to Mr. Dominic Slade. Beyond his initial conversation with Melissa he had kept Dominic's name to a minimum, only mentioning the fact, on his second visit, that he was staying with them and that he was quite a horseman . . . and that he too was thinking of setting up his own stud farm at a plantation named Thousand Oaks, which it just so happened was located less than two days' ride up the river. Wasn't *that* a coincidence! Who knew—he might even consider purchasing Folly for his own stables!

That information had not sat well with Melissa, and she had been aware of a feeling of great resentment. How dare this stranger ride into their midsts and decide to immediately set up in competition to her! Not, she admitted ruefully, that Willowglen was much of a threat to the newcomer. But it rankled, as did Josh's comment about selling Folly. She would *never* sell Folly and certainly not to some upstart, encroaching mushroom who might very well sabotage her fledgling attempts to establish her own stables! Irrationally, she even held his apparent wealth and handsomeness against him. It just wasn't fair for one person to have apparently been so generously endowed by fate! But she was curious about him and, to her shame, every time she had left Willowglen the past few days she had been secretly hoping to catch a glimpse of this paragon riding about the countryside. She wasn't, however, prepared to find him in her own stables—especially not when she was hot, dirty and sweaty and was holding a shovelful of horse, er, droppings in her hands!

One moment she was bent over her task, longing for

nothing more than a cool drink of water and a long, leisurely swim in the creek just over the hill, and the next
she was spinning around to stare at a tall, handsome
stranger. A stranger, she thought with a sudden, inexplicable tightening in her chest, who could only be Mr. Dominic Slade.

Coming in from the bright sunlight, Dominic took a
moment for his eyes to adjust to the quiet gloom of the
interior of the stable. He had been slightly relieved to see
that at least in this area *some* attempt at upkeep had been
made, but he was strongly of the opinion that when he
finally did view Folly he was going to be extremely disappointed. It was inconceivable that the horse he was
searching for would be found in this place of genteel pov-
erty, and he was fairly convinced that someone was enjoying a jest at his expense.

Seeing signs of movement at the rear of the stable, he
strolled in that direction. "Excuse me," he said as he
came closer, "but could you tell me where I could find
Miss Seymour?"

Unbearably conscious of her dishevelment, of the ugly
bun sagging at the back of her head, of the spectacles
sliding down her sweat-slick nose, of the shapeless unat-
tractiveness of the gown she was wearing and of the shovel
filled with horse manure in her hands, Melissa wished violently that she were anywhere but here. The fact that
Dominic was nattily attired in a superb-fitting jacket of
blue superfine—a jacket, she noted crossly, that did nothing to disguise his broad shoulders and wide chest—didn't
make her feel any better. With something between resentment and unwilling admiration, Melissa noticed the pair
of buff breeches that clearly revealed the muscled length
of his long, well-shaped legs and the pristine white cravat
which only called attention to the dark, handsome features
rising above its neat folds.

It was, she thought breathlessly, unfair for any man to look
as Dominic Slade did, to have such thick, curly black hair,
such long, luxurious eyelashes, such beautiful gray eyes and
a mouth . . . Melissa swallowed with difficulty . . . a mouth
that made the most erotic thoughts flash through her brain.

Appalled by and furious because of her unexpected reaction to him, she glared at Dominic and said stiffly, "I am Miss Seymour." With Uncle Josh's warnings about his libertine ways ringing in her ears, she decided that the sooner he was out of her barn the better. "Just who do you think you are, walking in here this way?" she asked rudely.

It was quick wits that prevented Dominic's mouth from falling open in astonishment. Not only did her appearance surprise him, but her hostile attitude caught him completely off guard. Surely, he thought with stupefaction, this unfashionably tall and scrawny creature in a deplorably fitting gown squinting so fiercely at him above a pair of ridiculously large spectacles could not be the Miss Seymour of Josh's descriptions! But it was her attitude that caused the polite smile to fade from his lips and the gray eyes to lose their usual good-humored glint.

Not in the best humor himself after his interview with Josh, and not at all pleased with what he had seen of Willowglen so far and most of all, not at all used to being greeted in such a fashion, *particularly* by the females of the species, Dominic asked with insulting disbelief, "Miss *Melissa* Seymour?"

Vividly aware of the frightful picture she must present, her shabby gown sticking unpleasantly to her back, through gritted teeth she got out, "Yes! Miss *Melissa* Seymour!" Confident of his identity but wishing to be positive, she asked, "And you are . . .?"

She wasn't the least surprised when Dominic said flatly, "Dominic Slade. Your cousin Royce and I are old friends, and I have been visiting at your uncle's plantation for the past several days."

"And—?" Melissa inquired hostilely, not about to fall victim to the perfidious charms that Josh had warned her about. But, to her dismay, that didn't stop her from wishing irrationally that she were wearing her best gown and that her hair were newly washed and curling about her shoulders!

Dominic's mouth tightened. What an ungracious witch! Resisting an urge to turn on his heels, he said grimly, "And, I have heard of a horse that you apparently own— Folly, a bay stallion. My brother Morgan saw the animal race in the New Orleans area several weeks ago and he was quite impressed by his speed and appearance. If you are agreeable I would like to see the horse with a view to possibly purchasing him.''

A gust of completely unreasonable rage swept through Melissa. After all she and Zachary had been through, after all the dreams they had shared, how dare this—this—popinjay speak so confidently of buying *her* horse! How dared he come uninvited and unannounced into *her* stables with his fine clothes and arrogant airs and act as if anything he wanted would be instantly forthcoming! She was dimly conscious that part of her hostile reaction to him was caused by embarrassment at being caught garbed as she was, and it didn't help her temper one bit for her to know that it was her own fault she looked as she did! Still, it wasn't just the awkward situation that prompted her hostility. There was something about the tall, darkly attractive gentleman standing in front of her which aroused an inexplicable animosity—and she never took instant likes or dislikes to anyone! He was far too handsome, she thought savagely, and far too confident and sure of himself.

A little ashamed and shocked by her uncharacteristically churlish reaction to a perfect stranger, but heedful of Josh's warnings and determined to get rid of Dominic's distracting presence immediately, she snapped ungraciously, ''If it was only to see Folly that brought you here, you have wasted your time as well as my own. Under no circumstances will I *ever* consent to sell Folly—not for *any* price you might care to offer!''

Thinking that Miss Melissa Seymour was one of the most unappealing, ill-tempered shrews it had ever been his misfortune to meet, Dominic nodded curtly. ''Then I would say that we have nothing more to discuss.'' With a derisive gleam in his gray eyes, he glanced at her shovelful of highly aromatic manure and drawled, ''I see that you have much more, ah, important things to do, so I shall not waste any more of your time.''

He took another long look at Melissa, his gaze moving slowly over the pulled-back hair of indeterminate color, the old-fashioned spectacles and the pinched mouth as he wondered cynically if it was common knowledge that Josh and Royce were mentally deficient. A beauty? Ha! If this was their idea of a beauty, it was obvious that they both should be shipped to England for a stay at Bedlam!

Shrugging his broad shoulders at the strange quirks in human nature, he was about to turn on his heel when from the front of the stable a voice called, "Lissa! I've brought a jug of lemonade. Do you want some?"

At the sound of her name, Melissa left off considering dumping her shovel of manure on Mr. Slade's highly polished boots, and a warm smile suddenly spread across her face. "Oh, Zack!" she cried in a far nicer tone of voice than Dominic had heard from her yet. "How did you know that I was longing for something to drink?"

Her brother laughed, and with a pitcher of lemonade in one hand and two glasses in the other, Zachary approached. Glancing at Dominic, he sent him a friendly smile and said, "Hello, you must be Dominic Slade."

It took Dominic a moment to register that he was being spoken to—he was still reeling from the fascinating change a smile made on Melissa's face. With an effort, he tore his eyes away from the delightful dimple that had appeared near her suddenly not-so-prune-shaped mouth, and looking at Zachary, he said politely, "Yes, I am." A faint expression of puzzlement showed on his handsome face as he asked, "But how did you know that? I don't believe that we have met."

Zack grinned. "Uncle Josh," he answered succinctly. "He was quite eager to tell us of his impressive visitor."

Dominic laughed deprecatingly, instantly liking this young man. "I would hardly call myself impressive, but then neither would I want to shatter your illusions."

Melissa's spinsterish expression returned firmly again, since she was not at all pleased with the way the two men were being so amiable with each other. "Well, you won't shatter *mine*, Mr. Slade!" she cut in sharply.

Ignoring Zachary's shocked *"Lissa!"* she put the shovel down perilously close to Dominic's booted foot. Her voice dripping with dislike, she said, "And since you were just on the point of leaving, we won't keep you any longer."

His smile fading, Dominic gave her a cool nod of his dark head. Deliberately turning his back on her, he sent a friendly glance toward Zachary. "Since it is obvious that I have come at an inconvenient time," he said to Zachary, "perhaps you would be so kind as to join Royce and me at the Whitehorn tavern in Baton Rouge tonight for dinner . . . we thought it would be a pleasant change to escape from the petticoats for a while."

Throwing his sister a defiant look, Zachary replied quickly, "It will be my pleasure, sir! What time do you suggest that I meet you?"

The two gentlemen, oblivious to Melissa's glowering figure, decided upon a time, and without another word or glance in her direction, Dominic sauntered out of the stable. Though he left Willowglen behind, that wasn't to say that the sharp-tongued Miss Seymour had vanished from Dominic's thoughts. Quite the contrary! He was convinced that she was everything unpleasant that he had first suspected and there was no doubt that she was a veritable termagant of the worst sort, but he was . . . he was, he admitted reluctantly, intrigued by her. Of course, he told himself cynically, it was only her *oddity* that intrigued him. Yet when she had smiled . . . when she had smiled he'd had a fleeting, baffling hint of the beauty that Josh had been babbling about. But those clothes and that hair! Not to mention her waspish attitude! Shaking his head in mystification, he slowly guided his horse toward the Manchester plantation. She was certainly a *novel* female!

Her flat refusal to even let him see Folly had angered him as few things had done in his life. While he had originally entertained only mild hopes of adding the horse to his stables, the unexpected and unwelcome setbacks he had received of late, specifically Miss Melissa Seymour's actions, had suddenly made him perversely determined to own the animal. She wouldn't sell the wretched horse at any price? Ha! He was going to buy her damned Folly and make her eat her insolent words! One day very soon, Dominic vowed grimly, Folly would be his, and it didn't matter very much to him just then if he paid a fortune for an unsuitable animal—he would have the great satisfaction of having bested Miss *Melissa* Seymour!

With just a hint of regret, he admitted to himself that his careless invitation to Zachary had been prompted as much by the unworthy impulse to annoy Miss Seymour as by a very real desire to further his acquaintance with the young man. He had liked Zachary on sight, something that couldn't be said of his feelings about Miss Seymour, but whether he would have sought out Zachary's company without the added pleasure of irritating Miss Seymour remained to be seen. Still, he was looking forward to the evening, and when he later mentioned Zachary's addition to their private dinner to Royce, Royce seemed rather pleased.

"An excellent idea—I should have thought of it myself," Royce said slowly as they walked from the stable at Oak Hollow where they had met. "Zack needs to get out from behind Lissa's skirts more. She tends to hover over him."

A glint in his gray eyes, Dominic began with mock wrath, "And speaking of 'Lissa,' would you mind telling me what in the hell you are playing at? I do not mean to offend you, but if your cousin is your idea of beauty, then I strongly suspect that you, my dear friend, have been rusticating here in the wilderness far too long!" Pretending to shudder, Dominic went on. "What a sharp-tongued vixen! She terrified me! And a dowdier, more unappealing creature I have never met!"

Having heard from his father about Melissa's changed appearance, Royce smiled enigmatically. "Ah, but there are hidden depths to Lissa."

"*Very* well hidden," Dominic retorted dryly, losing interest in the subject for the time being. Then, recalling that he had another bone to pick with his friend, he asked with deceptive mildness, "Would you like to explain to me why you went along with your father's little deceit about the horse?"

"Oh, that!"

"Yes, *that!*"

Royce shrugged. "I couldn't very well betray my father, could I? Neither could I call him a liar in front of you. It seemed simpler to let events run their course." Sending Dominic a limpid glance, he finished lightly, "You were never in any danger of any kind, and it seemed a harmless situation."

Dominic snorted, but he was willing to let it rest at that. However, as they entered the house he said, "For the present, it appears that Folly is out of my reach, and since I have spent several days longer than I had expected in this area, I'll be leaving for Thousand Oaks in the morning." Slanting a glance at Royce walking beside him, he asked, "Would you care to come with me? I cannot be sure precisely what sort of welcome we shall receive, but I'm certain, knowing my brother, that Morgan would not employ slovenly servants—even if he has not laid eyes on them in years!"

Royce looked thoughtful, but after a moment's pause, he accepted Dominic's invitation. "Why not? Things will be somewhat dull once you leave."

Dominic laughed and they parted to change for their dinner at the Whitehorn. But when Dominic reached for an elegant dark blue coat with gilt buttons, his good humor vanished as he reviewed the afternoon's events. Miss Seymour, he decided grimly, carelessly shrugging into the form-fitting coat, needed to be taught a lesson about the inadvisability of treating Dominic Slade so insolently! And, by God, he was going to enjoy teaching it to her!

Chapter Six

DINNER that evening at the Whitehorn was most pleasant. Dominic had requested the use of the only private sitting room, so the three gentlemen were undisturbed by other patrons of the establishment.

Dominic's initial liking of young Zachary Seymour was reinforced and he wondered, not for the first time, how this undeniably charming young man could have such a shrew for a sister. Listening to Zachary enthuse over a yearling colt that his stablemaster, Etienne Martion, had just convinced Melissa to purchase made Dominic smile, and he was reminded of himself at the same age—horse-mad and confident of his own ability to pick a goer!

They had finished their meal, an excellently done loin of beef, and were at present lingering over fine French brandy—smuggled French brandy. The conversation turned from horses to current affairs, namely the notorious pirate Jean Lafitte and his haunts off the coast of Louisiana.

Setting down his snifter, Dominic observed idly, "I suppose we should be thankful for Lafitte and his smugglers—if it weren't for them, we wouldn't be drinking this brandy. But it does bother me that our governor, Clairborne, seems unable to deal with the Baratarians. He tries his best, but no one really seems to want the smugglers stopped." Picking up his snifter once more, he continued. "I confess, though, that it occasionally worries me that Lafitte has such a well-armed group of pirates at his command. If the English were to enlist Lafitte and his men . . ." Dominic's voice trailed off. Soberly he finished, "God knows how much damage they could inflict upon Louisiana."

Royce nodded. "At least," he said reflectively, "General Jackson was successful at Horseshoe Bend and we no longer have to fear the Creek Indians attacking and pillaging at will as they did at Fort Mims last summer. I, for one, am glad the general can now bring his forces to bear against the British."

His eyes glistening with excitement, Zachary blurted out, "By Heaven, I'd like to see the British try to attack Louisiana—they would have a fight on their hands!"

Dominic's eyebrows rose. "Have you forgotten that not everyone feels as you do? There are some who would welcome the British. Aren't the Felicianas often called 'English' Louisiana because of the many British who have settled here? You are of British extraction—wasn't your grandfather a British officer?"

Zachary looked startled. "Well, yes, but that was long ago, and Lissa and I are American. *We* have no loyalty to England!"

"Which reminds me," Royce interjected with a pointed glance at Dominic. "Were you aware that our friend from London, Julius Latimer, is currently visiting the country? That he is, at present, staying with some friends who live a few miles south of Baron Rouge?"

The change in Dominic at the mention of Julius Latimer's name was emphatic. No longer did he lean indolently against the tall back of his chair, and wiped from his face was the expression of lazy good humor that so characterized him. Something savage leaped in his gray eyes, and his laughing mouth was held in a forbidding line, the very bones of his face seeming to suddenly have been molded from steel.

"Julius Latimer is here?" he asked silkily. "And you just happened to remember it? The evening before we are to leave?"

Watching Royce and Dominic, Zachary was aware for the moment that they had forgotten his presence, and in astonishment he kept his gaze locked on Dominic's dark face, unable to connect this dangerous-looking stranger with the smiling gentleman who had charmed him all evening. Even the long, elegant body seemed to have changed, and Zachary was reminded vividly of a sleek panther preparing to leap upon its prey.

Swallowing nervously, Zachary said into the tense silence that had fallen, "Do you know Mr. Latimer?"

As if suddenly recalling his presence, Royce and Dominic both stared at him, and before Zachary could blink, Dominic's face changed again, the handsome features once more showing only warmth and congeniality.

Dominic replied, "Yes, you could say that I am acquainted with Mr. Latimer. However," he added dryly, "one of the last times I saw him I was looking at him down the barrel of a rather fine dueling pistol!"

Zachary gasped, his youthful face alight with questions he was too polite to ask, but Dominic took pity on him. "In London some years ago, Mr. Latimer and I had a disagreement over a particular, ah, lady, and we vented our mutual feelings of dislike for each other on the field of honor."

"Dominic put as pretty a hole as I have ever seen right through Latimer's arm," Royce said with obvious relish. "But unfortunately, that wasn't the end of it. Two nights later Dom was ambushed as he came home from one of the gaming clubs and was beaten very badly. We have always suspected, but could not prove, that Latimer had hired the blackguards who attacked him."

"Oh!" Zachary breathed in a sigh. Sending a shy look at Royce, he said, "I've wondered why you never seemed to care overmuch for Latimer he has always been very polite to Lissa and me, especially since we owe him that money. Your manner toward him has puzzled me."

"You owe that swine money?" Dominic demanded bluntly.

"Regrettably," Zachary admitted, flushing a little. "Mr. Latimer holds a note that my father signed when he was in England. The note is long overdue, but Mr. Latimer has been very kind to us and has not sought an immediate payment, although it would be within his rights to do so." Reluctantly he added, "If he does demand his money, I have no idea how we would ever be able to raise it, since the sum is quite large."

"I wouldn't worry," Royce said carelessly, "but if he begins to pressure you for it, come to me immediately."

"Or me," Dominic drawled. "I have a few debts of my own to settle with Mr. Latimer, and it wouldn't bother me a bit to settle yours as well. It would, in fact," he confessed with a tight grin, "afford me great pleasure!"

Gratified and embarrassed at the same time, for the debt rankled, Zachary stammered, "Th-th-thank you! But Lissa says we shall come about under our own power."

"Just keep my offer in mind," Dominic said flatly. Then, seeking to divert the conversation, he added teasingly, "As for that sister of yours—why in the hell won't she even let me see that horse of hers, Folly?"

Zachary grinned, suddenly looking much younger than his nineteen years. "You put her back up," he admitted candidly. "She was really in a fury after you left. Etienne and I couldn't go near her all afternoon without having our heads bitten off!"

"Not her usual attitude?" Dominic asked with patent disbelief.

"Oh, no!" Zachary replied with a laugh. "Lissa is a great gun . . . except when she gets her feathers ruffled, and the one thing that will set her off for sure is any mention of selling Folly." His expression becoming serious, he added, "Even if our entire future were not dependent upon what we can earn from the stallion, Lissa would never countenance selling him—he is her horse and she has raised him from a foal and truly loves him."

"What mawkish sentimentality," Dominic said disgustedly. "I don't know what you plan, but I can tell you that without a great deal more money, you are not going to be able to fully take advantage of the horse your Folly is reputed to be." Giving Zachary a sympathetic look, Dominic continued carefully. "No breeder of any prominence will bring his best mares to a place that is run as Willowglen appears to be. I do not mean to offend you, but unless your entire establishment takes on a more affluent air and your stables are run more professionally, you are not going to have serious breeders flocking to your stud." A grin lurked at the corner of his mouth. *"Espe-*

cially not if they are greeted by a shovel-wielding, tart-tongued apparition, as I was this morning!''

Dominic's observations stung, but Zachary could not deny the wisdom in what he said. Dispiritedly, he admitted, ''I know, but Lissa and I have no choice but to try. Lissa says—''

''Spare me what Lissa says,'' Dominic interrupted with a shudder. ''What do *you* think?''

Never loath to give his own opinions, Zachary plunged into speech and the hours continued to pass enjoyably.

Unfortunately, neither of the two older men had taken into account that Zachary's drinking abilities did not match their own, and to their dismay, when at last they decided to call an end to the pleasant evening, they discovered that Zachary was foxed. It was glaringly apparent that he could not be allowed to ride home in such a condition—if, in fact, he could even remain on his horse.

Royce and Dominic wrangled amiably over who would escort their youthful inebriate home. Dominic finally said, ''There is no need for both of us to go with him, and since my valises are all packed and yours probably aren't, you're the one who should return to Oak Hollow.''

Royce's consumption of the potent brandy had not been light, and somewhat owlishly he regarded Dominic. ''You think I should rouse my servants at one o'clock in the morning and ask them to pack for me?''

Dominic grinned, haphazardly grabbing Zachary's limp form as the young man reeled in the saddle. ''No, but I do believe that you have had more to drink than I, and if I didn't know for a fact that you have a remarkably hard head, I would be concerned about *your* ability to find your way home without mishap!''

Looking offended, Royce wheeled his spirited chestnut gelding about. ''I am,'' he said, enunciating each word cautiously, ''quite, quite *un*affected by tonight's drinking. But since you seem determined to escort my cousin home by yourself, I shall not keep you.'' Giving his impatient horse a swift kick, Royce galloped away.

Smiling to himself, Dominic urged his own horse forward, keeping a judicious eye on Zachary as the young man rather ineptly rode off into the night. From the way he swayed in the saddle, Dominic seriously wondered if they would reach Willowglen before Zachary disgraced himself by falling out of the saddle.

Fortunately, Zachary was a better rider than Dominic gave him credit for, and they arrived at Willowglen sometime later without any mishap. The night air had sobered Zachary a little and his step was only a trifle unsteady as Dominic helped him up the stairs of the house.

Dominic had hoped that he could get Zachary inside and in bed without incident, but they had barely taken two steps across the wide gallery when one of the double doors flew open and Melissa whispered, "Oh, Zack! I am so glad you're home. I've been worried about you—do you realize that it is almost three o'clock?"

Although he might have recovered slightly, Zachary was not in full command of himself, and in thickly slurred speech he began to apologize.

Melissa hadn't been aware of Dominic's presence until he interrupted Zachary's incoherent words by saying softly, "I believe that he is too foxed to explain things at the moment."

There was only a partial moon, and in the shadowy darkness Melissa had not realized that someone else was on the gallery with Zachary, but with a funny little leap of her pulse, she recognized Dominic's voice instantly. Her first concern was for her brother, though, and angrily she hissed, "And whose fault is *that?* Must you attempt to corrupt him to your libertine ways?"

Melissa might have been unaware of Dominic's presence, but he had been all too disconcertingly aware of hers from the moment the door had opened. It was too dark to see very clearly, just outlines and shadowy forms, but he was distinctly conscious of her tall, slim body beneath the ghostly paleness of her night rail. From the silhouette barely discernible in the waning moonlight, it was obvious that her hair was loose and tumbling wildly about her shoulders and that she was not wearing the hideous spectacles. He could not see her features, but he was startled by an extraordinary, overwhelming desire to do so. Almost without thinking, he reached for her, his only intention in that first moment to pull her out into the weak glow of the moonlight, to attempt to satisfy his sudden curiosity. But her hot words infuriated him, and with a low growl he tightened his fingers on her slender arms and jerked her roughly up against his muscled length.

"Libertine!" he snarled softly. "If it is libertine ways you wish . . ."

Perhaps it was the brandy or the lateness of the hour, Dominic couldn't have said, but he was driven by a fierce, unexpected emotion that he had no control over. His mouth caught hers, his strong arms quelling Melissa's very natural struggles to escape. He hadn't meant to kiss her and certainly he hadn't expected to derive any particular pleasure from it, but to his intense astonishment, her lips were incredibly sweet, her young body warm and soft as he held her next to him, and he was suddenly gripped by a wave of battling, heady passion.

Melissa had been unprepared when his hands had closed around her upper arms, and the descent of his seeking mouth came as a total surprise . . . as did the hot rush of excitement that surged through her when his mouth pressed intoxicatingly against hers. She made an instinctive attempt to break free, but she could not, and as the seconds passed and Dominic enfolded her even closer to his powerful form, she was dimly aware that she didn't really want to escape . . . that she wanted him to kiss her, that she had thought of little else but him since this afternoon . . .

What he had intended to do, Dominic had no idea; he was conscious only of the soft, quivering lips under his and of the long, slim legs pressed against his own, of small, hard breasts pushing against his chest. Oblivious of the place and time, he gave a groan of pleasure and his hands traveled to her firm buttocks, pulling her even closer to him, forcing her warm softness against his instantly burgeoning manhood.

Lost in a dream, awakening to passion for the first time in her life, Melissa was unaware of anything but Dominic, of the sheer pleasure his touch gave her. Her arms crept around his neck and her fingers tangled in his dark hair, her mouth shyly opening before the demanding pressure of his. Fire seemed to leap in her veins, a shiver of excitement coursing through her as his hands caressed her hips and she felt the obvious sign of his desire against her belly. This was what her cousins had tried to tell her about, she thought hazily, helplessly arching herself closer to him, wanting this moment to last, wanting his hands to continue to evoke their magic on her body.

It was Zachary's voice that shattered the spell as he said confusedly, "I say, Dominic, are you kissing m'sister?"

Like scalded cats, Dominic and Melissa sprang apart, sanity reasserting itself. Ashamed and bewildered, Melissa reacted blindly. Catching Dominic completely by surprise, she slapped him with all her might, the blow rocking him on his heels.

"You monster!" she spat furiously. Her voice shaking with anger and embarrassment, her fists pounding on his chest, she raged, "How dare you touch me in that disgusting fashion! How dare you try to corrupt my brother with your disreputable ways!"

One moment she had been sweet, yielding fire in his arms, and then she had changed so swiftly into a spitting wildcat that Dominic was dumbfounded. His brain fogged by brandy and the so utterly incomprehensible passion she had aroused, he did not react as quickly as he would have done normally. Her slap had effectively killed his desire, but he was still reeling from the astounding knowledge that a woman he had freely stigmatized as a dowdy, overbearing shrew had quickened his body with a feverish passion that he had never felt for any other woman.

Almost absentmindedly, he touched his cheek where her hand had connected, so amazed by the situation that his usual quick wits deserted him. Even the small fists pounding somewhat painfully on his chest didn't really impinge on his consciousness as he stood silently before her, unable to believe what had happened. I don't even *like* her, he thought stupidly, so how can I want her?

Melissa was having no such conflicting thoughts, her anger at her own actions as well as his clouding any rational means to deal with the situation. Giving him a violent shove, she said wrathfully, "You, sir, are a blackguard, and if you ever come near me or my brother again, I shall shoot you on sight!"

Dominic had been standing near the edge of the steps,

and as she gave him one last, brisk shove he toppled down the stairs. He bounced and slid painfully down the three steps, landing with a thud on the soft ground. In stupefaction he lay on his back, staring up in her direction.

But Melissa had vented the worst of her rage. Grabbing the equally dazed Zachary, she whisked him inside, slamming the door resoundingly behind them.

Dominic lay for several seconds in the darkness, then gingerly felt his decidedly smarting face, a grin curving his mouth. "Well, I'll be *damned!*"

Inside the house, reaction had set in for Melissa and she began to tremble, her knees feeling weak and her hands shaking. Appalled at what she had done, she almost relented and went back outside to see if Dominic was hurt, but then she pushed the notion aside. He deserved it, she thought mutinously. He had no right to treat me like some . . . some slut found in an alehouse!

Zachary stumbled in the darkness, reminding Melissa that she was not alone, and groping her way through the pitch-blackness of the interior, she grabbed his arm.

"Come along, Zack," she said softly. "The stairs are this way."

"Have to say something," Zachary replied with quaint dignity. "Dom is m'friend." He spoke with a great effort, his words still thick and indistinct. "Don't think you should have hit 'im."

Exasperated, Melissa retorted sharply, "But it was all right for him to get you drunk . . . and kiss me against my will?"

Rather blearily, Zachary peered at her through the concealing darkness. Stiffly he said, "My business if I get drunk—I'm not a child! As for kissing . . . appeared to me that it wasn't against your will!"

Repressing an unsisterly urge to box his ears, Melissa jerked him toward the stairs which led up to their bedrooms. In a low, fierce voice, she said, "Well, it was! And I don't want you to have anything more to do with Mr. Dominic Slade!"

"Will if I want to!" Zachary insisted stubbornly. "Like 'im! A real gentleman! Could learn a lot from a man like him! Knows horses too!"

Biting back a furious denunciation of Mr. Dominic Slade's gentlemanly traits, Melissa grimly guided Zachary's faltering steps to his bedroom. She left him at the door, deciding sourly that he could manage to undress and put himself to bed.

In her own bed some minutes later, Melissa lay staring sleeplessly into the blackness, unwillingly reliving those passion-filled moments in Dominic's arms. How *could* she have acted in that reprehensible fashion? She who prided herself on her lack of romantic interest in men. On her ability to remain unmoved by the most ardent admirer.

Stifling a groan of self-disgust, she rolled over onto her stomach in an effort to escape the images that danced across her brain. What had possessed her? And after all of Uncle Josh's warnings about the man, what did she do? The first time he touched her, she fell into his embrace like a ripe plum! How shameful! And how, she wondered uncomfortably, was she going to look her brother in the eye tomorrow morning?

Fortunately for the relationship between the siblings, Zachary remembered very little of what had happened the previous night. He woke up late in the morning with an aching head and the firm conviction that never again would he allow himself to imbibe so freely. How embarrassing! Dom and Royce must think him the greenest cawker of their acquaintance. They'd never invite him to join them again!

Discovering that the slightest movement made his head feel as if it were splitting apart, Zachary made his way somewhat carefully down the stairs. A cup of steaming black coffee, served by an unsympathetic Ada, and a cold biscuit were all that he could face for breakfast.

Knowing there was work to be done and realizing that he had slept almost the entire morning away, Zachary doggedly walked toward the stable, despite the lurching of his stomach and the pounding in his head. The walk didn't seem to help his condition a great deal, but when he saw Melissa under a large oak near the stable, busily grooming one of the new mares, he sent her a weak smile.

That he was not feeling well was very apparent from the grayish cast to his face and the lack of jauntiness to his step, and looking at him, Melissa felt her heart melt. She loved him so much, and in spite of the chagrin and discomfort she was experiencing, she smiled back warmly.

Sitting himself gently down on the grass a little distance from the mare, he held his head in his hands and said, "Lord, Lissa! I feel terrible! I can barely remember how I got home." Glancing up at her, he asked, "Did you put me to bed?"

"Don't you remember?" she inquired softly, hope springing within her that her disgraceful behavior had indeed been forgotten by him.

Slowly, *very* slowly, he shook his dark head. "I remember getting on my horse outside the tavern . . ." He frowned. "I think Dom rode home with me, but I'm not sure."

Her mouth tightened and she began to brush the mare's already shiny chestnut coat with unneeded vigor. "He did escort you home . . . I met you both on the gallery."

Nervously Zachary looked over at her. "I didn't disgrace myself, did I? I wouldn't want Dominic or Royce to think that I am not up to their weight."

An angry sparkle lit her amber-gold eyes as Melissa rounded on him. "Is that all you're concerned about? Whether or not those two rakes think you are capable of keeping up with their licentious activities?"

"Doing it too brown," Zachary replied with a decidedly cynical tone to his voice. "You've taken a dislike to Dominic, and nothing he can do is right."

Stung, Melissa protested, "That's not true! Have you forgotten that Uncle Josh warned us against him? That he says the man is not to be trusted?"

"And since when have you ever paid any attention to what Uncle Josh says?"

Melissa flushed, and turning away from Zachary, she fiddled with a few strands of the mare's silky mane. Zachary had made a point and she had no ready argument. How could she explain to him the chaotic emotions that Mr. Dominic Slade aroused within her breast? How to explain the stinging joy she had experienced in his arms? The pleasure his mouth had given her? The excitement that had coursed through her veins when she saw him? How to tell him that the man both fascinated and frightened her?

More confused than she had ever been in her life, she glanced back at Zachary and said slowly, "You're right that I don't usually listen to Uncle Josh, but this time, I think that what he has to say has merit. There is something about Mr. Slade that . . ." She swallowed and then, taking a deep breath, she said in a rush, "I just don't like him, Zack! He is too sure of himself, too arrogant and certain that everyone will run to do his bidding!"

Zachary's eyebrows rose. That hadn't been his impression of Dominic. "Well, I like him! And I intend to pursue a friendship with him . . ." Glumly, he added, "If he'll let me after last night."

This was the first time that she and Zack had ever seriously disagreed on anything, and Melissa fiercely resented Dominic's apparent influence over her brother. She also didn't like to see him so uncertain, but stifling the words of denunciation she would have liked to utter, she said with forced carelessness, "Oh, I shouldn't worry. You didn't do anything so very awful, and I'm certain even the great Mr. Dominic Slade has been foxed on more than one occasion." She would have preferred to forbid him to have any further doings with the nefarious Mr. Slade, but she was unhappily aware that Zachary was now a young man and that she could no longer control his actions as she had when he was a child. Besides, she told herself miserably, she didn't want to be at daggers drawing with Zack, and it was glaringly apparent that any attempt on her part to stop his professed desire to see more of Mr. Slade would only cause more dissension between them. For the sake of their feelings for each other, she was just going to have to keep her mouth shut about Mr. Slade.

Pinning a determined smile on her mouth, she asked lightly, "Besides your having had too much to drink, how did you like your evening at the Whitehorn? Was it what you expected?"

Only listening with one part of her brain to Zachary's enthusiastic recounting of the evening's events, Melissa wondered dispiritedly if Mr. Slade had even spared them a thought. Probably not! Why, she would wager he would be hard pressed to even recall that he had kissed her!

Melissa would have been both thrilled and shocked to discover that Dominic had spent a great part of his waking hours doing nothing but thinking about her. Specifically, the moments when she had been in his arms.

All during the ride back to Oak Hollow he had thought of nothing else but his own incomprehensible reactions to a woman he didn't like, certainly didn't find attractive, and one, furthermore, who had all the charm and beauty of a flea-bitten camel! But he couldn't forget how she had felt in his arms—warm and pliant and oh, so desirable. He wondered briefly if he was growing senile or if there had been something in the brandy that had caused him to respond as he had. And, like Melissa, he found himself sleepless, his thoughts on that unforgettable embrace.

But sleep did come eventually, and although he did not awaken with the pounding headaches that had greeted both Zachary and Royce, he did not start the day with quite the zest he would have normally. Like Zachary and Royce, he had awaken late in the morning, which had annoyed him since he had planned on making an early departure for Thousand Oaks. He lay in his bed for several seconds, his thoughts going immediately to last night.

Good God! he mused ruefully. What had possessed him! His only interest in Miss Melissa Seymour was her damn horse! The situation was already difficult enough without the added complication of riling the wretched female! Deliberately, he did not think about the piercing desire he had felt for her. It was simply an aberration on his part and was unlikely ever to occur again.

With that notion grimly in place, he began to dress and finish preparing for the departure from Oak Hollow. To his surprise, Royce, though in a foul mood, was actually all packed and ready and waiting for him when he finally descended the curving staircase.

"And did you see your ewe lamb home safely?" Royce asked sarcastically, the throbbing in his temples not making him the best of company.

Dominic was familiar with Royce's ill temper after a night of deep drinking and he merely grinned. "That I did. And I suspect that his head is no better than yours is this morning!''

Royce shuddered. ''No doubt! And no doubt his sister will be ready to comb our hair with a cleaver, if I know Melissa. I do not look forward to the scolding we shall probably get from her the next time we see her! She has a viper's tongue when she's angry!''

Dominic gave him a sardonic look. ''What? The sweet beauty of whom your father sings such praises?''

Glaring at him, Royce snarled, ''I'm in no mood for your witticisms this morning!'' Turning on his heel, he muttered, ''Let's bid my parents adieu and get out of here.''

Chuckling to himself, Dominic followed Royce's less-than-charming lead. Bidding a polite good-bye to his hosts and promising to return for another visit took several minutes, but finally the two young men, followed by three horses which carried Royce's manservant as well as their trunks and valises, were able to effect their escape.

As they rode down the long driveway that led from Oak Hollow, Dominic was conscious of a queer reluctance to leave . . . not Oak Hollow, but this area—without one more look at Miss Melissa Seymour. He prided himself on being a discerning gentleman, and though he had stubbornly pushed thoughts of her to the back of his mind, the events of last night sat uneasily within him.

Turning to glance at Royce, he said slowly, ''I would like to ride by Willowglen . . . I believe that it is not too far out of our way.''

Royce sent him a considering glance. ''Now why,'' he asked derisively, ''would you want to do *that?*''

If it were possible for a man of Dominic's sophistication and years to blush, he did so, a dark red stain creeping up into his cheeks. ''I merely want to satisfy myself that Zachary is suffering no ill effects from last night,'' he relied rather stiffly.

Royce flashed him a look that spoke volumes. ''Very well,'' he said reluctantly. ''But I warn you, Dom . . . if I find that it is because you want to moon over Melissa, I shall not be responsible for my actions!''

''Moon over Melissa!'' Dominic grated indignantly.

"Don't be a fool!" That was the end of the conversation, but when they turned down the overgrown lane that led to Willowglen, Dominic wondered bleakly which one of them was the *real* fool!

They found Melissa and Zachary under an oak tree near the stables. Zachary was sprawled in the dappled shade of the tree, and Melissa appeared to be grooming an already immaculately groomed mare.

There was some constraint between Dominic and Melissa, but Zachary was so very pleased that the two older men had thought to call upon him that his obvious delight in their company covered any awkwardness that might have resulted. As the quartet stood there talking in the warm sunshine, some of Royce's surliness vanished, and by the time they were saying their adieus he was quite in charity with the world at large. In a much better frame of mind, his head finally not pounding, he was able to ride away from Willowglen, eager to begin the journey to Thousand Oaks.

Seated upon the fine black gelding that he rode, Dominic also bade the Seymours good-bye, but his mood was not improved by the event. The entire time that he had been talking to Melissa and Zachary, he had been surreptitiously studying her, seeking some clue to explain what had moved him to such stunning passion last night.

It was hopeless, he thought disgustedly, staring at the pinched face that met his gaze. The spectacles glinting in the sunlight made it impossible for him to even guess at the color of her eyes—and that hair! This morning it was pulled back in a bun every bit as ugly as the one she had worn the first time he had seen her.

Disparagingly his eyes traveled down the drab, shapeless gown, and he was unable to understand what had happened to him last night. So it was with great relief that Dominic said his good-byes and guided his horse away from the exasperating Miss Seymour. It *must* have been the brandy!

Chapter Seven

To HER chagrin, Melissa discovered that time seemed to drag unbearably with Dominic's disappearance from the neighborhood. Far more than she cared to admit, her wayward thoughts traveled often in his direction and she wondered, at least once every day, what he was doing and when he would return. *If* he would return.

It wasn't, she told herself viciously as warm May weeks gradually faded into even warmer June days, that she actually *missed* the beastly Mr. Slade! But she had to confess that his presence in the area had added a certain something to the even tenor of the days. She had been conscious of an eager anticipation within herself that had vanished when Dominic had ridden away with Royce.

Zachary, too, seemed to regret Dominic's departure, although his feelings on the matter were clearly expressed. While he echoed many of her own thoughts, there were times she was certain she would scream if she heard him say, once more, "I wonder when Dominic and Royce will be back. Things are so flat with them gone."

Of course, she betrayed none of her own longings for the absent Mr. Slade, grimly determined to push the memory of those passionate moments in his arms from her mind. She would rather have died than let Zachary know that she, too, wondered when Mr. Slade would return. Why she was so curious about his reappearance bothered her almost as much as the fact that she *did* wonder about him!

Convincing herself that she had only *momentarily* fallen prey to the practiced charms of a handsome Lothario was not easy, but it was the only way she could explain her reaction to him. It didn't help her state of mind, nor did it banish the embarrassingly explicit dreams that came to her at night, but she was able to gain some semblance of normality as the weeks passed.

There were other things to occupy her mind, so, busy and harassed as she was, she gradually came to believe that what had happened that night was just one of those odd, unexplainable events that occurred in everyone's life now and then. It certainly, she vowed sternly, would *never* happen again!

The constant struggle to maintain Willowglen was taking its toll of Melissa's slender resources, and the end of the second week of June found her seriously questioning her ability to accomplish little more than she had already. She was depressingly aware that what she and Zachary had done since their father's death to restore Willowglen's former elegance or even successfully implement their dream of running a stud farm was pitifully inadequate. Zachary had repeated some of Dominic's observations, and while Melissa had been infuriated with his comments, she had to admit that there was more than a little truth in what the annoying Mr. Slade had said. At least, she reminded herself with a disconcerting lack of enthusiasm, they were out of debt. . . . Not precisely, if she were to be totally honest. There was still that blasted note held by Julius Latimer, and she had the uneasy feeling that Mr. Latimer would not continue indefinitely to be so understanding about their inability to pay what was a disgracefully overdue debt.

This particular sunny morning, Melissa was perched on a wooden stool in the tack room, busily cleaning an old bridle, thinking about the debt and the attractive but slightly sinister Mr. Latimer, when as if her thoughts had conjured him up he suddenly appeared in the doorway of the small room.

She had been so lost in her unhappy musings that his voice startled her. She gave a frightened gasp as he said softly, "Ah, here you are, my dear. Miss Osborne told me that I might find you here."

Recovering herself quickly, Melissa put down the bridle

and slid off the stool. "I am afraid that I am to be found here most of the time," she replied ruefully. "It seems that there is always something that must have my attention. . . ."

Smiling at him, she made to move past him where he stood in the doorway, but he remained where he was, making no attempt to give way. Questioningly she glanced at him. His blue eyes held an odd expression, and suddenly realizing that he had not visited Willowglen since she had undertaken her disguise, she dimpled and murmured, "Does my appearance shock you?"

His lips quirking with amusement, he shook his blond head, his gaze traveling appreciatively over the untidy bun and the ugly spectacles which persisted in sliding down her delightful little nose. Laughter obvious in his voice, he declared, "You overwhelm me! I never would have recognized you. But tell me, what brings this about? Is there some costume ball that I have not heard of?"

Melissa giggled slightly. There were moments when she actually liked the Englishman. He was undeniably attractive with his deep blue eyes and wavy blond hair, and he could be quite entertaining when he chose to be. Standing just above six feet tall, Julius Latimer was slimly built, yet his shoulders were broad and there was nothing weak or effeminate about him. For some strange reason, he always made Melissa think of a rapier—slim, elegant and deadly. But when he was in a charming mood, as he appeared to be today, and wasn't, as was the case all too frequently, attempting slyly to let her know that there were other ways in which she could repay her father's debts, Melissa enjoyed his company. Nevertheless, his personal comments always disturbed her, as did the considering looks that came into those blue eyes. He had never come out and said exactly what he had in mind, but she was not so innocent that she couldn't guess. And yet he was so clever with his seemingly idle suggestions that she was never positive if he was serious or just teasing her—albeit in a most improper fashion!

She had never been entirely alone with him before, though, and she was suddenly uncomfortably conscious that they were very much by themselves—Zack and

Etienne had gone into Baton Rouge to the dry-goods store, Frances was up at the house with Ada, and the other servants were busy on the few acres of cotton which had been planted in the spring. The fact, too, that Latimer was effectively blocking the only way out of the tack room made Melissa a bit nervous. She didn't honestly think that he was going to attack her, but she would have preferred to have been out in the open—and within calling distance of the others.

Giving him a smile that betrayed none of her inner wariness, she said, "There is no costume ball. My uncle has been hounding me again about getting married, and I decided that if I made myself as unattractive as possible, the probability of finding a gentleman who wished to contemplate marriage with such a dowdy-looking woman would be greatly reduced."

"Hmm, I wouldn't say that," he drawled mockingly. "This disguise of yours might tempt a man to discover for himself the beauty that lies behind your outward trappings of homeliness." He moved slightly, his long fingers lightly touching her delicate jaw. "I have always thought that you are very lovely and, even looking as you do now, my opinion hasn't changed." He seemed to hesitate a moment, as if contemplating a course of action, and then a curious expression came into the blue eyes. "You know, there are all sorts of offers," he said softly, "besides marriage that a gentleman might make to a girl such as you. . . ."

An angry sparkle glinting in her amber-gold eyes, Melissa jerked her chin away from his caressing fingers. "A girl like me?" she said in a dangerous tone. "What precisely do you mean?"

Julius looked pained. Idly brushing away a nonexistent bit of lint from the sleeve of his elegantly cut bottle-green coat, he complained, "Oh, come now, Lissa! You must have some idea what I'm talking about. Lord knows, I've hinted enough these past weeks. Must I say it out loud?"

Her heart beating in thick, heavy strokes, her throat suddenly painfully tight, she said levelly, "Yes, I do believe that you must."

His aristocratic features stiffened and something very

unpleasant flickered in his eyes. "Very well, then, my dear," he said in a bored voice. "You owe me a considerable sum of money, and while I have been very patient, I'm afraid that my patience has run out, or rather, that my time here in America is coming to a close."

A frown between her eyes, Melissa said, "You're leaving?"

A cold smile curved his full mouth. "Not until the fall or early winter . . . it all depends on—" He stopped abruptly, before saying smoothly, "In the meantime, I am beginning to settle my affairs . . . which brings me to you."

Ignoring her attempt to escape his touch, he very deliberately grasped her chin and forced her to look up at him. "I find you extremely desirable, Melissa—even in this ridiculous garb—and for the pleasure of your charms over the next few months, I would be willing to tear up that voucher signed by your father." His lids dropped, his gaze fastened on her mouth. "I want you for my mistress. Our time together must naturally be of brief duration, but I'm sure that I shall find your many delectable attributes well worth the money."

Melissa tried to break his hold on her chin, but he tightened his grip brutally and her efforts were in vain. Latimer put his free arm around her waist and pulled her close to him. The desire he felt was obvious in his look, and a coaxing note came into his voice as he murmured, "I am prepared to be generous with you, my dear . . . and if you are, as I suspect, a virgin, I even would be willing to pay you for your loss. I want you very badly, and these weeks of biding my time have only whetted my appetite for you."

Outraged, insulted and frightened, Melissa acted without thinking, twisting her head and sinking her teeth into his wrist. A feeling of immense satisfaction swept through her when Latimer cursed viciously and instantly released her. Dancing several steps away from him, her bosom heaving under the faded material of her gown, she grated, "You'll be lucky if that is the only mark upon you before you leave here today."

Assessingly, he regarded her across the short distance that separated them, his handsome face marred by a black scowl. Rubbing at his wrist where her teeth had broken the skin, he snarled, "I had assumed we could discuss this politely, but I see I was wrong!"

Incredulously, Melissa glared at him. "Politely!" she echoed furiously. "I don't think your suggestion was very polite at all. In fact, sir, it was grossly insulting!"

"I'm sorry you feel that way," he replied coolly. "But since you find my offer not to your taste, I assume that you will be willing to pay your debt to me, in gold, before the week is out."

Melissa took a deep, steadying breath, her hand itching to slap the smug expression from his arrogant features. Trying not very successfully to keep her temper under control, she said icily, "You know that what you request is impossible. There is no way I can raise that amount of money in such a short time."

He raised a slender eyebrow. "Would you like me to give you an extension? I am a reasonable man, so shall we say by the first of July?"

Angrily aware that she was being baited, she lifted her chin pugnaciously and snapped, "You already know the answer to your question!"

"I'm afraid that I do, and if you do not have the money by then or are unwilling to take the alternative course I have offered you, then on that date I shall begin proceedings to have Willowglen sold under the gavel." Smiling mirthlessly, he added cruelly, "I always get my way, Melissa. One way or another . . . and if you would rather see your home sold out from under you"—he shrugged carelessly—"well, then, that is your choice."

Hopeless rage churned in her breast as Melissa glared at him with loathing. Either one of the choices offered to her was unthinkable. She could not bear to consider what would happen to her and Zachary and the others if Latimer carried out his threat, but the other avenue open to her was equally unthinkable. Whatever liking she might have had for the elegant Mr. Latimer had vanished the instant he had made his despicable suggestion; the thought of becoming any man's mistress, let alone a man she despised, was utterly repellent. Yet what could she do? The Manchesters could not give her the money, and a bank would certainly not loan such a large amount to her. She laughed bitterly to herself. Even if she could find a man willing to marry her in an instant, the trust could not be ended and dispersed in less than two weeks. Wild, impracticable schemes whirled dizzyingly in her brain as she sought some escape from the trap she saw closing in on her. There was only one way that she might be able to salvage the situation. Swallowing an acrid taste in her mouth, she said defeatedly, "Folly is worth a handsome sum, although not as much as my father's voucher. I could give him to you as partial payment."

"A horse? Partial payment, my dear?" Latimer drawled. Shaking his head, he said, "No, that won't do." Then he added harshly, "And I think you overestimate the value of your horse. But that aside, the entire debt must be paid—either in gold or by you—and by the first of July."

Melissa was almost relieved that he had turned down her desperate offer of Folly, and she wasn't at this moment exactly certain which would be more terrible to comtemplate—the loss of the horse which represented the only hope of keeping their home or the loss of her virtue. Despair filled her. What was she to do? Frantically in need of time in which to think, she asked reluctantly, "May I have some time to consider your offer?"

Relaxing slightly, Latimer smiled confidently. "Of course, my child! I am not a heartless monster!" His voice dropped and he muttered huskily, "Lissa, I want you very badly and I would treat you well. Our time together would be only a few months . . . I would be discreet—no one need ever know of our arrangement." When she remained silent, her face turned away from him, he grew bolder, sidling closer to her. "There is a cottage, not a mile from here. I could secure it for us and you could meet me there . . . it would be for our secret rendezvous."

Choking back the bile that rose in her throat, Melissa horrified herself by actually considering what he was saying. The greatest threat to her and Zachary's security would be gone, and since she didn't ever plan to marry anyway, what did it matter whether she remained a virgin or not?

It was Latimer's touch upon her arm that brought her unhappily back to the present situation, and with growing revulsion she stared at his slim, pale-fingered hand, imagining it upon her body. Violently, she threw his hand away. Driven by fear and anger, she snatched up a quirt that was lying nearby.

"Get away from me!" she raged, striking him soundly on the shoulder. "You're vile, and I will not listen to your wicked proposition any longer!"

He fell back in furious, painful surprise, but he made no attempt to fight with her. Eyeing the quirt held ready in her hand, he said grimly, "I would be careful how you deal with me. I am not easily thwarted and I will give you allowances by being surprised by my offer, but strike me again . . ." A dangerous gleam in his cold blue eyes, he promised, "I can make you very sorry, Melissa. There are so many things that can go wrong . . . a fire . . . a lamed horse . . . a word here, a word there. . . ."

Melissa's face was white and she stared at him as if she had never seen him before. He was, she realized, utterly ruthless.

There was an ugly silence and then Latimer said quietly, "Think about what I've said, Melissa. You may have a week to come to a decision, but on the first of July, either I have the gold owed to me . . . or you become my mistress." He gave her a polite bow, murmuring sardonically, "Good day, my dear. Pleasant dreams."

Stunned and sick, Melissa watched him walk away, almost not able to believe the repulsive scene that had just passed. Weakly she sagged onto the stool on which she had been sitting what must have been only minutes before. Despairingly she dropped her head into her hands. Dear God! What was she to do?

It was not her nature to listlessly allow others to rule her fate, but she seemed unable to think of any way in which she could avoid Latimer's plans for her . . . unless she was ready to sacrifice everything she and Zachary had worked for. So desperate was her situation that she seriously thought about what Latimer had offered, his comments drearily spinning in her brain.

Perhaps it wouldn't be too terrible, she mused misera-

bly. He had said it would be for only a few months . . .
he would be discreet . . . no one would know. . . . She
and Zachary would finally be free of the crushing burden
of debt left to them by their father.

Appalled at the nature of her reflections, Melissa shuddered and her mouth tightened. There *must* be some other
way out of her dilemma!

But by the end of the week that followed, she discovered that if there was another solution, she hadn't found
it.

Swallowing her pride, she dressed in her best gown and
rode into town to talk to the local banker. She could not
reveal why she so suddenly required such a large sum of
money, and in view of the circumstances, it was not surprising when Mr. Smithfield, who had known her since
birth, said kindly, "Melissa, you know that if I could help
you, I certainly would. But what you ask is impossible. A
small loan, yes, especially since you have been so diligent
in paying off your father's debts. But the amount you ask
for today is simply out of the question." He shook his
head sadly. "Even offering Willowglen as collateral would
not be enough. If the plantation were productive . . ."

"What about the horses?" she asked helplessly. "Folly
is worth several thousand dollars by himself, and we have
eight fine mares."

"My dear, I know that you have great hopes for your
horses, but I am in the banking business, not the horse-
breeding business. While Folly and the others are a good
investment, you simply do not have enough assets to sup-
port a loan of the size you request."

Hiding her growing agitation, she bent forward across
Mr. Smithfield's wide oak desk. "What about the trust?
If I could prove that I intend to marry soon—could I have
a loan against the trust?"

Worried about the desperation he could sense lay just
under the surface of her lovely face, Mr. Smithfield
frowned. "Melissa, are you in serious trouble? I thought
that the plantation and your horses were doing well for
you and Zachary. Perhaps I could personally advance you
a few thousand dollars."

Melissa bit back a bitter laugh. Mr. Smithfield was a

good man—he had been extremely understanding while she had struggled to bring Willowglen's finances into order. As her banker, he knew of the money owed Latimer and also how seemingly considerate the Englishman had been about not demanding payment. Telling fat old Mr. Smithfield about Latimer's demands would accomplish nothing—except to create scandal on a large scale. He would be outraged at Mr. Latimer's perfidious suggestion, but he would still be unable to loan her the money. And if the solutions offered to her were known, she couldn't bear to think of the speculation that would come about when July came and went and Latimer had still not been paid.

It was an ugly situation, and with a dejected slump to her slim shoulders, she left the banker's office. There was one other place to try, and with little hope of success, she guided her small black buggy down the red dirt road to Oak Hollow.

Smiling bravely, she sat sipping a tall glass of lemonade in her uncle's study. Josh was pleased to see her, and she was conscious that much of his pleasure was in her changed appearance, his fond gaze lingering on her tawny hair curling gently around her face and on the fairly stylish cut of her sprigged muslin gown. She had laid aside the large straw bonnet with its wide green satin ribbons that she had worn to avoid the heat of the sun, and setting down her glass on the table where the hat lay, she began quietly. "I suppose you wonder why I am here."

Josh smiled at her waggishly. "Come now, Lissa. Have we gone so far that you have to have a *reason* to visit us?"

A small smile curving her soft mouth, she shook her head. But her smile faded the next moment and her beautiful eyes fixed beseechingly on his. She asked breathlessly, "Could you lend me twenty-five thousand dollars?"

"Merciful heavens, Lissa, have you taken leave of your senses?" Josh bellowed, his air of joviality vanished. "You know that I cannot lay my hands on that sort of money right now." Almost peevishly, he added, "If I could, do you think I would be badgering you to marry as I have these past months?''

Desperately trying to act as if this were a perfectly normal conversation, she swallowed with difficulty before saying huskily, ''No, I don't suppose you would . . . and . . . I didn't really think that you could help me, but I had to try.''

Josh stared at her closely, seeing the lines of strain that were about her eyes and the pinched look to her mouth that had not been there the last time he had seen her. Something was obviously wrong. Gently, he asked, ''Lissa, what is it, child? I know that we have argued considerably of late, but you must realize that I have only your best interests at heart and will do anything within my power to help you.''

For one long moment, Melissa actually thought of telling Josh everything, of throwing herself across his broad chest and sobbing out the terms of Latimer's despicable offer. But she could not. The words would hardly leave her mouth before Josh would be bellowing for Latimer's hide, and although she was certain that her uncle was a fairly competent shot, she was equally certain that he would be no match for Latimer. Besides, she admitted tiredly, she couldn't take the chance. If Josh knew of Latimer's plans, then Royce would, too . . . and so would Zachary. The image of her young brother facing Latimer on the dueling field sent a shudder of fear through her. No. She dared not tell anyone.

Hiding the terrors that beset her, she smiled warmly at Josh. ''It is nothing, Uncle. I was just hoping that perhaps your own affairs were in better condition than my own and that you could forward me enough money to truly set up my stud farm.''

Josh was too familiar with Melissa to be entirely convinced by her reasonable statement, but Melissa could be utterly beguiling when she wanted and she deliberately set out to put his mind at ease. She succeeded admirably, and a scant hour later, a beaming and affectionate Josh escorted her to her buggy. She was even able to flash him a smile and say teasingly, ''I think I shall do as you say, Uncle, and catch me a rich, *rich* husband! I find I do not like being poor." She dimpled and added dulcetly, "Especially when such a simple solution is at hand!"

Extremely gratified, Josh helped her into her seat, approval showing in his blue-eyed gaze. Watching as she picked up the reins, he asked with apparent idleness, "What did you think of young Slade? I understand he rode over to Willowglen and talked to you about buying Folly."

Glad that her uncle didn't know of the *other* time she had seen the infuriating Mr. Slade, Melissa replied tartly, "He seemed precisely what you said—a rake and a bounder!"

"Eh?" Josh spluttered, dismayed. "Didn't like him?"

"Not in the least!" Melissa said with a snap of her perfect white teeth.

Wondering if he had overplayed his hand in blackening Dominic's character, Josh watched Melissa drive away, his mind already considering ways to rectify the situation. He'd have to be careful, he thought as he walked back into the house—couldn't, after warning her about Slade, suddenly start singing the fellow's praises to the skies!

Josh was a single-minded man, and by now he was so intent upon having Melissa marry Dominic Slade that his own personal reasons for desiring the marriage had almost slipped his mind. Melissa, he decided doggedly, *needed* to marry a man like Dominic Slade! Aside from the fact that Dominic was handsome, charming and wealthy, there was another compelling reason for the match as far as Josh was concerned—the chances of another eminently suitable suitor appearing so providentially on their doorstep were few. A good businessman wouldn't waste this wondrous opportunity, and Josh was going to see to it that Melissa didn't either—whether she wanted to or not!

Settling himself comfortably behind his massive desk, Josh reached for ink and paper. A letter to Royce wouldn't come amiss . . . and he could just ask, very casually, of course, when Royce intended to return and if Mr. Slade would be coming with him. So early the next morning a servant rode to Thousand Oaks with Josh's letter tucked securely in his saddlebags. But Josh's letter to Royce would not be the only one arriving at Thousand Oaks during the next few days. Melissa, her desperation great, was writing to Dominic.

It wasn't a decision that had come to her easily, and even as she stood at the long windows of the library at Willowglen the same afternoon composing the sentences in her mind, she doubted if this last frantic gamble would work. Time was running out, the first of July creeping steadily closer and closer, and she was nowhere nearer to raising Latimer's money now than she had been the day he had first suggested she become his mistress.

She had not slept well since the visit from Latimer, and whereas once she had been certain that she would *never* become his mistress, she now no longer believed that she could escape the trap he had set for her. It was obvious to her, in retrospect, that he had deliberately bided his time; that his overtures of friendship, the seeming consideration in not pressing for payment, had been to lull her into a false feeling of security. It also, she thought with bitterness, had given him time to ascertain the situation at Willowglen.

Even if Willowglen were sold, Melissa seriously doubted that its sale would raise the amount owed to Latimer. Oh, the land and the house were well worth a small fortune, but under foreclosure, the best price could not be gotten. Those prospective buyers bidding on the place would want to buy it as cheaply as possible, and she and Zachary would not get a quarter of what their home was worth. And Latimer, she realized with a quiver of helpless rage, *knew* it! He knew how she felt about her home, knew that she would do just about anything to save it. But become his mistress?

Shuddering, Melissa turned away from the window. Keeping feelings of fear and defeat at bay were becoming increasingly difficult, but gallantly, she endeavored to think clearly, to not overlook any possible way out of her dilemma.

If only it were just herself to consider, she'd throw Latimer's words in his teeth! But there were Zack and Etienne, and Frances and Ada and . . . Without Willowglen, they would all be homeless; their fate rested on her slim shoulders. In time, once Zachary turned twenty-one, or she married, their troubles would be lessened, but right now . . .

Her hands clenched in fists at her sides. She would not allow Latimer to ruin everyone else's life! As for her, what did it matter? Women had been bartering their bodies for centuries, and at least she would have the satisfaction of knowing that those dearest to her had benefited.

Melissa had longed to tell Zachary, longed to share the terrible burden, but just as she had dared not tell Josh, so she could not tell Zachary. It would put him in grave danger—his reaction would be far more violent than either of the Manchesters'.

There was one frail hope, she had finally admitted tiredly. Mr. Slade had made it clear that he was interested in Folly. Would he be foolish enough to buy the stallion for an outlandishly exorbitant sum of money? She didn't really believe that he would, and as she remembered her own insolent words that Folly was not for sale at *any* price, a wave of humiliation swept through her. But she had to try, it was the only path left to her and the first of July was only five days away. . . .

Chapter Eight

THE FELICIANA parishes of Louisiana, where both Willowglen and Dominic's Thousand Oaks plantations were located, were a vastly different area from the half-drowned marshes and swamps that inundated the lower reaches of the state. Away from the low land, the ground rose quickly into thickly timbered slopes, beautiful green valleys and fields. Here there were no murky bayous, no sluggish canals moving lazily between knobby-kneed cypress, only clear, sparkling blue creeks and lakes. An upland forest of thickly trunked beeches, yellow poplars, gloriously perfumed magnolias and spreading oaks flourished in the rich red-clay soil.

This was also fine cotton-growing country, and even before the Revolutionary War, the English had begun to settle on this lush, fecund land. When the War for Independence had broken out, many more English, loyal to the crown, had fled to the Felicianas; bewitched by the luxurious vegetation and the fruitfulness of the soil, they had been pleased to stay and build their homes and plant their cotton. Even when Spain had gained control of the area and it had been known as West Florida, the English had stayed, quietly and doggedly clearing and planting the land, their productive endeavors outstripping the French and Spanish settlers in the swampy lowlands.

The Felicianas had not been part of the historic Louisiana Purchase of 1803. Spain had retained ownership of the land, but, feeling strongly that their future now lay with the fledgling United States, the English settlers had coolly thrown off the indifferent yoke of Spanish rule. For seventy-four days the tiny area had been an independent republic, but when, somewhat belatedly, the Americans had arrived to annex the fertile pocket of land, the citizens of the Felicianas had thrown in their lot with the upstart Americans and the country blossomed.

It had been the idea of growing cotton that had originally drawn young Morgan Slade to the upper regions of the Felicianas, and the house he had built for his first wife was situated much like Bonheur, on a high bluff which overlooked the brown Mississippi River far below. Morgan had owned thousands of acres, some of his holdings stretching along both sides of the wide, muddy river and although he had had great tracts of the land cleared in those early days, the majority of it was still in virgin wilderness, filled with wild game and teaming with flitting birds in brilliant shades of scarlet, yellow and black.

Dominic had been enchanted by the area on sight when he had first visited with Morgan years ago, though it had not been the lure of cotton that had drawn him to it. He now threw himself, as eagerly as Morgan once had, into shaping the land to his own dreams. Fortunately, like his brother before him, he had the money and determination to rapidly accomplish what he set out to do, and in the extremely short period of time that he had owned Thousand Oaks, there were already ample signs of his stewardship.

Even before he had arrived as the new owner of the land, Dominic had sent ahead men and supplies so construction could start immediately on the sites he had selected for the new stables and paddocks which would soon house some of the finest horseflesh to be found in the entire Mississippi Valley. Since their arrival nearly a month ago, Dominic and Royce had spent their time overseeing, planning and discussing the progress which was moving along at an astonishing rate.

Neat white fences seemed to spring up overnight as the paddocks and pastures were laid out; the brood mare barns and the stallions' quarters were nearing completion, and the area being cleared for a long, sweeping racetrack was gradually taking shape. Small, brick servants' houses had been hastily constructed; fields of cotton, oats, corn and barley were under cultivation on the land which Morgan had originally wrested from the tangled wilderness. Everywhere one looked there were obvious signs of activity as Thousand Oaks shook off its sleepy air and came alive under Dominic's hand.

There was one area, though, that Dominic had left untouched, beyond the few extra necessities it had needed to make it more comfortable, and that had been the actual house at Thousand Oaks. Mrs. Thomas and her husband, the taciturn Mr. Thomas, the servants originally retained by Morgan, had kept the house scrupulously clean and tidy over the years—not such a hard task when all but a few of the many rooms in the house remained empty.

Morgan had overseen the completion of the construction of what he had dreamed would be his home, but he had deliberately left the interior of the house unfinished, thinking that his wife should have the pleasure of selecting the wall coverings, rugs, furniture and other amenities. Consequently, though the kitchen, situated a short distance away from the main building, as were all kitchens for fear of fire, had been fitted out properly, the inside of the house consisted of bare floors and walls. Two of the bedrooms had been hastily furnished for Dominic and Royce; a small table and chairs had been placed in the long dining room, and a few comfortable leather chairs, side tables and desk had been hurriedly introduced into the room Dominic had chosen for his office. For the two bachelors, gone most of the day from the house, these meager furnishings did fine—especially since Mrs. Thomas was such an excellent cook and the tasty meals she prepared and the fine liquors that Morgan had laid down in his wine cellar and liberally served by Mr. Thomas more than made up for the lack of elegant surroundings.

Dominic had much to be satisfied about as the days passed and he could see his dreams and plans gradually taking shape, but he was quite conscious of an annoying feeling of discontentment—and just when he should have been feeling very pleased with himself and his life. He could not put his finger on the source of his problem, but he was very aware, despite all the progress, of a lack of fulfillment. There was an unpleasant emptiness within himself that he had never experienced before, and it interfered with his unqualified delight in the revitalization of Thousand Oaks.

He could not even blame his odd dissatisfaction on loneliness. Royce was a most agreeable companion and they spent many enjoyable hours together, eagerly discussing the plans for Thousand Oaks and hunting in the game-filled forests. Everything was developing just as Dominic had envisioned—his own servants and personal belongings were even now on their way from Bonheur to Thousand Oaks. Within the next week or so, his stablemaster and the first of his horses would be arriving; he had even received a few letters from knowledgeable horsemen congratulating him on his undertaking and expressing interest in the fine-blooded stock they were confident that Thousand Oaks would one day produce.

So why did Dominic have this nagging sense of . . . of . . . of what? he had demanded angrily of himself more than once lately. Wasn't he doing precisely what he had said, time and time again, that he wanted to do? Wasn't everything going along just as he had planned? Just as he had expected it to? Of course it was! If anything, events were moving along swifter than his fondest hopes. So why did he have a damnably uncomfortable feeling that somewhere he had badly miscalculated . . . that he had somehow gone drastically astray? It was vexing, this strange feeling of hollowness within himself. And damned annoying, too! *Especially* when these odd sensations all seemed connected to an unsettling memory of that provoking Miss Melissa Seymour!

To his utter consternation, he could not push aside the memory of that night with her, remembering vividly the feel of her mouth beneath his. To his utmost frustration, he would find himself dwelling on the dowdy and unappealing Miss Seymour at the most inopportune times. Viewing the newly constructed brood mare stable with its wide alleyways and huge, freshly whitewashed stalls, the tack room filled with expensive leather saddlery and equipment, the bustling, neatly attired stableboys as they hurried about doing their tasks, he found himself brooding on the memory of the shoddy excuse of a barn that served

Miss Seymour. The contrast between the two buildings was ludicrous, but for some peculiar reason, Dominic took no pleasure in the differences. And idly watching the muscles ripple in the broad back of one of his field slaves as the man labored to even out the floor of one of the new stalls, he was irked to discover himself remembering his first sight of Miss Seymour, her slender body bent over as she cleaned out one of the dilapidated stalls at Willowglen.

Furiously he attempted to banish her from his thoughts, especially when he became conscious of feelings of admiration and sympathy. The woman was nothing but a stubborn, rude, sharp-tongued vixen! he reminded himself grimly. She was obviously content with her lot—he'd been willing to pay a goodly sum for Folly, and the money would have gone a long way in alleviating the necessity for her to work like a damned slave! But had she taken advantage of this opportunity? No! The stupid little shrew wouldn't even let him *see* the blasted horse, let alone consider selling the nag! Let her wallow in the uncomfortable bed of her own making, he thought wrathfully. *He* wasn't going to waste another moment thinking about her!

Which was far easier decided upon than done, he was to find to his growing resentment. At night when he lay in his bed, the seductive memory of her warm mouth responding so passionately to his kiss, the way her slim form had melted into his hard body, came back to bedevil him, to make him wonder if there were indeed such things as witches and spells that could snare the unwary male. Why else was she always at the back of his mind? Why else did he wonder even now what she would think of Thousand Oaks and his plans for the future?

It was unnerving, to say the least, made all the more so when he recalled his last sight of her. In the clear light of day her lack of obvious beauty had been glaringly apparent, and without effort he could see in his mind's eye the tight, unattractive bun anchored at the back of her head, the ugly spectacles and the drab, shapeless gown. For a man who prided himself on his superb judgment of beautiful women, a man whose mistresses were legendary for their charm and loveliness, his reaction to Miss Seymour that one evening was incomprehensible.

Annoyed with himself, Dominic vowed to stop this ridiculous fascination with Miss Seymour and channel his thoughts in a more pleasant direction . . . such as the success he would make of Thousand Oaks, or, if he wanted to think of women, why not the soft, yielding body of a certain young woman of easy virtue who resided in Natchez in a discreet little house owned by Dominic. . . . Smiling, he took a large swallow of wine. Yes, it was far more enjoyable to remember the buxom charms of the delectable Yolanda than it was to speculate about the infuriating Miss Seymour.

At present, on this fine June evening, Dominic and Royce were sitting on the broad gallery which ran across the front of the stately two-storied house. They were savoring glasses of port, having just finished another of Mrs. Thomas' tasty meals, talking idly of this and that.

Seeing Dominic's smile in the gloom of falling dusk, Royce asked lightly, "That's a very suggestive smile you have on your face, my friend. Any special reason for it?"

Putting down his glass, Dominic grinned. "I was just thinking of a particular soiled dove in Natchez and wondering if I wanted to visit her bad enough to leave here."

Royce chuckled, a knowing gleam in his eyes. "Yes, I had noticed that you have been exceedingly chaste of late and I've been curious to know if you'd taken a vow of abstinence! If I remember correctly from our London days, you were ever a man for the ladies."

"And *I* seem to recall that *you* were not backward yourself—remember that night in Covent Garden and the redhaired doxy you won in a card game?"

Royce laughed aloud, and for a while the conversation drifted back to their days in London, full of "Do you remember . . . ?" as they reminisced. But eventually the subject of Dominic's clash with Latimer came up, and some of the enjoyment of the evening vanished.

Dominic stiffened as Royce said Latimer's name; then he murmured, "I'm rather glad you introduced the subject yourself—I have not taxed you with it, but it did seem a bit underhanded that you made no mention of Latimer's presence until we were to leave the Baton Rouge area."

Grimacing, Royce admitted, "I know that hot temper

of yours and I didn't want you to challenge him to another duel—which you probably would have done if you had known where he was.''

''And now that I do know where he is?'' Dominic asked in a suspiciously meek tone. ''Aren't you afraid that I shall still challenge him?''

''No. Hot-tempered upon occasion you may be, but you're not a fool, and I have great hopes that now that you have gotten used to the idea that he is here in America, your own common sense will prevent you from doing something so singularly stupid,'' Royce replied tartly. Leaning forward in his seat, he continued. ''I know that few things would please you more than putting a hole through Latimer's black heart and I don't deny he deserves it, but that act would accomplish nothing—it wouldn't change what happened between you and Deborah.''

His features suddenly pale, Dominic said tautly, ''I don't want to talk about Deborah. Whatever I may have felt for her was long ago, and if she was willing to allow that bastard of a brother of hers to force her into a marriage with a man old enough to be her grandfather, then she wasn't the woman I thought she was anyway.''

''She never was,'' Royce remarked dryly. ''You took one look at that lovely face of hers and came as close to falling in love and committing yourself to the prison of marriage as you ever have—and don't try to deny it. I was there and I saw you making a cake of yourself over her.'' Royce grinned. ''A most stylish cake, but one nonetheless.''

Dominic moved restively in his chair, unpleasantly aware that there was more than a little truth in Royce's comments. He *had* been very near to falling deeply in love with Deborah Latimer that summer in London, and there had been a time, granted it had been an exceedingly *short* time, that he had actually contemplated the married state . . . until Julius Latimer had shattered his half-formed dreams. If the brief affair with Deborah Latimer had been his nearest foray into love, it had been her brother who had made him conscious of a darker side of his own nature.

Julius Latimer's reputation had been notorious in London. Even though he was tolerated by polite society, there were many doors of the ton that had been closed to him and, because of him, closed also to his sister. The Latimers were poor, distant relatives of a well-liked aristocratic family, and despite the fact that most members of society found Miss Latimer perfectly acceptable, they thought it a shame that such a shy, lovely young lady should have such a cold-blooded man like Julius for her brother.

It wasn't just that Julius had been prepared to sell her to the highest bidder. There had been more than one unsavory incident attached to his name. Too well did Dominic remember the scandal which had erupted when Latimer had fought a duel and killed a young man just up from the country, a mere boy too green to recognize a skilled and unscrupulous gambler like Latimer. There had been nasty whispers, too, about a beggar's maid who had died beneath the wheels of Latimer's carriage.

Reflectively, Dominic stared out into the darkness. He had not liked Julius on sight, and right from the beginning there had been a thinly veiled hostility between the two of them. Oh, they were civil to one another, but they tended to circle each other like wary cats, tensed for the first antagonistic move. It wasn't until Latimer had deliberately and maliciously filled Deborah's ears with wicked lies about him that Dominic had begun to fully realize just how totally unprincipled Latimer was, how determined he was to see that his sister married only the man of *his* choice—a rich man, to be sure, but one whom Latimer could control. Once Dominic had discovered the reason behind Deborah's sudden aversion to him, it had been too late to retrieve the situation between them, the mixture of lies and half-truths too cleverly interwoven to be unraveled. He had gained satisfaction, though, by challenging Latimer to a duel.

When they had finally met, his heart and pride smarting, suffering from the hurt caused by Latimer, for the first time in his life Dominic had let rage rule him—which was why his shot had gone through Latimer's arm instead of his heart.

Breaking the silence that had fallen, Dominic said suddenly, "I shouldn't have missed the bastard!"

Royce nodded in agreement. "If nothing else, it would have saved you from that beating by those rogues Latimer hired."

Dominic winced. The beating had not only left him sore and bruised for weeks, it had further dented his pride. He had been aware of an uneasy feeling that if some of his friends had not happened along when they did, Latimer's unsavory cronies would have finished their job and killed him. Aloud, he merely said, "I think that is what galls me so. We know that he was guilty of what happened, but there was nothing to lay before a magistrate, so he goes free as the air."

"I can countenance his freedom easier than I can meeting him in my mother's drawing room," Royce muttered. "It is all I can do to greet him civilly, but he has entrée *everywhere.*" Royce frowned. "I've tried to delicately warn my father that Latimer is *not* the sort of man one allows to run tame through one's home, but beyond telling him that Latimer's reputation in London was reprehensible, I have nothing tangible with which to back up my assertions. If anything, the fact that he is a well-known London rake gives him a certain cachet, and my reluctance to have anything to do with him makes me look churlish and jealous of his popularity amongst the local plantation owners." Cynically he finished, "Our countrymen are fascinated by what they think is a proper English gentleman in their midst—they hang on his every word believing he is an arbiter of fashion, a veritable Beau Brummell, if you will. The fact that he so strenuously espouses our cause in this ridiculous war with England makes him even more in demand with the gentlemen. And the ladies! They adore him!"

"Including Miss Seymour?" Dominic asked unexpectedly, startling both of them by his question.

An interested gleam in his eyes, Royce glanced at Dominic. "Now why would you want to know that, I wonder?"

Cursing his unruly tongue, Dominic replied stiffly, "I was just curious—Zachary didn't seem to dislike him, and I just . . ."

Royce looked so smugly satisfied that Dominic swore

aloud and said tightly, "Oh, never mind! I don't want to know anyway! I'm sick of talking about Latimer, and as for Deborah, I hope being married to the very old, very rich Earl of Bowden and being able to style herself 'countess' is worth having to put up with a half-mad husband!"

Hesitating a second, Royce finally asked quietly, "Dom, are you really over your calf love for Deborah?"

Surprise written across his face, Dominic stared at his friend. "Good Lord, yes!" he said wryly. "It was only a touch of madness, and you don't have to worry that I am secretly nursing a broken heart. The affair may have wounded me at the time, but it was not serious."

"I'm very glad to hear that. You are bound to meet Deborah here socially sooner or later." With no inflection in his voice, Royce added, "You may not know this, but the earl died rather suddenly, an indecently short time after he and Deborah were married—an accident, it was. It seems he drank too heavily one night and fell down a flight of stairs and broke his neck. He died instantly."

"And was dear brother Latimer visiting at the time?"

"How strange you should ask!" Their eyes meeting in perfect understanding, Royce said, "He had arrived just that evening, so I am told. It was he who discovered the body and broke the sad news to his sweet sister."

Dominic made an exclamation of disgust. "And so Latimer once again gets what he wants—not only his sister back under his hand, but control of a fortune in the bargain."

"Not quite. I have a friend in England, and he wrote me a most interesting letter about the entire affair, including the dispersal of the old earl's estates. There were no children of the marriage, naturally, and since most of the earl's fortune was entailed, the bulk of it went to his brother. The Lady Deborah was left only a small pension . . . which ends if she remarries."

A sardonic smile curved his handsome mouth, and Dominic muttered, "So there is justice of sorts!"

"I suppose one could say so," Royce admitted lightly. "But, like all cats, Latimer seems always to land on his feet. He may have been denied the earl's fortune, but I'm afraid he is still going to get his hands on a fortune, albeit a much smaller one.''

Frowning, Dominic asked, ''The note that Zachary mentioned? I don't mean to pry, but I don't quite understand the connection between Latimer and the Seymours. And from what I *do* know of Latimer, he never had that kind of money!''

''The original holder of the note was old Weatherby, Latimer's uncle. When Weatherby died, Latimer's inheritance was a *long* overdue voucher, and I suspect it will remain long overdue . . . unless, of course, Melissa decides to marry.''

At Dominic's look of total incomprehension, Royce laughed and briefly explained the trust that his grandfather had left for Melissa, Zachary and his mother, Sally.

Somewhat cynically, Dominic murmured, ''And you believe that Latimer is willing to wait two more years before laying his hands on money?''

''Well, he doesn't have to wait that long,'' Royce said coolly. ''He may decide to marry Melissa himself.''

For some unknown reason, Dominic found that idea extremely distasteful. He told himself it was because he objected to Latimer gaining a fortune so easily, although he was certain that marriage to Melissa Seymour would be a living hell for any man. Still, the thought of her married to Latimer rankled, and even after he and Royce had said good night to each other and sought out their separate rooms, the unpleasant notion lingered. Lingered to such an extent that he woke up the next morning with it in the forefront of his mind, and he was in rather a foul mood when he realized that once again he was wasting an inordinate amount of time thinking about Miss Seymour. What disturbed him most of all, though, was the fact that he could not decide precisely which aspect of a Seymour-Latimer alliance bothered him the most—Latimer getting his undoubtedly bloodstained, greedy hands on a fortune he didn't deserve, or Melissa being married to such a base creature. By Heaven, he vowed rashly to himself, before I'd let even an infuriating shrew like her be chained to a blackguard like Latimer, I'd marry her myself! The fact that he wouldn't object to Latimer marrying anyone else *except* Melissa didn't even cross his thoughts.

Entering the dining room, he discovered that Royce was already there ahead of him, perusing a letter as he drank a cup of black, steaming coffee.

Royce looked up and grinned at Dominic's entrance. "My father writes that I should invite you to come back with me."

Dominic smiled and shook his head. "No, thank you! I have too much to do here. Besides, I know a matchmaker when I see one, and your father has a gleam in his eye whenever he mentions Melissa's name that makes me nervous!"

"Ah, yes, of course." A suspiciously innocent expression appeared on Royce's handsome face as he added, "I wonder why she wrote to you."

"Melissa wrote to me?" Dominic demanded in a tone of great astonishment. "Whatever for?"

"I really don't know, but a letter to you from her arrived minutes after mine. Why don't you open it and read it yourself? It's lying there next to your plate."

With clumsy haste, Dominic tore open the letter, his heartbeat accelerating pleasurably . . . at first. Then, as the import of Melissa's letter sank in, his face darkened and in a voice filled with loathing he spat, "Your cousin is mad! After refusing to even let me see her precious damned horse, she now proposes to sell it to me—for twenty-five thousand dollars!"

Royce's eyebrows rose, as much because of Melissa's outrageous offer as because of Dominic's uncharacteristic rage. "I wonder why," he mused slowly.

"I don't give a damn why!" Dominic growled. "But we're leaving for Baton Rouge this morning. I'm going to see that blasted horse before she changes her mind—and then I'm going to tell her exactly what I think of her ridiculous offer! Twenty-five thousand dollars! he snorted. "She *must* be mad!"

Chapter Nine

IF ROYCE thought Dominic's sudden decision to return to Baton Rouge odd, especially in view of his flat refusal to do so only seconds previously, he wisely kept his own counsel. But he could not help the tiny grin that twitched at the corner of his mouth as Dominic immediately set in motion plans to leave Thousand Oaks. If he didn't know better, he would think that his friend was most *eager* to see his cousin once more—and this despite the curses Dominic called down upon Melissa's head as valises were hastily packed and horses saddled.

Within the hour they were ready to set out, Dominic leaving behind a stack of hastily written instructions for his overseer and stablemaster. He conferred briefly with the Thomases, giving them carte blanche for any necessities they deemed vital for the efficient running of the plantation. Feeling that he had everything under control at Thousand Oaks, with a strong sense of anticipation he mounted his horse and he and Royce departed.

They rode in companionable silence for several minutes as their horses trotted easily down the dirt road that led away from the plantation. Conversation, when it began, was desultory, but eventually the topic foremost in both their minds was introduced when Royce invited Dominic to stay at Oak Hollow while in Baton Rouge.

Sending Royce a wry glance, he murmured, "I think it best if I stay at the tavern where we dined with young Seymour." Then he added harshly, "I have no intention of remaining in the area longer than necessary—and what I have to do will not take very long!"

Looking across at his friend's dark face, Royce mused aloud, "I wonder what made Melissa change her mind about selling the stallion. She has always been very adamant about keeping him."

Dominic had his own ideas about why Melissa had done such a baffling turnabout; he had thought of little else since he had first read her letter. Even while he had been busily scrawling instructions to his retainers and speaking to the housekeeper and her husband, one part of his mind had been keenly reviewing all he knew about Miss Seymour . . . and Julius Latimer.

Keeping his voice neutral, he replied, "If I didn't know better, I would stick to my original assumption—that your cousin is mad, or merely doing this to annoy me. But I find it most peculiar that she would offer to sell the horse for such a ridiculous amount. No one will pay that kind of money for an animal—especially since the amount she asked for is *exactly* what is owed to Latimer."

Royce looked startled and then, as the significance of this sank in, his eyes darkened with anger. "You think that Latimer is behind this? That he is forcing Melissa to sell the horse?"

Dominic nodded slowly. "We both know that Latimer is a greedy bastard and we also both know that no matter how he may pretend to enjoy his stay here, it is just that— pretense." Smiling grimly, Dominic went on. "Latimer hates the country and he holds a scathingly low opinion of anything that remotely resembles bucolic pleasures. Remember how he could not be pried away from London no matter what the season, how he spoke so contemptuously of rustic bumpkins and the lack of amenities to be found in the country? Latimer is a dandy, a mincing fop—he is far happier in the sophisticated environs of London than in some provincial little town like Baton Rouge! New Orleans would be more to his taste, yet he has remained in what, to him, must be very inelegant and crude surroundings for several months. Only money," Dominic said flatly, "would keep him here, and I suspect that he has grown tired of waiting and has demanded that Melissa pay him."

"And since," Royce began thoughtfully, "the only thing Melissa owns of any value besides the plantation—

and that, technically, is Zachary's—is her horse, she is trying to meet his demands by selling Folly for as much money as she can get.'' He shot Dominic a speculative glance before saying slyly, ''Of course, she could marry him—that way he would get her share of the trust and the horse!''

Dominic had already considered that possibility and, to Royce's disappointment, showed no sign of expression as he replied blandly, ''Yes, it's true Latimer might be contemplating such an act. But the very fact that Melissa wrote to me makes it clear that she doesn't want to be married to him.''

Royce snorted. ''Melissa doesn't want to be married to anyone! She and my father have been arguing about that subject since she turned seventeen!''

''There is something else,'' Dominic said quietly, ''that we haven't discussed. Latimer may not have given her a choice. Can you see him married? He is far more likely to have offered to make your cousin his mistress rather than his wife!''

''By God!'' Royce blazed. ''If that blackguard has laid a finger on Melissa . . .''

Conversation lapsed after that, and it was with an increasing sense of urgency that the two men rode toward their destination. For Royce, the situation was simple: if Latimer had dared to make a dishonorable proposal to Melissa, he would kill him and that would be that! But for Dominic, there was no easy solution for the dilemma in which he found himself.

He was furious, annoyed, concerned and appalled at what was happening inside him, but those emotions did not disturb him as much as did the trickle of fear that slid down his spine whenever he thought of Melissa in Latimer's power. Fear was not an emotion with which he was familiar, nor had he ever experienced the surge of fierce protectiveness that swept through him when he reflected on what sort of pressure might have been brought to bear upon Melissa to compel her to write what must have been an extremely difficult letter. And paradoxically, because she aroused all those conflicting emotions within him, he grew even more furious about the entire situation. It was ridiculous! he told himself through gritted teeth. Ridiculous and incomprehensible that a woman he didn't even like, for God's sake, could cause him to act so precipitously. Damning her, damning himself, he rode steadily toward Baton Rouge, his mood growing surlier by the hour.

Royce and Dominic had not pushed their horses, although they had traveled at a brisk rate, and consequently it was nearing dusk the next day before they reached their destination. Despite Dominic's protestations to the contrary, Royce insisted upon accompanying him to the tavern where he planned to stay.

"I want to see you settled before I arrive home. My father will be disappointed that you are not with me, and I want to be able to soothe his ruffled sensibilities by assuring him that I saw you comfortably disposed before I left you," Royce told him with a smile.

Dominic sent him a dry look. "Hoping the tavern has no rooms?"

Royce laughed. "Ah, saw through me, did you? Oh, well, you can't blame a fellow for trying."

There was no difficulty in Dominic's procuring a room for himself, and shortly thereafter the two friends bade each other good-bye. Dominic promised that as soon as he had seen Melissa and spied out the situation, he would ride over and talk to Royce.

Royce had not disappeared from sight before Dominic was writing a note to Melissa, informing her of his presence in Baton Rouge and also explaining that he would be at Willowglen at eleven o'clock tomorrow morning to view Folly *if* she was still of a mind to sell him. A sardonic smile on his lips, he tossed a coin to a nearby urchin and requested him to deliver the missive to Miss Seymour at Willowglen.

If Melissa was surprised at the promptness of the reply to her desperate note to Dominic, she gave no sign of it when his letter to her was delivered that evening. She was startled, though, to discover that he was already here in Baton Rouge and that her outrageous price had not seemed to faze him.

The four days which had passed since Melissa had sent

off her letter to Dominic had not been easy ones for her, and with a feeling of impending doom she had waited almost apathetically for the first of July to arrive. Realistically, she faced the unpalatable fact that it was highly unlikely that she would escape from the trap Latimer had set for her. During the past four nights she had done nothing but lie awake and search frantically for some escape from the horrid fate closing rapidly in on her. Her skin crawled to think of Latimer touching her in an intimate way, and she spent a good part of each night dwelling fondly on ways in which to kill him before he dishonored her. She turned over wildly improbable schemes in her mind. The most obvious one was the ending of the trust, but even when she had made a second trip to see Mr. Smithfield, asking about the dissolution of the trust upon her marriage or proposed marriage, she had come away deeply depressed. It seemed that she had forgotten one minor clause: the trust would end upon her marriage, but the money would not be dispersed until thirty days *after* she married. A mirthless laugh had come from her. So even if she could have found a man willing to marry her within an indecently short time, it wouldn't have done any good. It was only later that she wondered if Latimer had known that fact when he made his infamous offer. . . .

Filled with anxiety and frustration, she began to show the strain she was under. There was a sharpness to her voice and a tight line to her mouth these days, but it was the dark circles under her eyes which revealed clearly that she had spent many a sleepless night of late. To Zachary's worried inquiries, to Etienne's gruff probings and to Frances' gentle questions, she returned soothing platitudes: "Why, no, nothing is the matter!" or "I didn't sleep well last night—an owl outside my window kept me awake," and "Good gracious, of course nothing is wrong!" Each accepted her word, but there were three pairs of very worried eyes that followed her about. She might try to hide it, but something was obviously very wrong, and they could not imagine what it could be.

All three had watched her face closely when the note from Dominic had arrived, and all three had noted the faint spark of hope that suddenly flickered in Melissa's topaz eyes. But when asked about the note, she had turned away, muttering some lame reply.

Melissa had never really expected Dominic to even answer her letter, and the fact that he had created another problem for her, one which she had to solve before he came to view Folly the next morning. She had deliberately not mentioned to anyone the possibility of selling the stallion, and with sinking spirits she wondered how she was going to explain to the others this inexplicable change of heart. Zachary was not stupid, nor were Etienne and Frances, and once they heard the amount she was demanding for Folly, she didn't doubt that one of them, if not all three, would guess that the voucher held by Latimer was behind her actions. But would they guess the alternative that Latimer had offered her? She didn't think so, but she was going to have to come up with a very good excuse for so suddenly deciding to sell the pride of their stable, their hope for the future. Lying in bed that night, she came to the dreary conclusion that she would just have to try to bluff her way through and hope that everyone would be too stunned to ask a lot of questions until it was too late.

Rising early the next morning, she dressed carefully for the coming interview with Mr. Slade, unconsciously choosing a gown of funereal black. After she viewed herself in the mirror, an unhappy sigh escaped her. She certainly looked as if she were going to a funeral, the pallor of her skin increased by the weeks of strain and worry, the severe hairstyle sharply defining the fine bones of her features, and the square-rimmed spectacles only bringing attention to the dark circles under her eyes. She made a face at her reflection; then, stiffening her shoulders, she marched from the room, feeling as if she were going to an executioner.

She put off telling Zachary and Etienne what she planned to do as long as she could. It was only after breakfast, as she accompanied the two men to the stables, that she said with a suspect airiness, "Oh, by the way, will you have Folly groomed and brought into the big box stall near the front of the stable?"

There was something in her voice that caused both men to look at her. Melissa could never tell a very convincing lie, and noticing the faint flush that stained her cheeks, Zachary asked suspiciously, "Why?"

Melissa swallowed and looked away. "Mr. Slade is coming to see him this morning," she muttered.

"What?" demanded both Zachary and Etienne in unison, but it was Etienne who recovered first. His eyes filled with speculation, he asked more quietly, "Why?"

Melissa kept her gaze averted, and in a low voice she got out, "I'm thinking of selling him . . . if Mr. Slade will give me a good price."

There was a thunderous silence, and Melissa wished miserably that she was anywhere but right there. She peeked at the two dearest men in her life, and her heart sank to her toes. Zachary's face was a mixture of angry disbelief, while Etienne stared at her as if she had gone mad.

It was Zachary who spoke first. "Don't you think we should have discussed this?" he asked in a deceptively mild tone, despite the clenched fists at his sides. "Folly is the entire basis of our stables. Without him we have nothing but a few brood mares—fine mares, to be sure, but none with the reputation that Folly has earned, and *will* earn."

Hiding her own dismay, Melissa lifted her chin proudly and replied with apparent carelessness, "I wouldn't worry about it. We have bred all the mares to Folly, and with the money I intend to get for him, we should be able to set ourselves up properly." Bringing the attack into Zachary's camp, she added tartly, "Besides, weren't you the one who said that without money it didn't matter what sort of stallion we had—that our ramshackle appearance would scare off a prospective breeder or buyer?"

Sullenly, Zachary growled, "I didn't say that—Mr. Slade did!"

"Well, there you are!" Melissa said with forced cheerfulness, but the expression of misery and chagrin on Zachary's face twisted her emotions and she desperately sought some way to comfort him. Her voice very low, she mumbled, "Someday we shall buy him back . . . once . . . once we are well established."

The look of scornful skepticism that Zachary shot her made Melissa even more grim, but she had no choice save to continue on the present course of action. Pasting a smile on her face, she said, "We'll come about, Zack! I know we will, and if selling Folly will help us right now, then that is what we have to do. I don't want to do it, but I see no other alternative."

"Strange, you've never mentioned it before," Zachary returned sourly. "I thought that things were going along well, and now, without warning, you tell me that we are going to sell the only thing of real value that we own—the one thing that will make all our plans and dreams possible. A horse of Folly's caliber and speed doesn't come along more than once in a lifetime—and you're going to sell him out from under us!" It was obvious that Zachary was upset, but he clamped his lips firmly together to keep from saying angry and hurtful words. Spinning on his heels, he turned away from Melissa, saying tightly, "I'll go get Folly. Since it seems that I am not worthy enough to be consulted on major decisions, I must by rights be the errand boy!"

Dismay clouding her features, Melissa watched him stride furiously away. One slim hand lifted as if to call him back, but then listlessly she let it drop to her side. She had handled this all wrong, but she didn't see any other way she could have done it without alerting Zachary to Latimer's ugly plans for her. Straightening her shoulders, she glanced at Etienne, who still stood nearby.

With an edge to her voice she demanded, "I suppose you intend to take his side?"

Etienne slowly shook his head, his black eyes shrewd and kind. "*Non, petite,* I will not add to your burden, but I think that you have not considered what you are doing when you talk of selling Folly. He is indeed a most uncommon animal, and once you sell him, you have no guarantee that no matter how wealthy you may or may not become, no matter how successful, you will be able to repurchase him, as you so blithely told Zachary."

Melissa glared at him, but the anguish she was experiencing was apparent when she said, "Don't you think I know that! And don't you think that if there were any other way, I would take it?"

Frowning, Etienne took a step forward. "Lissa, what is it? There is something that you are not telling us."

"I don't want to talk about it," she muttered grimly, frightened that Etienne might guess Latimer's involvement with her decision to sell Folly.

He started to say something else, but seeing the withdrawn, frozen expression on Melissa's face, Etienne gave a very Gallic shrug and walked in the direction that Zachary had taken. Through misty eyes Melissa watched him go, longing to call him back, longing to tell both Zachary and Etienne why she was acting in what must seem to them a foolish and contrary way.

A half hour later, her emotions fairly well under control, she walked into the barn, her heart a leaden weight in her breast. She stopped in front of the stall in which she had told Zachary to put Folly. With a mixture of pride and despair, she stared at the stallion as he whinnied and arched his neck. Moving closer to Melissa, he gently lowered his elegant head until it rested upon her shoulder, waiting for the scratching and petting he knew would be forthcoming. Fighting back an urge to cry, Melissa buried her face in his silky black mane, her arms creeping up around his long, powerful neck.

It wasn't just that she loved the horse and dreaded seeing him leave. He represented so many dreams for her; he was to have been the foundling sire of the grand stables that she and Zachary would build; he was to have made her and Zachary famous, his offspring adding to the luster of his name, bringing prosperity to Willowglen once more. And now she was going to have to let him go. Someone else would gain all that she and Zachary had hoped for. And for what? Her mouth twisted. So she could preserve her virtue?

Thinking of Latimer, thinking of what his perfidious actions were going to cost her no matter what she did, Melissa tightened her fingers on Folly's mane, and in a voice shaking with loathing, she cursed virulently. "Goddamn him! I hope he burns in hell!"

"Ah, I *do* trust that you aren't talking about me," Dominic said softly from behind her.

Startled, she spun around, her eyes widening when she saw him standing there, just inside the stable doorway. Trying to recover her composure, she nervously smoothed her full black skirt and sent him a small smile, not precisely a welcoming one, but not *un*welcoming either.

Dominic was dressed very smartly, she saw as he stepped closer to her. A coat of dark gray superfine fitted snuggly across his broad shoulders, his long legs encased in a pair of form-hugging nankeen breeches. Above the nattily arranged white cravat, his face was dark and vital, a lock of unruly black hair persisting in waving across his forehead, a quizzical smile curving his mobile mouth.

Melissa thought that she had hidden her distressed state well, but Dominic had seen the sheen of tears in her eyes and had noticed the faint tremble of her lower lip. His own smile faded just a little, and all the sarcastic remarks he had planned to greet her with fled. He was left with only a curious need to comfort her. Quietly he said, "It is obvious from the scene I just witnessed as well as what Royce has told me that Folly means a great deal to you. I promise that if I do buy him I will take good care of him and that he will not be mistreated in any way."

A spark of hope flickered in her breast, and forgetting that, according to Uncle Josh, Dominic wasn't to be trusted, she asked breathlessly, "You mean you really will consider paying my price for him?"

Compassionate he might be, kind even on occasion, but he disliked being taken advantage of as much as the next man, and his moment of madness disappeared. "I rather doubt it! But I thought I should at least see what I am turning down."

Melissa's features fell and Dominic knew an urge to call the words back, to tell her that he *might* be willing to meet her excessive price, willing to say anything that would remove the bleak, heartrending expression of defeat that had greeted his blunt statements. Angry with himself for this apparent weakness, horrified at this unexpected flaw in his character where she was concerned, Dominic reminded himself savagely that he had no intention of paying the exorbitant sum. He had not come here to comfort her, but to plainly let her know what he thought of her ridiculous attempts to rob him.

Stiffening his resolve, he stared at her dispassionately, wondering again what it was about her that stirred such strange emotions within him. God knew, it wasn't that she was a stunning beauty, he thought caustically as his jaundiced gaze traveled dismissively over the painfully severe hairstyle and the spinsterish spectacles. But his eyes lingered against his will on the curve of her mouth and the fragile bones of her jaw, and he was aware of a wild impulse to rip aside those spectacles and loosen the imprisoned hair and see for himself what might be revealed.

Suddenly conscious that Dominic was staring at her too intently, Melissa was instantly on her guard, her features automatically assuming the squint-eyed, pinched-mouth expression she wore in front of him. Determined to salvage her pride, if nothing else, she lifted her chin proudly and said frostily, "Very well, then, Mr. Slade. I'll show you the stallion."

Spinning around, she unlatched the lower half of the stall door, grabbed a lead rope hanging nearby and stepped inside. It took but a second to capture Folly's halter and to attach the rope. Squaring her shoulders and summoning up a careless expression, she gave the stallion a gentle pat and led him from the stall.

Folly was indeed a magnificent animal, his head finely formed, his neck proudly arched, the long, slender legs effortlessly carrying his elegantly proportioned body as he pranced by Melissa's side. Dominic eyed the stallion assessingly, privately thinking that he had seldom seen such a beautiful animal, but his face gave no sign of what was going through his mind.

Confidently he approached Folly, pleased that the stallion showed no signs of skittishness or nasty habits. With an expert touch, Dominic ran his hands along the straight back and down the strong legs. Folly stood quietly, his ears tuned to the soft sounds of Melissa's voice as she spoke to him, seemingly unconcerned about the stranger who moved around him. Even when Dominic checked his teeth, Folly remained calm and still, tossing his head only when Dominic let loose his muzzle.

Glancing at Melissa, Dominic said warmly, "He is quite the gentleman, isn't he?"

Forgetting just for a little while that Dominic represented an enemy, and proud of the stallion, Melissa smiled naturally at him. "Oh, yes! He has no real vices and has always been an absolute angel. Even as a yearling, he . . ." As she remembered why Dominic was here, her confidences stopped and her smile disappeared. Stiffly she said, "He is an excellent horse, as you can see for yourself."

Fascinated by the change the smile made of her features, Dominic stared at her for a long moment, thinking that she should smile more often, but seeing the pinched look that descended upon her, he sighed. He really must have had too much to drink that night—he could see no reason why she had affected him as she had, nor why it mattered to him that she *not* be unhappy. Shaking his head at his own folly, he said, "He is indeed a fine piece of horseflesh, but does he have the speed that I have been led to believe be possesses?"

Insulted that he should have doubts about Folly's abilities, Melissa glared at him, wishing that Mr. Dominic Slade were not quite so attractive and that she were not so very aware of him. But she was, and even though she was distressed and furious about the situation, she could not help be conscious of his tall, lean body and darkly handsome face. Reminding herself sternly that he was a rake and a trifler of feminine hearts and that his *only* reason for being here was to buy Folly, she replied icily, "If you will wait just a few moments, I shall have him saddled and Etienne can take him around our track."

Dominic nodded, watching with amusement and speculation as she marched away, leading the dancing stallion. When she returned, she had Zachary with her. There were a few moments of polite conversation, Zachary's dislike of the circumstances rather obvious from his tight-lipped expression and abrupt contributions to the words that were exchanged.

Thoughtfully Dominic followed the pair as they made

their way to the track that lay just beyond the main stable. It was glaringly apparent that no one was happy about the prospective sale, and having seen Folly, Dominic could understand Melissa's reluctance to part with the stallion. The love and pride she took in the horse had been more than obvious, he thought slowly, remembering the way she had buried her face in the horse's mane in the stable before Dominic had made his presence known. So why was she willing to sell him—even at her ridiculous price?

His thoughts busy on the puzzle, he stared out over the crude track that had been set up, the conviction that Latimer was somehow connected to this turnabout growing with every moment. From what Royce had told him, he knew that in less than two years, or sooner if Melissa married—which he could not conceive of any man being foolish enough to walk into *that* trap—the Seymours would have a fortune at their fingertips, even after paying off the voucher owned by Latimer. So what was it that had changed her mind this suddenly? It could only be Latimer demanding his money or threatening her with some action that she could not abide. And that had to be either demanding the sale of her home or . . . forcing his attentions on her. Dominic's mouth tightened and he glanced at her slender form in the shabby black gown. He could not understand it, but for better or worse, he seemed unable to banish Miss Melissa Seymour and her problems from his concern. He admitted disgustedly to himself that even if Folly proved to be tied at the knees and ran like a slug, he was probably going to pay the exorbitant price she had demanded.

Shaking his head at his own idiocy, he wandered over to stand near the peeling white railing that enclosed the track. The next instant, his gaze was riveted as Folly, Etienne upon his back, suddenly burst onto the race course, the stallion's long legs a mere blur as he displayed the style and speed that were making him famous. Folly ran with an effortless stride, his power and grace eloquent with every movement, and whatever doubts Dominic might have held about the horse's potential were forever banished. The stallion possessed incredible speed, and it didn't take a glance at his watch to have it confirmed—this was indeed a horse in a million!

His face enigmatic, his gaze followed the stallion around the track while Etienne gradually pulled the animal into a gentle trot. Folly would prove to be an outstanding addition to his stables, and Dominic was extremely pleased at the prospect of owning such a splendid horse—until he happened to look in Melissa's direction and saw the expression of misery and despair on her face.

Not giving himself time to think, certain that the sun had forever addled his wits, Dominic was stunned to hear himself say, "He is worth much more than you are asking, but if you will sell me a half interest in him for the amount you mentioned in your letter, I shall consider myself to have gained a bargain."

If his words stunned Dominic, they left Melissa utterly speechless. Her eyes locked painfully on his, searching desperately for any sign that he was toying with her.

Dominic met her gaze levelly, noticing for the first time the long, silky lashes that rimmed her slightly almond-shaped eyes. In her astonishment, Melissa had forgotten her disguise and her soft mouth was not in its habitually prim curve, the fullness of her bottom lip suddenly attracting Dominic's stare. Once again he knew that mad urge to take off those spectacles and to loosen her hair from its ugly confines. He couldn't even guess at the color, so tightly did she have it pulled back into the spinsterish bun, but he found himself wanting very much to know precisely the hue and texture of it.

Hope burgeoning within her breast, her hands clasped rigidly in front of her, Melissa finally managed to stammer, "A-a-are you s-s-serious? You are not j-j-jesting?"

One thick black brow flew up quizzically. "My dear, I do not jest about that kind of money." Putting on a fierce scowl, Dominic added, "And I will not pay you a penny more, so do not try to drive up the price!"

Melissa swallowed convulsively, visions of throwing Latimer's money in his face dancing before her eyes, joy at knowing that Folly would still be part hers causing a smile to tremble on her lips. "Oh, no! I wouldn't do that!'' Earnestly she said, ''You must believe me that I wouldn't have asked such a high price if it hadn't been of the utmost importance.'' She looked as if she might say more, but then she bit her lips and looked away.

Zachary, who had remained silent during all of this, finally spoke up. Addressing Dominic, he asked slowly, ''Does this mean that you are going to be a partner with us? That Folly will still be ours?''

''Half yours,'' Dominic replied, wondering how he was going to explain his incomprehensible action to Royce—and to himself for that matter!

Chapter Ten

DOMINIC ended up staying for dinner, and the midafternoon meal proved to be a singularly enjoyable one. He met Frances Osborne and found her to be a likable woman; Etienne, too, once he realized that Dominic was not going to take Melissa's beloved Folly away from Willowglen, became quite animated and friendly. And Zachary, reassured that the future he and Melissa had dreamed of and planned for was not to be destroyed, was further impressed by Dominic's easy conversation and manner.

Only Melissa remained apparently unaffected by Dominic's effortless charm as he complimented Frances on the excellent meal she had set before him and talked knowledgeably with Etienne and Zachary about horses. It was difficult for her to remain aloof, especially when she now had such strong reasons to be grateful to him for giving her the means with which to confound Latimer. Her resolution not to be bowled over by his mesmerizing presence would waver, though, whenever he would flash a warm, slightly teasing smile in her direction or his laughing gray eyes would meet hers. Sternly she reminded herself of everything that Josh had warned her about him, forcing herself not to notice the curly black hair or the handsome nose or the mobile mouth. She would *not,* she vowed grimly, prove to be just another silly female who allowed her head to be turned by a practiced rake. But it was a hard battle she was fighting within herself—particularly when she remembered what it felt like to be crushed in his arms and the intoxicating pleasure that same smiling mouth had given her.

Disliking the trend of her wayward thoughts, Melissa scowled fiercely at the remains of the chicken that had been served at dinner. It would make things so much easier, she admitted unhappily, if Mr. Slade were not quite so charming and attractive. And she suspected that even with Josh's warnings firmly in her brain, being around Mr. Slade very much was going to put a severe strain on her good resolutions.

Seeing her scowl, Dominic broke off his conversation with Zachary and murmured, "Is there something about my offer of a partnership in connection with Folly that displeases you?"

Melissa was instantly the focus of every eye, and a hot flush stained her cheeks. "Oh, no," she said quickly. Thinking that they should work out the fine details of their agreement, she added, "But I do think that we should discuss the actual arrangements in private before you leave this afternoon."

Dominic's expression grew quizzical. "Shouldn't your brother or your uncle be handling that sort of thing for you? I'm aware of the unusual circumstances that make you owner of the horse, but at this point, shouldn't the men of your family be the ones to decide the financial situation?"

Melissa gritted her teeth. She had long ago realized that her father had been extremely indulgent with her upbringing and that he had allowed her great license during his lifetime, but it wasn't until his death that she fully understood how little power she possessed in arranging the details of her own life. Although she had been forced by circumstances to take over the burden of decisions concerning Willowglen until Zachary reached his majority, she could not publicly carry out plantation dealings without a man's assistance—it was unthinkable that a woman could transact business without a male surrogate for court and legal proceedings. It was also a commonly held notion that women could not manage their own affairs without the help of men. She thought of the deplorable chaos her father had left for her and Zachary to muddle through, and her temper rose. So Mr. Slade didn't think she could handle her own money, did he? Topaz eyes blazing with swift anger, she replied to his question in a barely civil tone. "Mr. Slade! Folly is *mine,* and I'm afraid that whether you like it or not, *I* am the one you must deal with if you wish to buy him!''

Already familiar enough with her moods to see the signs of rising temper, but unable to resist teasing her, Dominic murmured dulcetly, *"Half* of him."

Melissa was not in a mood to be teased, but a faint smile tugged at the corners of her mouth. Rising gracefully from the table, she said, "If you will come with me?"

The glimpse of her smile was enchanting, he decided, and having noted the attractive flush to her cheeks before she turned away from him, Dominic was further intrigued. Without a word, he followed her lead, his gaze resting speculatively on her slim shoulders and narrow waist as she walked down the hallway ahead of him. Such a proud little tiger, he reflected with amusement.

He strolled into the room she had indicated and glanced around. This was obviously the library and it was a pleasant place, although everywhere Dominic's eyes traveled, signs of the Seymours' straitened circumstances could be seen, from the patched leather chairs to the faded velvet curtains which hung at the long windows.

After Melissa sat down on a chintz-covered sofa, Dominic settled himself in a chair across from her. With a faint smile curving his full lips, he asked, "What is it about my offer that you wish to discuss?"

Her resentment flaring at the sight of that half-indulgent smile, Melissa snapped, "I am not a child and I would appreciate it if you would take this conversation seriously and not treat me like an imbecile!"

His eyes narrowed, and in a much less friendlier tone of voice, he said, "Believe me, my dear, when I talk about spending twenty-five thousand dollars, I am *very* serious!"

Melissa bit her lip, miserably realizing that it would do her cause no good to antagonize Dominic—besides, this situation wasn't *his* fault! She just wished that she weren't so very aware of him, of the way his coat fitted across the broad shoulders, or the way his breeches stretched tautly against the long length of his muscled legs as he lounged across from her. It didn't help her peace of mind to find her eyes drawn repeatedly to his dark, lean face, to find herself dreamily going over each of his features—the proud arch of the eyebrows, the clear clarity of the teasing gray eyes, the mocking curve of his mouth and the hard line of his jaw. With an effort, she jerked herself back to the matter at hand. This was *business,* and so, sitting up even straighter on the sofa, she began to question Dominic about how he proposed that they share Folly.

While Melissa had been examining Dominic, Dominic had been doing a little surveying of his own, and what he saw still left him seeking a reason that this hostile, *plain* creature could cause him to act as he had. She definitely wasn't pretty, he finally concluded, having looked hard and long at her features, trying to imagine her without the spectacles, without the bun and without her mouth pursed in that depressingly prim manner, and he couldn't for the life of him picture her other than what she appeared to be—a somewhat dowdy spinster. So why did she hold such fascination for him? It was a question he couldn't answer, and Dominic intensely disliked unanswered questions.

The entire situation was ludicrous! he thought angrily. She wasn't pretty. He didn't like her. Yet he was prepared to spend an inordinate amount of money because he feared she was in some sort of trouble with Latimer. Inwardly Dominic snorted. What sort of fool was he? He wasn't altruistic. He had never been particularly obsessed with the plight of his fellow man, but this woman . . . this woman disturbed him and made him feel oddly protective. Hell! He'd bought only half a damned horse with his money! And that because he had seen how much she cared for Folly and hadn't had the heart to distress her further. Suddenly the unwelcome thought occurred to him that he'd had another motive: if he and Miss Seymour were partners, it would be only natural for them to spend a great deal of time in each other's company—and for some incomprehensible reason, Dominic discovered that he wanted to do just that!

Positive that he had entered his dotage, Dominic began to suggest several methods they could use to make the sharing of the animal easy for both of them. Melissa appeared to be reasonable about the subject, raising very few objections to his proposals. A bit suspicious of her meekness, Dominic wondered what was going on in her mind.

Busy struggling with the major problem of asking Dominic to pay her the entire amount within twenty-four hours, Melissa was only half attending to what he was saying. When he stopped talking, she suddenly blurted, "Could you pay me the money tomorrow? In gold?"

If Dominic had had any doubts that Latimer was behind her actions, this request settled it for him. Latimer must be demanding payment and must have set the first of July as the date the money should be paid or he would take some sort of action that Melissa could not countenance. Knowing Latimer, Dominic had a very good idea of what that action would be, although he simply could not understand *why* Latimer had designs on such an unattractive woman. Then he grimaced to himself. If she had *him* unwillingly fascinated, it stood to reason that she might have cast the same spell over Latimer.

Melissa's request for the money in gold by tomorrow created a problem, though. Dominic was a wealthy man, but laying his hands on that sort of cold, hard cash in the time given was damn near impossible. He hesitated and then said slowly, "I doubt very seriously that I could make arrangements that swiftly, but I can assure you that you will have your money before the end of the week." He shot her a keen look and, picking his words with care, added, "I'm certain that any, er, debtor who might be demanding payment from you would not be able to take any harmful action before you would have the money."

Melissa's eyes flew to his, her astonishment and fear obvious in the wide-eyed stare. She swallowed, then asked in a low voice, "How do you know I need the money for a . . . a . . . debtor?"

Carelessly, Dominic replied, "A mere guess, my dear; don't let it concern you." Driven by something he couldn't explain, he got up and stood in front of her. Bending forward, he picked up one of her hands as it lay limply in her lap, and holding it comfortingly in his, he murmured, "If there is some way I can serve you . . . ?"

His words were so tempting that for one insane moment, Melissa actually considered telling him of Latimer's dishonorable offer, but she was far too conscious of Dominic's disturbing nearness to think clearly. His hand felt warm and strong around hers, and her fingers seemed to tingle just from the mere touch of him, her heartbeat accelerating madly. Frightened that she might betray the tumult within her breast, she nervously jerked her hand away and stammered, "Oh, th-th-thank y-y-you, but there is no n-n-need for th-th-that!"

He remained unconvinced, but he could not force her confidences, and with a negligent shrug of his broad shoulders, he stepped away from her. Any chance for further private conversation ended when Zachary entered the room a moment later.

The three of them talked amicably for several minutes longer; then Dominic and Melissa signed an agreement stating the terms of the sale. With the paper safely tucked inside his waistcoat, Dominic took his leave. He was pleased with the morning's work, yet troubled, too. It went against his grain to know that Latimer was the one who would ultimately profit from the partnership between himself and Miss Seymour. If only there were a way, he mused idly, that he could put a spoke in Latimer's plans. . . .

Returning to his room at the tavern, Dominic found Royce waiting for him and, resigned to the teasing he was sure to receive, he succinctly told his friend what he had done. The knowing smile that quirked Royce's lips made Dominic's fists clench, but a reluctant grin crossed his own face. "I have gone mad," he admitted. "And I do not need you to tell me so!"

Royce's instant nod of complete accord did nothing for Dominic's self-esteem, but during the next few minutes he good-naturedly listened to Royce's mirthful comments about "addled wits" and "muttonheaded decisions." Eventually, though, Royce left off his mocking remarks and mentioned the reason for his visit. "My father invites you to partake of supper with us this evening." Giving his friend a rueful smile, Royce added, "He was *not* pleased that you preferred a public place to Oak Hollow, but I think if you come for supper, it will soothe his ruffled pride."

Dominic accepted the invitation, and shortly thereafter the two friends prepared to leave. They had just mounted their horses when Dominic got a brief glimpse of a gentleman entering the tavern. Frowning, he stared at the doorway, and Royce, noticing his expression, asked, "What is it? Something wrong?"

"I don't know," Dominic answered slowly, "but I could have sworn that I just saw Latimer go inside."

Royce shrugged. "And if you did? What are you going to do about it? The man has the right to go into a bloody tavern, for God's sake!"

Dominic grimaced, well aware of the truth of Royce's words. Without further conversation, he turned his horse away and headed in the direction of Oak Hollow. But he could not put the man he had seen from his mind. Was it Latimer? But even more importantly, was Latimer going to see Melissa tonight?

The answers to both questions was yes. It definitely had been Latimer whom Dominic had seen entering the tavern, and he wouldn't have been very pleased to learn that Latimer would be staying in a room just five doors up the hall from him, in room number three. Dominic would have been even more displeased to discover that once Latimer had procured his night's lodging, he had sat down and written a note to be delivered that very evening to Miss Melissa Seymour!

With relish and lewd anticipation, Latimer penned the words informing Melissa that he was in Baton Rouge and was looking forward to meeting with her. A malicious smile on his lips, he scrawled hurriedly that before they settled the terms for payment, he wished to see her to make final arrangements. He would be staying at the tavern tonight, he wrote in a barely decipherable hand, in room number three, and it would be to her advantage to see him this evening to make certain that they were in perfect accord concerning the "terms of their bargain."

It was an insulting missive, and reading it later that evening, Melissa shivered with revulsion. She had been expecting some word from him, so the receipt of his note was almost anticlimactic for her. Sitting on a small chair in her bedroom, she reread his letter, unbearably grateful that Mr. Slade had come to call today and that, thanks to his generosity, Latimer was no longer a threat to either her virtue or her peace of mind. If Slade had ignored her letter or had been tardy in answering it or unwilling to pay her exorbitant price . . . Melissa's mouth went dry as she thought of how she would feel if she had received Latimer's note without the comforting knowledge that she would be able to pay him off in gold coin by the end of the week.

She sat there alone in her room for a long time, staring blankly at Latimer's note, realizing sickly how close to ruin she had come, how she might very well have been forced to accept Latimer's degrading terms, if Dominic had not been willing to meet her unheard-of price for Folly. A soft smile suddenly curved her mouth as she thought of Dominic and his generosity. For several moments she was lost in a dreamy haze, remembering the way Dominic smiled and the way his clear gray eyes had twinkled with teasing laughter. Then with a regretful sigh she jerked herself away from such silly reflections, bringing her wayward thoughts back to the matter at hand.

She read again the part where Latimer had written that he wished to see her tonight. Why? she wondered suspiciously. What was he up to? Extremely mistrustful of him, Melissa considered different reasons that would make it imperative for him to see her tonight, but she could think of no satisfactory explanation for his request . . . except that he might wish to gloat at what he assumed was her predicament. Her eyes flashed with an angry golden fire and she considered letting him sit up all night waiting for her, but then her lips twisted. She dared not ignore his request—what if he should grow tired of waiting and show up here at Willowglen demanding to see her? A shudder went through her. If Zachary's suspicions were aroused . . . She glanced again at the letter, trying to decipher from Latimer's scrawl if it was number three or number eight. After careful scrutiny, she decided it was an eight.

Setting aside the letter, she got up and went to stand before the cheval glass, absentmindedly beginning to brush her long, wavy hair. She had washed it after Dominic had left and now it swirled about her shoulders in shiny honey-colored curls, the silky strands gleaming with a life of their own. The brush felt good as she rhythmically pulled it through the tawny mass, her mind still occupied with Latimer's note.

Why shouldn't she see him tonight? she mused grimly. It would be *such* a pleasure to watch his face when she threw his disgusting offer back at him! The more she considered it, the fonder she became of the idea. Why not? He had humiliated *her,* forced her to listen to his sordid plans, so why shouldn't she have the enjoyment of forcing *him* to listen to what she had to say? Why wait until tomorrow?

She smiled faintly, her first in many days, as she pictured Latimer's chagrin and—she hoped—disappointment when he discovered that she wasn't going to become his mistress.

Her mind made up, she spent several more moments planning how to get into town undetected and into Latimer's room without causing a most horrifying scandal. It wouldn't do to contemplate what would happen if it were revealed that she had gone alone at night to a tavern and, even more shocking, had actually been in a man's room alone with him!

Latimer had not stated any particular time this evening, and so she could ostensibly retire early to her room, slip out of the house and ride into town without anyone being the wiser. That part of her hastily concocted plan didn't worry her—it was getting into his room that gave her pause. She could hardly walk nonchalantly through the main area of the tavern! Then her face brightened as she remembered the outside staircase of the tavern. It had been constructed for precisely the reason Melissa needed it—to provide private access to the eight small rooms upstairs that were let out to boarders. She should have no trouble, she thought happily, in coming and going unseen.

A pleased little smile on her face, she looked inside the old mahogany armoire that sat in one corner of her room. There were few gowns in it and certainly none of those were particularly striking. Her smile faded. She wanted to look her best when she faced Latimer, wanted him to understand what he had lost. It wasn't very nice of her, but she not unnaturally wanted him to suffer a bit after all the anguish he had inflicted upon her. If she looked desirable when she told him just what she thought of his disgusting offer, well, so much the better.

Her hand brushed across an older gown of amber-colored silk, and with quickening interest she drew it from the armoire. Trying it on, she glanced at herself in the cheval glass. It would do admirably, she thought as she took in the way the snug fit of the bodice forced her breasts to nearly spill out of the soft material. She had owned the gown for a long time—her father had brought it back from England—and though it was almost too small for her, she could not bring herself to discard it. The gown flattered her, drawing attention to her creamy shoulders and high bosom, the amber shade of silk giving her hair the look of warm honey and deepening the topaz glow of her eyes. She twirled before the cheval glass, enjoying the way the silken material flared out from the high waist, the full skirt billowing out around her. It might be old, it might be a bit tight, but this was the most attractive garment she owned and she would wear it tonight.

Her plan proved lamentably easy, and her conscience pricked her at how concerned everyone had been when she had claimed a headache and retired early. With shaking fingers she had laid aside the ugly garment she had worn during the day and swiftly put on the amber silk gown. She gave her hair one last brush, and then, putting on a worn hooded cloak of brown velvet, she opened her door and peeked down the long hallway. It was deserted.

Quickly she made her way downstairs and outside, her heart beating uncomfortably fast. It took her but a moment to reach the stables and saddle one of the mares. Once she reached the main road, her heartbeat slowed and she took a deep breath of relief. She had done it! No one had seen her. Now for Latimer. . . .

Arriving some while later in Baton Rouge, she kept to the shadows, terrified that someone might see her and recognize her. Fortunately, the tavern was set near the edge of town, and Melissa quickly guided her horse deeper into the darkness at the rear of the rambling, two-storied wooden building. Sliding from the mare, she hurriedly tied the animal to a nearby oak sapling and with nervous steps approached the tavern.

Her heart had begun to pound painfully as she rounded the building and found the narrow staircase that led upstairs. It was one thing to contemplate confronting Latimer from the safety of her own home, and another to boldly march into his room. She hesitated, suddenly beset by the danger of what she was doing, as well as the impropriety. She very nearly turned back, but remembering the threat to Zack should Latimer come to Willowglen at an unseemly hour and in an ugly mood, she moved forward. No one would discover her, and it wouldn't be to Latimer's advantage for her presence here to become known. He would be labeled a blackguard of the worst kind, and she suspected rightly that he would prefer everyone to continue to think of him as "the charming Englishman."

Bolstering her waning courage, she sped up the stairs before she could change her mind. The door creaked when she opened it and her heart nearly leaped from her breast. Her face hidden by the hood of her cloak, Melissa slipped into the dimly lit, narrow hallway. To her relief and delight, room number eight was the first doorway she came to, and whatever reservations she had, vanished. Righteous indignation surged through her when she considered what Latimer had tried to do to her, and with golden eyes flashing, she opened the door and sallied forth to do battle.

To her dismay, the room was dark and empty. Rather taken aback, she stumbled inside, searching several minutes before she found a candle and lit it. In the flickering light she glanced around. It was a very small room, as were all the rooms at the tavern, these private chambers more resembling broom closets than actual bedrooms. But the bed was neatly made, a gaily colored quilt of yellow-and-green covering it, and a rudely constructed pine chair and tiny candlestand had been added for some extra comfort.

A bit deflated that her quarry was not in sight, Melissa gingerly set down the candle. Now that she was actually here, some of her nervousness was disappearing and her anger at Latimer's perfidious designs upon her virtue was growing. She paced the tiny confines of the room, going over the scathing words she would fling at Mr. Julius Latimer the moment he opened the door. But as time passed and there was no sign of him, she grew weary of her pacing, and she sat down on the pine chair, her hands clenched into fists in her lap as she continued to wait. She had no way of telling what time it was, but she realized that she had been here for quite a while and she began to wonder if she had misread Latimer's note. She had not brought it with her, but after mulling it over in her mind, she was positive she had not misunderstood him.

The initial rage that had prompted her actions gradually faded as the hour grew later and later and Latimer still did not appear. A mighty yawn suddenly overtook her and she glanced at the bed with longing. How much later would Latimer be? she asked herself half angrily, half wearily. It occurred to her that he was doing this deliberately—hoping, no doubt, that the long wait would be nerve-racking and intimidating for her. She straightened her drooping shoulders. By Heaven! She'd show him that such petty tricks didn't affect her!

But after another yawn escaped her, she decided it wouldn't hurt if she lay down upon the bed. She wouldn't fall asleep—she was too nervous and angry for that—but she could just rest her head for a few minutes. Convinced of the soundness of her thinking, using her cloak as a blanket, she lay down stiffly upon the bed. Without her even being aware of it, her eyelids closed and within minutes she was deeply asleep, her golden-brown hair splaying out from her head, the old cloak slipping down around her waist, revealing the sweet curve of her breasts as they surged up from the amber silk gown.

Downstairs, in the main room of the tavern, Dominic, Royce and Josh were cozily seated at a rough oak table, enjoying the latest of several snifters of brandy that they had consumed this evening. After dinner at Oak Hollow, the three men had returned to the tavern to celebrate Dominic's purchase of Folly. Josh had been most pleased by this turn of events, even more so when it was revealed that Dominic would share the ownership with Melissa—

anything that bound Dominic to Melissa was fine with Josh! Of course, Dominic had had to bear a great many jocular comments from both of the Manchesters, as well as sly teasings about his "intentions" toward Melissa.

Dominic had taken it all with his usual aplomb, but some of the remarks bit deep, making him wonder uneasily what his intentions toward the baffling Miss Seymour really were. But as the evening waned and he became increasingly mellow from the numerous snifters of brandy, he didn't really care that he might be marching inexorably down a road that he had sworn to avoid at all costs. Melissa fascinated him, he could not deny it, but *why* she fascinated him was almost more engrossing than the fact that she did! He could not explain his actions even to himself, and with a sigh, he pushed that particular puzzling aspect of the situation away, turning his wandering attention to what Royce was saying.

"I cannot believe that she actually sold you the horse. Even half a horse!" Royce said disbelievingly.

Dominic grinned at him. "Doubting my charm and grace with the ladies?"

An answering grin on his face, Royce slowly shook his tawny head. "Never that!" he admitted with a laugh. "When you decide upon a course, there are few, male or female, who would deny you."

"Perhaps," Dominic replied noncommittally. "But I can tell you that once I saw that horse I would have done anything within my power to own him. I was determined that, one way or another, your cousin was going to sell him to me."

"But at that price!" Josh exclaimed. "I have heard that you are an excellent businessman, but I must confess," Josh continued with a waggish smile, "that I have serious doubts about your abilities to strike a hard bargain after this morning's work!"

Dominic grimaced. He could not disagree with Josh— he had serious doubts about his own sanity of late! And as for what he'd done this morning, he had no answer or excuses. Shrugging his broad shoulders, he said dryly, "Be that as it may, I did accomplish what I set out to do."

"Half of what you meant to do," Royce reminded him with a roguish gleam in his eyes.

"Very well, *half,* but," Dominic said lightly, "who knows—I may not have to pay that amount in the end."

It was an idle statement, uttered without thought or reason, but Josh pounced on it. "Eh?" he questioned. "And why is that? Got some other ideas about my niece?" Privately, Josh was of the opinion that this co-ownership of the horse smacked of an imminent proposal, and Dominic's careless remark only confirmed it. Of course young Slade wouldn't have to pay the full amount in the end— not if he married Melissa! Be glad to have him in the family. Just wish they'd get on with it!

Royce wasn't overly concerned about Dominic's plans or lack of plans regarding Melissa, and leaning across the table, he demanded mockingly, "Where is that agreement you signed with Melissa today? I want to see with my own eyes proof that you did indeed strike that ridiculous bargain."

"It's upstairs in my room. If you really want me to get it I shall, but I don't think it's necessary." Ruefully, he added, "I can assure you that I did strike that 'ridiculous bargain.' " He had not forgotten how obstinate Royce could be in his cups, and when Royce doggedly insisted that he wanted to see the agreement, Dominic meekly complied. Rising to his feet, he said, "Very well, I'll get it. Order us another round of brandies while I'm gone."

A faintly cynical smile on his lips, he walked upstairs and down the hall to his room. He was already inside and reaching for his valise when he suddenly became conscious of the glow of the burning candle on the stand. Stiffening, he stared in bewilderment at the lovely creature sleeping in blissful abandonment on his bed. Hardly daring to believe what he was seeing, like a man in a daze, he slowly walked nearer, halting mere inches from the edge of the bed.

Spellbound by her golden beauty in the dancing light of the candle, he stared down at the sleeping woman, his gaze wandering over the profusion of honey-colored hair that spread wildly across the quilt, before traveling down to the creamy expanse of silken flesh which spilled invitingly out of the top of the gown. He couldn't seem to tear his eyes away from the gentle rise and fall of the woman's breasts, but finally, with an effort, he forced his lingering glance upward, past the firm chin and the full, tempting mouth, beyond the delightfully tip-tilted nose to the thick lashes that lay like black fans upon the delicate bones of her cheeks. She was utterly enchanting, he thought foggily, but what the hell was she doing in his bed?

Part Two

The Parson's Mousetrap

Marriage, if one will face the
truth, is an evil, but a necessary
one.

Unidentified minor fragment
—Menander

Chapter Eleven

How LONG he stood there staring down at the unconsciously seductive form of the young woman on his bed, Dominic couldn't remember; he only knew that as the moments passed, he was increasingly aware of his body's instant response to her nearness. Desire, fierce and compelling, surged through his loins; visions of making love to her, of kissing those provocative lips, of removing the material that stretched across her bosom, jostled in his brain. The intensity of his reaction to the mere sight of this undeniably disarming creature reminded him forcibly that it had been weeks since he had last lain in the arms of a woman—and it also reminded him of the teasing he had taken from Royce about his chaste state.

Enlightenment dawned and he chuckled softly. Of course—Royce had sent her here and then had cleverly manufactured a reason for him to return to his room to find this exquisite surprise. As he glanced again at the tempting curves plainly revealed by the tight, old-fashioned gown, sensual anticipation curled in his belly.

A lazy smile on his mouth, he absentmindedly sat down on the pine chair and with all his thoughts on the sweet charms that he would soon enjoy, he removed his boots. The jacket followed, as did the pristine cravat and embroidered waistcoat, but then, too eager to complete his undressing, he approached the bed, wondering fleetingly where Royce had found such a beauty.

It didn't really matter to him—she was here and he wanted her. Gently sinking down beside the sleeping woman, he nuzzled her neck and ear, one hand trailing across her shoulder. She smelled delicious, like sunshine and lavender, and he was amazed how potent an aphrodisiac such normal scents could be; hunger to know the delights of her body sent the blood thundering through his veins.

When there was no response to his light touch, Dominic softly teased the lobe of her ear with his tongue and murmured, "Wake up, sleeping beauty."

Dimly Melissa heard the words and struggled up through the layers of sleep that had overcome her. Slowly she became aware of her surroundings. She had been dreaming of Dominic, of Dominic kissing her, and when she opened her eyes and saw his face just above hers, it almost seemed like part of her dream. Her golden-brown eyes, drowsy and unknowingly seductive, widened slightly and a sleepy smile crossed her face. "You're here," she breathed huskily, still not fully awake.

Dominic was thoroughly enchanted. Asleep she had been lovely, but awake . . . His gray eyes, warm and caressing, traveled over her features, the tumbled golden-brown curls, the silky black lashes and the slightly slanted topaz eyes. Awake she was undoubtedly the most bewitching woman he had ever seen, his gaze riveted on the soft, beguiling curve of her mouth. And yet as he stared at her, he was troubled by an elusive sensation of familiarity—as if he had seen her before and should know her. Wishing his head were clearer, that he had not drunk quite so many brandies this evening, he frowned. He couldn't have seen her before, he finally decided—he would have remembered her!

Seeing his frown, Melissa lightly brushed back the lock of wavy black hair which persisted in falling across his forehead. "Is something wrong?" she asked, the remnants of her dream swirling hazily around in her brain.

Dominic shook his head. "Not now," he muttered thickly and brought his mouth to hers.

Sweet fire exploded in Melissa's body at the touch of his hungry lips, and with no will of her own, her arms went around his neck, pulling him closer to her. His kiss deepened and Melissa had no thought to deny him when his tongue sought entrance to her mouth, her lips opening eagerly for his possession.

A groan of pleasure broke from Dominic and he tore his mouth from hers, pressing hot, tingling kisses down her neck as he said roughly, "God! you're a sorceress—you make me mad!"

Feeling a little mad herself, a dreamy expression on her face, Melissa stroked his dark head, reveling in the sheer pleasure of touching him, of having him touch her. She didn't ever want to wake up from this blissful state, didn't want to open her eyes and discover that it was only her imagination. His searching lips found hers again and she ceased to think, conscious only of the taste and scent of him, of the sweet yearning that was building within her.

Even when his hands deftly undid her gown and she felt the garment slip down around her waist, her chemise following, she was unable to believe that this was anything but a dream. And since it *was* a dream, she could do whatever she wanted, and that included touching him freely and without shame, her questing fingers undoing his white cotton shirt and touching his bare skin. It was exciting to feel the leap his heart gave as her hands wandered over him, exciting to touch his warm flesh, to explore the hard, muscled chest and to discover the stiffened nipples surrounded by the crisp black hair. It was even more thrilling to hear his low growl of delight when her hands boldly traveled lower, and her own heart thudded in her breast at her wanton behavior.

His teeth gently caught her lower lip. "Don't!" he got out with an effort. "Don't tease me—I am too ready for you as it is."

A catlike smile of satisfaction crossed Melissa's face and with a sigh she arched her body nearer, longing for him to touch her, to explore her as she was doing him. But when he accepted her blatant invitation and his warm hand closed around her breast, she was unprepared for the sharp shock of pleasure that flooded her body. Gently those knowing fingers pulled and kneaded her breast as Melissa lay there breathless and stunned by the erotic sensations that were being created by that simple act, her flesh seeming to surge into his hands, tendrils of sweet desire burn-

ing in her blood. And when his head lowered and his lips
hungrily took one straining nipple into his mouth, his
tongue curling urgently about it, she thought helplessly
that nothing could ever feel as wonderful. But she had
been wrong. When his teeth lightly rasped the swollen
tips, a soft moan of pleasure escaped her. Gripped by half-
exciting, half-frightening emotions, she clenched his dark
hair, wanting more and yet not knowing what it was she
sought. She had never felt this way before, had never believed the depth of pleasure and yearning that could be
aroused so easily, so swiftly, by a man's touch. There was
a tight, almost painful ache centered at the junction of her
thighs, and unconsciously her hips pressed closer to Dominic's long, powerful length.

Groaning softly, Dominic endured the exquisite brush
of her body against his, the feel of her yielding flesh nearly
his undoing. He had wanted to savor this first joining, had
wanted to slowly bring them both to that final, mindless
pleasure, to kiss and fondle every delectable inch of the
intoxicating body moving so wildly under his, but the demands of his own body and the irresistibility of this sweet
wanton made it impossible.

Raising his head from her breasts, he stared down into
her face with passion-blurred eyes. A sensual smile on his
lips, he said huskily, "I see you can wait no longer than
I . . . but, sweet witch, I'm afraid that I shall be embarrassingly quick this first time. . . ."

Caressingly, his gaze dropped to her bare bosom, to the
upthrusting coral nipples, and a spasm of intense desire
made him tremble and groan in defeat. His mouth swooped
on hers, his lips crushing urgently against hers as his hands
pushed up her silken skirts in one almost violent motion.
He wanted her unbearably, could hardly prolong this sweet
torture another second, and shifting slightly, he settled his
hard body firmly between her thighs.

Melissa's eyes flew open with shock as she felt the un-
mistakable bulge press intimately between her thighs. Only
his breeches separated his naked flesh from hers, and suddenly, horrifyingly, she realized that this was no dream.
This was real and this was happening to her right now!

Reality shuddered through her, the events of the evening

flashing wildly before her eyes, and fright such as she had never known numbed the ardent cravings of her body. Yet when Dominic's searching fingers found the tight little curls between her legs, a gasp of mingled fear and melting delight came from her. But fear was the far stronger emotion, and she began to struggle frantically to escape from his seductive fondling, tearing her mouth away from his half-coaxing, half-bruising kiss.

Neither of them heard the faint knock on the door, nor the sudden opening of the door as Melissa cried out desperately, "Oh, stop!" Her hands no longer tangled in his black hair, she began to beat upon his back with clenched fists. "Oh, I beg you, you must *stop* this instant!"

Royce stood transfixed in the doorway, unable to believe the sight that met his eyes. His voice full of angry incredulity, he burst out, *"Good God! Lissa!"*

Melissa froze, her horrified gaze on Royce's pale, shocked features. She was only dimly aware of Dominic's instant tensing, of the sudden removal of his weight as he rolled away from her. Her cheeks flaming with shameful embarrassment, in great agitation she fumbled around, trying to straighten her clothing, to cover her naked breasts and exposed thighs.

There was a terrible silence and Melissa was certain that she would die of humiliation, that the ugly situation could not possibly be any worse than it was at this moment. But she was wrong. The three participants were still frozen in their revealing tableau when Josh's head appeared just beyond Royce's shoulder and he said jovially, "What is it, my boy? Dominic fall down drunk on his bed?"

Royce made an abortive movement to shield the occupants in the room from Josh's gaze, but he was too late, as Josh gently pushed his son aside and walked into the room. When the full import of the tawdry scene percolated into Josh's drink-befuddled brain, he made a strangled attempt to speak, but nothing came from his mouth save an odd gobbling sound.

It was Dominic who seemed to recover first. Rising swiftly from the bed, as if he wanted to put as much distance between himself and the deceitful, wanton little slut who sat there mute, Dominic snarled, "For God's sake, shut the damned door! We don't have to put on an exhibition for everyone in the tavern!''

His voice seemed to release the others from their dumbfounded state. Josh bellowed furiously, "Now see here, young man! Don't you take *that* tone with me—particularly when it is *my* niece you have cravenly attempted to seduce!" Averting his gaze from Melissa's disheveled state, he muttered, "And, *Lissa!* What were you thinking of to come to a man's room alone! The shame of it! We are disgraced! *You* are ruined!"

Royce, his face hard and set, his eyes gleaming with a golden fire, growled dangerously, "But that is easily remedied. My *friend* can name his seconds, and we can settle this insult with pistols at dawn.''

"Don't be a fool, Royce," Dominic said coldly. "I have no intention of blowing your brains out—or allowing you to do the same to me over what is an unfortunate mistake."

"*Mistake!*" Josh nearly shrieked. "How can you call it a mistake? Is that not my niece there on your bed, and were you not in the process of ravishing her when we arrived?''

A grim smile quirked Dominic's lips. " 'Ravish' is not the word I would have chosen—and I did not know that she was your niece."

Royce's common sense began to reassert itself, and as his initial outrage and stunning fury abated somewhat, he asked in a calmer voice, "Perhaps you would like to explain to us *precisely* what was going on?''

It was a most embarrassing predicament, but embarrassment was the least of the emotions that Dominic was feeling at this moment. He was furious at the entire situation; furious that he had not instantly recognized Melissa Seymour, if by no other clue than the almost uncontrollable passion that had assailed him the second his mouth had touched hers—a passion that only she seemed to provoke; furious that he now found himself in the unpleasant position of having to explain to two very justifiably angry gentlemen exactly what he had been doing with one of the ladies of their family; and furious because he very much feared that he had allowed lust to lead him blindly into a very clever trap. Silently he cursed himself for not having been more wary; he *knew* Josh had been eagerly match-making, but he would never have suspected that Manchester would go this far to get a husband for his niece!

Dominic threw Melissa a look of bitter dislike. She had caught him in one of the oldest snares known to woman, and that perhaps infuriated him most of all. His gaze decidedly hostile as it roamed over her rumpled state, the amber gown now clutched protectively in front of her, her legs hidden beneath its folds as she crouched there against the headboard watching this drama with a glassy-eyed stare, he felt something stir within him. But then, reminding himself that she was *very* adept at disguise, he squashed the slight softening he sensed within himself and said icily, "I would be happy to explain my part in this whole ugly affair, but I think that we would all find it far more interesting to discover why Miss Seymour came unknown and *un*invited by me to my room and bed this evening."

"What?" Royce and Josh demanded in unison, Royce's eyes narrowing speculatively and Josh's blue orbs nearly starting from his head.

Dominic smiled tightly, his gaze hard on Melissa's white face, lingering for a second on her passion-bruised mouth. "Exactly what I said. I came up here with no other purpose in mind than to get the document about which we had been speaking. You may well imagine my surprise when I discovered an attractive young woman asleep on my bed." He flashed Royce a wry glance. "I thought that you had sent her up here—and that you had manufactured a reason for me to go to my room so that I could find her."

His voice tightening, he looked again at Melissa, the contempt he felt obvious in his face. "I had never seen your cousin without her, shall we say, disguise, and so I did not recognize her. Why should I even connect the seductive creature I found with the prim Miss Seymour? It is not the habit, I believe, for most proper young ladies to come calling alone, at night, to the room of a man they barely know . . . nor do they usually offer themselves so freely to the demands of strangers."

Each word was like a savage blow to Melissa, and as

each one fell, she shrank closer to the headboard as if this way she could escape the pain they brought. She could think of nothing to say, her brain numb, her tongue stuck to the roof of her mouth. This must be a nightmare, she told herself half hysterically. It *must* be! This could not be happening to her! She would wake up any moment and discover that she was at home in her own bed, *not,* please, dear God, at the Whitehorn tavern, in Dominic Slade's room in this degrading situation. But her prayer went unanswered and she was certain that her heart stopped beating when she heard Dominic say caustically, "But that is enough of my explanations. I think it would be only fair if we let the *lady* tell us what she was doing here at this time of night."

Melissa suddenly found herself the focus of three pairs of eyes, and if she had thought that nothing more terrible could happen, she discovered that she had been very wrong. She didn't know which was the worst to bear—the disappointment and embarrassment in her uncle's eyes, the cynical speculation in Royce's or the furious contempt in Dominic's cold gaze. Wishing she were dead, she stared back at them in misery, her thoughts whirling through her brain like autumn leaves as she tried frantically to formulate some reasonable explanation for her presence. Never mind about why she had responded so ardently and wantonly to Dominic's kisses; *that* was something she would never discuss, even if they applied red-hot pincers to her flesh!

The silence spun out, the three men waiting in varying degrees of impatience. Melissa swallowed with difficulty, then licked her dry lips, desperately hoping that inspiration would come to her. And just when she was positive that she would disgrace herself by having a case of the vapors, something that Dominic had said earlier popped into her brain. Not meeting the gazes of any of the men, she looked down at the hem of her gown and stammered, "It—it w-w-was the a-a-agreement."

"What agreement?" Dominic snapped, wondering precisely what sort of a trick she was pulling now.

Josh's expression was gentle as he coaxed, "You had an agreement to meet with Mr. Slade tonight in his room?"

Horrified that her words would be interpreted that way, Melissa opened her mouth to protest, but it was Dominic who said explosively, "That is a damned lie—I do not go about seducing innocent young women! I never made *any* assignation with your niece!"

Josh sent him a cold glance. "You, sirrah, are already on dangerous ground. I would not compound your errors by calling my niece a liar!"

Dominic's mouth shut with a decided snap, and from the furious glance he sent her way, Melissa knew that he would like nothing better than to wring her neck. This was an appalling set of circumstances in which to find oneself, and though she sympathized with Dominic's position, at the moment she was far more concerned with concocting a plausible explanation for herself. She risked a look at her uncle and regained a little of her courage from the encouragement she saw in his eyes. He was, she knew, shocked and revolted by the state of affairs, but he would help her in spite of where her own stupid folly had taken her.

Actually, once his first astonishment and dismay had waned, Josh was quite delighted with the situation and could barely control the urge to rub his hands together with glee. He had been plotting and scheming for years to get Melissa married to a wealthy, aristocratic gentleman, and now, just when he had been about to give up hope, she had plunged into a most compromising situation with a most eligible gentleman! If he had arranged the affair himself, this little contretemps couldn't have turned out better, and it was only by exercising the greatest self-restraint that he prevented a satisfied smile from creasing his mouth. Since one of his fondest dreams was about to be realized, he could afford to be magnanimous. His voice soothing, his manner warm and confiding, he said, "Come now, Lissa, tell us what happened tonight. You don't need to fear us—we are your family and we will do our best to shield and protect you from any disagreeable results that might arise from this unfortunate incident." He bent Dominic a telling glance. "We will *all* do what is expected of us!" Looking back at Melissa, he continued. "You have nothing to fear. Whatever you say will go no further than these four walls. Speak freely, my dear, and tell us about the agreement.''

Melissa licked her lips again, wondering helplessly what would happen if she just flatly refused to say anything. For a long moment she considered the idea, but then rejected it, having the lowering notion that if she refused to offer some sort of reason for being in Dominic's room, the four of them would be there indefinitely.

Keeping her eyes averted from Dominic's half-naked form as he stood there beside the bed, his white shirt still gaping open to reveal the black, curly hair which covered his muscled chest, she said in a rush, ''It was the agreement about Folly. I wanted to talk to him about some of the things that we had discussed this afternoon.''

It was an extremely feeble excuse, almost nonsensical, but it was the best that she could come up with under the circumstances. She dared not reveal that she had made a terrible mistake, that it had been Julius Latimer she had come to see and *not* Dominic Slade! She shuddered as she imagined the expressions on their faces if she blurted out *that* information! But it was apparent that the explanation she offered found no favor with the gentlemen, and she wasn't really surprised at the look of patent disbelief that Dominic shot her or the mocking skepticism she saw in Royce's eyes. Josh, however, betrayed no lack of mistrust in her statement, and with relief, hating herself for having to lie so blatantly to him, she continued doggedly.

''I only meant to speak a moment with him—I—I—I n-n-never intended to—to . . .'' Her throat closed up and she could not force another lying word from her mouth. The entire situation was too humiliating, and she wished desperately that this embarrassing inquisition could be put off until tomorrow. She felt soiled and tawdry. It didn't help her state of mind to have two of the gentlemen in the room staring at her as if this ugly situation were completely her own fault. That most of the blame clearly lay at her feet she was more than willing to admit, but not all of it was her doing, and as the minutes passed, she was conscious of a stirring of angry resentment. How dare they look at her this way!

Her chin lifted proudly and she said stiffly, ''I never

meant to put myself in a compromising position, and if Mr. Slade had been a gentleman''—she slanted him a haughty glance—''instead of a rutting boar, then none of this would have happened.''

Dominic's face darkened and his hands clenched into rather formidable fists. Why, that lying little slut! he thought furiously. She comes uninvited to my room, arranges herself seductively on my bed, returns my kisses with avid enjoyment and then has the gall to say that *I* am the one who is at fault! With a great effort he kept himself from speaking his angry thoughts aloud, but he promised himself savagely that he very definitely had a score to settle with Miss Melissa Seymour!

His eyes narrowed, he drawled mockingly, ''But what else could I do—especially when I find a sow in heat in my bed!''

Melissa gasped with outrage, her topaz eyes flashing with molten golden sparks, her cheeks flushed with fury. ''A sow in heat!'' she hissed. ''Th-that's a disgusting thing to say!''

Dominic's eyebrow flicked upward in cynical surprise. ''Surely no more disgusting than what you said?'' Only by the most tremendous willpower having gotten his own flaming temper under control, he was almost enjoying himself now, wondering idly how he could have been so misled by something as simple as an untidy bun and a pair of disfiguring spectacles. Seeing Melissa as she really was, he understood now the comments about her loveliness that the Manchester men had dropped. And he would be the first to confess that she was indeed lovely. His gaze resting on the enchanting sight she presented, the honey-colored hair tumbling in wild abandon about her shoulders, her lovely eyes bright with temper and her delightful bosom heaving with suppressed anger, Dominic thought that he had never seen another woman who appealed to him so powerfully. It was, he decided with a sudden sensual twist to his lips, truly unfortunate that Royce had arrived so inopportunely—it would have been *very* interesting to see how far the little minx would have gone in order to snare a husband! Realizing grimly where his musing had taken him, Dominic cursed under his breath and his enjoyment vanished. He had been neatly jockeyed into an untenable position, and here he was mooning over the very creature who had applied the whip!

Josh had concluded that enough insults had been traded and it was time both principals became aware in what direction their duty now lay. Clearing his throat portentously, he said quietly, ''This is a most distressing affair, but I am exceedingly thankful that there is an honorable solution for us all.''

Dominic stiffened, surmising where Josh was leading. It didn't come as any surprise to him—he had been expecting it from the second that Melissa's identity had been revealed. He shot the source of his predicament a dark look. She was clever, he'd grant her that, but although he might be forced by circumstances to make an honest woman of her, she wasn't going to find him a complacent husband! He was furious that after having escaped the most elaborate traps set out by some of the most expert matchmaking mamas and their daughters, he had been well and truly snared by such a seemingly artless country miss. Not that she had responded so very artlessly to his embraces! Dominic thought savagely. His only consolation, and it was poor comfort at best, was that at least he'd be able to take pleasure from her body, if nothing else! With arrogant thoroughness, his gray eyes moved slowly over Melissa's slender form. Marriage was something that he had sworn to avoid at all cost, but perhaps it wouldn't be too hellish, he decided coldly, *if* she lived up to the promise of passion her wanton responses to his kisses had revealed.

Melissa was so embarrassed and shocked by what had happened that she had not given much thought to her situation beyond the most pressing problem: explaining her presence in Dominic's room. Somewhat naively, she was hoping that now, having given her explanation, no matter how weak it sounded, Josh would escort her home. She expected to get the worst scolding of her life and she was prepared for Josh to be very angry with her for a while, but that would be the end of it. Of course, it was going to be very uncomfortable the first few times she was in company with Mr. Slade, but that too, she was foolishly confident, would pass in time. After all, she reminded herself optimistically, no irreparable harm had been done. Yes, it was a disgraceful position to have found oneself in, and there was no doubt that she would ever forget this humiliating experience, but Royce *had* appeared at a most opportune moment and in spite of how sordid it seemed, her honor was still intact. About why she had so ardently returned Dominic's kisses she perversely refused to speculate, yearning only to put this mortifying experience behind her. Later, when she wasn't so sensitive about it, wasn't so inexplicably attracted to the disruptive Mr. Slade, she would examine her perplexing and uncharacteristic reaction to him. For now, though, she just wanted to go home.

A brief silence had fallen after Josh had spoken, and it was Royce who eventually broke it. A sardonic smile on his mouth, he said to Dominic, "It seems that we are about to become more than just friends."

His lips slanting into a derisive smile of his own, Dominic nodded his dark head. Glancing at Josh, he stated coolly, "Naturally, I will marry her."

"You will not!" Melissa said forcefully, her eyes wide with astonishment. "I have no intention of marrying anybody, and certainly not *you!"*

Gray eyes gleaming cynically, Dominic regarded her flushed features. What sort of game was she playing at? he wondered. He had agreed to marry her, so what more could she want? Thinking that she was overplaying the outrage just a bit, he drawled wearily, "Oh, come now, my dear, wasn't that the point of all this?"

"Don't be ridiculous!" she snapped, rising from the bed in one graceful motion. Grabbing her cloak from the chair, she faced her uncle and demanded furiously, "Take me home! I don't want to spend another moment in the same room with him!"

Levelly, Josh stared back at her. "That's unfortunate . . . since you *are* going to marry him. After tonight's happening you have no other choice."

Melissa blinked at him, hardly able to believe what he said. "You cannot be serious, Uncle!" she finally got out when she realized that Josh did not seem to share her feelings about the situation.

"He's very serious," Dominic replied dryly. "There is

no other solution. If word of what occurred here were to be bandied about, our reputations, yours in particular, would be ruined.'' Sneeringly, he finished, ''But I'm sure you knew that before you came here.''

Furious at his insinuations, Melissa spun around and slapped his mocking face with the open palm of her right hand. ''That's a lie!'' she spat, golden-brown eyes blazing. ''I don't want to marry you—you conceited lout!''

This was all that was needed to cap a thoroughly infuriating situation, and her hand had hardly connected with his cheek before Dominic's fingers closed painfully around her shoulders. Shaking her violently, he snarled, ''Well, believe me, I don't want to marry you either—a more hot-tempered, ill-mannered shrew I've never met!''

Josh intervened hastily, fearful that all his plans were about to come tumbling down around him. Jerking Melissa away from Dominic, he said quickly, ''Royce, get Dominic out of here for a moment or two. I wish to speak to Melissa alone.''

''Intending to remind her of what a catch she's on the verge of throwing away?'' Dominic remarked snidely.

Moving indolently across the room, Royce murmured, ''Be a good fellow, Dom, and put on your boots and come with me.'' He smiled angelically. ''We'll drink a toast to your betrothal.''

Dominic sent him a look, but then a reluctant grin crossed his mouth. Without a word, he swiftly pulled on his boots, buttoned his shirt and dragged on a coat. A second later, Melissa and Josh were alone in the tiny room.

A hint of despair in her eyes, Melissa demanded almost fearfully, ''You don't really mean to try to force me to marry him, do you?''

Her obvious distress at the idea worried Josh. He was a kind man and he had never wanted to hurt Melissa. But she had to be made to see reason. Stifling the faint pangs of his conscience, he said heavily, ''Melissa, dear, you really have no other choice. You must marry Mr. Slade. You have disgraced yourself, and the only way out of this shameful affair is for you and Mr. Slade to marry. This is not the way I would have preferred your betrothal to come about, but I'm afraid that I must insist upon your doing the honorable thing."

Melissa's mouth tightened, and with Dominic's insulting words burning in her brain, she was not in any sort of mood to think rationally. Besides, she insisted stubbornly to herself, nothing had happened! Josh was using this unfortunate situation to further his own gains—well, she wasn't about to let him sacrifice her happiness just so he could get his hands on the money from the trust! Her chin raised pugnaciously, she stated grimly, "I am *not* going to marry Mr. Slade and you cannot make me!"

Josh regarded her sadly. "But I can, my dear," he finally said in a tired voice.

"How?"

"Simply by exercising my right of authority over your brother. Your father's will named me joint guardian, and while I have allowed you to have full control, if you defy me in this I shall have no choice but to remove Zachary from your, ah, lascivious influence."

"*Lascivious!*" Melissa breathed, incensed, the furious expression on her face making Josh take a nervous step backward.

But he was determined, and telling himself uneasily that Melissa could be made to see reason, he said firmly, "Yes, lascivious! I didn't want to say anything in front of Dominic, but, child, what you did tonight is scandalous, and you should be thankful that he is willing to marry you."

Melissa thought she would explode with wrath. Thankful! Ha! *Insulted* would be more like it, she reflected indignantly. If Josh thought for one minute . . . "I won't let you browbeat me into doing this! *I will not marry Dominic Slade!*"

Josh shrugged. "Very well, then, don't. But don't come crying to me when I remove Zachary from Willowglen and when I refuse to let you see him."

"You can't do that!"

"I can," Josh replied in a hard voice. "I can and I will." When Melissa still stood glaring at him, obviously not believing what he said, he explained quietly. "If you do not do as I say, I will go to Judge Hartley in the morning, and as much as it will pain me, I shall tell him of tonight's doings.'' He cocked an eyebrow at her. ''After that, do you think he will allow you to have control of Zachary? Of course,'' Josh added fairly, ''it will be for only two years. When Zachary is twenty-one, I cannot stop him from living where he wishes, but until then . . .''

With a painful thump of her heart, Melissa realized sickly that Josh meant every word he said. He *would* take Zachary away from her—her father's will gave him the right. She swallowed back the sudden tears that clogged her throat. The two years didn't matter, but the loss of her reputation did, and she could just imagine the gossip and speculative stares that would follow her once tonight's event became common knowledge. That it would become common knowledge was a foregone conclusion, especially when Zachary was removed from her care—even if Josh swore the judge to silence.

Her face pale, Melissa looked away from Josh. Zachary would hate living at Oak Hollow, hate having Josh supervise his activities—he might even hate *her* for being the cause of his removal from Willowglen. Another, more terrifying thought occurred to her: Zachary might even challenge Dominic to a duel, feeling that Dominic had dishonored his sister and brought shame to all of them. Miserably conscious of the trap closing in on her, Melissa frantically sought some other solution. There was none. Unless she married Dominic Slade, she would be labeled a fallen woman, her brother would be taken from her and whatever dreams or hopes they'd had for the future would be destroyed. It was unlikely that any reputable horse breeder would wish to deal with a woman whom scandal had marked.

It wouldn't matter what she did with her life; there would always be those who would whisper behind her back, those who would refuse to let their wives, daughters and even sons associate with her. Bitterly she acknowledged the unfairness of it all—she would be condemned, but Dominic Slade would be allowed to walk blithely away from the incident untouched, perhaps even gaining the admiring stares of some of the gentlemen.

Realizing that she had no alternative, Melissa met

Josh's stern gaze and said crisply, "Very well. I will marry Mr. Slade." A surge of angry pride brought a militant sparkle to her topaz eyes and she vowed huskily, "But I promise you—Mr. Slade will not find *me* an obliging wife!"

Chapter Twelve

"OBLIGING" was not a word that Dominic had ever associated with the provoking Miss Seymour, and he certainly did not apply it with regard to tonight's unfortunate affair.

Seated in one of the darker corners of the main room of the tavern, Dominic had few doubts that his bride, and there was never any question in his mind that she *would* marry him, would prove to be very disobliging! She might have put on an excellent performance about not wanting to marry him, but he grimly assumed that it was just another example of her contrary nature. And even though the prospect of marriage brought him little joy, there were two things of which he was quite confident—that he was going to thoroughly enjoy exerting his husbandly rights and that his cantankerous, willful, disconcerting and utterly fascinating bride-to-be would never bore him. That thought brought a rueful smile to his mouth, and seeing it, Royce asked, "A little more resigned to your fate?"

Dominic grimaced. "Yes. But I'll admit that I'm not particularly enamored of the idea and that if she were any other female except your cousin, I would have found some way out of the tangle!" He turned serious. "You do believe me when I said that I didn't realize who she was, don't you? I am capable of many things, but not, I hope, of deliberately seducing a relative of one of my most intimate friends!"

"I believe you," Royce answered without hesitation. "And I'm sorry that Melissa's actions have created this

168

situation." He frowned. "I wonder what in the hell she was doing in your room."

Cynically Dominic drawled, "Oh, come now! We are both men of the world. You know damn well what she was up to—neatly springing a trap for an unwary fool—me!"

Reflectively Royce stared at his glass of ale. It could be. He and Melissa had been close when they were younger, but there had been little contact between them for the past several years. What did he really know of her? Her situation certainly did lend itself to desperate schemes. Perhaps Dominic was right; perhaps she had seen a chance to snare a rich husband and had coolly seized it. It wouldn't be the first time that a marriage had been engineered by a calculating female. He didn't want to believe that of her, but in the face of no other evidence to the contrary, he couldn't see any other logical explanation for her having put herself in such a damning position.

Sighing, he remarked, "Well, at least you'll get something out of it. As her husband, you'll have Folly to control and you won't have to bother with the nonsense of being a partner in connection with the stallion." A gleam in his eyes, he added slyly, "And from what I saw when I entered the room tonight, you are not exactly immune to my cousin's considerable charms. You might even find that you'll enjoy being married to her."

Dominic scowled. "Not bloody likely! As for the horse, I've already agreed to buy half the animal, and whatever else I do, I will keep my word on that. She'll get her damn money and I will honor the bargain that we struck this afternoon." He grinned. "I'm not saying that I won't occasionally, er, overrule my 'partner,' but I'll not come the heavy-fisted husband with her."

"Just as well," Royce replied, grinning also. "Melissa would more than likely comb your hair with a stool if you applied too much of a curb to her activities. She is not going to be a meek, biddable bride."

"No, she isn't," Dominic murmured with an odd smile. "And I am sure that I will rue the day I ever laid eyes on her, but I think I shall also enjoy taming her to my hand."

A companionable silence fell, and for several moments the two young men sat there, quietly drinking their ale, each one busy with his own thoughts. Suddenly, something occurred to Dominic and he chuckled aloud. At the sound Royce looked up at him.

"I was just thinking," Dominic began, "that there is going to be one person who will be over the moon about the results of tonight's doings—my brother's wife, Leonie! She had been scheming to get me married for years, and when she learns that I am at last going to be leg-shackled, she will be beside herself with elation. She will," he added with a wry grin, "be quite certain that she willed it to happen!" Seeing the expression of curiosity on Royce's face, he explained, "Before I left Château Saint-André to come to Baton Rouge, she laid a curse on me—that I would find a female who would lead me a merry dance."

His eyebrows raised quizzically, Royce asked, "And you think Melissa will do just that?"

"*Precisely* that!" Dominic replied with feeling. "Marriage is not something that I ever contemplated, but if I had been hanging out for a wife, I definitely would have wanted a congenial and submissive one—not the vixen I am to be saddled with!"

"While you have my sympathies," Royce said dryly, "I think you are not as opposed to this marriage as you would have one believe. In fact, I have the greatest suspicion that you are actually viewing the prospect with some pleasure!"

Dominic smiled that odd smile again. "Perhaps." Then he added dulcetly, "After all, marrying her *will* gain me Folly."

Royce snorted and the two began to talk of more practical things, such as when the wedding would take place and where. Between them they decided that the middle of August would be the earliest date and that Melissa would probably want to be married from her home—if it could be refurbished in time for the event.

"If not," Royce said lazily, "I'm sure that Oak Hollow could be substituted. Nothing would give my mother more pleasure."

Once the initial plans had been made, Dominic became

bored with the subject, and glancing at his gold pocket watch, he murmured, "Shouldn't we rejoin my bride-to-be and your father? I think that we have been gone long enough for Josh to have convinced her of the wisdom of marrying me. Not," he finished darkly, "that I believe she needed much persuading!"

Royce nodded and the two men rose and began to walk across the room. The area was dimly lit and Dominic looked idly around. It was only when they had reached the door that he saw someone he knew. Freezing, he stared hard through the smoke-filled gloom, recognizing instantly the elegantly attired gentleman sitting in the corner by himself—Julius Latimer. Dominic made an instinctive movement in that direction, but Royce, having just then spotted Latimer himself, quickly grasped his arm.

"Stop, you fool!" Royce hissed in Dominic's ear. "I know you would like nothing better than to throttle the bastard, but at the moment you have no grounds to charge over there and challenge him to a duel."

Knowing that Royce spoke the truth, unpalatable though it was, with an effort Dominic stilled the rage that had erupted within him at the sight of his enemy sitting there so calmly. Latimer had not seen them, and from the expression on his face it was obvious that the man had other things on his mind than an old enmity. A black scowl darkened his blond handsomeness, and briefly Dominic wondered who or what had caused Latimer such fury. There was an air of savage anger which fairly radiated from him, and from the manner in which Latimer slammed his tankard of ale on the scrubbed pine table, it was apparent to even the meanest intelligence that *something* had displeased him greatly. After one more glance, Dominic allowed Royce to hustle him from the room. Latimer would wait—there were more pressing matters to attend to tonight. He had a prospective bride waiting upstairs in his room, and with a quickening step he left his old enemy behind.

On the surface, Dominic might have seemed to have accepted his fate rather tamely, especially considering his oft-expressed contempt for the married state, and although there was a part of him that didn't find the idea of being married to Melissa Seymour *too* arduous, he did deeply resent the means she had used to trap him. Admittedly, there were aspects of the coming marriage that intrigued him, but he was not overjoyed at the prospect, nor did he expect his wedded life to be anything but a damn nuisance once his inexplicable passion for his bride faded—and he was still convinced that it was only a passing caprice on his part. He didn't like Melissa; she did not, he was quite confident, like him; he had never planned to marry, and if he had ever seriously contemplated marriage, it wouldn't have been to someone like *her!* Dominic might smile and jest about this evening's debacle and its ruinous effect, but inwardly he was furious.

He could not deny, however, that there was something about Miss Seymour that had caught his attention from the very first, and it was equally undeniable that when he kissed her, when he touched her, when she came into his arms, something utterly incomprehensible happened to him. He was suddenly possessed by a yearning, primitive desire—everything faded from his mind but the intoxicating sweetness of her lips and the seductive lure of her slender body. That type of uncontrollable passion was something new to him, and it both excited and galled him. Consequently it was with a mixture of anticipation, anger and speculation that he entered his room. Standing just inside the doorway, he stared coolly across the room at the conniving creature who had brought about his downfall.

Melissa was seated primly on the only chair, her hands stiffly folded in her lap, her worn cloak covering the delectable charms that Dominic remembered far too well for someone who assured himself that all he felt was rage and disgust for her actions this evening. She met his stare with one equally cool, the topaz eyes icy, the soft coral lips held tautly and the set of her narrow shoulders making it abundantly clear that she was not pleased with the situation. Still pretending not to want to marry him, was she? Dominic thought cynically.

Josh beamed at him and said happily, "Ah, there you are! You'll be pleased, I'm sure, to learn that Melissa has seen reason and is aggreeable to the match."

Dominic wasn't surprised at her capitulation. Why else, he wondered sourly as his gaze traveled over her set features, had she come to his room tonight, if not to snare a wealthy husband? Yet even as those thoughts crossed his mind, he was conscious of a feeling of unreasonable disappointment. It would appear that his suspicions about her were correct, and he admitted for the first time that he had been hoping that she would prove not to be such a calculating female. Testily he said, "Well, I'm delighted that's settled! Now if we can come to some understanding about the actual wedding and such, we can put this less-than-pleasurable evening behind us." Not looking again at Melissa, he added, "Royce and I have been discussing the matter and, under the circumstances, we feel that the middle of August would be a likely date for the wedding."

Melissa had been vibrantly aware of him the instant he had opened the door, and she had been mortified at the leap her heart had given when their eyes had met. She should dislike him; after all, wasn't he the cause of one of the most humiliating moments of her life? He was, she thought waspishly, arrogant and far too sure of himself. He was also the most fascinatingly appealing man she had ever encountered.

She was beset by a volatile concoction of attraction, rage, resentment and tingling excitement just being in the same room with him. Mutinously, she tried to deny feeling anything but wrath and bitterness toward him, and Dominic made it childishly simple for her when he made his presumptuous statement about the date of the wedding. Outraged that he and Royce had arbitrarily decided upon *her* wedding date without even so much as a by-your-leave, Melissa flashed him a look filled with golden fire and snapped, "I believe that the bride should at least be consulted about the date of her wedding!"

Reading the signs of the impending explosion clearly, Josh said in a nervous tone of voice, "There, there, my dear. I'm sure that your, er, bridegroom meant no discourtesy."

Watching interestedly the various expressions that chased themselves across Melissa's revealing face, Dominic suggested mockingly, "Perhaps my bride has a better time in mind? I should warn you, however, that the sooner we are married the less likely there is to be any scandal from this evening's affair. None of us intends to speak of it, but even the best-kept secret has a way of revealing itself when least expected. The middle of August is far enough away not to cause too much speculation about our, ah, sudden desire to marry, yet far enough away to allow us time to notify all our friends and relatives."

There was much sense in what Dominic said, but the middle of August was too terrifyingly near for Melissa to accept with equanimity. Though she argued vehemently against the middle of August, it was to no avail, Josh ending the discussion by saying exasperatedly, "Melissa, this is no ordinary marriage! We are trying to avert a possible scandal here, and you *will* marry on the sixteenth of August."

Impaled by three pairs of eyes, Melissa bowed her tawny head, the frightening sensation of having no control over her own life sweeping through her. Blinking back angry tears, she got out in a muffled voice, "Very well. The sixteenth of August."

There was such obvious unhappiness and despair in her tone that Dominic found himself strangely moved. Instinctively, he walked across the room to stand beside her and reached for one of her cold hands, holding it in his warm fingers. She glanced up at him in surprise, and when those incredible topaz eyes met his, he felt his pulse accelerate. Huskily he murmured, "The circumstances of our marriage may not be the most fortuitous, but if we both try, perhaps something good will come of it." Slanting her a crooked grin, he added, "I will attempt to be a reasonable husband, and if you will meet me halfway, I believe that we can rub along tolerably well together."

It wasn't the most romantic statement, but it gave Melissa a feeling of hope, a feeling that they might just contrive to find, if not the bliss her heart yearned for, that at least they could live together peaceably. A tremulous little smile flitted across her generous mouth and she said softly, "I shall try . . . but I do not think that it will be easy for either one of us."

Dominic cocked a black eyebrow. "But then," he drawled wryly, "nothing that is worth anything ever comes without effort. Sometimes it requires a great deal of effort."

Melissa slowly nodded, and Josh decided sagely that it would be wise to bring an end to the evening while they were still talking to each other.

"See there, my dear," he said heartily, "I told you everything would work out for the best. Now come along, we must get you home as soon as possible."

It was in a state of numbness that Melissa accepted Zachary's elated congratulations the next day when the Manchester family arrived with Dominic, and Josh made the announcement. She knew she smiled and nodded her head at the appropriate moments, and she knew she appeared to listen alertly as plans were made and discussed, but none of it seemed real; it all might have been happening to someone else. Even that evening when a servant from the inn delivered a note to her from Latimer, she could only stare at it blankly, unable to comprehend his angry threats. It didn't matter anymore—nothing mattered anymore; in a matter of weeks she would be married to a man she barely knew, and Latimer's threats paled to insignificance in the face of that fact. Almost without being aware that she did it, she wrote him a reply, telling him of her engagement and that he would get his money soon enough.

In the weeks that followed, she was increasingly thankful for her seeming inability to feel anything but indifference to everything that was happening around her. Comfortably cushioned by this sense of unreality, she listened with detachment to Zachary explaining excitedly how Dominic was forwarding him a large sum of money so that some repairs and refurbishing of the house could be completed before the wedding.

His eyes sparkling with delight, Zachary stated, "I'll tell you this, Lissa—I'm damned glad you're marrying him—he's a great gun! He said that since the trust will be ending in just a few months now, he saw no reason he couldn't advance me enough money to start getting things in order. I'm especially happy that on your wedding day, with all our friends and family gathered here, you won't be ashamed of your home.''

Deep within herself she was conscious of a prick of resentment—she had never been ashamed of her home! How dare this, this *intruder* put such thoughts in Zachary's head! But the feeling passed in an instant, and she merely smiled vaguely at Zachary and wandered down to the stables. The stables these days seemed to be the only place where she could gain any sense of reality, and with the army of workmen whom Dominic had helped Zachary hire swarming all over the main house, it wasn't surprising that she escaped to the serenity of the place she loved best.

Nothing seemed to touch her greatly. She could listen unmoved to Aunt Sally's and Frances' happy chatter about the coming nuptials; she could be easily persuaded that a wedding gown of sheer Indian muslin embroidered with silver thread would be most attractive; she could view without flinching the growing horde of gifts and missives of well-wishers that began arriving at Willowglen once the invitations of her coming marriage had been sent. She seemed to glide effortlessly through it all, smiling at the correct time, inclining her head politely when needed and generally managing to convince everyone that she was a young lady dazed by love and her sudden, unexpected good fortune.

Yet as the date of the marriage drew nearer, the cocoon of numbness that had been wrapped protectively around her began to unravel, and there were increasing moments as the second week of August sped by that she would wake in the night, filled with a feeling of despair. The wedding day was no longer weeks away; it was now only a matter of days until she would be married to Dominic Slade, and she was finding it harder and harder to pretend that this was happening to someone else—more and more difficult to tell herself that she would soon wake from this particularly vivid nightmare and discover that everything was just as it had been before that fateful night.

It became more impossible to pretend otherwise as the changes the horde of workmen produced began to near completion. The house and its furnishings were no longer shabby and worn; the exterior glistened with several coats of white paint, the fan-shaped windows and doors were trimmed in a delicate green shade, and inside . . . Inside, luxurious window coverings of velvet and damask hung against the windows, newly arrived carpets now lay upon the recently refinished floors, and the walls and ceilings glowed softly in newly painted shades of pale blue and peach. There were even some new pieces of furniture which had only a few days before arrived from New Orleans, and the once-tattered lawns and shrubs were now meticulously and tidily trimmed and scythed. Willowglen was rapidly being restored to the state it had been in Jeffery Seymour's time, and though Melissa was conscious of a slight sensation of indignation that it was at her expense that all this was happening, deep within her heart she could not but be happy for Zachary, happy for all the inhabitants of Willowglen. At least, she thought moodily, her foolishness had brought some good.

Yet even Latimer had been paid his beastly money—Dominic had very graciously paid her the gold on the date he had promised. It had given her a wrench to realize that Folly was no longer solely hers, but she had also been conscious of the lifting of a great burden when she had sat down with Mr. Smithfield and made arrangements for her father's final debt to be paid in full. Fortunately, Mr. Smithfield had handled everything for her and she had not been forced to actually give Latimer the money herself, which was just as well—she might have scratched his eyes out!

Yet even with the debt paid, she had the uneasy feeling that she had not heard the last of it. There had been that peculiar expression on Dominic's face when he had paid her the money, almost as if he had found her eager acceptance of it distasteful. She had made no mention of what she intended to do with it, and she wondered if Dominic thought that she was being unduly greedy—he was to be her husband and perhaps he had assumed that she would not press him for the money. But she had, and the unpleasant idea had occurred to her that mayhap all she had done was change one debt for another, another with a much higher price to pay. . . .

Resolutely she refused to think about it, just as she refused to think beyond each day, stubbornly continuing to pretend that soon enough she would awaken from this nightmare and discover that it all had been a bad dream.

Perhaps the fact that Dominic had been gone until well after the first of August was what had made it so easy for Melissa to push reality aside, to keep up the pretense that none of this was real. Within three days of the announcement of their betrothal, he had left for Thousand Oaks, where he had been overseeing some hasty improvements to the living arrangements of the main house, and he had only just arrived back in Baton Rouge on the eleventh of August. Melissa had forgotten the unpredictable impact he made upon her senses, and watching his dark face across the linen-covered table from her as they dined at Oak Hollow on the evening of his return, she was shaken by the sharp feeling of delight which coursed through her.

It was a small supper party that Aunt Sally and Uncle Josh had arranged to toast the betrothed couple, but Melissa was conscious of only one person in the room—her far-too-soon-to-be-husband. Her eyes traveled over Dominic's lean, mobile features, noting the arrogance and pride that was inherent to him, and she shivered slightly. Would he be a kind husband? Or a cruel one? A spendthrift like her father? Or a generous, astute man like her grandfather? She was bitterly aware that he could move her to great passion and that she found him utterly fascinating, but was that a basis for marriage? A basis enough to entrust her life to him? She didn't believe so, and even though she could admit to his handsomeness and charm, she mistrusted it; too much of what Josh had said about him earlier remained unpleasantly clear in her mind. With something perilously close to open hostility, she stared at him, unwilling to let herself be distracted by the warm curve of his mouth, or the gleam of teasing laughter in his gray eyes, or the beguiling dimples that came and went as he smiled. She would *not* like him! she vowed fiercely. She might be forced to marry him, but she was not going to be an adoring slave at his feet! Other women might be bedazzled by his roguish charm, but not she!

Dominic was very aware of her unfriendly stare and it baffled him. He had not expected her to greet him with rapture, but then again he had not been prepared to have his bride-to-be welcome him back in such an icy manner. What did she have to be displeased about? he wondered caustically. She was getting a wealthy husband! While all he was gaining was a beautiful, completely confusing shrew! Surely, he mused as he shot her a swift glance from beneath his unknowingly haughty brows, she wasn't *still* pretending to be against this farce of a marriage?

It would appear that she was, and as the last remaining days before their nuptials flew swiftly by, Dominic could feel his frustration growing. He was seldom allowed to be alone with Melissa, but if she had been agreeable, they might have managed to steal a few moments of privacy. Obviously that was not what she wanted and he found her singularly elusive, any attempt on his part to talk intimately with her being instantly averted. Not once was he allowed even a glimpse of the vibrant, irresistible creature he had held in his arms, and as their wedding day approached he was aware of increasing dismay within himself. He was thankful, however, that someone had made her see sense and she was no longer decking herself out like a prune-faced spinster. It gave him sardonic pleasure to watch the bemused expressions on his relatives' faces when they were introduced to Melissa. All his family, presently domiciled in various places around Baton Rouge, seemed to be bewitched by her dazzling smile and lissome form. Leonie, having arrived with Morgan two days before the wedding, was entranced.

Rushing up to him after meeting Melissa for the first time, Leonie flashed him a radiant grin and murmured, "See, *mon ami!* I told you that all you lacked was a wife. And, Dominic—she is lovely! Just what I would have wished for you." There was a mischievous glint in her green eyes as she added slyly, "And I am most happy to see that she does not dote on you! It would be ruinous for you to marry a woman who thought your every whim was law."

Dominic had hoped that Leonie would not notice that Melissa did not seem to care overmuch for his company, but trust his irrepressible sister-in-law to put her finger on the sore part. Slightly nettled, he muttered, "A biddable wife would bore me, Leonie, you know that." With heart-felt certainty, he said, "And Melissa will never bore me, of that I am positive!" He wouldn't add that he was very much afraid that she would exasperate, enrage and keep him thoroughly captivated!

And he was captivated. She might treat him with indifference, but that didn't stop him from gazing possessively at her or from remembering distinctly the sweetness of her mouth or the intoxicating softness of her body. It was the haunting memory of the two times that he had kissed her that had given him comfort during the passing weeks and enabled him to view his approaching wedding day, if not with delight, at least with anticipation for the night which would follow it. Privately he could wish that there was more than physical desire which bound him to Melissa, but if desire was all they shared, then he fully intended to take complete advantage of it. And with that in mind, he had already made several arrangements which, oddly enough, he hoped would please his wayward bride.

Almost with exhilaration, later that same night he contemplated Melissa's probable reaction to the outrageously sumptuous bed which he had commissioned for their bedroom at Thousand Oaks. He'd had to send to Natchez for his requirements, and the bed and its attendant furnishings had not yet arrived at the plantation before he had to return to Baton Rouge; but thinking of it, of the wide, down-filled mattress, of the rich sensuousness of the gold silk hangings which surrounded it, and vividly picturing Melissa lying naked in the middle of the bed, Dominic felt his entire body convulse with hungry desire. He might not wish to marry, but his body burned with an aching desire to possess her—and that, he told himself cynically, was nearly worth putting his head into the parson's mouse-trap!

The day before the wedding finally arrived. All the guests had been assembled and were presently staying with various friends and neighbors of the Seymours and the Manchesters. Even the meager public accommodations had been commandeered by the friends and relatives of the bridal pair, and there was hardly anyone up and down the river between Natchez and New Orleans who didn't know that on the morrow Dominic Slade would take Melissa Seymour as his bride.

Julius Latimer certainly knew of it—he could hardly not have known of it since receiving both Melissa's note and his money. And then there was the fact that he and his sister had been invited to attend the gala reception honoring the newlyweds that would be held at Oak Hollow after the actual wedding at Willowglen. Melissa would have preferred for him not to have been invited, but in the small, close-knit society of the river towns, it was impossible to voice an objection without explaining precisely why. She had consoled herself with the knowledge that she had no need to fear him any longer, and surely she could force herself to meet him in polite company.

That last afternoon before the wedding, Dominic made arrangements to take Melissa for a ride, and she pushed any thought of Latimer aside. Dominic acted very mysterious, saying with a faint smile that he had a surprise for her. Zachary grinned and Melissa suspected that her brother knew exactly what the ''surprise'' was. She wasn't the least interested in any surprises and, more importantly, she wasn't about to go anywhere alone with Dominic Slade. To Dominic's frustration, she quickly turned what he had hoped would be a private affair into something more public by inviting Morgan and Leonie, Royce and Zachary to accompany them. It was while the two ladies were waiting on the gallery for the men to come with the horses that Latimer chose to intrude once more into Melissa's life. A second note from him arrived just then.

Melissa excused herself from Leonie and went to the end of the long gallery to read Latimer's missive in relative privacy.

My dear Melissa, Latimer wrote, *you cannot imagine my heartache and dismay when I received word of your impending marriage to Dominic Slade. I had thought to keep silent, but I cannot! I know now that my offer to you was misguided and crude, and I apologize most humbly for my actions, but was a month or two of my company worth selling yourself for life to a blackguard like Slade?*

I, at least, was honest with you about my intentions, wrong though they were, but can you say the same for him? He is not to be trusted—there are things I could tell you about him that would cause my regrettable actions to seem like a mere schoolboy prank! If you doubt me—and I would not blame you if you did—talk to my sister. She knows what he is, and she has great fears for you. Once she fell for his spurious charms, and she knows to her cost that he is a vile seducer and a trifler of affections. I repeat, he is not to be trusted.

It pains me to tell you this, but you must be on your guard with him at all times or you will be like my poor, deluded sister, who, even knowing that he is a bounder and a clever schemer, still yearns for him. And worse, he knows it and continues to play upon her ill-advised affection for him. (He visited with her just yesterday at the plantation where we are staying. I find it curious that he chose to call at a time when I was away and unable to deny him my sister's company.) It is not pleasant for me to write to you of this, but if I can prevent you from falling under his wicked spell, then it shall be worth whatever shame I shall suffer for it.

I could have wished that things would have been different for us, but please believe me, Melissa, when I say that I do care deeply for you and that I hope, in spite of all that has passed between us, that you will consider me your friend and know that I sincerely hope that should you ever need help, you will turn to me. I may have failed you lamentably by what I realize now was a most dishonorable offer on my part, but I shall not fail you in the future. And if you go ahead with this terrible misalliance, I know in my heart that someday you will need my help and that I will be able to redeem myself by proving to you that I will stand by you in your hour of need.

Latimer.

Crumpling the letter in her hand, Melissa stared blindly out over the green expanse of lawn, wishing violently that she had not read Latimer's words. She mistrusted him, she suspected that much of what he wrote was a tissue of lies, but she could not forget his warnings. A bitter laugh escaped her. There wasn't, as far as she could see, much difference between Latimer and Dominic, and she thought it particularly ironic that Latimer should warn her against the man she was to marry on the morrow. There was little in Latimer's letter that she did not already know. Hadn't Josh, when he had first told her of Dominic's presence in the neighborhood, warned her about him? But the information about Dominic's past relationship and yesterday's visit with Deborah, Latimer's sister, disturbed Melissa more than a little. As a matter of fact, for one mad moment she was eaten alive with sheer jealousy, and it was only the sound of the approaching horses and men that brought her back to reality.

Composing herself with a struggle, Melissa ripped the letter into shreds, thinking that she would like to do the same to Dominic's heart. Scattering the scraps, she walked toward Leonie and the others. If she had thought Latimer's letter ironic, that was nothing to the caustic amusement she felt when Dominic's surprise was revealed. By some evil coincidence, he had bought as a wedding present for her the very cottage Latimer had proposed as a love nest.

As the others exclaimed and commented on the pretty little building—newly painted and refurbished for the bride—Melissa stood there staring blankly at it. Thinking his bride-to-be was overcome with delight, Dominic said softly as he stood near her, "I know that we will come often to visit your brother, and I thought that you might like to have your own place to stay. It is small but very comfortable, and if you like, in the future we can make some additions to it."

Diffidently he added, "There are fifty acres with it, and I have hired some men to start construction of a small stable and some paddocks—we may decide to keep some of our horses here at certain times."

When Melissa still remained silent, Dominic glanced around, and seeing that the others were already climbing up the steps that led to the small gallery, he caught her shoulders between his strong fingers. "The cottage and the land are yours, Melissa. They are my gift to you."

His words startled her and she stared dumbly at him,

her black-lashed, golden-brown eyes widening in astonishment. It was the first time that she had looked directly at him since the night at the tavern, and Dominic felt himself drowning in the mysterious depths of her lovely eyes. His gaze dropped to her mouth, and remembering its warmth and sweetness, he muttered huskily, "We will stay here tomorrow night after the wedding. . . ."

Chapter Thirteen

SOMEHOW, Melissa was never certain how, she kept from laughing aloud hysterically. It seemed that this place, this quaint little cottage with its rose-covered gallery, was destined to be the site of her loss of innocence, and it gave her absolutely no comfort at all to realize that it would be Dominic, as her husband, who initiated her into womanhood rather than Latimer, as her so-called protector. For one wild moment she considered telling Dominic why she was not precisely thrilled with his choice of a wedding gift, but common sense, something Melissa felt strongly she had been displaying a decided lack of lately, exerted itself and she merely flashed Dominic a false smile.

Knowing that something more was expected of her, she grimly kept the smile pasted on her lips and said brightly, "How very thoughtful of you! Thank you!" She searched desperately for something more to add to what was undoubtedly meager thanks for such a munificent and unexpected gift, but her brain seemed to have frozen, his statement about tomorrow night blotting out all else. The sensuous expression in Dominic's eyes as he continued to stare at her mouth made Melissa feel weak. To her horror she could feel her breasts tingling with anticipation of his lips on her nipples, and she was unbearably conscious of a sudden tremor of insistent desire fluttering low in her abdomen. Helplessly she swayed nearer to him, her lips unconsciously parting, and her pulse leaped as his hands tightened on her shoulders and the gray eyes darkened with passion. . . .

"*Dominic!*" Leonie called out from the shade of the

gallery. "Aren't you going to even let Melissa see the inside of the house before tomorrow?"

As if stung, Melissa jerked away from Dominic, and Dominic, murderous thoughts concerning his favorite sister-in-law sliding through his mind, slowly pivoted to face Leonie. A tight smile on his lips, he said darkly, "Someday, Leonie, I am going to strangle you—especially if you don't cultivate a bit more tact!"

A saucy grin on her face, Leonie said airily, "Melissa, don't pay him any heed. He is always threatening me, but as you can see, I have survived—and prospered wonderfully!" She turned a limpid gaze on Dominic's handsome features and added dulcetly, "Please, dear Dominic, may we see the interior?"

A reluctant laugh came from Dominic, and as the moment of intimacy with Melissa was clearly shattered, he took her arm and escorted her toward the cottage. "I hope you approve of what I have done. There wasn't much time, but I left fairly comprehensive instructions about what I wanted while I was gone. If there is anything that you don't like, we can always change it later." He cast Melissa a bone-melting smile. "I believe that it will prove to be sufficient for our needs, though."

Still shaken and flustered by her reaction to him, Melissa kept her face averted and mumbled some reply. She hoped it made sense—certainly nothing else did these days!

The interior of the cottage was delightful, but Melissa was so acutely conscious of the fact that she would share this house with Dominic tomorrow night that she didn't really remember much of what she saw. She knew the front parlor was quite spacious considering the small size of the building, and she vaguely remembered some rooms with cream-colored walls and window hangings of pale rose, but of the downstairs furnishings she couldn't recall a single item. In addition to the parlor, there was a decent-size dining room, a small breakfast room and an even smaller room that could be used as an office, and upstairs were two comfortably large bedrooms connected by a tiny dressing room. It was the bedrooms that attracted her attention most. Alone in her bed that night at Willowglen, she could suddenly see in clear detail the carved rosewood bed with its deep lavender satin coverlet, and remembered Dominic's voice saying huskily, "This will be your room and bed . . . I hope you will allow me to share it with you . . . frequently."

In the darkness of her room, Melissa realized that this was the last time she would ever sleep here . . . alone. Her breath caught painfully in her chest. Tomorrow and for all the tomorrows that would come she would be Dominic Slade's wife; she would share a bed with him for the rest of her life. She was aghast at how much that knowledge excited her. Aghast and furious! Her fists clenched at her sides, and she stared sightlessly up at the ceiling. He must never guess, she thought feverishly, at the tumult his touch aroused within her. No matter if there were times that her body betrayed her, she must always be on her guard and never let him see into her foolish heart. Almost with relief she turned her thoughts to Latimer's letter. For the first time she wished she hadn't destroyed it, wished she had it in her hands right now so that she could read and reread the ugly words that he had written about the man she was to marry.

Unfortunately, though she tried earnestly to believe evil of Dominic, she found it hard going, particularly when she remembered how kind he had been to Zachary, and of course, there was the cottage. . . . How many men, even those besottedly in love, would present their brides with such a tasteful little house and fifty acres? And then there was Folly. Dominic had been very fair about his purchase of the stallion, even when their coming marriage would seem to make his offer unnecessary. How kind and generous he had been.

Suddenly angry with herself for entertaining such charitable thoughts about Dominic Slade, Melissa scowled. It was his unfair charm, she decided darkly. And his laughing eyes. And that mocking mouth and . . . Gritting her teeth, she deliberately made herself remember some of the nastier things that Latimer had written about him. Such as the way Dominic was still working his perfidious charm on Deborah, even when he was betrothed to another woman! Uncle Josh's early comments about him floated unpleasantly through her brain, and with a muffled groan she sat up in bed.

There was no use pretending. Despite all she knew about him, Dominic Slade fascinated her as no other man ever had, but much worse, in her opinion, was that just his slightest touch, even though she knew he was a caddish womanizer, could fill her with all sorts of wild longings. She must protect herself, must remember that he was not as he appeared; and she must guard herself against falling under his wicked spell—she was *not* going to be enslaved like poor Deborah! Oh, no! She was going to show Mr. Slade that not all women were such silly susceptible creatures as foolish Deborah!

Her mouth set in a stubborn line, she contemplated the future. It was not a pleasant task, and she was extremely conscious of the unpalatable fact that not only would she be battling the beguiling influence of Dominic's spurious attractiveness, but battling the dictates of her treacherous heart and body too. She began to consider ways to accomplish her aims, finally hitting upon a scheme which she hoped would keep him at a distance.

The seesaw of emotion that had kept her awake until nearly dawn did not diminish as the hours of her wedding day sped by. She had dutifully allowed Frances and Aunt Sally to coo and flutter about her as they decked her out in the lovely high-waisted muslin gown with its delicate silver threads and wound sweet-scented orange blossoms through her tawny curls. It was difficult not to share their excitement, and despite her best efforts to the contrary, when Zachary finally placed her hand in Dominic's as they stood before the local preacher to say their vows beneath one of the soaring mimosa trees near the house, her cheeks were attractively flushed, her eyes shining and there was an endearingly tremulous curve to her rosy mouth.

Dominic looked devastatingly handsome in his wedding finery, the dark blue cloth coat fitting his broad shoulders admirably, the snowy whiteness of the fine cambric stock and ruffled shirt enhancing the natural darkness of his skin. Short, buff kerseymere trousers revealed the lean, muscular shape of his thighs, and his white silk stockings fitted snugly against his elegantly formed calves. But it was his face which captured Melissa's gaze, the full force of those sometimes haughty, sometimes laughing and at all times strikingly handsome features suddenly hitting her like a blow. His black hair was neatly brushed, but one errant lock persisted in waving near his temple, and Melissa knew an impulse to reach up and brush it back. As soon as the idea crossed her mind, her heart sank. Oh, dear! How was she going to resist him if at the very sight of him she could feel all her hard-won resolutions crumbling?

The ceremony was brief and the kiss they exchanged before the assembled family and guests was chaste, betraying none of the hot surge of passion that Dominic experienced when his lips touched hers. The blood hammering in his veins, he lifted his head and tucked her hands beneath his arm, turning coolly to present his bride. In seconds they were engulfed by a laughing, congratulating mass of relatives and friends.

During the festivities that followed, Dominic tried very hard not to reveal his growing impatience for the moment when he would have his bride to himself; when he would not have to share her attention with others, especially what suddenly seemed to him an inordinate amount of gentlemen who appeared determined to wrest his bride from him. Every time he sought her out, invariably some rackety fellow would be there to claim her regard—and to his jaundiced eye, the fellow was always young and handsome! Even Jason Savage, who was in attendance, had deserted Catherine's side to spend several moments in teasing conversation with Melissa. Not that he blamed him; Melissa's radiant loveliness left him breathless, and no matter whom he was talking with, no matter how interesting the conversation, his eyes kept searching the milling crowd for her tawny head, his ears constantly attuned for the sound of her voice.

No matter what she had vowed to herself in the darkness of her room, as the afternoon passed Melissa discovered that Dominic could tangle her emotions without even lifting a finger. All he had to do was smile beguilingly at the various, clinging females or bend his dark head confidingly to speak to this one or that, and she would be quite certain that he was a perfidious scoundrel weaving his dark spell on unwary innocents. But then across the room his gray eyes would meet hers and she would find herself beset by a melting desire, a desire for the numerous toasts to be over, for the congratulations to be said, for Dominic and her to be alone. . . .

Finally her wish was granted. The last toast, the last congratulation, had been given and she and Dominic drove away with shouts of good wishes and laughter ringing in their ears. They had not gone fifty feet before the realization suddenly hit her that this man, this tall, distinguished stranger sitting beside her in the smart new gig, was actually her husband and that he now virtually owned her. Legally he now had the right to control her possessions; even more frightening, he had the right to do *anything* he wanted with her body. . . .

She stared at the strong tanned hands as Dominic expertly guided the high-stepping gelding along the red-dirt road, visualizing those same expert hands on her body, removing her clothing, touching her shoulders, her breasts, her stomach, her . . . Melissa's heart pounded erratically, and she angrily wrenched her gaze away from his hands and stared stonily ahead. This *must* stop, she furiously berated herself. She had to remember not to weaken, not to let him bewitch her!

If Dominic noticed that his bride was unusually stiff and silent, or if he had thought to comment on the way it had seemed to him that she had smiled and flirted outrageously with every man under the age of one hundred on her wedding day, he kept it to himself. He slanted a glance in her direction, noting with a curious sense of pleasure the sweet curve of her cheek and the delicate line of her jaw. She was enchantingly lovely, he thought not for the first time today, remembering the way his pulse had leaped when he had watched her approach him before the preacher. He had told himself repeatedly that she was a deceitful, conniving baggage and that this was simply a marriage of convenience, that it was only her manipulations that had brought it about. Yet he could not help the wave of possessiveness that flooded his body whenever he looked in her direction or the odd feeling of pride he felt when he saw how effortlessly she charmed his family . . . and, he recalled blackly, any man who came near her. *That*, he vowed, was going to stop immediately! She was *his* wife and he wasn't going to have a bunch of pining, lovesick fools hanging about his household. Jealousy was an emotion he had always scorned and one that he had never before encountered. That might have been why it never occurred to him that for a man who scoffed at the green-eyed monster, he was displaying clear signs of having been bitten—badly.

It had been a long, tension-filled day for both of them, and Melissa was almost glad when the cottage came into sight. Dusk was just beginning to fall, and she welcomed the slight coolness that the increasing darkness offered from the humid heat of the day. Longing for nothing more than a refreshing wash and a soft bed, she said unthinkingly, "Oh, I can hardly wait to be out of this gown and in my bed."

Flushing wildly when she realized how her words might be interpreted, she waited in an agony of embarrassment for Dominic to reply. There was a suspicious twist to his lips, but he only murmured gently, "Yes, I imagine so. I have taken the liberty of hiring a maid for you, and I trust that she will have everything you require ready and waiting for you."

Melissa digested this information in silence. She hadn't had a personal maid in years and she didn't know that she necessarily wanted one now, but against her will, she was touched by his apparent thoughtfulness. Then she sighed. If he was going to continue to be nice, he was going to make her task of withstanding him even harder than she had imagined. Perhaps, she decided bleakly, this was how he had managed to enslave Latimer's sister.

Determined to let him see that she was unaffected by his actions, she gave an impudent toss of her honey-colored curls and said airily, "Thank you—that was very kind of you."

Although Dominic might have hoped for more of a response than a casual thank-you, he was not dissatisfied with her acceptance of his gift. She baffled him and he never quite knew what to expect from her; she could just as easily have been offended by his gesture. It was her changeability that both fascinated and infuriated him; one moment she could be all melting smiles and the next she would flash him a look that would have sent a lesser man staggering to his grave. She had obviously planned and schemed to entrap him, and yet once the deed was done, she had pretended that marriage to him was the last thing she wanted. He shook his head at her contrary nature, wondering, as he had so often since he had first laid eyes on her, precisely what sort of game she was playing. At least tonight, he thought with a sudden tingle in his loins, he'd reap some reward for having allowed himself to be so stupidly caught in a snare so conspicuously baited that even now he was positive that his wits must have gone wandering.

The next hour or so they were busy settling into their new home. Preoccupied by the visions of physical delights that were soon to be his, Dominic voiced no objection when, after a light repast served in the dining room by one of the several new servants he had engaged, Melissa disappeared upstairs to her bedroom. A lazy smile on his mouth, he lingered over his brandy, imagining his bride undressing and donning some flimsy apparel for his delection. Increasingly aware of the insistent demands of his body, after several moments he set down his brandy snifter and left the dining room.

In his bedroom, he hurriedly stripped out of his wedding finery, and after a hasty rinse in the tepid water left in a china bowl on a blue marble washstand, he shrugged into his dressing gown, which had been laid out by his manservant, Bartholomew. His heart beginning to beat faster in anticipation of what was to come, he swiftly crossed the tiny dressing room that separated their bedrooms. With fingers that shook slightly, he grasped the crystal doorknob and opened the door.

He'd furnished Melissa's chamber with her in mind, and he was understandably pleased with the results. The room was large, and the soft yellow and pale lavender colors that he had selected gave it an inviting warmth. A satinwood armoire and a delicate dressing table of rosewood had been introduced into the room, as well as two pretty chairs covered in willow-green silk. The bed he had finally chosen did not have the sumptuous decadence of the one he hoped would be waiting for them at Thousand Oaks, but he was not displeased with it. The canopy was a graceful swathe of gauzy material which gave the tall, carved posts an airy look, the gleam of the deep lavender coverlet hazily glimpsed through the misty folds of the gossamer curtains that draped all four corners of the bed. Seeing that his bride was not waiting for him in the bed, Dominic scanned the room for sight of her, his gaze finally finding her where she stood by one of the long, narrow windows which lined one wall of the room.

Melissa had not been idle in the time since she had left her husband in the dining room. Suspecting that Dominic would linger over his brandy, she had indulged in the refreshing bath which had been waiting for her and had even succumbed to trying one of the many containers of powder that Dominic had bought for her use. Liberally dusting herself with a sandalwood-scented powder, she then began to prepare for bed . . . and Dominic. Scandalizing the proper and efficient maid, Anna, whom Dominic had hired for her, Melissa had dismissed the young woman, stating quite firmly that for tonight, at least, she had no desire or need for Anna's services. Once Anna had gone, Melissa had wasted a few minutes searching for the trunk which held the meager items she had brought with her from Willowglen. Finding it at the back of the armoire, she had dragged it out and with relish she began to properly prepare for her wedding night, wishing with a pang that she had not been tempted by the bath and the powder—smooth, silken skin, enticingly scented, was *not* what she had in mind for Dominic tonight!

Precisely what she planned to do she didn't really know; she only hoped to somehow keep a barrier between them. To tamely accept his presence in her bed and in her arms would be to acknowledge defeat, to admit for all time that she was his property and that her purpose from this day forth would be merely to serve him. Her spirit rebelled against such an idea and her mouth tightened into a stubborn line. No matter what ultimately transpired tonight, she must salvage something for pride's sake.

She had few illusions about her ability to withstand indefinitely Dominic's sensuous appeal to her senses. After

all, wasn't it that same inability to resist him that had
gotten her into this situation in the first place? If she'd
been made of sterner stuff, wouldn't she have slapped his
face and pushed him away the instant he had touched her
in his room at the tavern? Remembering the way she had
melted beneath his kisses, she grimaced. The really dam-
nable thing, she thought glumly, was that she had no indication which way her treacherous body would react
tonight.

Her defenses were frail, and the most she could hope
for was a postponement of the inevitable, for if Dominic
touched her, if he took her into his arms and kissed her
and awoke that sweet fire she had experienced only in his
arms . . . She sighed gloomily. No matter how she protested to the contrary, she was dismally aware that her
wretched body would probably betray all her plans, and
she was desperate to prevent that from happening.

The effect upon Dominic when he entered the room and
saw the results of her ministrations was everything that
Melissa could have wished for, and for one moment she
was certain that he would erupt into fury—which, of
course, would give her the excuse she needed to create a
disagreement of epic proportions. The moment his eyes
found her, the lazy smile that had curved his mobile mouth
was instantly wiped clear and the warm light in his gray
eyes vanished. He looked, Melissa thought with satisfaction, exceedingly displeased.

Her heart pounding with a queer excitement, she waited
breathlessly for the explosion of wrath she was certain
would now occur. She wanted him to be angry, because
then it would be so much simpler for her to be angry too;
but to her consternation, a slow smile of sheer appreciation
suddenly spread across his face, and with a thread of
amusement in his voice, he drawled, "Miss *Melissa* Seymour, I presume?"

It was indeed the sour-faced, prim and spinsterish Melissa Seymour of his first meeting with her at Willowglen
who faced him across the short distance of the room. Staring at her, knowing now what lay behind the disguise, he
wondered how he had ever been taken in so easily. Even
with her hair pulled back into that ridiculously unattractive

bun, the fragile beauty of her face would have been obvious to anyone who knew her. Naturally the fierce scowl she was bestowing upon him made that beauty a trifle harder to see, but still to him, at least, she looked utterly adorable. He was going to take great enjoyment in discovering, layer by layer, the loveliness and the warm, yielding body he knew lay beneath this absurd disguise.

At his expression of amusement, Melissa felt a tremor of pure fright skid down her spine. Oh, dear! she thought distractedly, her eyes helplessly caught by Dominic's dark, compelling features, this isn't going to work! She made a game attempt to press on. Ruthlessly tearing her eyes from his faintly curved mouth, she put on her haughtiest air and said frostily, "You know very well what my first name is! And since we were just married this afternoon, you are perfectly aware that I am now Mrs. Melissa *Slade!*"

Not the least put off by the haughty tilt of her gently rounded chin or by the icy tone in her voice, Dominic gave her slender body a long, thorough appraisal, his gaze lingering on the rise and fall of her bosom. Purposefully he began to close the distance which separated them. "How could I forget," he murmured huskily, "when I've thought of little else for the past several hours."

Melissa's pulse gave a funny little leap at his words, and a feeling of breathless anticipation slowly eddied through her. She knew she should do something, that she should move or speak, do anything but stand there frozen in one spot, staring at him as if mesmerized by his steady approach. Against her will her eyes clung to him, skimming over the unruly black hair which persisted in waving near his temples. Deliberately she avoided meeting the stare of those long-lashed gray eyes, her wandering look sliding down the length of his regal nose and remaining for a breathless moment on the wide, full-lipped mouth. Unwillingly she remembered the taste and texture of that warm, exciting mouth, remembered the heat of it, remembered the slight abrasiveness of his tongue as he had kissed her deeply that night in the tavern. . . .

Only when he stopped directly in front of her was Melissa able to gain some remnant of control over her unruly thoughts, and it was then that she realized belatedly that

she had chosen her site of confrontation badly—she should
have stood in the middle of the room, where she would
have had easy maneuverability. As it was, her back was
pressed against the wall and Dominic was planted squarely
in front of her, cutting off all avenues of escape, standing
so close to her in fact that the lapels of his dressing gown
nearly touched her breasts. Vexedly she bit her lip and
glanced away, unwilling to see the triumph she was certain
would be on his face.

"Shy, Melissa?" he asked softly, the faint breath from
his mouth brushing against her cheek.

"Of course not!" she maintained stoutly, sending him
a freezing glare.

"I'm pleased," he replied lightly, "that you are not
shy. Seducing virgins has never been to my taste, and as
for bedding a shy virgin . . ." A rueful gleam appeared
in the gray eyes. "Bedding a shy virgin might very well
tax even my ingenuity!"

In confused astonishment Melissa stared at him, only
vaguely aware that he had placed a hand on either side of
her head, *very* aware of the heat and power that radiated
from Dominic's deceptively relaxed body. "Since virgins
aren't to your taste," she began recklessly, "perhaps we
shall simply dispense with consummating our marriage!"

With a frankly sensuous curve to his mouth, Dominic
shook his dark head. "No," he said bluntly. "The thought
of being your first lover, of simply being your lover, has
kept me awake for far too many nights. Now that there
are no longer any impediments to that taking place, I shall
not deny myself. . . ."

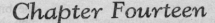

Chapter Fourteen

HER MOUTH suddenly dry, the blood in her veins thudding violently through her body, Melissa watched dumbly as Dominic slowly lowered his head, the slight brush of his lips against hers sending a jolt of feverish excitement down her spine. Ignoring the eager response of her body, she deliberately turned her head aside, breaking the contact of their mouths. In a stifled tone, she asked, "Suppose I don't want you to be my lover?"

She wouldn't look at him, finding it far easier to concentrate without his handsome features blocking out every other sight from her gaze. But his lips were still faintly touching her cheek, and she felt rather than saw the smile that curved his mouth. His breath, warm and brandy-scented, wafted against her skin as he said softly, "Oh, you will, sweetheart, by the time I'm finished with you."

Melissa tried very hard to be insulted by the confidence in his voice, but mingled with her feelings of insult was a giddy sensation of anticipation. Ignoring the flutter in her stomach, she risked a glance at him and then wished she hadn't—the teasing expression in his gray eyes increasing her agitation. Desperate to break the spell that he was so effortlessly weaving about them, she said breathlessly, "That's arrogant of you!"

"Mmm, it might seem so, but you forget that I've kissed you and held you in my arms before—on at least two occasions that I can recall quite vividly—and you didn't seem averse to my advances then," he commented dryly.

"It was d-d-different then," she stammered helplessly. "We w-w-weren't m-m-married!"

A gleam of amusement lit the gray eyes. "I see," he said slowly. "You only welcome my embraces when we *aren't* married?"

"That wasn't what I meant and you know it!" she exclaimed.

"Then precisely what do you mean, sweetheart?" he asked dulcetly.

Melissa took a deep breath and began earnestly, "I mean that we didn't really *want* to marry each other and that . . . that . . ." She hesitated, then ended in a rush, "And that consummating our marriage right now would be a mistake."

Some of his amusement vanishing, Dominic asked idly, "And when *do* you propose we do consummate our marriage?"

Feeling a bit more confident, she said airily, "Oh, perhaps in a few weeks, after we know each other better."

Dominic snorted. "I'm willing to indulge you in several areas, my dear, but since it was our mutual desire for each other that put us in this position in the first place, I have no intention of denying myself my connubial rights."

Her heart gave an uncomfortable leap within her breast, but assuming a martyred expression, Melissa said dramatically, "Since you feel that way, there is nothing I can do to stop you from having your way with me." She sighed heavily. "I shall just have to dutifully endure your presence in my bed."

She was prepared for some sort of reaction from him, either anger, disgust or disappointment, but to her astonishment, he merely chuckled. "Very well," he said calmly. "You have warned me, and since you have no intention of joining me in this endeavor, I shall just have to please myself." Before she realized his intent, he had reached out and whisked away her spectacles. A satisfied smile on his handsome face, he stared down into her widened eyes. "Getting rid of your ridiculous disguise will be only the first of many pleasures that I plan on enjoying."

He glanced at the offending spectacles and then, as Melissa watched transfixed, he opened the window near where they stood and with one powerful movement flung the spectacles far out into the darkness. "There," he said smoothly. "That was one thing I've wanted to do for a long time." He looked at her, the narrowing of his gaze causing her breath to suddenly constrict in her chest. "And now," he said slowly, "for the rest of it."

Like a frightened doe confronted by a dark predator, Melissa attempted a frantic leap away from him, but his hands caught her slender shoulders and with an infuriating economy of effort, he brought her struggling form up next to his hard body. Laughter in his voice, he murmured, "Remember, you are supposed to *dutifully* endure, my dear, not fight me."

Furious and, to her mortification, excited, Melissa glared up at him, unbearably conscious of his warm, hard length pressed so intimately against her. Quelling the treacherous response of her body to his nearness, she said angrily, "How dare you destroy my spectacles!" And when he remained unmoved, only grinning down at her with that thoroughly disgusting satisfied expression on his face, she added, "I need them!"

He shook his head. "Not for what I have in mind," he murmured softly, one hand already traveling upward to pluck the pins from her hair. Despite Melissa's best attempts to avoid his exploring fingers, in a matter of moments her tawny hair was tumbling wildly about her shoulders, the ugly bun ruined. Both hands once again on her shoulders, Dominic surveyed his handiwork, noting with pleasure the flushed features that she raised to him, her freed hair curling like golden silk near her cheeks, her rosy mouth full and tempting just below his and the amber-gold eyes dark with some indefinable emotion. Fear? Desire? Anger? He didn't know and at this moment he didn't care; the movements of her body against his as she had sought to escape had made him compellingly aware of the demands of his own body. Unable to resist the sweet lure of those lips, Dominic gave a low groan and found her mouth with his. Hungrily he kissed her, surrendering himself to the driving, primitive emotions that suddenly flooded through him at the touch of his lips against hers. He wanted to tease her, taste her, explore her slowly, but he found that he could not, that she was too tempting, too intoxicating for him to think clearly, and he urgently deepened the kiss, forcing her lips to part for him, boldly invading her mouth.

Trapped as much by the restraining hands on her shoulders as by her own wayward body, Melissa trembled from the force of the emotions that racked her as Dominic's warm, questing tongue filled her mouth, the velvet length of it stroking seductively against her own tongue, blatantly inviting her to follow suit. Her head swimming, a curiously weak feeling creeping through her very bones, she swayed nearer to him, unconsciously offering herself to him, her lips helplessly parting even further before his demanding kiss.

Greedily he took what she bestowed, his lips hardening, his tongue moving feverishly within her mouth, arousing her, making her unbearably aware of the reckless desire that curled and eddied deep within her. She was powerless in his embrace, unable to even conceive of the idea of resisting him, her thoughts becoming increasingly fuzzy and indistinct, until the only thing that she was aware of was Dominic, the passionate enchantment his mouth was wrecking upon her, the wanton desires that were clamoring in her veins.

She had thought that there could be nothing more thrilling than his kiss, but when his hands dropped to her slender hips and he pulled her hard against him, making her intensely conscious of the heat and size of his swollen manhood beneath his silk robe, she realized that she had been wrong. She was swamped by a heady sensation of delight, of sweet power to know that she had brought him to this state, to know at this moment that it was *her* body he desired. But that satisfying thought disappeared almost the instant it occurred—his hands had found the fastenings at the nape of her neck, and with a sudden lurch of her heart, she felt her gown slipping away from her.

Shaken at how easily she had allowed herself to nearly be seduced, she jerked her mouth from his and jammed her arm between their locked bodies. Half angrily, half pleadingly, she got out, ''Oh, stop it! Please!''

Through half-shuttered eyes, Dominic gazed down at her, the expression on his dark features hard to discern. Does she realize the impossibility of what she is asking?

he wondered helplessly. He ached to the very marrow of his bones with wanting her; she was his wife; this was their wedding night, and she wanted him to stop? He shook his head slightly and muttered, "I cannot. I want you . . . willing or not." His gaze dropped to the creamy shoulders and the slight swell of her breasts that his seeking hands had revealed, and he knew an urge to touch those same places with his mouth, to rip the concealing, offending garment from her body, to have all the secrets of her flesh laid bare before him. With a concentrated effort, he raised his eyes from temptation, but his gaze lingered for a long second on the faintly bruised fullness of her mouth. His eyes on hers, he finally said, "Melissa, whatever the reasons for our marriage, we *are* married—we will be man and wife for the rest of our days. I didn't want this marriage—I never thought to marry at all—but since, through my own folly and a certain amount of encouragement from you, we found ourselves forced to comply with tradition, I fully intend to make it a real marriage." He grinned ruefully. "It's odd, but while I envisioned our marriage to be filled with all sorts of difficulties, I never counted bedding you among them. *That,*" he concluded wryly, "was the one and only place I assumed we would have no trouble."

His words stung, but Melissa had to admit to the justice of them. Certainly her reactions to him every time he came near her would lead one to suppose that she was *more* than agreeable to join him in bed, she thought disgustedly. But she could hardly confess that she found him utterly fascinating and that becoming his wife, his *beloved* wife, held a great deal of appeal to her. Since it was depressingly clear that he felt none of the more tender emotions that she did, she was going to have to make certain that he never discovered just how hard it was for her not to fall under his mesmerizing spell. Giving a saucy toss of her honey-colored curls, she said bluntly, "Well, it would appear that you were mistaken!"

He smiled slowly, and Melissa felt her traitorous heart beat a little faster at the sight of that beguiling curve of his lower lip. "Mistaken?" he repeated lightly. "No, not mistaken—I merely forgot how infuriatingly contrary you can be!''

There was far too much truth in what he said for her to deny it, and to her horror, instead of the anger she was desperately longing to feel, she was conscious of a foolish compulsion to giggle. She could actually feel her lips start to twitch in an answering smile before she remembered herself and quickly pursed them into a tight, disapproving line.

But Dominic had seen the slight quiver of her mouth and, laughing delightedly, he swung her up in his strong arms. With mischief and something else dancing in his gray eyes, he murmured against her ear, ''And now, sweetheart, there will be no more talking . . . unless, of course, you wish to tell me what a wonderful lover I am!''

Torn between the desire to soundly box his ears and the equally appealing desire to join in his laughter, Melissa gave up all pretense of resistance. He was irresistible, and she suspected that she had lost this particular battle the moment she had first laid eyes on him. But the memory of what he had admitted about not wanting to marry lingered with painful intensity. Determined to protect her silly heart from further hurt, she said formally, ''I just want you to know, Mr. Slade, that it is only because it is my *duty* as your wife that I am consenting to this.''

Dominic grinned down at her as he placed her gently on the silk coverlet. ''And I,'' he murmured with a wicked gleam, ''will only *dutifully* exert my husbandly rights!'' As he had lowered her to the bed, her gown had slipped farther down her body, the tip of one small breast peeking above the lace of her chemise. His smile faded, and as if mesmerized by the sight of that rosy nipple, he said thickly, ''*Very* dutifully.''

With one careless movement, he loosened the sash of his robe and shrugged out of it. Melissa had a brief glimpse of a muscled chest, thick dark whorls of hair spreading across its hard width; and then his face and head blotted out everything as his mouth sought hers and she gave herself up to the enchantment that was Dominic.

She had been half fearful that he would fall upon her like a ravening beast, but now that all the words had been said between them, he seemed in no hurry to claim what was rightfully his. Instead he took keen pleasure in merely kissing her, long, deep, drugging kisses that sent her blood spinning dizzily through her veins, blocking out any idea of resistance. But kisses soon didn't satisfy him and his mouth traveled slowly across her jaw, his tongue tasting her flesh, his teeth gently nibbling as he explored the shape and texture of her silken skin. It was a delicious sensation, and Melissa shivered with pleasure when his teeth found her earlobe and he bit it lightly, his tongue circling and probing.

If his exploratory kisses had made her dizzy, the touch of his questing hands sent a jolt of sheer animal enjoyment right through her bones. She had been so caught up by his seductive kisses that it was a shock when she felt his hand close over her breast, his thumb rubbing persistently across the nipple. With breathless anticipation, she lay there oddly acquiescent, unable to move or think of anything but what he was doing to her, his warm mouth slowly sliding down her chest, his lips moving unerringly toward her aching nipples. Unable to help herself, she moaned softly as he cupped her breast and his mouth fastened hotly over the rosy tip, his tongue curling with obvious relish about the straining flesh. Desire, instinctive and compelling, washed through her, the hungry suckling movements of his tongue and mouth dragging her deeper into the erotic whirlpool he was deliberately creating between them.

Melissa had foolishly thought that she could maintain some sort of composure, to merely submit to his demands, but she discovered that it was impossible to remain un-moved by his arousing caresses. Helplessly, her fingers tangled in his dark hair, unconsciously pulling him closer to her breast, her body arching up slightly toward his tan-talizing mouth. At her betraying movement, his hand tightened fractionally on her breast and his teeth grazed the swollen nipple gently, intensifying the already plea-surable sensation, and she moaned again, unknowingly en-couraging him to continue this tender assault.

Time and again his lips would leave her breasts to fasten demandingly on her mouth, his hands moving feverishly across the soft skin that he had exposed. Half shyly, half greedily, Melissa returned his kisses, her tongue seeking to explore his mouth as he was exploring hers, her hands sliding wonderingly across his broad shoulders, feeling with delight the muscles tense when her fingers brushed against his spine. His skin was warm and firm and she discovered that it gave her great pleasure just to touch him, to feel the reaction of his body as her hands grew bolder, slowly wandering down his back to his waist.

Groaning softly, Dominic suddenly raised his mouth from hers and his bright gaze moved sensuously over her flushed face before it dropped to the small breasts with their upthrusting coral nipples. Her crumpled gown and chemise hid the rest of her body from his searching eyes, and pressing a kiss between her breasts, he muttered, "I want to see all of you . . . to see if reality is as beautiful as my dreams of you."

Before Melissa had time to protest, if the thought had even occurred to her, Dominic swiftly pushed away her offending garments. He shifted slightly and with one final movement, gown and underclothing were totally removed and tossed carelessly onto the floor. In the faint dancing light of the candles which had been lit earlier with a possessive glitter in his gray eyes, he boldly surveyed her slender shape as she lay there, her skin gleaming like sunwarmed honey against the deep lavender coverlet. Her breath trapped in her chest, Melissa froze, unable to move, inherent modesty warring with an odd shamelessness as his gaze moved slowly across her bared flesh.

Unhurriedly Dominic viewed her nakedness, the slim ankles and long, shapely legs, his gaze riveted for several seconds on the soft tangle of tawny curls at the junction of her pale thighs before he was able to wrench his eyes away and continue his leisurely appraisal. She was everything that he could have wished for, and unable to just merely look upon her, he reached out and pressed one hand on her flat stomach, letting it sweep up past the slender waist to the soft swell of her firm breasts. "Lovely," he said thickly. "Far lovelier than even my dreams."

His mouth swooped down upon hers and he kissed her fiercely, his tongue plundering between her lips, his arms closing around her strongly. The warmth and hardness of his powerful body startled Melissa, her breasts crushed against the unyielding wall of his chest, her legs intertwined with his; and between them . . . between them, stabbing against her belly with a heat and force of its own, was the swollen, imposing length of his manhood. Melissa knew a quiver of excitement and fear when his hands moved to her hips and he jerked her closer to him, making her even more aware of the strength and power of his big body.

Lost in the wild turbulence of new emotions that stormed through her body, Melissa responded blindly to Dominic's increasingly urgent kisses, her arms closing about his neck, her body instinctively pressing intimately against him. Her nipples tingled from the rough caress of the crisp hair that covered his chest as they lay there locked together in a passionate embrace, and she was more and more aware of an insistent yearning ache deep within her. The touch of his roaming hands as they traveled over her slender hips, fondling her buttocks while he rhythmically rocked against her, only served to excite her further, to intensify the spiraling need that was inexorably surging through her slender body. She ached with an elemental need; the kisses and the arousing caresses were now not enough. There was a hunger for something more, driving her to seek a closer intimacy, her hips arching up to rub erotically against him.

Dominic groaned with satisfaction at her actions, his hands clenching convulsively into the soft, pliant flesh of her buttocks as he held her motionless against him, just savoring the sensual experience of her delicately formed body pressed so close to his. Her hard little nipples were burning into his chest like points of fire, and the excited brush of her body against his was an incredibly carnal pleasure. She was an enchanting, intoxicating creature, everything about her pleasing him, from the passionate kisses she returned to the obvious signs of her own arousal. He wanted her, needed urgently to bury himself deep within her, to find relief from the aching, throbbing demands of his body, and so gently he pushed her back into the softness of the mattress, his hands sliding to the tight curls between her legs.

At the first touch of his hands in so intimate a place, Melissa stiffened, the instinct to protect herself momentarily allowing coherent thought to filter through her consciousness. She made a tiny movement to escape, but Dominic was prepared for it, and lifting his mouth from hers, he muttered huskily, "Ah, no, sweetheart . . . don't close me out. Let me . . ." His mouth slid to her breast and he muttered against the silken flesh, ". . . let me pleasure you, let me teach you . . ."

A shudder of happiness went through her at the need and desire clearly evident in his voice, and with a small moan of mingled defeat and excitement, she relaxed against him. His lips closed almost painfully around her sensitive nipples and the hungry, yearning ache in her loins sharpened instantly, nearly making her cry out at the intensity of emotion that flooded her being. But it was the probing caress of Dominic's knowing fingers between her thighs that shattered her inhibitions and had her writhing like a wanton, possessed creature as, tenderly, he taught her the secrets of her body. With an excruciatingly sweet deliberation, he stroked and teased that most sensitive flesh, and pleasure such as she had only guessed at exploded throughout her body with every erotic movement of his fingers. Gripped by a fierce onslaught of desire, she pushed up frantically against his invading exploration, her hands rubbing feverishly across his broad back.

"Oh, Dominic," she moaned softly, "I want . . . oh, please . . . please . . ."

Her words were very nearly his undoing, the throbbing demands of his hungry, straining flesh almost destroying whatever restraint he still possessed. Her scent was in his nostrils, her yielding, sweet body was eager and aroused beneath his touch and her honeyed kisses nearly drove him mad with the compelling desire to plunge his body into hers, to make them one. Aware that he would lose total control of the powerful needs that were swamping him if he did not end this delicious torment soon, he captured her wandering hands in his and quickly covered her with his body, sliding between her legs.

The warmth and weight of him both thrilled and agitated Melissa, her breath suddenly catching in her throat as she felt the burgeoning pressure of his swollen organ between her thighs. She twisted against him, wanting his possession and yet frightened of it too. He seemed so big and intimidating as he loomed over her, and with a leap of her heart she became aware of the strong grip of his hands holding her own prisoner on either side of her head. She could feel him trembling against her, could sense his driven passion from the hungriness of his fierce kisses, and her apprehension fled. He was her husband, the only man who had ever aroused her to passion, the only man whose kisses and caresses had shaken her, the one man who had made her giddily aware of the delights to be found in physical love, and helplessly she melted against him. Her lips against his firm mouth, she murmured gently, "Take me, Dominic . . . make me truly your wife."

She felt the quiver that knifed through him at her words, but she could never guess at the deep pleasure they gave him. Unable to think clearly any longer, the urgent demands of his body pushing all thoughts but one from his mind, he kissed her passionately, his hands tightening on her wrists, and with one swift lunge, he buried his aching flesh within hers.

Racked by a sudden, sharp burst of pain as his body thrust into her virgin one, Melissa shivered violently, her fingernails digging into the backs of his hands as she choked down a cry of intense hurt. Her body heaved upward in protest at the pain he had so unexpectedly given her, but Dominic's hands clamped even more securely around her wrists, holding her prisoner beneath him.

He remained motionless within her, deliberately giving her body time to adapt to this new intrusion, and gently he kissed her cheeks and the tempting outline of her mouth. "I'm sorry," he breathed huskily, "but there was no other way. . . ." He kissed her deeply, only by the greatest effort able to control the elemental compulsion to seek his own release. It was ecstasy to lie here like this, to feel his body locked with hers, to feel the heat and silkiness of her all around him, and a surge of incredible tenderness eddied through him. She was fire and wine in his arms, everything that he had ever wanted in a woman, and helplessly, his kisses became more demanding, his body moving slowly, gently, within her.

In a welter of confusion and shock, Melissa felt the pain ebb, felt her body widen to accommodate his possession. She was a woman now, Dominic's woman; that one thought banished the last remnants of her pain, and mindlessly she let him wrap them both in the heady pleasure to be found between lovers.

Bemused by the frankly sensual experience of his hard body driving urgently into hers, intensely aware of his strong hands clasping her buttocks, holding her tight against him, instinctively she matched him movement for movement, her slender hips eagerly rising to meet the downward thrust of his. Dominic's powerful lovemaking was intoxicating, the demanding pressure of his mouth sweeping her violently along with him, a soft ripple of tingling pleasure unexpectedly shooting through her as he increased the tempo. Breathless and wide-eyed, she lay there stunned beneath him, unable to understand how such a simple act could bring this much delight.

Dominic had been uncertain whether he could bring her fulfillment this first time, but he felt that faint quiver her body gave, and a surge of exultance raced through him, pushing him over the edge to find his own ecstasy. And afterward, afterward, there was her sweet, soft body to pull next to him, his hands compulsively tangling in the tousled curls that tumbled wildly near her temples, his mouth, gently, thoroughly, searching hers as he plainly enjoyed the aftermath of lovemaking.

Melissa lay silent beside him, shyness and confusion sealing her lips. What did one say after such an event? *My, wasn't that enjoyable? Thank you very much?* A nervous giggle threatened to escape her and she burrowed her head deeper into his warm shoulder, unbearably conscious of their nakedness as they lay there together on the satin coverlet.

It would have come as a great surprise to her to learn that Dominic was suddenly, paralyzingly, at a loss for words. He had made love to several women in his life, although he had never had quite as many mistresses as had been attributed to him by the gossips, but this was the first time that he had ever made love to a virgin or to a woman who was his wife. What, he wondered uneasily, did he do now? Ordinarily, he would have dropped an affectionate kiss on her head, mentioned a future meeting and then discreetly taken his leave, but this was his wife, for God's sake! He couldn't treat her like a damned mistress! Besides, he discovered to his astonishment, he didn't really want to leave her bed; he rather enjoyed lying here with her tempting body pressed against him. More to the point, he was extremely conscious of the renewed stirring of his body—not since his hot-blooded youth had he felt this compelling desire to taste again the delights that he had experienced only minutes ago. And that rather alarmed him. As a matter of fact, his whole reaction to Miss Melissa Seymour, now Mrs. Dominic Slade, alarmed him.

Frowning, deliberately ignoring the urgings of his body, he considered all his uncharacteristic actions of late—particularly since he had first laid eyes on the bewitching, infuriating creature at his side. He could in part, now that her disguise had been dispensed with, understand the attraction he had felt for her . . . except it nagged him that even when he had thought her a sharp-tongued dowdy, he had still found himself drawn to her. He hadn't been aware of her beauty the night Zachary had gotten drunk. Nor had he plumbed the depths of her disguise when he had made the ridiculous offer to buy a half interest in Folly. In the darkness, he smiled wryly. Folly. That was what this entire episode had been, pure folly. But calling it folly didn't satisfy him, and his sensation of disquietude grew. He could convince himself, in regard to the purchase of the horse, that he had allowed compassion to move him; he could even tell himself that it had been simply to rescue her from what he was fairly positive had been an unpleasant situation involving Latimer. He would have done a lot to thwart Latimer. . . . But that still didn't explain everything. Nor did it answer why he had meekly stood by and let Josh Manchester coerce him into marrying her. . . .

It had been an unfortunate situation that night at the inn, of that there was little doubt, but marriage . . . He moved uneasily on the bed, his hand unconsciously caressing Melissa's arm. Marriage was something he had sworn to avoid, and he was dimly aware that had the woman he had found in his room that night been anyone other than Melissa, he would never have lost his head that way, nor would he have let any number of angry relatives force him to take such a drastic step. Not liking the trend of his thoughts, he scowled. *Why* he had acted as he had on numerous occasions in connection with Melissa wasn't important, he told himself doggedly. The important thing was that they were married and that it would behoove them to make the best of a bad situation. But even coming to that sensible conclusion didn't quell the uneasiness within his breast. He had the unwelcome premonition that if he were not *very* careful he would commit the greatest folly of all—falling madly in love with his wife and turning into as besotted and doting a husband as his brother Morgan! It was only natural that his young bride should fascinate him, but loving had *absolutely* nothing to do with it. As for the desire she aroused, well, that was perfectly normal—he wouldn't be male if his body didn't respond as it did to the warmth and silky feel of her soft flesh. Resolutely, he pushed aside any further thoughts on the subject. What if he did want to make love to her again? She was his wife; this was their wedding night and he *had* been a long time without a woman. Convinced for the present that he had explained everything away, with renewed hunger stirring in his veins, he tightened his clasp on Melissa and fervently sought her mouth with his.

Melissa responded blindly to Dominic's kiss, the touch of his lips on hers plunging her once again into the relentless whirlpool of physical desire. He was not quite as gentle with her this time, his movements hurried, as if he were driven by a strange urgency, but she didn't care, her own newly awakened desires rising up swiftly to meet his, and for the second time she discovered the magic to be found in a lover's arms.

But when it was over, when their heartbeats had stilled once more and the passion that clouded rational thought ebbed, Melissa returned unpleasantly to her present predicament. Her cheek resting against the gentle rise and fall of Dominic's warm chest, she was miserably conscious that nothing had changed. He still didn't love her; he still hadn't wanted to marry her, and she didn't know if she could bear to have him come to her bed, aware that it was not love but mere, common lust that brought him there.

To her horror, she felt tears prick at the corners of her eyes and for an awful moment she was afraid she was going to burst into sobs. Biting her lip, she blinked several times, berating herself for being a fool and for allowing herself to be beguiled by his undoubted charm. There was no use pretending to herself after tonight that she would ever be able to deny him anything. Her sweet mouth twisted. Certainly she wouldn't be able to deny him her bed—all he had to do was touch her, and her bones turned to milk pudding, she thought disgustedly. But if she was willing to admit that Dominic utterly fascinated her, she wasn't about to let *him* know her feelings—then all *would* be lost.

Tears gone, she lay there for several seconds, her thoughts busy with ways to hide the silly yearning of her wayward heart. It wouldn't do to sigh and beg for the moon. She would have to act as careless and indifferent around him as she could. Not for her languishing looks and soulful eyes! So she had lost this first skirmish between them; that didn't mean that she should simply surrender and turn into a meek, biddable mouse of a wife, did it?

A sparkle in her amber-gold eyes, she began to formulate plans to make it abundantly clear to her new husband that, while he might command her body, he had not conquered either her heart or her spirit! If he wanted a mewling, clinging vine, he should have continued his pursuit of the fair Deborah, she thought tartly. But she was aware of an odd constriction in the region of her heart at the thought of Dominic with Deborah, and she sighed faintly, suddenly depressed about the future.

Dominic heard the soft sound she made, and remembering her virgin state and concerned that he might have hurt her this last time, he brushed a kiss across her forehead and inquired quietly, "Shall I leave you? I did not mean to act in the manner of a rutting boar—I hope I did not hurt you."

Still very shy with him, she shook her head, not able to

look at him. But it seemed that Dominic suffered from no such niceties, and before she could protest, he had shifted their positions until she lay flat on the bed and he was propped up on one elbow, lounging there beside her and gazing down at her wary features.

A thread of laughter in his voice, he murmured, "What did that shake mean—no, you don't want me to leave? Or no, I didn't hurt you?"

Staring up at him in the flickering light of the candle, Melissa wished vehemently that he didn't look quite so appealing with his curly black hair ruffled from her caressing fingers and his gray eyes full of lazy amusement. There was a frankly satisfied smile curving his mobile mouth, and that more than anything strengthened her resolve not to let him know precisely how *very* attractive she found him.

Pretending an indifference she did not feel, she smiled carelessly at him and shrugged. Not meeting his eyes, she replied lightly, "Take it to mean whatever you like—it really doesn't matter to me."

That wasn't what he wanted to hear, and her infuriatingly cool smile made him a trifle annoyed. He had hoped that she would want him to stay with her, and even in spite of her less-than-inviting attitude, he found himself reluctant to move away from her seductively warm body, much less her bed. With an edge to his voice, he muttered, "Then I'll take it to mean no . . . to both questions."

Hoping he would not guess at the effort it cost her, she shrugged again and yawned delicately. "Whatever you wish. I for one am quite fatigued and would like to sleep now." She opened her eyes wide and said innocently, "Since I have proved myself to be a dutiful wife and endured your demands, I *do* think that I should be allowed to sleep alone in my own bed . . . don't you?"

Chapter Fifteen

"BY GOD, I sure as hell don't!" Dominic burst out furiously, all signs of lazy amusement gone. An angry glitter in the gray eyes, he jerked upright and in one lithe motion leaped from the bed. Snatching up his robe from the floor where he had thrown it in what seemed only moments before, he glared at Melissa. "*Endured!*" he snarled, wounded pride battling with the strong inclination to grab her into his arms and kiss her mindless. How dare she act this way! He had given her pleasure, he knew he had, and now the brazen little baggage was trying to pretend that it had meant nothing to her!

He stood there glaring at her for a long moment while he considered climbing back into her bed and proving to her that *enduring* was not quite what she had done during their lovemaking. But there was an uncomfortable niggle at the back of his brain that questioned his assumption that she had enjoyed what they had just shared. . . . Perhaps, he thought with a sudden sinking feeling in his midsection, she really *had* simply endured; that, her actions to the contrary, she truly found his touch repulsive and had merely suffered his presence.

It was, for Dominic, one of the most painful moments of his life, and if Melissa could have guessed the hurt she was inflicting by her facade of indifference, she would never have been able to carry it out. As it was, she met his look squarely, and continuing with the role she had selected, she replied with a remarkable amount of composure, considering the tumultuous beat of her heart, "Yes, endured!"

Jaw taut, Dominic said acidly, "Very well, madam wife, you have made yourself abundantly clear—I will not *inflict* my company on you any longer—and rest assured that while you find my lovemaking distasteful, there are many women who don't!" His gaze raked her naked body. "And although your charms are delightful, I'm sure that I shall find others who are just as pleasurable! Good night, dear wife!"

Her topaz-colored eyes appearing huge in her pale face, she watched as he stalked from the room, the urge to call him back very strong, the desire to retrieve every word she had spoken almost overpowering. In trying to protect herself, had she made a mistake? Had that been a flicker of pain she had glimpsed in the depths of those usually laughing gray eyes?

Miserably she stared at the door that Dominic had slammed behind him. To add to her feeling of guilt and unhappiness, the memory of all the kind things that he had done for her since she had first known him came rushing back. Oh, my wretched, *wretched* tongue! she thought forlornly, wishing that there were some miraculous way to call back the last few minutes.

Unfortunately, Melissa's abject state didn't last very long. Though she remembered the kind things that Dominic had done for her and Zachary, she also remembered Josh's early comments about Dominic and the ugly content of Latimer's letter. Reminding herself that he had made it very apparent that he'd had no desire to marry her and had done so only out of a sense of honor helped to lessen some of the guilt she was experiencing. After all, she mused slowly, she hadn't said anything *vicious* and she *had* warned him that she didn't want to consummate their marriage, so he shouldn't have been surprised at her actions. And since he obviously didn't feel any deep emotion for her, it shouldn't have bothered him very much that his lovemaking apparently left her unmoved. . . .

She wasn't exactly comfortable with her line of thought, but it did give her some solace and it did dilute her awful feeling of having wounded Dominic's sensibilities. But it didn't explain away her growing uneasiness that she had made a terrible miscalculation and that she was going to pay a dear price for tonight's works. With a lowering spirit she recalled his final words to her about finding other women who didn't find his lovemaking distasteful.

Angry with herself for even caring that he might seek the charms of other women, Melissa sat up in bed, pulling her knees up to rest her chin on them. Wrapping her arms around her legs, she stared blankly at the door from which Dominic had departed so abruptly such a short time ago. It didn't really matter, she told herself for perhaps the tenth time. This was a marriage of convenience—they both knew *that!* There was no love between them; they would probably live separate lives, each one busy with his or her own pursuits. Melissa grimaced. Somehow that wasn't how she had expected her marriage to be; it was precisely to shun such an empty life that she had refused to marry in the first place.

A bitter laugh escaped her. It was ironic that after all the machinations she had gone through over the years to avoid being forced into a loveless marriage, she should find herself in just that position. Conscious of the tiny ache in the region of her heart, she felt a tear trickle slowly down her cheek.

She wished she knew what Dominic was thinking; wished she had some inclination of his feelings for her. She knew he desired her, or *had* desired her, she thought with an unhappy twist of her mouth, and she knew that he had been both generous and indulgent with her during the brief time they had known each other. But just because he had been generous and indulgent didn't imply that she meant any more to him than . . . than his horses! He was a wealthy man, he could afford to be generous, and as for indulgence—sometimes indulgence merely masked indifference!

A militant sparkle appeared in the golden-brown eyes. She was *not* going to brood over tonight! She would be very polite and very proper with her husband, but she was not going to allow herself to be hoodwinked by his spurious charms! Hadn't Latimer written in his letter that Dominic had been seeing Deborah only days before the wedding? And hadn't dear Uncle Josh warned her repeatedly that Dominic was a bounder, a womanizer of the worst kind? Oh, no, she wasn't about to allow her foolish heart to be captured by such an unworthy creature!

Giving her tawny head a defiant toss, she decided that she had not been wrong to act as she had tonight. Her husband was already too arrogant, too confident of his own worth and handsomeness, and it was just as well, she told herself staunchly, if she *had* punctured his pride a little. Certainly it would *never* do to let him have a hint of the sweet turmoil he created so effortlessly in her breast by a mere look, a touch, a smile. . . .

Melissa took a deep breath. She wouldn't think about *that!* She concentrated instead on what she had gained. The worst hurdle was over; she had made her position clear, and it was time that she stopped yearning for something she couldn't have and set about finding some even ground on which to base their marriage. Having convinced herself of the soundness of her reasoning, she lay back down and prepared to sleep.

But sleep came hard, the memory of Dominic's ardent lovemaking causing her body to ache for his touch; the memory of the expression in his eyes just before he had turned away from her making her doubt the wisdom of the stance she had taken. It wasn't at all surprising that she awoke depressed and unrefreshed at the first light of dawn, her thoughts going instantly to her husband, all the uncertainties she had assumed she had resolved within herself rushing to the forefront of her mind.

At least Melissa had been able to sleep, even if only for a little bit, but such had not been the case for her very new and very angry husband. Dominic had spent the hours since he had stormed from her bedroom alternately cursing her and yearning to creep back into her bed and press her sweetly perfumed flesh next to his, to know again the intoxicating wonder of making love to his wife.

It was, to say the least, one of the most unsettling nights of his life. Everything he had ever wanted had come to him easily. His charm, his handsome face and form, his powerfully connected family and his fortune had made few things beyond his grasp, and now to discover that a woman he found wholly enchanting, if exasperating, was completely indifferent to him was a devastating blow.

Over and over again, he reviewed those moments in Melissa's bed, remembering her every reaction to his touch, trying desperately to prove to himself that she had lied to him, that she had *not* been unmoved by his caresses. She must be lying, he muttered to himself furiously. Lying through those honey-sweet lips of hers. The problem with that particular line of thought was that he could think of no reason, other than sheer perversity, for her to do so! And while he wouldn't discount just such a reason for her actions, he finally decided gloomily that she must have meant every word she had hurled at him.

But he could not accept that notion, telling himself repeatedly that her responses to him had been too eager, too natural and uninhibited to have been calculated. Though he tried to convince himself of the soundness of his reasoning, he found little comfort in his musings.

Leaving Melissa's room, he had dragged on a shirt and a pair of breeches, and finding a pair of boots in his own room, had hastily put them on before departing from there. Downstairs and outside on the surprisingly spacious gallery of the cottage, he had paced back and forth, oblivious to the warm, magnolia-scented air that wafted gently around him.

What a devilish tangle! he thought viciously. Married to one of the most infuriating yet utterly beguiling women he had ever met in his life, and she was, or claimed to be, totally indifferent to him! His pride was stung and his faith in his own physical prowess was thoroughly shaken. His expression grim, he continued to stalk back and forth along the gallery, trying to make sense of what had happened tonight, and why—since he was positive she wielded no power over his heart—Melissa's rejection of him should matter so very much.

It wasn't as if he hadn't had his advances rebuffed before; granted they had been few and far between, but there *had* been those rare women in his life who had spurned the lures that he had thrown out to catch their attention. It had never disturbed him in the least—he had simply shrugged his broad shoulders and gone on to find another who caught his fancy. Except for his brief and mad involvement with Deborah, he had never given those instances much thought, no one woman ever touching his finer emotions . . . until he had laid eyes on the aggravating, enraging and wholly enchanting Miss Melissa Seymour!

His ambulations had brought him to one end of the gallery where a few chairs and a small, square table were situated. Conveniently there was a slim case filled with the thin black cheroots that he smoked upon occasion, and idly he selected one. Lighting it, he began his restless pacing once more, a tobacco-scented cloud of blue smoke following him about the gallery.

While Dominic was willing to admit to several things, such as his seeming inability to deal rationally with the amber-eyed, tawny-haired witch who was no doubt sleeping dreamlessly in her bed upstairs, he was not about to admit to himself or anybody else that he had fallen into the same trap that had snared his brother Morgan. He would *not*, he swore with his teeth clamped tightly around the black cigar, fall in love with Melissa. He would not allow himself to become so besotted with any female that his life revolved around her and that there was an emptiness without her at his side. And he was most definitely *not* in love with the infuriating little baggage he had just married this afternoon!

Having convinced himself that he was utterly untouched by Melissa's advent into his hitherto well-ordered existence, he proceeded to find perfectly logical reasons for his incomprehensible actions these past few months. His physical response to her, he was positive, was simply because he had been a long time without a woman and she *was* desirable—why, he'd wager that he would have responded to *any* personable young woman! As for offering that ridiculous sum of money for *half* a horse, well, that was easily explained too—it had been merely an act of kindness; the Seymours had been in desperate straits and he'd seen a way to help them. That philanthropy had never before figured high on his list of pleasures, he resolutely ignored; besides, in addition to helping them, there had been the wicked enjoyment of being fairly confident that he was also thwarting Latimer. But it didn't *really* matter why he'd done it—the money was a paltry sum to him anyway, and if he wished to throw it away, it was no one's business but his own. The marriage itself was not so remarkable to understand—marrying her had been the only honorable thing he could have done considering the circumstances. Stubbornly he closed his mind to the sure knowledge that had it been a female other than Melissa he'd found in his room that night at the inn, he would not have been willing to offer himself as hostage for honor.

Satisfied that he had explained his seemingly eccentric behavior of late, Dominic was in a much better frame of mind and leisurely he filled his lungs with the rich smoke of his slim cheroot. But as his thoughts drifted irresistibly back to tonight's debacle, his hard-won satisfaction fled and a black scowl darkened his fine brow.

Usually, Dominic was able to see the humor in most situations, but he was finding it devilish hard to see anything amusing about being found wanting by one's wife. He was not an overly vain man, although he *did* have a good opinion of himself, but he found it impossible to believe that Melissa had been as indifferent as she claimed. He'd made love to too many women not to know when he had also given them satisfaction, and he discovered that he was deeply affronted by the notion that he was such an inept lover that he could not bring pleasure to his own wife! Time and again he relived those sweet moments of passion that he had shared with her, and to his utmost disgust, his body would instantly harden, the desire to seek her out and prove her words lies nearly overpowering.

The first pink-and-gold signs of dawn were streaking across the horizon when Dominic came to several discomforting conclusions. For whatever reason, his wife of mere hours had taken it into her lovely head to repulse his attempts to make their marriage real and, worse than that, he was going to have to tread very lightly if he ever hoped to share her bed again. He could force his attentions upon her and the law would be on his side, but he found such an idea distasteful—rape had never appealed to him. More importantly, he had remembered something that he should never have forgotten: Melissa had trapped him into marriage and her reasons for marrying him had nothing to do with the finer emotions; she had seen the opportunity to snare a rich husband and she had not hesitated to strike. He must take partial blame for her success—if he had not been so blinded by her beauty and the baser promptings of his body, he would not be in this situation right now.

A thoughtful expression upon his handsome face, Dominic lit another cheroot and stared blindly out at the dawn-gilded oak and magnolia trees that dotted the view in front of him. If there were certain things, such as a wife, that he knew he hadn't wanted, having committed himself to this marriage he knew there were other things that he also didn't want, and one of those things was the cold and empty relationship he had seen amongst several acquaintances who had married for money and position. Melissa might have married him for just those motives, but he saw no reason that he couldn't change her mind.

He wasn't precisely certain what it was that he wanted from his marriage—having coolly rejected Morgan's brand of marriage and the silken bonds of love—but while he might not be willing to risk his total happiness in the hands of just one woman, he most definitely did not want the sort of marriage that Melissa must envision for them, a frigid, passionless existence in which they both lived their lives separately, joined only by a name and a fortune. Or a horse, he thought ruefully, an irrepressible grin suddenly breaking across his face. By God! he swore softly, he wasn't about to let Melissa condemn them to a barren fate devoid of warmth and laughter . . . and passion. There *was* passion between them—even if she chose to deny it— and he had no intention of letting her pretend it didn't exist, or worse, trying to extinguish it. No, he thought with suddenly narrowed eyes, he wasn't going to be shut out of her life, her room or her bed. For a while, perhaps, but in time . . .

Unaware of her husband's midnight musings, somewhat apathetically Melissa allowed Anna to dress her that morning. Despite all her rationalizing of the previous night, she was still nagged by guilt at the way she'd acted—both her responses to his caresses and then the way she had sent him from her bed. But since it was not her nature to spend a great deal of time repining over fate, she straightened her slender shoulders, lifted her chin bravely, and ignoring the inward quaking of her spirit, left the sanctuary of her bedroom.

She was not yet overly familiar with the house, but since it was small, she found her way down the stairs and into a delightfully sunny little breakfast room, the bay window that curved across one end of the area overlooking a tidily planted rose garden. Crisp white muslin curtains adorned the windows and contrasted nicely with the pale apricot color of the walls. Because of its size, the room was sparsely furnished; a small oak sideboard and a spindle-legged table of the same wood with four simply designed chairs were its only furnishings. A painted canvas rug in shades of russet and green lay on the floor, and an oblong gilt mirror hung above the sideboard and gave the room an inviting appearance.

But Melissa was only vaguely aware of her surroundings, a faint flush stealing into her cheeks the instant her eyes met those of the man sitting in one of the chairs apparently enjoying a cup of coffee. Wishing her heart would not jump so wildly in her breast at the mere sight of him, Melissa kept her expression neutral and said woodenly, "Good morning, Mr. Slade."

One of Dominic's thick black brows shot upward and a mocking smile tugged at the corners of his mouth as he murmured, "Mr. Slade? So formal, my dear . . . and after last night?"

The faint flush became bright pink, but Melissa stubbornly refused to drop the course she had decided upon, and somewhat stiffly she asked, "What should I call you, then?" The instant the words left her mouth she knew she had made a mistake, the gleam that entered Dominic's eyes making her wish she had bitten off her tongue.

Rising belatedly from the table, he walked over to where she stood just inside the doorway of the small room. Running a caressing finger down her hot cheek, he offered, "Lover? Darling? Sweetheart? You choose, my dear."

He was irresistible, the imp of mischief dancing in those gray eyes calling to her own sense of amusement, and for just a second she very nearly abandoned her stance, but then, remembering that he was an expert at wooing the unwary, she pursed her lips and muttered, "You're not *my* lover!"

"Oh?" he replied lightly. "I'm certain that you are wrong. I distinctly remember last night. . . ."

Laughter brimmed his eyes and Melissa very nearly stamped her foot with vexation. How could one resist him? Especially looking as he did this morning, the dove-gray broadcloth jacket fitting smoothly across his broad shoulders and the dark blue breeches clearly defining the long length of firmly muscled legs? The black hair was carelessly brushed and waved near his temples; the pristinely white cravat was neatly tied and made the skin of his freshly shaved jaw look healthily bronzed. But it was the teasing expression in those long-lashed gray eyes that disturbed her the most, and she decided with an unexpected lift of her spirits that if he could treat what had happened last night so mockingly, then she could too!

Demurely lowering her eyes to hide the sudden glint of amusement stirring in their amber-gold depths, she said breathlessly, "A—a—a considerate l-l-lover would not embarrass me so."

His teasing behavior vanished, and with a keen look at her lovely features enchantingly framed by the curling mass of tawny hair, he asked huskily, "Is that what you want, Melissa? A considerate lover?"

This was hardly the way she had expected their first meeting to progress. With her blood thudding so loudly in her veins she was positive that he could hear it, she got out, "I—I—I th-th-think that this is not the time to discuss such things." She didn't really know what she was saying. Dominic's mocking manner as well as his nearness had her feeling dizzy and confused.

Not wishing to start an argument after such a promising beginning, Dominic retreated, saying carelessly as he led her to the table, "It is most *in*considerate of me to pounce on you before you have even had a chance to drink your coffee . . . or would you prefer some chocolate?"

"Oh, no, coffee will be fine," she answered quickly, dreading the enforced intimacy of the small breakfast room. Despite having known him as a lover, she was still shy and uncertain in his presence, and though they were now married, since their engagement they had spent very little time in each other's company. They were strangers to each other, strangers who had been compelled by reasons other than love to marry, and Melissa was very conscious of that fact.

Silently she watched as he politely poured her cup of dark, steaming coffee from a tall silver pot, wondering wildly what she should talk about to him. Certainly not about last night! she thought with a half-hysterical urge to giggle.

Dominic did nothing to help ease the situation, but then he was struggling with his own unruly thoughts, paramount among them the strong urge to kiss that sweet, temptingly soft mouth of hers. He had been taken aback at the thrill that had shot through him when he had glanced up and seen her hovering in the doorway. She looked, he decided bemusedly, utterly bewitching in a new high-waisted gown of rose-colored jaconet. Blond Mechlin lace trimmed the modest neckline, and the elbow-length sleeves were also lavishly adorned with the same lace. Dominic was quite pleased to see that the gown was as attractive on her as he had imagined it would be when he had selected it from the many color plates shown to him by the expensive modiste patronized by Sally Manchester. His gaze riveted by the rhythmic rise and fall of her delectable little bosom, he also recalled the negligee of nearly transparent gossamer satin he had chosen at the same time, and his chest grew tight at the image of the filmy material resting where his eyes did now.

An uncomfortable silence stretched out, each of them lost in thought yet unbearably aware of the other. With an effort Dominic tore his attention away from the erotic fantasy he had been enjoying, and clearing his throat, he said blandly, "Since our wedding was so hastily arranged, and considering that it is not a particularly healthy time of the year to do much traveling, I'm afraid that I did not make plans for us to go on any sort of honeymoon. If you like, once the fever season is over, perhaps we shall go to New Orleans for a month or so. In the meantime, you'll have the pleasure of fitting out your new home at Thousand Oaks to occupy your time." He would have preferred to have taken her to London, but with the damned war dragging on, it was an impossibility. Someday, he thought, I'll take her to England. . . . A faint smile flitted across his face. Knowing his bride, he was fairly confident that he would spend more time visiting the various excellent Thoroughbred stud farms to be found there than he would the salons and soirees that would have appealed to a more conventional wife. And that, he admitted to his surprise, suited him perfectly!

Since the circumstances of their wedding had been anything but romantic, Melissa had not thought a great deal about her honeymoon, but she had harbored the faint hope that they would go away together for even a short time to some place that would offer several pleasant distractions from the enforced intimacy being married engendered. Time spent together in the congenial company of others, with the days spent in enjoying entertaining pursuits as they gradually became more familiar with each other, would surely have lessened the strain between them and would have given them a chance to become better acquainted. She hadn't realized how much she had longed to learn more about her new husband in less confining surroundings until Dominic so coolly dismissed the idea of going anywhere. She wondered briefly if he was ashamed of her and if, now that they were married and the marriage consummated, he would bury her in the wilds of upper Louisiana for the rest of her life. With a wistful droop to her normally laughing mouth, she admitted forlornly to herself that after last night that was probably *exactly* what he wanted to do with her—that, or strangle her! Inexplicably feeling even more guilty about her actions the previous night, she confessed to herself that she wouldn't blame him in the least if he did exile her indefinitely in the country—what else did one do with a recalcitrant wife?

As Dominic noted the disconsolate curve of her lips, an extremely unpleasant idea occurred to him. Of course, he mused cynically, I should have been prepared for this—no doubt she has been expecting an elaborate and expensive honeymoon. How could I forget that she *did* marry me for money, and now I've already failed to live up to her expectations. A harsh note in his voice, he said, "Don't look so downcast, sweetling. I'm sure that if you are very good to me, and naturally if you change your mind about *enduring* my caresses, I shall make up for your disappointment in not having an extravagant wedding trip."

It was an ugly thing to have said, but then Dominic was feeling in an ugly mood, all sorts of decidedly unpalatable notions suddenly running rampant through his mind. Throwing down his linen napkin, he rose from the table. "I'm going for a ride. I find myself in need of fresh air."

Astonished, Melissa stared after him as he strode rapidly from the room, her pretty mouth forming an O of surprise. But as his words sank in, a frown curved her brow. He had been insulting, she thought with growing anger, all guilt about their previous parting vanishing in an instant, but along with her anger there was a strong sense of bewilderment. He couldn't possibly believe. . . ? Oh, surely not! she told herself uneasily. He couldn't believe that she was only interested in what he could give her. Or could he?

He had certainly reacted like a man faced with a money-grubbing little slut whose favors were easily bought by the highest bidder, she acknowledged with increasing agitation. And her behavior last night . . . She swallowed uncomfortably.

Miserable and uncertain, Melissa stared down blindly at her fragile china cup, the thoughts going through her brain exceedingly distressful. Josh had clearly indicated that Dominic was a bit of a bounder when it came to women, and Latimer's letter had certainly confirmed the fact that her new husband was a notorious womanizer and was not to be trusted in affairs of the heart. And yet, she admitted to herself, Dominic had never shown her anything but kindness . . . and, she confessed wryly, a great deal of patience, all things considered.

There were so many wonderful qualities about him, aside from his handsome face and charming personality, Melissa thought painfully. He had been very kind to Zachary; he had been overwhelmingly generous in connection with the purchase of Folly—and he had done the honorable thing and married her under circumstances that did not cast her in the best light! She sighed wistfully. Could Josh have been wrong about him? And Latimer? Couldn't Latimer's accusations have been motivated solely by spite? Had she entirely misjudged Dominic? Cast him as an unfeeling monster when he was actually a more-than-considerate gentleman?

Assailed by the increasing conviction that she had completely misundertsood everything about Dominic, she jumped up from the table, her one thought to find him and attempt some sort of new beginning between them. She had been a fool! she berated herself angrily as she flew out the front door and ran toward the tiny coach house at the rear of the main building. She must see him and try to explain, try to find a way across the ever-widening breach between them.

Her thoughts in a jumble, she paid no heed to the fact that she was not properly dressed to go riding, and ignoring the scandalized stare of the groom, hastily ordered a horse saddled. Riding astride in a fashion that would no doubt provoke comment up and down the river, she kicked her horse in the ribs and swiftly rode in the direction the groom had indicated that Dominic had taken several moments earlier.

Impetuous and headstrong as Melissa was, she had ridden only a half mile down the road before it dawned on her that explaining her actions was going to be rather awkward. How did you tell your husband that you were sorry about the way you had been behaving, but you thought that he was a debaucher of innocents and a philandering womanizer?

Slowing her horse to a walk, she bit her lip uncertainly. She could apologize for last night without giving too detailed an explanation about what had prompted her actions. Her mouth twisted. That should be easy enough—even now *she* couldn't explain the conflicting emotions that had raged through her. Closing her mind to the difficulties that lay ahead, she finally decided that she would simply lay all her contrary and undoubtedly infuriating behavior on the natural anxieties of a new bride and, she admitted ruefully, that was a great deal of the truth. She would also, she thought with a sudden rising of her spirits, clear up any misconceptions he might harbor that she had married him only for mercenary reasons.

If he realized that she had been as trapped as he by what had happened that night at the Whitehorn tavern and that his money did not appeal to her, might they in time learn to trust each other . . . and even love? A wistful glow entered her eyes. She didn't think that she would find it frightfully arduous to fall deeply in love with Slade! In fact, she very much feared that she was already halfway there!

But first, she thought apprehensively, she *must* convince him that his fortune had nothing to do with their marriage. Hopeful and yet nervous about the coming confrontation, she urged her horse into a gallop, eager to make peace between them.

Chapter Sixteen

MELISSA might have had thoughts of peace on her mind, but Dominic was grimly considering ways of wreaking sweet revenge on the unfairly seductive body of his bride. She was not going to be the only one to get what she wanted from this farce of a marriage, he thought blackly as he guided his bay gelding along the gently meandering road that led to Willowglen.

When he had ridden away from the cottage, he'd had no particular destination in mind; he'd simply needed to put some distance between himself and his calculating little bride before he did her a violence! His pride had taken quite a beating of late at the hands of the new Mrs. Dominic Slade, but it was not his nature to suffer such slights and insults meekly, and he'd consoled himself by thinking of various means to bring to her knees the mercenary, conniving baggage he'd had the misfortune to marry. He discovered, curiously enough, that his most satisfying visions of revenge were those in which a sweetly contrite Melissa pleaded frantically for his caresses and affection. Of course, he would turn an indifferent shoulder to her pitiful entreaties for his affection—at least he hoped he would, but he was aware of an uneasiness on that point.

By the time he'd relished quite a few scenes concerning the subjugation of his bride, he'd begun to feel slightly better, his first burst of dark rage having abated somewhat. It was then that he discovered that he was almost halfway to Willowglen. Having no desire to return home at the moment, he continued on his way, thinking that he'd enjoy a chat with Zachary and that he wouldn't mind looking Folly over again.

Certainly Dominic had not thought of meeting with Deborah Latimer, or rather Lady Deborah Bowden, as she now styled herself. But he had just turned down the lane leading to Willowglen when he came upon her, closely followed by her groom.

Despite being in no mood to exchange polite pleasant-ries, Dominic had no choice but to stop and greet her. And then there was the fact that he was just a bit curious about what she was doing visiting with young Zack.

Smiling, he said, "Good morning, Lady Bowden. Out for a morning ride?"

Her delicate features framed by guinea-gold curls, the wide blue eyes limpid and inviting, Deborah sent him a wistful little smile. "Good morning, Dominic," she said in her soft, lilting voice. Sending him a reproving glance, she added, "Must you be so formal with me? Especially since once . . ."

It was amazing, Dominic thought with astonishment as he sat there easily controlling his restive horse, how in-different he was to her now. Curiously he let his gaze run over her, noting how skillfully the attractive riding habit of sapphire-blue cloth revealed her ripening curves, idly aware of how gracefully she sat upon the dainty black mare she was riding—and how completely unmoved he was by her fragile loveliness.

At twenty-five years of age, Deborah was undoubtedly lovely, her small face perfectly heart-shaped, all her fea-tures from the spiky-lashed blue eyes to the Cupid's bow, pink mouth exquisitely formed. She was not very tall, but she had a lushness of figure that Dominic had always found vastly appealing, and though he could admire her appear-ance, he'd learned from experience that little intelligence existed behind the lovely facade. Once he had thought she was the embodiment of everything perfect, but Latimer's machinations and Deborah's own actions had shown him the error of his thinking. He no longer bore her any malice because she had taken his youthful dreams and trampled them; as a matter of fact, the only emotion Deborah Bow-den aroused within him these days was pity. And he did pity her. Pitied the lack of spirit that had enabled her to be bullied by her unscrupulous brother into a marriage to a man old enough to be her grandfather. Pitied the lack of courage that would not even now let her break free of Latimer's grasp. Pitied the absence of backbone and mettle to fight for her own happiness. . . .

Gently he asked, "Is everything all right? Latimer hasn't . . . ?"

The lovely eyes brimmed with tears, and cursing himself for a softhearted fool, Dominic dismounted swiftly and walked to stand beside her horse. Glancing back at the sober-faced groom, he muttered, "Ride ahead, James—I would like to talk with your mistress in private."

The groom had hardly disappeared around a bend in the lane before Deborah threw herself into Dominic's arms, great sobs racking her body. "Oh, Dom!" she wailed. "If only I had listened to you in London all those years ago."

His arms reluctantly filled with yielding feminine flesh, Dominic flung a harassed look around, cravenly hoping that no one would come upon this embarrassing scene. Resignedly he said, "Now, Deb, we've been through this before. I don't blame you for what happened, but it was a long time ago and you made your choice and there is no going back to yesterday . . . as I told you just last week."

Her arms creeping around his neck, she pressed her face against his chest and gave a tiny heartrending sniff. "You're right, I know, and I should not have written you, asking to see you when you were an engaged man," she got out mournfully. "I impose too much on our old friendship and your kindness."

Privately Dominic agreed with her—she'd written him three or four times since she'd discovered he was in the area, and they had been such sad and helpless little letters that he had finally felt compelled to see her, to offer his help. And seeing her, watching the play of unhappy emotions run across those lovely features as she had poured out her tale of woe, of Latimer's abuse of her, his threats, her fears, Dominic had been greatly moved and filled with pity for her plight. His first impulse had been to get her away from Latimer, and he had extravagantly offered to take her to his parents' home in Natchez—she would be safe there, he had urged. When she would hear none of that, he had vowed that he would settle a sum of money on her, not a grand sum, but enough to give her independence as long as she spent her money wisely; but that too she had refused, staring up at him with those big, trust-filled blue eyes.

Incomprehensible to him, rather than take his money, she was willing to let Latimer continue his nefarious ways, and it appeared that once again brother Julius had his eye on a doddering, *rich* old man who would make, from Latimer's point of view, an excellent second husband for her. Dominic had argued vigorously with her, telling her not to be a fool, to simply refuse to do as Latimer demanded. But Deborah had slowly shaken her beautiful head. "Oh, I could not!" she had exclaimed breathlessly. "He is my brother and he would beat me unmercifully if I didn't do what he wanted. That, or throw me penniless out in the streets. You just don't understand."

Dominic wouldn't have argued with *that*—he didn't understand her reasoning at all. Didn't understand why she apparently allowed Latimer to browbeat and manipulate her, or why, since she had spurned him in London, she now viewed him as her only savior. He knew that in part it was his own fault—he should never have answered that last letter of hers. But once she had meant everything to him, and although she no longer held any allure for him, the memory of what had been prompted his desire to help her. Royce, he admitted wryly, would twit him unmercifully for his soft head, but he did feel sorry for Deborah and wanted to see her happy. If only, he thought impatiently, she'd let me send her to London, far away from Latimer's influence.

Sighing, he absently put his arms around her waist and rested his cheek on the top of her small riding hat of black beaver. "Deborah," he murmured, "you have to leave Latimer! Let me take care of things for you."

It was just as well that Melissa couldn't hear what he had said, for the mere sight of *her* husband standing in the middle of the road *embracing* Deborah Bowden was enough on its own to make her teeth snap together nastily and her golden-brown eyes blaze with a decidedly feral light. Jerking her horse to a standstill, she sat there in stunned fury, her bosom heaving. Any idea of peacemaking and any hope she had held that Josh and Latimer had been mistaken about her husband's womanizing proclivities vanished in an instant. Which one of the two transgressors she would have liked to take her riding whip to first was questionable, but realizing with extreme reluctance that to do so would only complicate the situation, she checked this immediate impulse with a *great* effort. And as the seconds crept by and she sat there glaring at the oblivious pair, something of vital importance occurred to her: even if Dominic *was* a womanizer, and of that she no longer had any doubts, he was still her husband, still the only man who had come near to touching her deepest emotions, and she wasn't about to stand meekly by and let Deborah Bowden fawn all over him. Nor, she admitted with narrowed eyes, was she going to quietly abandon the field to the other woman!

A dozen impractical schemes flashed through her mind, but she had no time to examine each one, and giving rein to her impetuous nature, she kicked her horse forward. Forcing a lighthearted smile on her lips, she called out gaily, "Oh, Dominic! There you are! How mean of you to race off ahead of me that way." Approaching the undeniably wary pair, she smiled benignly down at them, acting as if she found it perfectly acceptable for her husband of less than a day to be publicly embracing another woman. "Hello, Lady Bowden. How are you this morning?"

To say which of the two principals was more taken aback would have been difficult to ascertain; certainly Dominic knew that he would not have acted so tamely if he had caught Melissa in this sort of compromising position. Of Lady Bowden, it was difficult to say what was going through her mind, the blue eyes resting guilelessly on Melissa's vibrant features, a tremulous little smile curving her bow-shaped mouth.

"Oh, Miss Seymour," Deborah began breathlessly, then, giving a small giggle, amended gently, "But, of course, you are now Mrs. Slade. How silly of me."

Unhurriedly Deborah removed her arms from around

Dominic's neck and stepped slightly away from him. Smoothing out the creaseless skirt of her riding habit, she murmured, "You mustn't mind me crying on Dominic's shoulder. We are old friends and habits die hard, as I'm sure you understand."

Smiling, Melissa replied dulcetly, "Of course I wouldn't want to do anything to come between such *old* friends."

Stifling the grin that twitched irrepressibly at the corners of his mouth at the chagrined expression on Deborah's face, Dominic glanced quickly away, his heart unexpectedly lifted by the implications of this exchange. His young bride might act indifferent to him, but if he was any judge, from the militant glint in those incredibly colored topaz eyes, he was quite confident that she was very definitely jealous—and prepared to do battle on his behalf!

His first reaction to the sight of Melissa bearing down on them had been one of anger and despair, anger at his own folly and despair that he could ever explain how innocent this situation really was. There had also been a strong inclination to wring the clinging Lady Bowden's slim white neck for having put him in this unfortunate position. He had suffered momentarily all the natural embarrassment and uneasiness of a man caught in such a compromising predicament, but at Melissa's pleasant greeting, other emotions had taken control—admiration for both her beauty and her poise, and sheer delight that she was displaying such obvious signs of jealousy. If she were as indifferent to him as she had claimed, why would she be jealous if he sought consolation in the arms of another? And if she *were* jealous, then a whole host of interesting possibilities presented themselves to Dominic.

With difficulty he refrained from grinning idiotically and was even able to find it in his heart to be grateful to Deborah for engineering this little scene. Hiding both his amusement and his pleasure in the circumstances in which he suddenly found himself, he turned away from Deborah and walked over to Melissa.

Laying a warm hand on hers as she tightly gripped the reins of her horse, he murmured, "It is kind of you to be so gracious and tolerant." A mocking light entered the gray eyes, "Most brides would not be so understanding

. . . but then you have made it clear that what I do doesn't concern you, haven't you?''

Melissa gave a funny little choking sound as she bit back the urge to tell him *precisely* what she thought of his deplorable actions, and lying through her pretty, white teeth, she finally said mildly, "If you are discreet, my dear . . .'' She glanced across at the avidly listening Deborah. "You may have all the doxies you want!" And with that parting shot, she dug her heels viciously into the sides of her horse and wheeled away, her gown billowing out behind her as she kicked the animal into breakneck speed.

Bemusedly Dominic watched her disappear down the lane, thinking to himself that she had looked magnificent, with her tawny hair tumbling wildly about her cheeks and her eyes flashing with a golden fire. Even the ruched-up gown, which displayed an immodest amount of her slender calves and ankles, had only added to her captivating beauty, giving her the air of some untamed creature that appealed powerfully to his senses. He continued to stare after her receding figure until Deborah's voice brought him unpleasantly back to the present.

"What a hoyden you have married, Dominic!" Deborah said with gentle malice. "I've heard tales that her father simply let her run wild, but I never believed it before. Did you see the improper way she was garbed?" She gave a scandalized cluck and went on spitefully. "You're going to have your hands full with that one!"

An odd smile on his chiseled mouth, Dominic turned to look at her. "Yes, I am . . . and believe me, dear Deborah, I shall enjoy every moment of it! Now, shall I help you to mount—or would you prefer that I find your groom?"

Aware that for the moment he would not fall victim to her wiles, Deborah smiled winsomely and murmured, "Oh, my, I have made you angry, haven't I?"

Glancing at her coolly, he said politely, "Why, no. But you will understand that I must be on my way?"

Deborah shrugged her slender shoulders good-naturedly and said sunnily, "Of course, how foolish of me—you wish to be with your bride."

Dominic merely nodded his dark head and effortlessly

lifted her back into the saddle. Remounting his horse, he said impassively, "Good day, my dear. I hope that you will not allow your brother to take advantage of you as he has in the past . . . and remember, my offer to send you either to my parents' home or to London is still available."

Her lashes lowered demurely, Deborah responded cloyingly, "You are too generous, Dominic. I shall never forget your many kindnesses to me. I count on you as my only friend."

Dominic shrugged his shoulders uncomfortably and, shaking his head, muttered, "Deb, do not say such things. There are others, I am sure, who will stand by you, should the need arise. Now, if you will excuse me?"

Sending him a wistful smile, she nodded her head. "Good-bye, my dear. Go to your bride, and I . . ." She sighed heavily. "I shall go to my brother."

Ordinarily, Dominic might have been moved by her words, but his thoughts were already on Melissa and he answered almost absently, "Yes, you do that. Good day." And without another glance or word, he kicked his horse into a gallop, eager to find his *jealous* bride.

He found her as he had suspected he would, down at the stables at Willowglen. She was in one of the paddocks, Folly tied to the whitewashed fence, industriously brushing the stallion's already burnished coat, a ferocious scowl on her face.

Dismounting, he threw his reins to one of the stablemen and strolled over to her. Leaning his arms on the top rail of the wooden fence, he stood there for several moments, watching idly as she continued to brush Folly, her strokes becoming stronger and faster as the minutes passed.

Melissa had been vividly aware of him from the instant he had ridden into view, but stubbornly she had refused to acknowledge his approach, even when he had come to lean on the fence. She had been dwelling on the pleasurable fantasy of shoving Lady Bowden's face into the manure pile when he had arrived, but his disruptive presence ruined her enjoyment in that pastime. She had not been able to think of a punishment horrid enough for him, and deliberately turning her back on him, she continued to vigorously groom Folly, considering and discarding several rather disagreeable fates for her errant husband. As he remained imperturbably leaning on the fence, apparently absorbed in watching her brush the horse, her sense of ill-usage grew, until finally she could stand it no longer. Violently throwing down her brush, she spun around to face him. Hands on her hips, topaz eyes glittering angrily, she demanded, "How could you! We are not married twenty-four hours and you are out, out . . ." Words failed her and she glared at him in silent rage.

Helpfully, he said, "Womanizing?"

Nearly exploding with wrath, she hissed, "Yes, womanizing!"

His face the picture of innocence, he murmured, "But surely you are not upset. I warned you last night that there were others who would not find my advances so distasteful." His gaze slid sensuously down her body. "Or have you changed your mind?"

"Yes! No! Oh, you confuse me!" Melissa muttered distractedly, angrily conscious of the leap her heart had given at the expression in his eyes. Furious with herself for betraying the agitation she felt, she met his interested gaze squarely and said rudely, "Go away. I don't want to talk to you."

She looked so fetchingly angry and bewildered at the same time that Dominic had a hard time suppressing the urge to jump over the fence and take her into his arms. Giving no hint of what he was feeling, he remarked carelessly, "Very well, sweetheart, since that is what you wish. Just remember that if you have second thoughts, do let me know. Until then, I assume I have your permission to amuse myself?"

Caught in the trap of her own making, Melissa could only stare miserably at him, debating the two courses open to her. She could sink her pride and admit that she wanted him on any terms, or . . . She swallowed painfully. Or she could salvage her pride and pretend indifference.

Neither choice particularly appealed to her, and she asked in a small voice, "May I have time to think it over?"

Dominic had never seen Melissa in such a subdued mood, and for just a moment he seriously considered her request, but then, reviewing all her baffling actions during the brief time he had known her, he came to the conclusion that it might be dangerous to let her dwell on the subject for too long. God knew, he thought sardonically, what sort of twisted logic might govern her answer if he didn't press his unexpected advantage. Shaking his head, he said levelly, "No, I believe that this is something we should settle now."

Perhaps if he had shown some sign of guilt or had been more encouraging, Melissa might have given him the answer he craved so intensely. But as it was, his arrogant words were like hot knives in her flesh and she stiffened. Her eyes flashing dangerously, her chin held at a haughty angle, she spat, "Then my answer is yes!" Spinning around, she began to furiously brush Folly. "Go *amuse* yourself—it doesn't matter to me!"

For a long moment Dominic stood there staring at her straight back, fighting a powerful demand to tip her over his knee and beat her soundly—and he was not normally a violent man! Disappointment made his voice harsh as he answered, "Very well, madam, since that is your wish— don't expect me home this evening!" And wheeling on his heels, he walked stiffly away, anger in his every movement.

Melissa didn't see him leave—she was too busy fighting back the bitter tears that threatened to spill down her cheeks. But the tears finally won, and a few minutes later Zachary found the bride of less than twenty-four hours sobbing her heart out on Folly's shiny neck. In one swift bound, Zack was over the fence and his strong arms were wrapped comfortingly around her slender body.

"What is it, Lissa?" he demanded urgently. "What has happened between you? I just passed Dominic and thought he was going to tear out my liver!"

Melissa had frozen at the first touch of Zachary's arms, thinking unbelievably that it was Dominic, but at the sound of Zack's voice she went limp. Turning in his arms, she lifted a tearstained, heart-wrenchingly miserable face to him and choked, "I hate him! He is an unfeeling, unprincipled monster! I will *not* stay married to him one minute longer than it takes to get a divorce!"

Zachary was appalled. He couldn't help but be aware that his sister's marriage was not the love match it was rumored to be. He knew Melissa too well, and while he had gone along with her subterfuge, he had often wondered what had really prompted the sudden engagement. But he liked Dominic very much, and since Melissa had appeared willing to marry him, he had youthfully assumed that all would be well. But now . . . now with Dominic in such a foul, unapproachable mood and his dear sister in tears, Zachary was very much afraid that he had badly miscalculated the situation. As for a divorce, he shuddered at the thought of it. Even if Dominic were the unprincipled monster that Melissa labeled him, a divorce was not to be considered lightly. In fact, divorce was almost unheard of, and it invariably brought shame and disgrace to both parties—especially the woman.

All his protective instincts aroused, Zachary held Melissa gently against his chest, murmuring soft words of encouragement, but his mind was racing. What the devil had Dominic done to make his sister so unhappy? And what had Melissa done to make Dominic so furious? And how was *he* going to resolve it? *If* it could be resolved? Even though Zachary was willing to abet Melissa in whatever action she desired, he wasn't altogether convinced that whatever problem existed between the newlyweds was one-sided. Despite the gravity of the situation, he smiled faintly. He knew Lissa's flaming temper and stubborn nature and he suspected that Dominic, too, possessed a formidable temper and could be equally as stubborn. Not the best combination for a tranquil marriage, he mused uneasily, his smile fading. But . . . But twenty-four hours was hardly long enough to give the marriage a chance, and looking down into Melissa's face, he said quietly, "I think you need to consider more fully what you want to do. Those vows you took yesterday are not to be lightly discarded."

The memory of Dominic embracing Deborah searing across her brain, Melissa snapped, "Well, I wish you would tell my husband that!"

At Zachary's speculative look Melissa bit her lip, longing to call the words back. The last thing she wanted was to involve others in the disaster of her marriage. Besides, Zachary might take it into his head to confront Dominic; even, she realized with a sickening thud of her heart, challenge him to a duel!

Deciding that she had to distract Zachary, she wiped away the last of her tears and smiled tremulously at him. With more than a little truth, she got out in a shaky voice, "Oh, Zack! You know my wretched tongue and temper, and I am afraid that I have, as usual, let them run wild without considering the consequences. You'd think I'd have learned my lesson after all these years, wouldn't you?"

Zachary wasn't completely convinced, but he was agreeable for the moment to go along with whatever Melissa wanted. And if she wanted to prevent him from probing too deeply, then he would allow her to do so—for his age, Zachary was a *very* astute young man.

Cocking an eyebrow, he asked, "So what are you going to do about making up with your husband?"

Melissa had no intention of "making up" with Dominic—at least not at the present time. Her pride was too deeply wounded, and the knowledge that her husband had immediately sought out another woman had been a painful blow to her wary heart. But she had to say something to Zachary which would ease his mind about this morning's events. "Well, first I shall have to apologize for my regrettable temper, and then . . ." She shrugged carelessly. "I shall think of something!"

Not at all deceived by Melissa's words, Zachary murmured dryly, "Oh, I'm sure you will. I just hope it isn't something that drives an even wider chasm between the two of you!"

Despondently Melissa turned away. She rather doubted that anything she could possibly do could make matters worse. What, she wondered miserably, could be worse than being married to a man who didn't love you, hadn't wanted to marry you and was a blatant libertine in the bargain! The future looked very bleak indeed from where she stood. Hiding the distress that suddenly filled her, she kept her face averted from Zachary and said with an attempt at lightness, "Don't worry, Zack. It is just a lover's

quarrel.'' And until she said it out loud, she had not realized how desperately she wished it *had* been a quarrel
between two lovers; at least then there would have been
the possibility of a reconciliation.

That thought stayed with her throughout the long,
wretched hours that followed. She didn't remain long at
Willowglen—she dared not, fearful that Zachary would
pry the truth out of her, and after chatting desultorily with
him for several minutes, she departed. He had asked no
further questions, although she could tell that he was consumed with curiosity and he even limited his opinion about
her unorthodox riding apparel to a few brief comments as
she prepared to ride away. A teasing glint in the topaz
eyes so like hers, he drawled, ''You look quite fetching
in that new gown, Lissa. Shame you got it all covered
with horsehair.''

She grimaced as she glanced down at the once-immaculate
gown but made no reply. Then she guided her horse away
from the plantation. She was in no hurry to arrive back at
the cottage—what waited for her there? Nothing but empty
rooms and empty hopes and dreams. But eventually she
did return to the cottage, and leaving her horse with the
groom, she wandered dispiritedly up to her room.

Strange, to think how hopeful she had been when she
had ridden away from here this morning, and now . . .
now she thought her heart would break.

Listlessly she allowed Anna to help her out of her dress,
completely oblivious to the woman's scoldings and
shocked comments about the deplorable condition of the
expensive garment. The soothing bath that Anna had prepared helped restore her physical well-being, but nothing,
she thought soulfully, could ever heal her heart. And it
was in those dark moments that she began to examine her
feelings about Dominic Slade more fully. What she discovered did not help her dreary spirits in the least. To her
dismay and horror, she realized that she had inexplicably
fallen in love with her husband, womanizer or not, and
she wanted him . . . wanted him in all the ways a woman
in love could want a man.

But how, she wondered painfully, could she attract his
interest, let alone his love? If only I had acted more wisely

last night . . . if I had not sent him away so cruelly. . . .
Yet even if I had acted differently, would it have mattered
at all? She sighed gloomily.

Blindly she wandered around her pretty bedroom, her
thoughts on her erring husband. She had accepted the unpalatable notion that Dominic did not love her and that
their marriage was not going to change his dissolute ways.
Now all she had to do, she mused drearily, was to conceive of some way to change his nature . . . to make him
fall in love with her and to renounce all other women for
the rest of his life. Ha!

Growing more depressed by the minute, she sank down
gracefully on one of the green velvet chairs, the filmy
skirts of her amber robe rippling around her feet. A length
of black silk ribbon had been woven through Melissa's
tawny curls by Anna, and leaning back comfortably in the
chair, she began to absentmindedly play with it, her
thoughts still hopelessly muddled.

Should she pretend that last night and this morning had
never happened? Greet Dominic when he finally came
home with courtesy and affection? Her mouth twisted.
Knowing her own volatile temper and incendiary nature,
she rather doubted she could play such a meek role. She
was far more likely to break something over his head than
to meet him with gentle smiles and open arms. Besides, if
she seemed to accept his actions, wouldn't that encourage
him to continue with his deplorable behavior? More than
likely, she admitted with an unladylike snort of indignation. But she couldn't rail and scream at him either—*that*
might lead him to believe that she cared about him. Which
she did, she conceded miserably. Terribly.

Well, if she couldn't act as meek as milk or like a jealous fishwife, what was she to do? Some sort of peace had
to be established between them before she could even begin to think of some way to gain his affection. There had
to be some middle ground for her to travel; some way to
salvage her pride and put a good face forward, yet not
appear to merely condone his actions.

Frowning, she stared off across the room, wishing she
were more sophisticated, that she had had more dealings
with men, that there were an older, experienced woman

she could talk to about this dreadful situation. For a brief moment, Leonie Slade's face danced before her eyes, but then she shook her head. No. Leonie would invariably be on Dominic's side—the deep affection between them had been very obvious to Melissa. And then there was the fact that she dreaded the idea of another person being involved in this painful state of affairs. The problem was between her and Dominic, and at all costs she wanted it to stay that way.

She sighed heavily. Perhaps she should just accept her fate and resign herself to being an unloved, neglected wife with a philandering husband who treated her kindly and generously. She shuddered at the vision of the long, empty, joyless years stretching before her.

If only there were some way to catch Dominic's interest. To make him look at her with new eyes. To challenge him . . .

Eyes narrowed in thought, she considered the possibilities, her mood beginning to lighten a little. The majority of men, even the most apathetic, tended to be extremely possessive of their wives. Did she dare hope that she could arouse a jealous streak in Dominic? And if he *did* prove to be jealous, could she build upon that particular unstable emotion? It could be a dangerous and possibly foolish path that she was thinking of treading, but none of the alternatives—meek acceptance or constant battles—appealed to her.

Nervously chewing on her bottom lip, she continued to ponder the situation, a faint glimmer of a plan occurring to her. If she were to act politely indifferent to his philandering and suggest that they *both* be allowed to pursue their own interests, provided, of course, that they were discreet . . . If he had the slightest flicker of feeling for her, wouldn't he object to such a distasteful arrangement? And if he did object, perhaps she could nurture his feelings of possessiveness into something deeper and more lasting.

Melissa was uncomfortably conscious that there was an inherent riskiness in her plan and that she was not following the wisest course. But Dominic's actions this morning had hurt her badly, and then there was her stubborn pride and a very real need to protect her newly acknowledged love for him. She was confused, jealous, hurt and angry all at the same time; considering that this was her first foray into the lists of love, she could be forgiven for choosing such a foolhardy method of attracting a husband's roving eye. With a sudden sparkle of mischief in her topaz eyes, she smiled faintly. She would neither argue with nor reproach her errant husband, but would let him believe that she had decided to follow the old adage—*what was good for the gander was good for the goose!*

Chapter Seventeen

DESPITE the misgivings she might have harbored about the wisdom of her plan, Melissa felt much better for having decided upon some course of action. She had never been one to repine and wring her hands, being far more likely to leap first and then look later, and so it proved on this occasion. But before she could put her desperate scheme into operation, she had to decide upon which gentleman of acquaintance she could safely embroil in her plan.

Her first choice was her cousin Royce, but since she had no intention of telling whichever gentleman she finally selected why she had so suddenly become interested in him, it made things a bit awkward. Royce, she admitted ruefully, would know what she was playing at the instant she fluttered her lashes at him. And she dared not choose someone who might take her attempts at flirtation seriously. She did not want to find herself in the ridiculous situation of having to fend off amorous intentions aroused by her seeming encouragement of them, nor did she wish to inadvertently cause some poor gentleman to think that she was truly in love with him. Having discovered how painful it was to love someone who didn't return that love, she was not going to condemn some unsuspecting devil to that same fate.

After selecting and discarding several gentlemen, including her previously rejected suitor, John Newcomb, she finally and reluctantly settled on Julius Latimer as her unknowing foil. Latimer was old enough and sophisticated enough to handle a flirtation lightly, and she strongly suspected that although he might have wanted her for his mistress, she had not touched his heart—nor could she. If he even *had* a heart, she thought darkly.

Latimer might have written her an exceedingly contrite and apologetic letter in an attempt to smooth over his dastardly actions, but Melissa wasn't about to forget those anxious days before Dominic's offer to buy Folly had saved her from the fate Latimer had planned for her. She didn't trust him one little bit . . . but she wasn't above entangling him in her rash scheme to make her husband jealous. It would serve him right, she decided with a spurt of righteous indignation, for having treated her so insultingly.

Melissa had no fear that she could keep Latimer at a distance when she chose to do so—she was far more adept at repulsing advances than she was at making them! But she was a trifle uneasy about using him in this way, astute enough to realize that she might set in motion events over which she had no control. If she could have thought of anyone other than Latimer with whom to embark upon an apparent flirtation, she certainly would have, but no one else presented himself to her mind. It would, she conceded unenthusiastically, have to be Latimer who became the object of her seemingly amorous interest.

After she had come to those conclusions, all that now remained was for Melissa to inform her husband of her decisions concerning the tenor of their marriage, and she grimaced. For one long, yearning moment she considered simply throwing her arms about her husband's neck and begging for his love, but eventually she put this from her mind. Beyond being a generous gentleman, he had never given any indication that he particularly cared whether his wife loved him or not, and she wasn't about to leave herself open to rejection by Dominic.

As the hours passed and she waited anxiously for Dominic's return, her resolve to fight fire with fire hardened. And by the time the clock struck the hour of four in the morning, she came to two rather unpleasant determinations: her husband of less than forty-eight hours really was *not* coming home this night, and she really had no choice but to go ahead with her reckless plan. Dry-eyed and miserable, she finally sought out her lonely bed.

Dominic would have given much to find himself in a lonely bed, any bed, for that matter, than the one in which he found himself. Which really wasn't a bed at all, merely a handy pile of clean straw on the ground.

He had spent the hours since he had parted so furiously with Melissa wandering morosely about the countryside, avoiding contact with his fellow man. No more than Melissa did he wish to involve others in their quarrel, and as no ready explanation for his presence alone in the neighborhood occurred to him, he had decided it would be best if he simply remained unseen by anyone. And since he had sworn to his shrewish wife that he would not be home this evening, he thoroughly intended to do just that—hence his rather uncomfortable bed of straw.

Longingly he thought of his soft feather bed with its clean linen sheets as he tossed and twisted, trying to find a position in which to sleep. But sleep proved impossible, and finally, hands behind his head, he gave up the pretense and lay there staring up at the star-sprinkled, black sky.

For the life of him, he could not understand where he had gone wrong or what he had ever done to deserve the position in which he now found himself. Married, which was bad enough, but married to a witch who both infuriated and enchanted him. And if he had ever envisioned being married, he had certainly not intended to spend his second night of marriage hiding like a felon in a bed of straw behind his own stable!

His sense of humor, which had deserted him since the argument with Melissa this morning, suddenly came forth and a smile twitched at the corners of his mouth. Lord, Royce and Morgan would tease him unrelentingly if they ever found out—which, he admitted wryly, was the least of his problems.

He could not blame Melissa for being upset about the scene with Deborah, and he acknowledged fairly that she had behaved far better than he would have if he had come upon such a seeming tryst. But the very fact that she *had* handled it so well depressed him—not even the hopeful suspicion that she had been jealous comforted him at the moment. If she cared even just a tiny bit for him, could she have acted so coolly? If he had found her in such a compromising position, there would have been little doubt about his reaction—he would have challenged the other man to a duel and then taken his errant wife home and made love to her so fully that she would *never* stray again!

Though the facts stared him straight in the face, he could not believe that Melissa had married him solely for money. Whether it was his pride or instinct, he did not believe that she could respond so freely to him and yet have no feeling at all for him. It *could* be simple lust that motivated her, but again Dominic could not believe that it was solely lust that had her warm and pliant in his arms. Lust was an emotion with which he was quite familiar; he had felt it for several women during his lifetime and had satisfied it on more occasions than he cared to think about, and he was quite certain that what Melissa and he had shared had not been mere lust. He would not name it, though, unwilling to look deeper into his heart, only willing for the moment to blame everything on Melissa's seemingly unpredictable, wayward willfulness.

When dawn came, his thoughts were no more ordered or clear than they had been when he had first lain down, and with a frustrated groan, he sat up, running a hand through his hair. Well, he could not delay his return home any longer, and as he rose to his feet and ripped off his crumpled cravat, he decided that with his unshaven jaw and straw-covered, wrinkled clothing, Melissa was sure to think that he had spent the night in a drunken stupor somewhere. At least, he thought with a cynical smile, she can't possibly believe that I spent the night in the arms of another woman.

If the servants thought it strange that the master of the house, a bridegroom of less than forty-eight hours, should return home in such a bedraggled condition, there was no sign of it; not by as much as a lifted eyebrow did the new butler who opened the door, nor the upstairs maid Dominic passed on the stairs, betray surprise as he entered the house and made his way to his room. Even his English valet, Bartholomew, who had been with him for years, did not venture a comment as he helped Dominic undress a few minutes later.

His long, sallow face perfectly expressionless, Bartholomew asked with suspect meekness, "And will you require a bath now, sir?"

Dominic sent him a wry look. The two men had been together since Morgan, on Dominic's twenty-second birthday, had decided that it was time his younger brother gained his own gentleman's gentleman. Dominic had been dubious about the idea, especially when it turned out that Bartholomew was a nephew of Morgan's own valet, Litchefield. And since Litchefield inspired a sensation close to terror in young Dominic, he had been less than pleased to have one of his relatives foisted off on him—especially in the guise of a present! But despite his early misgivings, the arrangement had worked surprisingly well; Bartholomew, in spite of his melancholy features, proved to be a rather amusing fellow and, more importantly, one who was able to gauge his master's moods with an uncanny accuracy.

While Litchefield was short and stout, Bartholomew was tall and thin. He kept his dark, lank hair neatly clubbed, and his one vanity was a slim, impeccably trimmed black mustache. He affected a suit of plain, unrelieved black clothing which did nothing for his sallow complexion, and one was inclined to overlook him completely, unless the more discerning person happened to look into Bartholomew's dark, lustrous eyes. They were very knowing eyes, but they also held warmth and amusement, and those qualities far more typified Bartholomew than any others—although Dominic, when nursing an aching head from a night of deep drinking, had been known to refer to him as "that damned, dark cadaver!" Still, the two men were very close and enjoyed something more than merely a master-servant relationship. A fact that was instantly obvious when Bartholomew twitched his long nose and answered his own question by murmuring, "Ah, yes, I can smell that you do." With a measured tread he left the room to oversee the preparations as were needed for the master's bath.

Watching him leave the room, Dominic grinned. It was good to have Bartholomew in residence once again, and he wondered what would have happened that night at the tavern if Bartholomew had been traveling with him rather than tending to odds and ends in New Orleans. Who knew?

Kicking off his boots, Dominic relaxed back on the bed, relishing the thought of his bath.

Actually, it was some hours before Dominic had his bath. When Bartholomew returned, he found his master deeply asleep, and noting the dark circles under the eyes and the haggard lines which had only recently apeared, he quietly withdrew. But with that uncanny ability of his, Dominic had barely awakened from a long, refreshing sleep when Bartholomew appeared at the side of his bed and said, "Your bath is ready, sir."

Consequently, when Melissa and Dominic finally faced each other again, he was feeling greatly rejuvenated, which could not be said for Melissa. While he had been sleeping blissfully in his room, she had been pacing the floor, trying to gather her waning courage before confronting her husband and telling him that she saw nothing wrong with their seeking separate pleasures!

She was not happy with her course of action, but she could see no other that she could take. And there was the frail hope that if he saw her paying attention to another man, it might arouse some sort of possessive spark within him. Yet she hesitated to put her plan in action. She had made so many mistakes in dealing with Dominic that she was terrified of making another one, one that could drive a final wedge between them. If only she had not sent him so cruelly from her bed. What did it matter if he didn't love her—at least it would be *her* bed in which he slept! And why, she wondered wretchedly, couldn't I have let him know that I *had* changed my mind?

She pulled a face. She knew the answer to that question—pride and a strong sense of ill-usage. She could hardly have capitulated and agreed to share his bed again only moments after finding him with another woman—particularly since he'd made it clear it didn't matter to him one way or another! But ultimately, Melissa knew that she had complicated the problem between them, and she was sickly aware that she had inadvertently placed herself on a very high horse with no acceptable way of climbing down. No way, that is, except abject surrender, and she had not come to that point yet.

From Anna she had learned of Dominic's return and the

information that he was sleeping in his room. For one wild moment, she seriously considered going to his room and joining him in bed, letting her eager young body say what her lips could not. But then she turned away from their connecting doors dejectedly; after enjoying the charms of the beauteous Deborah all night, he wouldn't want her. . . .

A surge of jealousy shot through her at the idea of Dominic in Deborah's bed, and her despondent mood vanished. By Heaven, she would show them that she was no meek little mouse to be treated this way!

The topaz eyes flashing dangerously, she walked over to the armoire filled with the lovely gowns which Dominic had purchased for her. But with images of Deborah kissing Dominic searing across her brain, Melissa was hardly aware of what she was doing. Certainly she was not full of gratitude at this further sign of Dominic's unfailing generosity. Did he think that costly silks and laces could make up for an adulterous husband? she fumed as she scanned the expensive garments. Was he fool enough to believe that mere *objects* could console her?

A magnitude of emotions churned in her breast as she finally selected a gown, but mostly she was simply miserable. Trying to push away the lowering knowledge that much of her predicament was her own fault, she spent an inordinate amount of time on her toilet, letting Anna fuss over her, needing the added confidence of knowing that she looked her best when she finally faced Dominic. But even dawdling with her hair and attire, she found herself restlessly pacing the floor, wondering what she would say to him when they met. And although she was still resolved to stick to her plan, doubts about the wisdom of it had begun to creep into her thoughts. By the time Dominic finally joined her in the small sitting room at the front of the house, she was wavering between a desire to furiously denounce him for his bestial behavior and an equally strong desire to seek some sort of peace between them, all the pitfalls and foolishness of her plans to make him jealous having presented themselves to her—vividly.

Unfortunately, Dominic seemed intent upon playing the role of an errant, unrepentant husband, and strolling into the sitting room, he said mockingly, "Ah, there you are, my dear. I must apologize for having allowed you to spend so much time by yourself, but I'm afraid that last night's, er, activities expended all my energy." With interest, he watched her small bosom swell with indignation, completely missing the stricken expression in her lovely eyes.

His very actions sealed his fate, and turning away to hide her hurt and jealousy, she said with apparent airiness, "Oh, it doesn't matter. I am used to amusing myself—our marriage won't change *that!*"

That wasn't the reaction Dominic wanted, and he was conscious of a compelling urge to cross the short distance that separated them and kiss her so thoroughly that she'd never treat him with indifference again! With an effort he restrained himself, deciding that when he was through kissing her, he might very well throttle her for the havoc she had created in his hitherto well-ordered life. Almost resentfully, he glared at her, wishing that even now, with the suspicion that she had married him for his money tearing at his gut, he didn't find her so damnably attractive.

Melissa did look very lovely this evening, the high-waisted gown of pale lilac sarcenet, trimmed with black satin ribbon, complimenting her tawny coloring wonderfully, giving her complexion a pearlescent glow, intensifying the contrast of those startling black lashes against the jeweled hue of her golden-brown eyes. Even her hair seemed brighter in color, the tawny strands arranged stylishly in loose curls, divided by a tortoiseshell comb. But it was the gown which held Dominic's attention, or rather the sweet body it clothed, and appreciatively his gaze ran over the lovely expanse of shoulder and back that the low cut of the garment revealed. The flared skirt gave little indication of the slim hips and slender legs beneath its soft folds, but too well for his peace of mind could Dominic remember them.

There was an awkward pause, but Dominic recovered himself first, and deciding to test just how far her indifference went, he drawled, "How very accommodating of you, sweetheart. There are few brides who would be so understanding. I'm pleased that you are not going to be a jealous wife."

But I *am* jealous, Melissa thought furiously. I am so jealous I want to scratch out Deborah's eyes and make you oblivious to all other women except me! Concealing her inner turmoil with an effort, Melissa swung around to face him, and forcing her lips into a semblance of a smile, she murmured, "I trust that since I have proved to be most obliging in this matter, you will grant me the same prerogatives."

Melissa had not been able to hide every trace of her unhappiness, and Dominic, watching her closely, had known a second of hope when she had first turned to look at him, the jealousy she was fighting to hide clearly evident in the angry sparkle of the topaz eyes. Well, well, he had mused cheerfully, she is not as detached and disinterested in the possibility of my having spent the night in the arms of another woman as she would pretend. But he had barely been able to savor this encouraging discovery when Melissa's words sent an icy trickle down his spine. Did she mean what he thought she meant?

His face unreadable, the gray eyes hard, he stared at his wife. "And what," he asked in a dangerously soft voice, "do you mean by that?"

Melissa swallowed nervously, thinking that it was all very well to consider beating him at his own game and quite another to actually do it. Forcing herself to act nonchalantly, she shrugged her shoulders and replied, "Why, just exactly what it sounded like. We are both adults, and I see no reason for us to pretend that this marriage was what either of us wanted. And since our marriage was not by choice, I see nothing wrong in each of us seeking his or her own, er, companionship."

"*Companionship!*" Dominic spat, the expression on his handsome face making Melissa waver between fear and delight. He crossed the short distance between them, and grasping her shoulders, gave her an ungentle shake. "You're my wife, you little fool, and if you think that I am going to let you ride roughshod over me and plant a pair of horns on my head, you have badly mistaken your man!"

The golden hue of her topaz eyes very pronounced, Melissa lifted her head. Her heart beating fast as much from his violent action as from the powerful surge of hope that thudded through her at his words, she asked innocently, "Let me see if I understand you correctly—it is perfectly acceptable for you to seek the company of others, but it is not acceptable if I do the same?"

Acutely aware of the pit opening under his feet, Dominic smothered a curse. The little witch! How cleverly she had twisted his words! She also, he thought wryly, had him neatly trapped. Either he could confess that nothing had happened between him and Deborah and that he had spent the night sleeping *alone* in his own hay pile, or . . . He hesitated. Or he could tell her that she was driving him mad and that even the mere thought of another man touching her was intolerable to him. He would have liked to be able to do both, but Melissa's previous actions made it rather difficult for him. She had not been exactly encouraging, and the very fact that she had hinted at a desire to seek her pleasures where she might did not engender feelings of trust or optimism within him. He was not at all inclined to leave himself open to ridicule and what he suspected might be a nearly fatal blow to his uncertain heart by admitting at this moment that she had no cause to be jealous . . . that there was no other woman he wanted but the one in his arms right now. . . .

Unknowingly, his grip lessened, and there was a caressing quality to his fingers as they lightly kneaded her silken shoulders. The delicate moss-rose scent of her perfume drifted tantalizingly into his nostrils and he became tormentingly conscious of the warmth and nearness of her soft body. Memories of her nakedness pressed ardently against him flooded his mind and he could feel his body quickening with desire. He smiled mirthlessly. She was indeed a witch—in the middle of an irritating disagreement, she could effortlessly arouse him.

Both his hesitation and his smile made Melissa's heart sink. She had prayed for a sharp denial, but as the seconds passed and he remained silent, she felt something shriveling inside her. He was actually considering giving her license to pursue other men! she thought incredulously. She didn't want to believe he was that amoral, but as the silence stretched out and he simply continued to stare at her, she could think of no other reason to explain his behavior. She came very close to hating him in that moment and she fought the urge to slap his arrogant face and to scream at him that *she* was not inclined to act the part of a promiscuous slut—even if her husband chose to be a whoremonger!

To her utter fury, not only did it appear that he was contemplating making a mockery of their marriage vows, but suddenly, vibrantly aware of the change in Dominic's touch, of the sensuous gleam she detected in the gray eyes, she realized that he was attempting to seduce her! Disgusted, she jerked away from him and muttered fiercely, "Didn't Deborah satisfy your lusts last night? Must you subject me to more of your unwanted attentions?"

Dominic stiffened, the warm light in his eyes dying. "Forgive me!" he snarled. "I had forgotten how distasteful you find my touch. A pity you didn't have such scruples that night at the inn!"

Fighting back angry tears, Melissa glared at him. "At least I didn't commit adultery within twenty-four hours of becoming your wife!"

Her words cut through him like a knife, and the sight of her tears effectively killed his own anger. Words of denial hovering on his lips, he took a hasty step forward, his arms reaching out for her, but furiously Melissa avoided him, dancing nimbly away.

Roughly dashing away the humiliating signs of her distress, she said in a low, scathing tone, "Don't touch me! I never want you to touch me again—*especially* not after you have just come from another woman!"

Consideringly, Dominic stared at her. Although the situation was not to be made light of, he could not help the faint smile which tugged at his lips, and some imp of mischief drove him to murmur, "Just? But I assure you, my dear, that I have *just* come from the hands of my valet. If you wish to question him, I promise you that I shall make no objections."

Openmouthed, Melissa stared at him, unable to believe that he could tease about something this vital. It only confirmed her darkest fears—he had no feelings whatsoever for her! She meant nothing to him! Recovering herself instantly, she closed her mouth with a decided snap. The topaz eyes glittering with wrath, she said through gritted teeth, "I am pleased that you find this situation so amusing! I hope that you will continue to do so when I am the one who has spent the night in the arms of a lover!"

Even enraged as she was, Dominic found her utterly enchanting and he noted admiringly the furious gleam in the amber-gold eyes and the telltale flush that made roses bloom in her cheeks. But the notion of her taking a lover was not to be tolerated. His smile disappearing, he said unwisely, "There is only one lover you will ever find in you bed, sweetheart . . . and you are looking at him right this minute."

"Oh!" Melissa burst out indignantly, suppressing the foolish urge to tell him that he was the only lover she had ever wanted or would ever want. He looked so appealing as he stood there in front of her, the dark, curly hair carelessly brushed and waving over his forehead, the expertly tailored dark blue jacket fitting his powerful shoulders admirably and the form-clinging black knee breeches hugging the smooth muscles of his thighs. With his patrician features, laughing eyes, arrogant nose and mobile mouth, he was the embodiment of a maiden's dream. Unfortunately, Melissa decided bitterly, his handsome features hid a black heart, and she snapped, "You are arrogant and abominable! I wish that I had never laid eyes on you!"

"If it had been only your eyes that, er, laid on me," Dominic said dryly, "we wouldn't have found ourselves in this position."

Her temper soaring, hands on her slender hips, Melissa flashed him a scorching glance. In a voice of dangerous calm, she demanded, "Are you blaming me for this disaster?"

He lifted a thick dark brow. "You did come to my room that night at the inn and you did accept my advances. *Encouraged* them, as a matter of fact." His mouth twisted. "Something that you seem to have changed your mind about now that we are married."

It was the opening that once Melissa would have seized upon eagerly. While she could not explain away her presence at the inn that fateful evening, she could have at least made amends for her rash words of last night, but in view of his flagrant intrigue with Deborah and his obvious unremorsefulness, the words died stillborn on her lips. She would rather die than explain *anything* to him! Putting on her haughtiest airs, she said regally, "I see that we will gain nothing by continuing this unpleasant discussion. But before we part, I should like you to know that I do not intend to sit meekly by watching your antics with that—that woman! Since you have made it clear that you feel free to indulge yourself in such pastimes, I feel it is only fair that I have the same liberties."

Thoughtfully, Dominic regarded her, wondering how much of what she was saying was the truth and how much sheer bravado. Did she really want another lover? Or was all this outrage real and her professed intention to seek a lover merely a mask to disguise what she was truly feeling? Jealousy, perhaps?

Dominic wanted desperately to believe that it was pure jealousy that was prompting Melissa's actions, but he could not be sure—certainly during the time that he had known her, she had given him few clues to her inner emotions. So. Was she merely bluffing, hoping to provoke some sort of revealing action on his part? Or did she mean every word she said?

There was, he finally decided sardonically, only one way to find out. His voice carefully indifferent, he asked, "Since you seem to have expended a great deal of thought on the subject, has your fancy alighted on any particular man?"

His careless attitude was the final goad, and before she even realized what she was doing, she announced rashly, "Yes! *Julius Latimer!*"

Part Three

Of Intrigue and Desire

Pains of love be sweeter far
Than all other pleasures are.

Tyrannic Love
—John Dryden

Chapter Eighteen

THE TIME which passed after Melissa's announcement in the sitting room was rather peculiar. Dominic had gone pale at the mention of Latimer's name, and with a mixture of elation and fear she had watched, mesmerized, as he had marched up to her. Melissa had had no idea of the effect her words would have on him and she was totally unprepared for the depth of his reaction. Certainly she hadn't deluded herself into thinking that it was because he had any depth of feeling for her. It was something much more acute than mere jealousy that had prompted his words and actions.

Dominic's handsome features had been cold and set, and his voice had been icy as he had snarled, "If I ever find you in Latimer's arms, I'll kill him on the spot and then make you regret for the rest of your life that you ever even knew his name!" Without another word he had stalked from the room.

It wasn't precisely the reaction that Melissa had yearned for, but she tried to console herself by clinging to the thought that at least he had not laughed at her, nor had he been indifferent. It was small comfort, though, and she had been dreading their next meeting, wondering how he would treat her—coldly, indifferently, or pretending the incident had never happened?

Dominic chose the latter path, and Melissa could not decide whether she was dissappointed or grateful. Joining her the next morning in the small breakfast room, he greeted her cordially and, to her astonishment, actually spent part of the day at her side. No mention was made of the ugly scene of the previous night, and while she waited nervously for him to make some comment or raise the subject again, he did not. Instead, he acted like any new husband, showing his bride over the premises, calling her attention to changes that could be made and soliciting her opinion on renovations he planned.

Bewilderedly Melissa followed his lead, occasionally even allowing herself to forget for several minutes at a time the seemingly insurmountable obstacles that lay between them. At first she was optimistic about the state of affairs—if he was spending the majority of his waking hours with her, he couldn't very well be seeing the odious Deborah, could he? And since she now had his attention, perhaps she could begin to smooth over their disastrous beginning and create some sort of lasting harmony between them.

It took almost a week before she realized that she had nothing to be optimistic about. Dominic might not, at present, be continuing his flagrant meetings with Deborah, but he certainly did not seem at all inclined to pursue his wife either! He was so polite to Melissa that gradually she began to feel like a visiting guest, rather than the lady of the house.

He had subtly withdrawn from her; no longer were there any teasing smiles, and the expression in those eloquent gray eyes remained the same—coolly polite, no hint of the sensual glitter that could make her heart beat fast, no indication of a passion barely leashed. He was extremely careful in the way that he touched her, his hand lingering not one second longer than necessary on her arm as he escorted her about the grounds, and Melissa tried to convince herself that this was exactly what she wanted. Hadn't she told him *not* to touch her? But since he was now doing precisely as she had requested, why was it making her so unhappy?

Not only did he appear to want little physical contact with her, he also, she observed miserably, swiftly turned the conversation away from anything remotely personal, and so her few uncertain attempts to discuss their difficulties were smoothly brushed aside.

By the time another week had passed, she was acutely

dejected, certain that she was condemned to spend the rest of her life tied to the cool, austere creature Dominic had become. She was so dejected, in fact, that she had even managed to make excuses for his apparent affair with the beauteous Lady Deborah, berating herself for having acted so hastily and wrongly on their wedding night. Wistfully, her eyes would follow his broad-shouldered form about, and she yearned for the chance to start anew. How differently I would act, she thought forlornly. I would control my wretched tongue. And my lamentable temper. I would try to be more understanding. Less inclined to leap to conclusions . . .

The situation was not any easier for Dominic, particularly since he would have liked nothing better than to encourage Melissa's tentative advances. But the murderous rage which had exploded through his body at the mere thought of Latimer even touching her had shocked him, making him realize that what he felt for Melissa was no passing fancy. He had never been possessive of a woman in his life, and to discover that she aroused such primitive, uncontrollable emotions within him had been a confounding experience.

After leaving Melissa in the sitting room that evening, he had spent another sleepless night, this one, at least, in his own bed, where he had lain staring blindly at the canopy overhead, his thoughts chaotic and rambling. He had made all manner of excuses to explain away his behavior, but even though he was eventually able to rationalize things to his satisfaction, he was left with the uneasy sensation that he was only fooling himself. Melissa had enraged him and befuddled him from the moment he had first seen her, and he finally decided, with great distaste, that her suggestion on their wedding night that they become more acquainted with each other before plunging into physical intimacy had not been the ridiculous notion it had seemed at the time. Besides, he conceded grimly, she had made it quite clear she didn't want him in her bed! And for the present he was willing to respect her conditions, infuriating though they were.

A bit of breathing room, he admitted reluctantly, is what we need. Some time to learn more about each other . . .

time to discover if she did marry me for my money . . .
time to discover if she does have some feeling for me. . . .

If he could maintain an air of sedate politeness, perhaps
he would be able to discover a way to make their marriage, if not happy, at least bearable. But how, he wondered, was he going to keep his hands to himself when
every nerve in his body tingled with pounding desire
whenever she was near him? He snorted. He was deluding
himself. It wasn't just her nearness—she didn't even have
to be in the same room with him for him to react to just
the *thought* of making love to her! But conceding that a
bout of chastity might do them both some good, he grimly
resigned himself to the part of pleasant host.

It was not a role he relished playing, but Dominic had
always been a man in full control of his emotions, and he
needed, just now, to prove to himself that he was perfectly
capable of behaving with his usual, well-known sang-
froid—no matter how much he might desire Melissa, nor
how ridiculous the situation. She's my *wife,* for God's
sake! he thought irritably, and I should be able to make
love to her if I want! But to his intense annoyance, an
unwelcome voice whispered in his brain: *But she doesn't
want you. . . .*

The days that had followed were a curious blend of delight
and agony for Dominic, Melissa's tremulous attempts to
breach the distance he had deliberately created between them
putting a tremendous strain on all his good intentions. In the
beginning it had not been difficult; he had been too angry
and, yes, hurt about her threat to take Latimer for a lover to
either encourage or discourage her overtures of peace. But
as the days had passed, he had found it harder and harder to
maintain his aloof posture.

While he played his role of polite host, they had spent
many hours exploring the property adjoining the house,
and quite a bit of time had been idled away abstractedly
discussing the plans for the outbuildings that would be
built to accommodate whatever animals would be housed
here instead of at Thousand Oaks. Gradually, though,
Dominic's iron control slipped, and he was angrily conscious of a thawing on his part; all too soon, as they were
talking about additions to the cottage one afternoon, he

caught himself thinking Melissa utterly enchanting when she blushed charmingly at his matter-of-fact mention of a nursery wing. He felt light-headed for many minutes after, finding the idea of being the father of Melissa's children vastly appealing.

The long summer evenings might have been the hardest to get through if they hadn't been able to while them away by speculating about the various lines of the different horses Dominic owned and the possible impact Folly's breeding would have upon the resultant offspring. They spent an inordinate amount of time talking about horses, as much because it was a safe subject as the fact that they were both "horse-mad." To his pleased surprise, Dominic discovered that Melissa was indeed very knowledgeable when it came to prime horseflesh and was not the least hesitant about stating her opinion.

"How can you dismiss the Godolphin Barb's get so cavalierly?" she had demanded one night as they had sat on the gallery, arguing enjoyably about the history of Thoroughbred horses. "Look at Cade. And what about his son Matchem? They've all contributed hugely to the breed." Shaking her head, she had said decisively, "Your comment that the Darley Arabian has had the most effect has yet to be proved."

He was impressed by the amount of information she had learned over the years, particularly when he considered that she had never traveled widely, and then just to race meets. Seeing the wistful expression that crossed her lively face when he had talked about attending the Derby at Epsom in England, he vowed to himself that once this blasted war with England was over, he would take her there to see that greatest of horse races at the first opportunity.

But although she was passionately interested in horses, she wasn't, he found out to his amusement, particularly obsessed with the fripperies and gowns that commanded the intense interest of many of his female acquaintances. She had thanked him very prettily for the lovely things he had bought for her, and though he had few doubts that she was grateful for them and enjoyed wearing the beautiful garments, seeing the blithe disregard with which she treated her apparel made it quite clear to him that she would have been perfectly happy in the dowdy gowns in which he had first seen her. He supposed that he should be thankful that he would not be receiving exorbitant bills for trunkloads of feminine furbelows which would seldom be worn at Thousand Oaks with its limited society, but her reaction left him even more bewildered. She was *not* behaving like the mercenary little witch he had named her.

As for housewifely zest, Dominic found out immediately that his bride wasn't the least bit concerned with the running of the household. As long as eatable food appeared at reasonable hours and the house was maintained in a tolerably clean manner, she seemed perfectly content. Always having had an impeccably run household, Dominic prided himself on having had the excellent foresight to hire a competent housekeeper and staff. Left to Melissa's tender mercies, he was positive that he would dine frequently on stale bread and moldy cheese in a dining room decorated with cobwebs and dust!

Watching one warm, inviting morning as Melissa's tapping foot betrayed her impatience to be off while the housekeeper, Mrs. Meeks, went over the daily tasks to be done about the premises, Dominic had to turn away to hide his amusement. Melissa was obviously more interested in trying out the new mare he had purchased for her than in whether the house was properly run! And it came as no surprise to him when she smiled sunnily at Mrs. Meeks and said cordially, "Mrs. Meeks, I leave it all in your capable hands. *You* decide on today's menu. And as for the other things, I'm certain that Mr. Slade and I will be *most* satisfied with the way you carry out your duties."

Putting her arm confidingly in Dominic's, she glanced up at him. "Shall we go now? I know that the horses are waiting for us."

A teasing glint in his gray eyes, Dominic murmured, "Such a house-proud wife I have! Are you positive that you can bear to tear yourself away from the fascinating chores that Mrs. Meeks has outlined?"

Melissa looked enchantingly guilty. Doubtfully she asked, "Do you think that I should stay? Perhaps it is wrong of me to make Mrs. Meeks see to everything."

Dominic laughed. "My dear, that is precisely why I pay her the ridiculously high sum that I do."

Melissa's expression of guilt increased. "Oh, dear!" she exclaimed. "I hadn't thought of that! I am being most unthrifty, am I not? Would you prefer that I take a more active hand so that you wouldn't need her services?"

Giving her a thoughtful look, Dominic finally said gently, "If you were here at the house, then I would be deprived of your very charming company, wouldn't I?"

Blushing delightfully, Melissa nodded shyly, her heart thumping rather pleasantly within her breast. It was at times like these that she found it extremely difficult to believe him the womanizer she knew him to be, and she wondered wistfully how much longer she could hold his undivided attention. How much longer before he grew bored and began casting a roving eye about, searching for the next woman to enslave with his mesmerizing charm?

If Melissa had trouble reminding herself of Dominic's philandering propensities, he was having an equally difficult time reconciling the captivating creature who was deepening, day by day, the spell she had cast over him with the seemingly calculating hussy who had so cold-bloodedly trapped him into marriage. It was true that beyond that one night of ecstasy she had denied him the rights of a husband, but other than that particularly disagreeable fact, he could find no fault to lay at her door. She was a delightful companion—warm, amusing and unfailingly bewitching to him. Though he believed that she had married him for money, she displayed no signs of being a greedy harpy; if anything, the many gifts that he had given her seemed to make her slightly uncomfortable. She made no monetary demands upon him; had, at present, given no hint of being either impressed or attracted by his wealth. Surreptitiously, he had stared at Melissa time and again, puzzling over her motives for being in his room that night at the tavern, and because he could think of no reason other than his original assumption that she was determined to snare a rich husband, he came to the unpleasant conclusion that perhaps she was playing a game with him, deliberately trying to disarm him.

Grimly he admitted that she was succeeding beyond her

wildest dreams. He could almost believe that there was some other motivating factor that he did not know of that had caused her to place herself in such a damning position. *Almost*.

And so the days drifted by, Melissa hoping that she could hold her husband's fancy and mayhap woo him away from his libertine ways, Dominic thoroughly baffled and beguiled by his tawny-haired bride.

If they had been able to remain secluded in their own little world at the cottage, the misunderstandings they each harbored about the other would have been explained in a relatively brief time. Melissa had been bracing herself to come out and bluntly ask him about Deborah, and Dominic, driven half mad with longing to hold his wife in his arms again, had for the past few days been on the point of attempting a bit of gentle seduction to see if she was still determined to keep him from her bed. If she showed any signs of relenting, his next step would be to find out, if he could, precisely what her motives had been when she had agreed to marry him. But before either of them could take the first tentative step toward the other, the world in the guise of a servant from Morgan came knocking at their door. After presenting Dominic with a note, the man waited patiently for a reply.

Morgan had written that Jason would be departing tomorrow for Terre du Coeur, but before he left he wanted very much to talk to Dominic. Morgan was asking him and Melissa to dine at Oak Hollow that night.

Thoughtfully Dominic stared at the bold handwriting, wondering what had prompted this apparently urgent desire to see him by Jason. Apart from Jason and Catherine wishing to bid them farewell, he could think of no other reason. Shrugging his broad shoulders, he turned to Melissa and said, "My brother would like us to dine with him at your uncle's home tonight. Have you any objections to accepting the invitation?"

With mixed emotions Melissa considered the invitation. By accepting, it would signal the end of their privacy and she wasn't quite positive that she was ready for that; these days alone with Dominic had become precious to her and she didn't want them to end. On the other hand, they could not remain sequestered from the world forever, and sending him a smile, she replied lightly, "No, of course not. I'd be delighted to see your brother and his wife again."

Dominic had half hoped that she would not wish to break their sylvan isolation. Once it became known that their self-imposed, supposedly romantic seclusion was over, he was certain that they would be the recipients of numerous invitations, everyone wanting to entertain the new bride and groom. And yet he almost welcomed the end to this charade—being cloistered in such an intimate setting with a woman he desired passionately, but dared not possess, was becoming increasingly wearing on all his good intentions. It would almost be a relief to join the company of others. At least that way, he told himself wryly, when the urge to make love to her became nearly overpowering, he could seek distraction amongst his acquaintances. Then, too, it might be just as well to have the opportunity to observe his young wife in less intimate surroundings. Perhaps by her actions as she mingled with her family and friends, he might be able to settle the ugly controversies that raged in his own mind—was she a calculating, grasping doxy who had married him for what she had gained, or was she the utterly beguiling creature whose image drifted seductively through his dreams?

Only time would supply the answer to his dilemma, and resignedly he found some ink and paper and wrote an affirmative answer to Morgan's note. Watching the servant ride away, he frowned. Somehow he didn't think Jason's request to see him was one of mere politeness. He sure as hell hoped that Morgan and Jason weren't going to embroil him in some sort of political intrigue, but even as he and Melissa left the cottage that night to drive to Oak Hollow, he could not shake the uneasy feeling that whatever Jason wanted to see him about, he wasn't going to like!

He wasn't wrong, but he was surprised at the direction of Jason's thoughts. Dinner had been most pleasant—Josh, an affable, congenial host; Sally, serene and slightly bemused as usual; Royce, amusing; Morgan and Leonie affectionate; Jason and Catherine, charming; and the inclusion of Zachary, a welcome and not unexpected guest.

It was only afterward, when Jason, having made previous arrangements with Josh, commandeered the library at Oak Hollow, that Dominic discovered the reason for the dinner. There were only four gentlemen in the library, Royce, Dominic, Jason and Morgan, and as they sipped appreciatively on some of Josh's finest brandy, Royce remarked, "What did you tell my father and Zachary to make them so willing to leave us alone?"

Jason smiled, his dark face sardonic. "Merely that I needed to discuss something of great governmental importance with you."

Dominic grimaced. "And have you really something of 'great governmental importance' that Royce and I *must* know? Couldn't we remain in blissful ignorance?"

"Well, I haven't that much to tell you, but I'm hoping you two can tell *me* something." At the expression of wariness that crossed the faces of the two younger men, Jason's green eyes gleamed with amusement. "Rest easy, it is nothing very personal. I merely wish to know about the Englishman, Julius Latimer. I understand that you two are fairly well acquainted with him?"

"In a manner of speaking," Dominic conceded dryly, carefully setting down his half-filled snifter of brandy on a polished mahogany table. "But whether we can be of any use to you . . ."

Leaning forward from the comfortable leather chair in which he sat, his bold features intent, Jason asked, "What sort of a man is he?"

Without hesitation, Dominic said, "A scoundrel, a liar and a cheat."

He had barely gotten the words out of his mouth before Royce echoed them, saying bluntly, "Unscrupulous, dangerous and not to be trusted."

Jason's thick black brow arched. "That much of a blackguard?"

Two heads nodded in swift unison. But it was Dominic who spoke. "His reputation in England is not the best—it is only because of his family connections that he is, or was, tolerated by the ton. I'm sure what family he has breathed a sigh of relief when he came to America."

Morgan, who had remained silent up until now, entered

the conversation, asking quietly, "Your opinion of him is based on mere rumor and gossip?"

Royce and Dominic exchanged glances. "No," Royce said when Dominic showed no sign of explaining. "Latimer and your brother have faced each other on the dueling field—I was Dom's second. I don't think that you need to know all the reasons why they fought, but one of the causes of the duel was the fact that Latimer had vilified Dominic's character and spread some outright lies about him, painting him as a libertine and a fortune hunter and all manner of nonsense—so we *know* that he is a liar. As for the other . . . Dominic gave him a nasty wound and Latimer was carried from the field swearing all kinds of revenge. Something that might be discounted if it weren't for the fact that two days afterward, in one of the most select areas of London, *not* a place where one would expect to find rascals and thieves, Dominic was set upon by several rogues whose only intention seemed to be to kill him."

Morgan's blue eyes narrowed. "That doesn't prove that Latimer had anything to do with it."

Wearily, Dominic said, "No, but that seems to be the way in which Latimer works—no one has ever *proved* anything against him—there had been other, similar incidents connected with him. Fortunately for me, Royce and a few other friends showed up in time to save me from having my skull bashed in, and we were able to capture one of the bullies." His face reflective, Dominic went on. "He was a crafty fellow, and while he would not name who had hired him, he did admit that he *had* been hired to kill me and that it had been a 'fine swell' who had done so. Now, I don't go around making that many enemies, so we all came to the same conclusion—Latimer had to have been the 'fine swell.' "

"But you didn't question the rogue further?" Jason asked sharply.

Dominic shrugged. "We turned him over to the watch and he was taken to Newgate. We intended to, er, convince him to tell us the name of the man who had hired him, but the fellow just *happened* to get into a fight while waiting to appear before the judge and was stabbed to death.''

"I see," Jason murmured softly, absently rubbing his chin. "Our charming Englishman does not seem to be the sort of man one would like at one's back in a tight situation. . . ." He glanced across at Dominic and Royce. "Is he very wealthy? He has given that impression, and I would like very much to know how he manages to keep himself in such an elegant style so far from home."

Thoughtfully Royce said, "In England, neither Julius nor his sister had much of a fortune; it was common knowledge that both were hanging out for a rich husband or wife." Very deliberately, Royce did not look at Dominic as he continued. "His sister, Lady Deborah, was finally able to snare a wealthy old man, but it did her little good. When he died she discovered the estate was entailed, and she was left with only a small sum of money. As for Julius, I don't think he particularly wants to find his fortune in the marriage bed. In London it was the gaming halls that held his attention, rather than the sedate rooms at Almack's. He is a very good gambler, although there are those, myself among them, who would say that he is also a *very* clever cheat. I know what I say because I watched him one night gull a young cawker up from the country out of a sizable sum. And as for what Latimer may or may not have inherited from his uncle, Weatherby, gossip has it that the only thing he got from that estate was the gaming voucher of Hugh's . . . and a paid trip to America.''

Jason and Morgan looked blank at the mention of the voucher, and briefly Dominic and Royce explained about the debt that Melissa and Zachary had inherited upon their father's death. When they had finished speaking, Jason nodded his dark head, as if their words had confirmed some inner conclusion of his own. "So it would appear that our Latimer has found some way of living quite elegantly without any money."

His face sardonic, Dominic said dryly, "Well, that has changed—he was finally able to collect on Hugh's note."

"And," Royce added slowly, "he has not had to expend a great deal of money while he has been in this area—

he and his sister have been staying with Colonel Grayson down the river.''

"Ah, yes, Colonel Grayson," Jason murmured smoothly. ''The dear colonel who was once an officer in the King's Army and whose outspoken Tory sympathies caused him to be driven out of Virginia at the beginning of the War for Independence. A most interesting situation, wouldn't you say?"

Both Dominic and Royce were obviously startled as the implication of Jason's words occurred to them. "Are you hinting that you think that Latimer is a spy?" Dominic asked incredulously. "He would make a poor tool, I would think."

"Think again, my young friend," Jason replied tartly. "Unscrupulous, a liar and dangerous; these would be definite virtues in a spy. And his supposed advocacy of our cause would give him a perfectly legitimate, even admirable excuse to be here in the United States for the duration of the present unpleasantness with England. And since he appears to have unlimited funds, he is also able to move about the country at will, traveling here and there . . . visiting with this one and that. . . ."

His skepticism apparent, Dominic remarked sharply, "You have more information than that on which to base this theory of yours."

Jason grinned. "And I thought I was going to impress you with my omnipotency."

Gray eyes dancing with laughter, Dominic admitted, "Ten years ago, yes, but not now." The laughter fading from his eyes, Dominic said seriously, "Now tell us what you know."

"Actually very little, but it is because of a letter I received from our former President Thomas Jefferson that my suspicions have been aroused about Mr. Latimer's activities. It seems that from other sources Jefferson has been alerted about Mr. Latimer's discreet visits to many former Tories who since the war have ostensibly thrown their lot in with the Republic. The visits that most concern him, however, are here in Louisiana, where so many previous British officers have chosen to settle. Mr. Jefferson, as you know, has a great fondness for Louisiana. It was his administration that brought about the purchase of these vast lands, and he wouldn't want anything to happen that would see even a portion of these lands fall into British hands. . . ."

Being the intent focus of three pairs of eyes didn't faze Jason in the least, and in the suddenly tense silence that had fallen, he took an appreciative sip of his brandy. Then he said quietly, "If rebellion could be fomented here in the north to coincide with a British attack of the city of New Orleans, we all might find ourselves under English rule before we had time to realize what had happened. Defending New Orleans is going to be difficult enough, but if we have to fear betrayal at our back . . ."

The conclusion was blatantly obvious, and, his voice tight, Dominic growled, "I could kill him. Our dislike of each other is not so well known here." He threw Royce a cynical glance. "And while I have been advised to greet him politely, it still shouldn't be very difficult for me to find an excuse to challenge him to a duel."

"No," Jason said forcefully. "We don't want him dead—yet. We want to find out just how serious his activities really are and who may or may not be agreeable to his treasonous talk. We need you and Royce to keep an eye on him for us and to find out what you can."

Dominic pulled a face. "Royce will be far more likely to be of any help to you. Latimer would be suspicious the instant I acted toward him in a friendly manner."

"But you are quite friendly with the sister, aren't you?" Morgan asked slyly, reentering the conversation.

If it were possible for a man of Dominic's years and sophistication to blush, he did so. Feeling like a youth caught in a misdemeanor, he sat there helplessly wishing he could simply sink through the floor or forcibly deny Morgan's statement. A spot of dark red color burning high on his cheekbones, he muttered, "That was a long time ago. She is a mere acquaintance now."

"Ah, that doesn't seem to be my understanding of the situation," Morgan persisted lightly, the sapphire eyes alight with affectionate amusement. "At your wedding, I spent some time with the young lady, and she made it quite clear that she considered you a *dear* friend and that she had been overjoyed to make her reacquaintance with someone for whom she had once harbored, er, warm feeling."

Dominic was not about to discuss his relationship with Deborah with Jason and Morgan. His chin set at a pugnacious angle, he demanded, "And? Is it a crime to have known an attractive woman in the past?"

"Absolutely not," Jason said. "But since you cannot claim a friendship with Latimer, I would like to suggest that Royce attempt to insinuate himself into the Englishman's circle and that you concentrate on making yourself agreeable to the sister. She may not know everything that her brother is up to, but I am quite sure that she will prove a fount of interesting information about his activities."

Distaste was clearly displayed on his handsome face as Dominic asked levelly, "Are you suggesting that I commit adultery? That I start an affair with her?"

Understanding in his eyes, Jason said gently, "No. But it would be helpful if you could remain on good terms with her and keep your ears and eyes open. I realize that I'm asking a great deal of you, especially since you have not even been married a month, and I would not want you to do anything that would endanger your marriage, but if you could encourage Lady Deborah's interest in you and keep up some sort of sense of intimacy with her, I think that it would be a good idea." Commiseration in his voice, Jason continued. "I know that the timing is deplorable, but the situation is fairly urgent. If it is any consolation to you, this particular facade should not entail more than a few weeks, perhaps just a month or two of your time." When Dominic's face remained hard and set, his intense dislike of the proposition obvious, Jason added quietly, "Ask yourself whether you would prefer to participate in this unpleasant little charade for a short while or possibly see Louisiana lost to the Republic. . . ."

There really was only one answer to Jason's question, and, his voice harsh, Dominic snarled, "Oh, very well! I'll do it—I just hope to God that when this is over I still have a wife!"

Chapter Nineteen

IF MELISSA noted her husband's surly mood after the dinner at Oak Hollow, she wisely made no mention of it, but she was most curious about what the gentlemen had discussed. Perhaps even more curious since Josh and Zachary had obviously been banned from the discussion. Her tentative attempts to find out what they had been talking about had been met with such black looks of anger that her curiosity was even more aroused than it would have been normally.

Melissa had enjoyed the evening at Oak Hollow. She had been dreading this first public appearance since her wedding, particularly because the situation between her and Dominic was so unsettled, but whatever reservations or fears she might have held were quickly dispelled as she was enveloped in Josh's hearty embrace and he boomed out his pleasure at seeing her. Josh's greeting set the tone of the evening which followed, and she found herself relaxing and entering eagerly into conversation with the other guests; and since, except for Jason and Catherine Savage, the others were all members of the family, it was quite a lively and informal evening. Thinking back over it and how much she had enjoyed talking with Leonie and Catherine, she was a bit saddened to realize that in a few days her new friends would be leaving—Catherine and Jason, in fact, had bidden the newlyweds good-bye that evening, extending a warm invitation for them to come and visit at Terre du Coeur when time allowed. And all too soon, Leonie and Morgan would be returning to Château Saint-André in the southern portion of the state.

The next morning, as she and Dominic enjoyed a cup of fragrant coffee on the gallery at the front of the cottage, Melissa asked almost wistfully, "Do you think that we shall really visit Terre du Coeur and Château Saint-André someday?" The notion that Dominic might intend to sequester her at Thousand Oaks had not been entirely dispelled, although she felt certain that he would never be *deliberately* cruel to her.

His thoughts dwelling unpleasantly on last night's conversation with Jason and Morgan, Dominic replied testily, "It'll be a damned long time before I see that sly brother of mine and his crafty friend again, I can tell you!"

At Melissa's look of astonishment, he added hastily, "Merely jesting, my dear! If you like, we may very well spend our first Christmas together at Château Saint-André. The house at Thousand Oaks will still probably be only half put together, and I'm sure that you will enjoy shopping in New Orleans for some new furnishings and whatnots."

It was the first time that Dominic had mentioned Thousand Oaks in several days. Setting down her china cup, Melissa asked softly, "When do you intend for us to go to Thousand Oaks?" Shyly she added, "I should very much like to see my new home." Then, afraid that she might have slighted their delightful present abode, she said quickly, "Not that I am not quite happy right here!" Twisting slightly in her chair, she gazed with open pleasure at the front of the cottage. "It's such a dear little place, and I am sure that I shall miss it tremendously at times."

For reasons of his own, Dominic suddenly found the idea of going to Thousand Oaks immensely appealing, and pushing aside the thought that he might be acting in a craven manner, he said brightly, "What a splendid notion! I should have thought of it sooner! Of course you want to see your new home. We can leave just as soon as possible."

Nearly prattling with delight at the prospect of putting several miles between himself and Deborah Bowden and the danger she represented to his fragile marriage, he stated happily, "The house there is in utter shambles, but you can make up a list of the most immediate items that you need, and then we shall travel to Natchez and see what is available. You may buy whatever you like.''

Melissa might have been taken aback by his enthusiasm, but she certainly harbored no suspicions of an ulterior motive being at the root of his ready agreement to remove to Thousand Oaks. Her eyes alight with mischief, she murmured, ''You should not be so free with your promises—I may prove to be a very greedy wife!'' She had said the words in jest, but at the suddenly cynical expression that crossed his face, she wondered if she had been unwise. Some of her lightheartedness fading, she added quietly, ''You need not fear that I shall be a spendthrift.'' Her soft mouth tightened. ''My father's way of life taught me to be quite careful with money—I will not be wasteful with yours.''

The subject was dropped, but her words gave Dominic much to puzzle over, and leaving her a few minutes later, he walked away with a frown on his face. One moment it seemed that she was indeed a grasping harpy, and the next . . . A faint, tender smile tugged at the corners of his chiseled lips. And the next she completely disarmed him, making him believe that the ugly idea of marrying him for his fortune had never even occurred to her. Which, he wondered, not for the first time, was the real Melissa?

Deciding not to waste more time in fruitless speculation on her motive, he turned his thoughts to more pleasant topics, such as their removal to Thousand Oaks. It appeared to be an excellent solution to many of his problems—he and Melissa would be so busy making the house habitable, it would eliminate some of the strain that presently existed in this intimate setting . . . and it would place *him* out of Deborah Bowden's path. Which particular aspect of the situation appealed to him more was hard to say, and he was whistling cheerfully by the time he reached the small stables.

Unfortunately, his optimistic mood did not last, and before ten minutes had elapsed, as he rode toward Oak Hollow to tell the family of their plans, he realized reluctantly that he and Melissa could not leave for Thousand Oaks. To do so would be tantamount to ignoring a call to duty, and no matter how distasteful he found the prospect of encouraging Lady Bowden's friendship to learn what he could of her brother's activities—activities that could endanger his country—it was a task that must be done. How would he feel, he wondered heavily, if Jason's fears that Latimer was inciting rebellion here in the northern reaches of Louisiana proved to be true and he had blithely turned his back on the situation and run away to hide at Thousand Oaks? His mouth twisted. He had never run from a duty or a fight in his life, and resignedly, he knew that he could not and would not run from this one—no matter what strain it put on his marriage.

Perhaps it was just as well that they stay near Baton Rouge for a while longer, he finally concluded. Until he had settled all his own doubts about Melissa and her reasons for marrying him, it might be best if he allowed her to intrude no further into his life. Thousand Oaks was at present untainted by her presence; he had no memories of her there, nothing of her to haunt him, should she prove to be the calculating creature he had called her.

Then, too, it would be easier to observe her here, where her family and friends were and where she would be more at ease, less careful in their company, and he might discover some clue to explain her inconsistent conduct around him. Certainly she would feel less isolated, less cut off from all that she knew than she would in the half-tamed wilderness area of Thousand Oaks.

Not relishing having to tell Melissa of his sudden change of mind, particularly when he could not tell her *why* he had changed his mind, he sighed and slowly turned his horse around, riding back in the direction from which he had just come. He was, he decided irritably, going to be seen to be acting in as capricious a manner as his bride!

Leaving his horse in the hands of the startled groom, he walked unhurriedly toward the cottage, considering several different reasons to present to Melissa to explain his apparent erratic behavior, but none of them found much favor with him. And when he caught sight of Zachary's bay gelding and Royce's big chestnut tied to an iron hitching post near the corner of the house, his heart sank. Lord, he hoped that Melissa hadn't yet told her brother or Royce about going to Thousand Oaks! His dismay increased even further as his gaze fell upon a jaunty cart of scarlet and yellow and the dainty black mare which pulled it standing securely tied in the shade of one of the big oaks at the front of the house. It would seem that in his brief absence company had arrived, and he smothered a curse under his breath.

Not having recognized either the cart or the horse, he was curious about the owner. He had known that as news of their attendance at dinner last night at Oak Hollow spread through the countryside, the privacy afforded them during the first weeks of marriage would vanish, but he had hoped that he and Melissa would still have some time to themselves before company came calling to wish them well. It would seem, he thought dryly, that he was wrong.

As he quietly entered the house, a sudden prickle of unease slid down his spine. Beyond the family, there was only one other person he knew who might be brash enough to come calling so soon, and he wasn't precisely surprised when he walked into the main salon and discovered Deborah Bowden sitting on the tapestry sofa, fastidiously sipping a cup of freshly brewed tea. Zachary was lounging in a damask-covered chair which looked exceedingly fragile under the weight of his powerful body, and Royce was standing near the fireplace, one arm resting negligently against the mantel. Melissa, her expression polite and wary, was sitting directly across from Deborah, and at Dominic's entrance she looked up at him with a mixture of relief and something else that made him decidedly uneasy. His bride, it would appear, was not pleased with the situation either, and if he read the signs right, he was going to find himself in a *very* uncomfortable position.

Smiling warmly at the room in general, Dominic said lightly, "How nice to see you all." Looking directly at Royce, he added, "I was on my way over to see you this morning when my, er, stirrup broke and I had to return. We must have just missed each other on the road."

A sardonic gleam in his eyes, Royce murmured, "How fortunate that you have returned. Melissa was just regaling us with the news of your imminent departure."

Zachary, looking very handsome in a snug-fitting coat of bottle green, said with a grin, "Yes, and my sweet sister has just invited me to come with you—I hope you don't mind?''

Inwardly groaning, Dominic smiled faintly and was just on the point of trying to extricate himself from what was becoming a stickier situation moment by moment when Deborah set down her cup of tea, and rising to her feet, ran girlishly across the room to him and said breathlessly, "Oh, Dominic, do say that you will change your mind and stay for a while!" Sending a limpid glance in Melissa's direction, she continued softly. "I have barely gotten to know your bride, and if you whisk her away so soon, we shall not have a chance to become friends."

Turning away from Dominic, her blue silk gown floating behind her, she drifted over to where Melissa sat. Patting her lightly on the shoulder, she murmured, "She is such a dear creature, and I think it is unfair of you to take her away to that wretchedly remote plantation of yours. She would much prefer to stay here, I am sure."

The expression on his face revealing nothing, Royce said carelessly, "I do think that Lady Bowden is correct— you *should* stay here for a bit longer." Casting Dominic a meaningful look, he added, "There are certain demands on your time which you could not meet while at Thousand Oaks."

"See!" Deborah cried gaily. "Even Royce thinks that you should stay!" An entreating smile on her face, she danced over again to Dominic. "Oh, *do* say that you will remain here a while longer!"

Cursing Jason, Royce and Deborah, Dominic kept his eyes averted from Melissa and said half angrily, half laughingly, "Oh, very well! We shall remain here a bit longer." Risking a glance in Melissa's direction, he asked gently, "That is, if my bride does not mind?"

A polite smile was frozen on her lips, but Melissa said with outward graciousness, "Why, of course, my dear! Whatever you please." Only Dominic noted the outrage and, yes, pain in her golden-brown eyes, but he could do nothing at the moment to alleviate either.

Having accomplished what she had set out to do, Deborah returned to her seat on the sofa, and smiling happily, she chatted away. "Oh, it will be so wonderful. We shall have picnics and go for drives along the river and do all manner of pleasant things.''

"Is that what you were doing this morning? Driving along the river?'' Dominic asked as he helped himself to a cup of tea, wishing it were strong, burning whiskey.

Deborah looked demure. "Well, not exactly . . . I was just out for a morning drive when I remembered that I had left one of my gloves at Willowglen the other day. When Zachary realized that I was all alone, he *insisted* upon escorting me on my drive. We met Royce on our travels, and when we learned that he was coming here we thought it would be nice to join him.''

"Well, I for one am disappointed that Melissa and Dominic are not going to Thousand Oaks. I was quite looking forward to seeing the place,'' Zachary said, a troubled expression in his eyes as he glanced at his sister.

"Oh, Zachary!'' Deborah cried with a pretty pout on her lips. "How could you think of going off and abandoning me that way?''

Zachary laughed self-consciously and made some idle comment, and the conversation moved on to other topics. A short while later, bidding her first guests good-bye, Melissa decided ruefully that she deserved some sort of award for polite behavior under duress. If she had had to listen to Deborah's artless prattle one moment longer . . . If she had had to watch her brother stare besottedly in Deborah's direction one more time . . . And if she had had to sit there smiling, acting as if nothing in the world were wrong, while her husband let that, that *hussy* wind him around her finger . . . Her bosom heaved and some very unladylike thoughts were whirling around in Melissa's head as she watched the trio disappear down the long driveway.

Any doubts she might have nurtured that Dominic's meeting with Lady Bowden had been innocent, or any hopes she might have had that there was nothing between the two of them, had been shattered the instant Dominic had allowed himself to be talked into staying here near Baton Rouge . . . and Deborah Bowden. Of course he didn't want to go off and leave his mistress, she thought viciously, her slim fingers clenching into two fists at her sides. Uncertain which of the two she wished to wreak violence on first, Melissa angrily swung around, the glint of battle shining brightly in her topaz eyes.

One thing had become crystal clear to her. Dominic might not love her, he might even have been compelled to marry her, but she could not simply give him up—certainly not to Deborah Bowden! At least I *care* about him, she told herself forlornly, and if he'll let me, I'll make him an exemplary wife. I'll *try* to be an exemplary wife, she amended, unhappily conscious of her wayward temper.

Melissa would be the first to admit that she had made many mistakes during her brief marriage, but the situation was not an easy one for her. It was bad enough being married to a man one knew hadn't wished for marriage, but to have fallen in love with that man and to realize that there would always be other women who would attract his attention were indeed painful. If Dominic had loved her, if their marriage had come about under normal circumstances, if she had known herself loved by her husband, she was quite positive that she could have faced Deborah's threat to her happiness with equanimity, but as it was . . . As it was, not only was she going to have to fight for his love, but she would also have to engage an enemy who, if Deborah's antics this morning were anything to go by, did not know the meaning of fighting fair. She sighed heavily. The worst of it was, she didn't have a clue to how Dominic felt about the situation. Would he care one way or the other whether she vanquished Deborah or not?

Throughout the visit of the others, Dominic had warily observed his wife and he had been steeling himself to face her justifiable wrath as soon as the unwanted company had departed. Deciding that now was as good a time as any to let her vent her spleen, he said mildly, "Well, that was a pleasant visit, wasn't it? It was rather, er, nice of Lady Bowden to come to call on us."

Melissa stubbornly kept her face averted from him, thinking that she would like to tell him exactly how *nice* she thought it was, but instead, she replied woodenly, "Yes, wasn't it." Unable to control herself, in a voice dripping with sarcasm, she muttered, "I'm sure that since we shall no doubt see a great deal of *dear* Lady Bowden in the future, it is a good thing that she has taken such a wonderful liking to me, don't you agree?''

Dominic had to smother a laugh, although he could sympathize heartily with what Melissa must be going through. He turned her around to face him, one finger lifting up her chin, and murmured, ''Are you very disappointed that we are not going to Thousand Oaks immediately?''

Determined not to betray the agitation within her breast, and acting with a nonchalance she did not feel, she met his amused gaze and said with considerable aplomb, ''Of course not! It doesn't matter in the least.'' Continuing to appear indifferent, she added lightly, ''I shall probably always prefer here to Thousand Oaks—it was going to be difficult for me to say good-bye to all my friends.'' Putting on a dreamy expression, she murmured softly, ''It will be most pleasant to continue to visit with the young men . . .'' She gave a fleeting peek at Dominic's face. ''. . . and women, too, whom I have known since birth. I was dreading leaving them all so soon. I'm sure that several young men will be happy we are staying.''

She cast him a limpid glance, much in the way that Deborah would have done, and suddenly very aware of what she was playing at, Dominic was hard pressed not to burst out laughing at her excellent mimicry. The little witch! She was trying to make him jealous! He could understand very well what she was trying to do and she had his wholehearted enthusiasm, if she but knew it. Thinking that under different circumstances he would enjoy watching her antics a great deal, Dominic fought down the urge to take her in his arms and kiss her senseless.

But some of his enjoyment at this gratifying situation faded as he realized that the following days were going to be very tricky. How was he to win Melissa's heart—and he suddenly realized that he did indeed want Melissa's heart—when he had to appear to be fascinated by another woman? He scowled. Jason and Morgan had a lot to answer for, he decided grimly.

Seeing Dominic's scowl and mistaking the reason for it, Melissa felt her heart leap. Obviously the mention of other men in her life had not sat too well with her husband.

Good! Continuing with her role with increased excitement, she said gaily, "Since we are not leaving for Thousand Oaks any time soon, I suppose that we should have a party to let our friends and neighbors know that we are now receiving guests." She paused, sent him a demure look and added, "Of course we will be sure to invite Lady Bowden . . . and her brother."

His face expressionless, Dominic replied dryly, "Whatever pleases you, my dear. I'm sure that if you discuss it with Mrs. Meeks, she shall see to everything. All you will have to do is prepare the guest list."

Melissa had hoped for some sort of reaction from him at the inclusion of Latimer, and she was aware of a pang of disappointment at his calm, disinterested words. With less enthusiasm than she had displayed so far, she muttered, "Very well, then, I *shall* discuss it with Mrs. Meeks! Do you have any objections to next Thursday evening? A party of fifteen to twenty for dinner?"

With an eyebrow cocked at the slight bite to her words, Dominic shook his dark head. "No. Whatever you fancy, sweetheart."

Melissa could have stamped her foot with vexation. Then, her chin set at a stubborn angle, she swept regally from the room in search of Mrs. Meeks. Abominable man! she thought with irritation. She'd show him that she could act just as coolly and carelessly as he! Why, she might even smile and become very friendly with Lady Bowden!

After a series of meetings with Mrs. Meeks, the party was planned to everyone's satisfaction; the invitations were written and duly delivered by one of Dominic's servants. To Melissa's delight, everyone accepted immediately, and with a happy smile on her face she set about overseeing the preparations for her first party. She had not expected to feel excited about the affair under the circumstances, but she did, taking shy pleasure in the final results of all the eagerly discussed plans.

Since the weather was very fine and the dining room at the cottage was exceedingly small, it had been decided to hold the dinner party outside. To prevent the guests from being eaten alive by the swarms of biting insects which inhabited the area, with the help of several servants an elegant, exotic-looking room had been formed with hundreds of yards of gauzy netting hastily purchased in Baton Rouge. A long, white-linen-draped table had been placed in the middle of the structure, and several chairs had been borrowed from both Willowglen and Oak Hollow; although they did not match one another, the effect was quite charming. Silver bowls filled with fragrant gardenias graced the tables; garlands of glossy green leaves were artfully arranged near the bases. Gleaming crystal candelabra with tall, slim, cream-colored candles had been placed strategically in between the silver bowls, and on several small tables that had been scattered about the room more candles had been put. Lanterns had been strung from several of the magnolia and oak trees nearby, and the entire area had taken on a fairy-tale setting, causing the guests to exclaim with delight.

It was a predominantly family party, Zachary naturally being invited, as well as the senior Manchesters and Royce. Daniel Manchester, Royce's younger brother, who had been away visiting with his bride-to-be in Mobile, had come home for Melissa's wedding and had been included in the party. Morgan and Leonie Slade had also been invited, and with the exception of Lady Bowden and Julius Latimer, the remainder of the guests were old family friends and neighbors. As the evening progressed, Melissa's initial nervousness vanished, and to her astonishment, she actually found herself enjoying the party, forgetting for the moment that she was not the radiant young bride she appeared.

And she was radiant. Dominic, despite his best efforts, could not keep his eyes off her vivacious countenance, her tawny hair gleaming like sun-warmed honey in the candlelight, the creamy white flesh of her shoulders and bosom which rose above her low-cut gown of bronze silk taking on a golden glow. For tonight Anna had arranged Melissa's hair high on her head, a cascade of curls flowing onto one smooth shoulder. Dominic seemed fascinated by a lone little curl that rested in that delicate place where her shoulder and neck joined, and he spent a good part of the evening imagining his lips pressing against that same spot. So entranced was he by the erotic thoughts chasing themselves through his brain that he was unaware of half the conversation sent his way.

After dinner, deserting Zachary who had claimed her attention up until then, Deborah swam up to Dominic in a sea of rustling blue satin to claim his attention. Her wide blue eyes full of promise, she murmured, "Oh, Dominic! Do walk with me! The grounds look so inviting in the light from the lanterns that I feel almost compelled to go exploring. Do say that you shall come with me!"

"What a capital idea!" Royce concurred smoothly, and grasping Melissa's arm, he said, "Come along, my dear. Since Dominic is properly escorting your guest, it is my privilege to have you with me."

Any chance of Dominic's refusing Deborah's request had been neatly scotched, and as the other guests fell in with the suggestion, Dominic sent Royce a look that was *not* fond. Royce smiled angelically.

Whatever enjoyment Melissa had been taking from her highly successful dinner party vanished the moment Deborah laid a decidedly familiar hand on Dominic's arm, and blindly she allowed Royce to lead her from the gauzy room. Her heart a bag of stones in her breast, she walked through the warm, magnolia-scented night, the laughing voices of the other guests barely impinging upon her consciousness, her mind full of definitely ugly ways of teaching Lady Bowden the *un*wisdom of the commandeering other women's husbands.

Royce allowed her some minutes of silence and then he said gently, "Lissa, don't take it so much to heart. Any fool can see that Dominic would far rather be here at your side than putting up with the inane chatter of that simpleton. Have more faith in yourself . . . and in him."

Melissa stiffened and she shot her favorite cousin a markedly hostile glance. Under her breath, she hissed, "I should have guessed that you would stand up for him! Tell me, are you also willing to lie to me and deny that they are lovers?"

There was a glitter in her lovely eyes that gave Royce pause, and hastily pulling her into the shadows, he said, "Don't be a little fool! I know that it looks bad, but trust me—Dominic's apparent interest in Deborah is not what you think!''

Melissa laughed bitterly and jerked free of his hold on her arm. "Naturally! I never doubted it for a moment," she said with obvious disbelief. "Now if you will excuse me, I shall mingle with my guests—especially with the male ones!''

Impotently Royce watched her stalk away and for the first time he realized why Dominic had not been so keen on Jason's suggestion. Well aware of Melissa's volatile temper—he possessed a similar one himself—he didn't envy Dominic in his predicament. Smothering a curse under his breath, he hurried after Melissa, hoping that she wouldn't do something foolish . . . or dangerous.

Approaching the group that Melissa had joined, Royce was conscious of a sinking sensation in his chest. Jesus Christ! She *would* choose Latimer!

Her hand resting as confidently on Latimer's arm as Deborah's rested on Dominic's, Melissa was smiling warmly up into Latimer's face, the inviting expression in the glittering topaz eyes making Royce distinctly uneasy. And watching the lascivious avidity with which Latimer accepted her attention, Royce cursed again. If this continued, there was going to be hell to pay!

The group that gathered around Melissa and Latimer consisted of Morgan and Leonie, Zachary, Anne Ballard, the daughter of a neighbor, and Daniel Manchester. The conversation at the moment was about Daniel's nuptials, which were scheduled to take place in early November, and as Royce approached them, Daniel sent him a grin and murmured, "Well, old man, now that Dominic has been caught and I am to take the plunge in just a few months, can you expect to escape the parson's mousetrap much longer?''

Daniel was very like the Manchester side of the family, being a younger, slimmer version of Josh. His eyes were very blue, his thick chestnut-colored hair stylishly arranged à la Brutus and his manner confident and easy. He had a ready smile that sat well on his jovial features, and being the youngest in the family, he had always been greatly petted and pampered all of his twenty-three years. But he was possessed of such an amiable, even-tempered personality that he had not been the least spoiled by all the attention lavished upon him by his doting parents and siblings. From the expression on his face, it was quite clear that he admired and adored his older brother, and despite the dark look Royce sent him, Daniel laughed out loud, obviously not at all abashed by Royce's expression.

"And you," Royce retorted bluntly, "would be well advised to think twice before putting your head into the trap!"

Daniel shook his head. "Not me! Unlike you, I am eager to be married and set up my nursery. You can remain a crusty old bachelor if you like!"

There was a general titter of laughter since Royce, tall and commanding in his evening clothes of form-fitting dark blue jacket and black satin breeches, looked nothing like anyone's version of a "crusty old bachelor." The conversation became general after that, and winthin a few minutes, to Royce's frustration, Latimer and Melissa drifted away.

Melissa felt a momentary qualm as Latimer deftly guided them into a shadowy area that the flickering light from the lanterns barely penetrated. But then she gave a saucy toss of her curls. Her husband was so obviously amusing himself in some darkened corner, so why shouldn't she? It had been anger that had driven her to Latimer's side and it was anger that kept her there, even if every bone in her body yearned to be with Dominic— but a Dominic who loved her.

Although anger might have caused her to act rashly, it did not make her a fool, and the instant the obscuring darkness closed down around them, she stepped away from Latimer, her hand falling to her side. Like a wary young animal, she stood there in front of him, poised to run at the first sign of danger.

Noting her stance, Latimer said dryly, "I am hardly likely to pounce on you here, you know."

In the darkness Melissa flushed. "I realize that!" she replied sharply. "But you have to admit that I have little reason to trust you."

There was a long silence, as if Latimer were turning over several avenues of thought, before he said softly, "I've asked your forgiveness for my odious behavior. Is there nothing that I can do that will let us be friends again?"

Yes! Melissa wanted to scream. Take your sister and leave! Go far, *far* away and never let me hear either of your names again! But she could hardly say such things. Sighing, she muttered, "I don't know. I had thought that you were my friend, and then for you to act in such a despicable manner . . ."

"My dear! You must understand that I went a little mad. I was a fool—I freely admit it—and if I had not been so rash, so blinded by my desire for you, it is I who would now be your husband instead of—"

"Dominic," Melissa finished dully, the misery she was experiencing evident in her voice.

Taking encouragement from the fact that she had not thrown his words back in his face, Latimer very gently said, "I did try to warn you, my child. But you did not listen, did you?"

Momentarily overcome, Melissa glanced away, fighting the tears that unexpectedly threatened to fall. His apparent kindness was nearly her undoing. It would have been such a relief to share her misery with someone who understood Dominic's true nature, but loyalty, caution and an instinctive mistrust of Latimer's motives held her back. She had noted the look that he and Dominic had exchanged when Latimer and Deborah had arrived; she had felt the tension that had coiled in her husband's tall body as the two men politely traded greetings, and there had been little doubt that Dominic's dislike of Latimer had deeper roots than merely her professed interest in the other man.

Taking Melissa's continued silence for encouragement, Latimer stood behind her and laid a hand on her naked shoulder. "I never meant you any harm, my dear," he murmured. "It is true that my offer was a dastardly one, but if you will forgive me, I will try to be your friend and help you in any way I can." His voice taking on an emotional intensity, he added, "You can trust me . . . *I* would never betray you!"

Pride stiffened her shoulders, and in a distinctly cool voice, she asked, "Are you so very sure that Dominic will?"

A bitter laugh came from Latimer. "Can you doubt it? You forget that I have known him a long time—longer than you!" Swinging Melissa around to face him, he demanded harshly, "If you doubt the truth of my words, tell me—where is your husband now?"

"Mon Dieu!" exclaimed Leonie gaily behind them. "That is something that I would like to know myself." Pretending not to see Melissa's start of surprise or the misery in her face, Leonie went on lightly. "Where *is* that husband of yours?" Shaking a teasingly admonishing finger in Melissa's face, she continued. *"Petite,* you must treat these Slade men sternly, right from the beginning. Otherwise, they will rule you . . . just as Morgan does me!"

Royce and Morgan materialized out of the darkness from behind Leonie, and Morgan said with a grin, "She's absolutely right, you know—from the moment I laid eyes on her, she has commandeered my life."

Melissa made some polite rejoinder, the obvious happiness between Dominic's brother and his wife a twisting knife in her already wounded heart. And the pain became almost unbearable when only moments later, Dominic with Deborah clinging to his arm strolled over to join them.

Dominic's once-immaculate cravat was slightly askew, and Deborah's face wore such a look of smug triumph that Melissa had little doubt that they had just shared a passionate interlude in the darkness. She would have been astonished, however, if she had known that, far from sharing a passionate moment with Deborah, Dominic had spent the entire time drying to defend his honor, and his cravat had become disarrayed when he had somewhat forcefully jerked Deborah's clinging arms from around his neck and informed her harshly that he was a married man and would she please not be so forward in his presence!

Chapter Twenty

EXCEPT for the disagreeable necessity of having to suffer Latimer's presence and of having to act politely to the man he despised, Dominic had actually been enjoying his wife's first attempt at entertaining. Before their guests had arrived he had nicely complimented Melissa on her appearance, thinking to himself that he had never seen her look lovelier . . . or more desirable, and as the evening had progressed, he had allowed himself to be encouraged by her soft smiles and wistful glances. He had been quite pleased with the state of affairs until Royce had practically thrust Deborah into his arms and he had seen the stricken expression which had flashed across Melissa's face.

Well aware that common politeness prevented him from flinging Deborah's hand from his arm, and also well aware of the reasons behind Royce's actions, Dominic had grimly allowed Deborah to maneuver them into a secluded spot. Barely listening to her inane chatter, he had scanned the concealing darkness, hoping for a glimpse of his wife, and it was only when Deborah mentioned a name that he knew very well that she had his full attention.

"Roxbury? The Duke of Roxbury?" he demanded. "Jason's uncle paid your passage to America?"

Startled, Deborah looked up at him. "Jason? Who is Jason?"

Impatiently, Dominic replied, "My brother's friend . . . and the nephew of the Duke of Roxbury."

"Oh! Didn't I meet him at your wedding? A tall, distinguished man with very green eyes?"

"That sounds like Jason Savage, but how is it that you know his uncle, the duke?"

Giving an airy shrug, Deborah ran a caressing hand up his chest to his shoulder. "I don't know him—it is Julius who is acquainted with him." Forming her lips into a pretty pout, she murmured, "I don't want to talk about Roxbury or Julius. I want to talk about us. . . ."

Stifling a sigh, Dominic unobtrusively removed her hand from his shoulder and said very gently, "Deborah, there is no *us*. Once there might have been, but that is in the past—as I've told you repeatedly. You must not dwell on what happened in London; it was a long time ago."

Sulkily, she muttered, "Not such a long time ago, Dominic—less than four years ago."

"That may be, but times change. You married another man, and I am a married man now myself."

"How pompous you sound! Nothing at all like the ardent young man I fell in love with in London!" Deborah said with a slight edge to her voice.

"If you fell in love with me, then why did you believe your brother's lies about me? And loving me, why did you marry Bowden?" Dominic retorted, slightly stung at being called "pompous."

Dropping her gaze, she moved her hand restlessly along his arm. "I didn't want to believe him, but he *is* my brother and I didn't know you very well. You could have been every vile thing that he claimed you were. How was I to know?" she asked softly.

"Didn't your heart tell you anything?" he inquired sardonically, not really caring how she replied, but unable to think of a way to change the subject to the far more interesting one of why the Duke of Roxbury had seen fit to expend his gold on strangers.

"Oh, Dominic! I was young and unsure of myself—you were a brash American, so different from any man I had ever met. How was I to know that my brother's motives were not the highest? How was I to know that he wished me to marry that horrible old man?"

Increasingly bored by the conversation, especially since he had heard it all before, Dominic said coolly, "It doesn't matter, Deborah. You did what you felt was right at the time—there is no use pining over what is done with—I bear you no animosity about what happened in the past.''

''Darling Dominic! You have no idea how happy it makes me to hear you say that! I have brooded many an hour over the injustice of my actions and I was thrilled when Julius told me that we were coming to America— my first thoughts after hearing the news were of you.'' She glanced up at him, the blue eyes wide and pleading, her Cupid's bow mouth soft and inviting.

Unmoved, Dominic asked dryly. ''Were they, my dear?''

''Oh, yes! All I could think of was that at last I would see you again and that I would have a chance to make amends . . . and perhaps . . .'' She sighed heavily. ''But it was not to be. You were engaged to be married, and Roxbury's generosity came to naught.''

Pleased that Roxbury's name had been introduced once again, Dominic said quickly, ''I am most curious how it was that Roxbury came to arrange your passage here, and at a time of war between our two countries. It is most peculiar.''

An expression of annoyance flitted across her perfect features. ''Not so peculiar when you understand that old Weatherby and the duke were close friends. When Roxbury learned that Julius' inheritance was here in America, he very kindly offered to pay our way. He said he was doing so because he believed that it had been an oversight on Weatherby's part not to have left us the money to reach here.''

Keeping his face carefully bland, Dominic listened to her tale with growing astonishment. Of all the cock-and-bull stories that he had ever heard! He didn't know Roxbury intimately, but having observed the older man when in London and having heard tales from both Jason and Morgan on Roxbury's machinations, he had come to the firm conclusion that Roxbury *never* did anything idly! Certainly, though the man was reputed to be generous, it sounded completely out of character for him to squander a large sum of money on virtual strangers to help them gain a dubious inheritance! But it was definitely very interesting. . . . With only polite inquiry in his tone, he asked, ''And money to live on? Where did that come from?

Not to touch on a delicate area, but I seem to recall that in London you and your brother were always rather hard pressed for money, and yet, since you have been here, money appears to be no problem for you.''

"How rude of you to mention such a thing!" Deborah cried angrily, her lips thinning unattractively.

"You're absolutely right," Dominic admitted, aware that in his quest for information he *had* been rude. "It was most ungentlemanly of me, but I could not help wondering about it.''

"There is nothing so very odd about it," Deborah said sulkily. "As you know, there are many people in America who still have a certain loyalty to the crown—who felt then and still feel that the War for Independence was a mistake. Roxbury is a member of a philanthropic organization in London which is most interested in the fate of those Britons who opposed the rebellion but remained here afterward.'' At Dominic's skeptical look, she said moodily, "I don't care if you believe me or not! It is true! Roxbury merely wanted Julius to talk to some of these people, and he was willing to pay my brother a handsome sum to do it! I think it is all very silly. Especially since nothing can be done until after the war.''

"Pardon? I'm afraid I don't understand.''

Deborah shot him an irritated look. ''After the war Roxbury's organization is willing to pay the passage home to England of any indigent, former British soldier so that the doddering simpletons can die in Britain. I told you it was silly!''

"Silly" wasn't precisely the word that Dominic would have used to describe the situation. Deborah was certainly silly if she believed one word of the nonsense that she had just spouted, and as for Roxbury . . . Dominic felt a chill slide down his spine. He'd wager his birthright that Roxbury cared not one whit for the fate of some elderly, former British soldier who wished to return to the land of his birth to die. But how clever to concoct a valid reason for his own man to call upon those men who had once sworn to serve the British crown. That sly, sly old fox! he thought with a mixture of anger and admiration.

Dominic couldn't be positive of Roxbury's motives and

plans, but he didn't believe for one moment that it had
been altruistic reasons that had prompted the duke to enlist
Latimer's aid. Still, it was a piece of information that they
had not possessed before, and eager now to discuss the
matter with the others, Dominic attempted to guide Deborah away from the little nook where they were standing.
Smiling heartily at her, he said glibly, "I agree with you
completely, my dear; it does sound rather silly. Now shall
we join the others? I'm sure that they have missed us."

"Oh, Dominic! You cannot mean it!" Deborah wailed,
and throwing her arms around him, she lifted her face to
his. "We have so few moments alone, and I cannot bear
to share you with the others just yet. Please, dear Dominic, kiss me once again."

Thoroughly uncomfortable and exasperated, Dominic
retorted sharply, "Good God, Deborah, I am a married
man! When will you accept that fact and stop creating
these embarrassing scenes. I do not remember that you
used to be so forward!"

With a less-than-gentle motion, he jerked her arms from
around his neck, thinking viciously that he'd like to put
Jason Savage in this position and see how *he* enjoyed it!
But mindful of the need not to completely alienate Deborah, he said more gently, "You are a very attractive
woman—far too attractive to waste yourself on an ineligible fellow like me." Smiling faintly at her, he murmured, "You must not tempt me, my dear."

Her ruffled feathers slightly soothed, some of the fury
died from Deborah's eyes and she asked coyly, "Do I
tempt you, Dominic?"

Relieved that she seemed to be taking his rebuff so well,
he said with complete truthfulness, "Oh, yes, you do tempt
me, indeed." What he didn't tell her was that she tempted
him to wring her neck!

Deborah seemed pleased with his words and there was
a decidedly smug smile on her face as Dominic guided her
over to the small group which contained Melissa. Dominic
might be married, but Deborah didn't see how that presented a problem; he was still the most exciting man she
had ever met in her life, and now that she was no longer
an innocent miss, she was determined to experience the

full power of his passion. Besides, Julius had asked her to remain on friendly terms with Dominic, and she had every intention of doing so to the extreme!

There had been a pleasant smile on Dominic's face as he had approached the group, but when his eyes fell upon Latimer standing so close to Melissa, his expression hardened and he was conscious of a strong inclination to snatch Melissa close to his side, to make it clear to everyone, especially Latimer, that Melissa was his! Unfortunately, that was a little difficult to do, considering that he had another woman clinging tightly to his arm and was surrounded by guests who would no doubt find his actions amusingly childish. Once again his thoughts of Jason and Morgan were not kind, not at *all* kind!

His already exacerbated temper was not helped in the least when Leonie, a determined glint in her sea-green eyes, leaned over and tapped him sharply on the arm with her ivory-and-gold fan. "For shame, *mon cher!* To desert your young bride this way at her first dinner party! What are you thinking of?" Turning to a frozen-faced Melissa, she dragged her forward and said half seriously, half laughingly, "You must not let him continue with his old tricks, *petite*. It is imperative that you make him understand immediately that his days of rakish behavior are over."

While the others watched with varying degrees of amusement and chagrin, Leonie stepped up to Dominic and in one swift, skillful movement disengaged Deborah's hand from his arm. In a voice of teasing reproof, she said, "And now, my dear Lady Bowden, you must not take up any more of his time. He has a sweet bride who commands all of his attention these days."

Before anyone could lodge a protest or even knew what she was about, Leonie had grabbed Melissa's cold hand and placed it firmly on Dominic's arm. Like a farmer's wife shooing chickens before her, she turned them around and pushed them away, saying merrily, "Away with you two! There is a wonderful golden moon shining above, and it is a perfect night for lovers. Go. Go and enjoy yourselves."

Having no other choice under Leonie's expert generalship, Dominic and Melissa slowly disappeared into the darkness. Her face filled with satisfaction, Leonie turned to look at the others. "Wasn't that very bad of me?"

There was a general ripple of laughter, although Leonie noticed that neither Monsieur Latimer nor Lady Bowden appeared to gain much enjoyment from it. But the approving gleam in Royce's eyes and the loving laughter in Morgan's dancing blue eyes were all she cared about. Deciding that it was time to follow her own excellent advice, she grasped Morgan's arm and murmured impishly, "Excuse us, *s'il vous plaît?* It *is* a night for lovers, and I wish to spend it with mine!"

The silence which fell in the wake of their departure was both angry and diverting—Latimer and Lady Bowden were barely able to conceal their anger, and Royce had found the entire situation wholly diverting. His voice full of suppressed amusement, Royce said, "I do believe that the newly named Duke of Wellington could have used Leonie's tactics against Napoleon, don't you?"

Her lovely face marred by a haughty expression, Deborah replied tightly, "She is certainly very forward! I do not believe that you Americans have any manners at all!"

"Perhaps not," Royce agreed amiably. "But if you think that way," he added slyly, "why do you punish yourself by remaining among us?"

Deborah flashed him a glance of active dislike and answered stiffly, "I should have said *some* Americans. There are many who are obviously aware of how to act in polite society, but Leonie Slade is not one of them."

"Oh, my! She really did ruffle your feathers, didn't she?" Royce observed with relish. Then, mindful of the fact that he would do their cause no good by unduly infuriating Latimer's sister, he smiled at her charmingly and murmured, "You must forgive me, Lady Bowden, for teasing you so—it is, I'm afraid, a *very* American habit."

Deborah sniffed disdainfully but did not return an answer. Instead, looking pointedly at her brother, who had remained curiously silent during this exchange, she commented waspishly, "I think it is time that we left—and I doubt that our host and hostess will think of us at all!"

Deborah erred in her assumption. Melissa was thinking quite a lot about the other woman, and her thoughts were not in the least bit pleasant—nor were the various grisly fates she had considered for *both* her husband and his inamorata. It was only by concentrating on the as-yet-undecided glorious revenge that she was going to take that Melissa was able to prevent herself from soundly whacking her despicable husband about the head and shoulders with the nearest weapon she could find. Rage like she had seldom experienced in her young life was billowing through her, and she was inordinately grateful for the concealing darkness and for these few moments in which to gather her composure before returning, like the good hostess she was, to her guests. As for her husband . . . Her teeth grated together with an almost audible fury. She would like to . . . Unable to think of any fate satisfyingly wicked enough for him, she stared stonily ahead.

If Melissa had assumed that her rage was not obvious to her husband, she was mistaken. Dominic was very conscious of the strong emotions that fairly radiated from her slim body, and he was certain that if there had been enough moonlight for him to see more clearly, his wife's form would no doubt be vibrating with suppressed fury. He didn't blame her for feeling the way she did, and a sensation of frustrated dismay washed through him. Somehow he had to make amends. Sending her averted profile an uneasy glance, he took a deep breath and began tentatively, "Melissa, I know that the situation looks damning, but I'd like to try to explain matters to you. Believe me, you have nothing to fear from Lady Bowden, and if I seem at times to prefer her company unduly, it has *nothing* to do with you!"

"Well, thank you very much!" Melissa burst out stormily as she swung violently around to glare at him, her normally topaz eyes a bright, burning golden color in her pale face. With fists clenched at her sides, she said hotly, "I don't think that I really want to hear any of your explanations! Your conduct this evening has made it clear that you care nothing for my feelings, and in the future you can be certain that I will care nothing for yours! Now if you will excuse me, I have guests to see to—something you seem to have forgotten!"

His own temper rising mercurially, Dominic's eyes were

equally bright with anger as he snarled, "Goddammit! Listen to me! I know it looks bad, but at the moment I have to—" He stopped abruptly, sickly aware of the fact that he had no idea if he could trust Melissa with the reasons behind his actions. If he were to tell her, and if she were to act in the manner of several women whom he could call to mind, it wouldn't take too long for word to reach Deborah's ears and then everything would have been for naught. Worse, Latimer would *know* that they were suspicious of him.

Foot tapping furiously, arms closed rigidly across her small bosom and her chin set at a stubborn angle, she inquired ominously, "Yes? You have to . . . ?"

It was obvious that she wasn't going to believe a word of what he said anyway. Dominic smothered a curse, dwelling lovingly on telling Jason Savage precisely what to do with certain intimate parts of the human anatomy! Feeling as if his cravat were going to choke him, he vented some of his thwarted spleen by snapping with frustrated rage, "It doesn't matter! In the mood you're in right now, you wouldn't listen to reason anyhow."

"And I suppose, if positions were reversed, you would?" she asked with deceptive sweetness.

"Yes! No!" he shot back harshly, uncertain whether he could ever act in a rational manner around this beguiling little shrew whom he had married. With difficulty he tried to get his fraying temper under control, and reaching for Melissa, he caught her shoulders and shook her gently as he said in a less heated tone of voice, "We can't continue this way . . . we must talk—"

It had been a mistake to touch her, as he soon found out to his cost. Melissa's frail composure snapped when he laid hands on her, and flinging aside his hold in one furious motion, she said in a voice of icy fury, *"Don't touch me!"*

If her composure had cracked, Dominic's fairly exploded at her angry words. Not touch her? When she was his wife? When he ached for her? When she filled his every thought? When he had lain awake night after night, his body burning with desire for her? Forgetting every promise he had made himself, forgetting that now was not the most propitious moment, allowing anger to give him the excuse he needed to break the bonds he had placed upon himself, he grabbed her upper arms in a secure hold and yanked her roughly against him. His mouth mere inches from hers, he breathed thickly, "Not touch you? You ask the impossible, madam." And his mouth came down crushingly on hers, his lips hard and demanding, permitting no escape from his fierce kiss.

At first too blinded by her flaming temper to feel anything but sheer rage, Melissa fought him, twisting wildly in his powerful embrace, her fists, doing as she had longed to do earlier, striking him about the head and shoulders. It was all to no avail. Dominic seemed oblivious to anything but forcing a response out of her, his hands tightening bruisingly around her arms, his mouth moving with urgent hunger against hers.

For perhaps thirty seconds longer the battle raged between them, Melissa driven by pure fury and Dominic goaded by base instincts he had not known he possessed. Suddenly, treacherously, Melissa became aware of the familiar, sweet tide of desire that was flowing with increasing power through her body, felt the hot ache in her loins, felt herself straining urgently closer to Dominic, not in anger but in wanton hunger. Appalled, she tried desperately to still the urges which had sprung violently to life within her body at Dominic's brutally potent kisses, but the pull between them was too great, too inevitable to ever be destroyed.

Mind spinning, she knew she had to escape from him, but now for a totally different reason, and her movements became nearly frantic as she made several futile attempts to break his hold upon her. And all the while she could feel her resolve slipping, feel herself sliding helplessly deeper into desire's dark, mesmerizing web. She made one last valiant effort to get away, but Dominic's arms only held her more securely, his ravishing kisses smashing through the frail barriers she had erected between them. Shame and desire mingled together as, with a little sob of defeat, she gave up the battle and began to passionately return his kisses, her arms circling his neck, her body arching up provocatively against him.

Her surrender was his undoing, and he became blind to everything but the warm, yielding body in his arms. Only Melissa's sweet response held any meaning for him; only her soft lips and teasing little tongue impinged upon his consciousness; that, and her arousing body and the fierce desire that flooded his entire being. Nearly mindless with passion, he slid his hands to her hips, pulling her closer to him, maneuvering his body in carnally explicit rhythms against her. He ached for her, wanted her with such a burning intensity that he was certain that if he could not have her he would die with wanting. Lifting his head slightly, his voice husky and blurred by passion, he muttered, "You're driving me insane! You must let me. . . ." His eyes were claimed by the expanse of creamy flesh that rose above her gown, and unable to resist the lure, he pressed hot, tiny kisses across her bosom, saying thickly, "I've never felt this way before—you're all I can think of. I lie awake remembering what it felt like to have your naked flesh next to mine . . . the sweet taste of your breasts . . . the pleasure you give me. . . . I want you so badly, I cannot think. . . ."

His words were bittersweet to Melissa, and if there had been one word of love, one hint that he felt more for her than a moment's bodily gratification, she *might* have been able to forget all that had gone before. But she could not, and with every word he uttered, it became painfully clear that he felt absolutely nothing but animal lust for her. Any woman would have done for him, and though it was her body of which he spoke, she could easily envision him saying the same thing to Deborah—perhaps he had earlier. That knowledge was as effective as a dousing of icy water, and her once-unbridled passion vanished as if it had never been. Dispiritedly she tried to push herself away from him, humiliation and despair coursing through her.

Instinctively Dominic resisted her first attempts to free herself, but something in her manner, something about the *way* she was struggling, got through to him and he finally, reluctantly, released her. His own passion ebbing slowly as the moments passed, puzzlement apparent in his voice, he asked, "What is it? You wanted me . . . as desperately as I wanted you."

Not looking at him, she kept her face averted as she distractedly smoothed her gown, seeking unhappily for the right words. Suppose she were to say, "Wanting isn't enough. I want your love?" A bitter little smile curved her mouth. How easily it would be for him to simply reply, "But I do love you!" She wasn't so naive that she didn't know that men said all manner of things in the throes of desire. How could she believe him? Especially after her statement would make it obvious what she wanted to hear. But she had to say something, and some of the fury she had felt earlier came seeping back into her consciousness as she said bluntly, "You're a very practiced lover. I'm sure that you can make most women want you . . . for a while at least." Hiding her pain and bitterness, she ended coolly, "I'm afraid that your, er, expertise momentarily overcame my scruples. But do not concern yourself about it—it won't happen again. And if it's a woman you want, I'm sure that Lady Bowden will be more than happy to supply your wants." Giving him an infuriatingly indifferent smile, she murmured, "And now I do believe that we should rejoin our guests, don't you?"

Melissa might have acted cool and indifferent, but inside she was a quaking mass of nerves, and her composure was not helped at all by the icily contemptuous gaze that Dominic raked across her slim body. Why? he wondered with caustic anguish. Why does she do this to me? Warm and eager in my arms one minute, and the next as cold and unfeeling as an alabaster statue? She *had* wanted him, wanted him as passionately and desperately as he had wanted her, and yet . . . Yet for some reason of her own, she pretended that the hunger they felt for each other did not exist. Why? But even as he stood there, fury and resentment building in his breast, it never once occurred to him that in all their dealings together he had never mentioned love, had never given her any clue that there might be something deeper in the emotions that flowed so powerfully between them than just the desire to slake the body's carnal needs.

With a narrowed gaze he watched her, thinking savagely that he'd like to teach her a lesson about the foolishness of playing such a dangerous game—tantalizing and teasing him with that pliant, delectable body and then denying him what had been so freely offered only moments before. Did she do it for some perverse pleasure? Or was it simply sheer, spiteful willfulness?

The sound of muted laughter drifted through the warm night air, and knowing that she was right, that they did have guests, he smothered a curse under his breath and angrily offered her his arm. The gray eyes unfriendly and scornful, he said sneeringly, "By all means, madam, let us rejoin our guests! At least there I can enjoy myself!"

They played their roles very well for the remainder of the evening, and most of the guests were not aware of any sense of constraint between their hosts. But Leonie had noticed that something wasn't quite right, and as she and Morgan rode slowly toward Oak Hollow in the small buggy Josh had lent them during their stay in the area, she commented on it. Her sea-green eyes troubled, she said, "Morgan, what is wrong with Dominic? I do not understand him. He has a lovely young bride and yet he allowed that harpy Deborah Bowden to command his attention." She scowled. "And even after I went to so much trouble to put him and Melissa together, something was very wrong between them as they were bidding all their guests good-bye."

Morgan laughed softly. "I wouldn't let it worry you, my dear. I'm quite certain that Dominic can handle his own domestic problems." Somewhat thoughtfully, he added, "Although I wouldn't want to be in his shoes right now. It's a very tricky path that he must traverse."

"Why?" she asked, her frown deepening. "All he has to do is stay away from the harpy and behave like an honorable and loving husband." Her frown vanished and she flashed her husband an elfin grin. "Just like mine!"

"Well, there is a bit more to it than that," Morgan answered unwisely, his attention on the horse as he guided the animal along the moonlit road.

"Oh?" Leonie asked, her interest piqued. "And what is that? Does it have anything to do with that meeting you two had with Jason at Oak Hollow last week?"

Wishing his wife wasn't quite so observant, Morgan stifled a sigh. He and Leonie had no secrets, and he had complete trust in her ability to keep her mouth shut, if need be, but for reasons he didn't care to examine too closely, he had not told her what had transpired that night at Oak Hollow. Perhaps he'd had the uneasy suspicion that she would not look at it the same way he and Jason did; perhaps he had known that what they were asking of Dominic was unfair.

Suddenly uncomfortable, he muttered, "Jason has this notion that Latimer and his sister, for that matter, might be here for reasons other than the ones stated. And he wanted Royce and Dominic to keep their ears open."

"And?" his wife demanded.

Morgan cleared his throat nervously. "And, um, Jason thought it might be a good idea, since Dominic bears Latimer no love, if Royce concentrated on Latimer and Dominic, ah, concentrated on Deborah."

"What?" Leonie shrieked, sitting up very straight beside her husband. Her eyes beginning to flash dangerously, she inquired in a tone of voice that made Morgan's heart sink, "Are you telling me that you allowed Jason Savage to convince Dominic to pay attention to that harpy and ignore his bride?"

"Not exactly," Morgan retorted angrily, his own temper beginning to rise. "No one expects Dominic to sleep with the woman. We thought that there would be no harm if Dominic merely remained on friendly terms with her. She's made it embarrassingly obvious to everyone that she harbors, er, warm feelings for him, and we didn't see why we shouldn't take advantage of those feelings."

"*Mon Dieu!*" Leonie burst out furiously, her face alight with all the contempt she felt for this idea. "I cannot believe what I am hearing! He is a newly married man, you dolt! How can you ask him to pay attention to a woman other than his wife? No matter what the reason!"

"Goddammit, Leonie! We're not asking him to sleep with the bloody woman—only to be on good terms with her and to keep his ears open."

"And not his breeches?" she inquired tartly, not the least impressed by her husband's arguments. "Ah, bah! It is no use talking to you. I am very angry with you! After all the years that I have wished and waited and yearned for Dominic to fall in love and marry, you do *this!* You and Jason will ruin his life! No wonder poor Melissa appears unhappy!''

Jerking the horse to a standstill, his conscience stabbing him more than a little, Morgan glared at his wife. ''You will *not* mention a word of this. I doubt that she is, but Melissa could be a prattle-trap, and until we know that she can keep her mouth shut, she isn't to know what Dominic is about.'' At his wife's cold silence, he added in a more conciliatory tone of voice, ''I know that the timing isn't the best, but it is important that we know what Latimer is up to. There is good cause to believe that he is a spy for Britain and that his reasons for being here aren't in the best interests of our country.''

Leonie was unmoved by his statement, and her chin lifted mutinously. ''I am so angry with you,'' she muttered furiously. ''In fact, I am so angry with you I do not even want to discuss this distasteful subject any longer. In fact . . .'' Her eyes narrowed and Morgan should have been on his guard, but he wasn't, and when she said vexatiously, ''Oh, dear! I have dropped my reticule on the road. Will you get it for me?'' he should have been warned that his sweet wife was up to no good.

Cursing under his breath, Morgan handed her the reins, jumped down from the buggy and walked around to the other side. Reaching down to the ground, he found Leonie's beaded silk reticule and thrust it into her hand. ''There, madam, your reticule,'' he growled exasperatedly.

Leonie smiled coolly. ''Thank you, monsieur, but I am still angry with you . . . and I don't want to see you anymore this evening.'' Before Morgan's dumbfounded gaze, she gave the horse a smart slap with the reins and left him standing alone in the middle of the road.

Turning the night air blue with curses, Morgan swore long and loud, promising himself that when he laid hands on his wife . . .

Since Leonie had left him a scant quarter mile from Dominic's place, and uncomfortably conscious of his wife's temper, Morgan deemed it wiser to seek other accommodations for the night. Grumbling all sorts of reprisals, he began to walk down the way he had just come.

He and Leonie had been the last of the evening's guests to depart, and he consoled himself with the knowledge that at least he wasn't going to have an audience to watch his ignoble return.

The cottage came into sight in just a few minutes, and Morgan was further relieved to discover that Dominic had not yet retired for the evening. As he walked up the steps, he spied Dominic sitting on the gallery, a full crystal decanter of brandy at his elbow, a half-filled snifter in one hand and a black cheroot in the other.

At the moment, Dominic bore little resemblance to the nattily attired host to whom Morgan had bidden farewell only minutes before; his cravat was gone, his jacket had also disappeared and his white cambric shirt was open nearly to his waist. He evinced no surprise at his brother's unexpected arrival, merely cocking one eyebrow, gesturing to a nearby seat and saying mockingly, "Leonie kick you out, did she?"

Morgan grinned, not at all abashed. "Yes, she did, the little devil! But I can't say that I exactly blame her, although I intend to take full revenge for her antics."

Without further ado, Dominic rang for a servant, requesting another snifter, some more cheroots and that a bed be prepared in his study for his brother. Within seconds, Morgan was leaning back in a chair, his own jacket and cravat dispensed with and a snifter of brandy in one hand.

There were a few minutes of silence as the two men contemplated their fate. It was not pleasant. Morgan might have grinned and made light of his disagreement with Leonie, but he was not looking forward to the next few days. He knew full well that Leonie was not about to let things lie. He didn't fear that she would tell Melissa what they had discussed, but she was sure to meddle . . . and make life miserable for him! As for Dominic, he was grimly aware that until he could detach himself from Deborah, any hope of mending the ever-widening chasm between him and Melissa was impossible. It was a bleak future that faced both men, and almost simultaneously, they burst out, *"Goddamn Jason Savage!"*

Chapter Twenty-one

THE WORDS hung for a second on the night air and then, both men aware that their thoughts had been following the same path, laughter suddenly erupted between them. Shaking his dark head, Morgan remarked, "Jason's ears must be burning, and I can hardly wait for Leonie to divulge to Catherine all that has transpired. Then *he'll* be the one banished!"

Good humor restored, they sipped their brandies in relative quiet until Dominic began to tell Morgan what he had learned from Deborah this evening. Morgan listened intently, whistling softly when Roxbury's name was mentioned. "That old fox!" he said half admiringly, half disgustedly. "I had never considered his fine hand in the scheme of things, but I am not surprised and I doubt that Jason will be when he hears that his wiley old uncle is behind Latimer's trip to America." His face thoughtful, he added, "I am a bit surprised, though, that Roxbury chose a rascal like Latimer—usually his tools are men of character."

Dominic grinned. "Like you and Jason?"

Morgan smiled sweetly. "My point exactly."

They continued to discuss the matter for several more minutes, but eventually, having exhausted the subject, and neither in a particularly jovial mood, they sought out their lonely beds, each wishing he were somewhere else—in the warm, welcoming embrace of his wife, to be precise.

If Melissa found it strange to be greeted by her brother-in-law in the morning, when she could clearly remember bidding *both* Morgan and Leonie good-bye and watching them disappear down the carriageway together, she gave no sign. She smiled politely and did all the usual things that a good hostess would do. As for her husband . . . well, she treated him in the same impersonal manner.

And no one, least of all Morgan, was a bit surprised when Leonie, a half-defiant, half-contrite smile on her lips, drove up just as they finished breakfast and were enjoying a cup of rich black coffee on the gallery. Graciously allowing her husband to help her from the buggy, she murmured lightly, "Ah, good, you are all awake. I did not want to arrive too early and rouse the household."

Shooting a skittish glance at her husband and being met with a bland smile that, after years of marriage, she knew promised retaliation for last night's prank, Leonie sat down in a chair next to Melissa's. Leaning across, she patted Melissa's hand and asked brightly, "And how are you this morning, my dear? Worn out from your first party?"

Ignoring the gentlemen, the two women proceeded to spend the next half hour in a moment-by-moment dissection of last night's dinner. Aware that he was still in his wife's black books, but growing tired of her antics, Morgan suddenly said, "Leonie, I'm sure that you and Melissa will have other times in which to discuss this fascinating subject, but I for one would like to leave." Sending her a look that brooked no argument, he explained, "As you can see, I am still in last night's clothing, and before the day is much older I should very much like to be wearing something else."

It was a somewhat subdued Leonie who sat beside her husband as they waved good-bye once again to Dominic and Melissa. They rode in silence for several moments until Leonie said nervously, "Are you very angry with me?"

"Should I be?" Morgan asked.

Leonie gave it some thought. "Probably," she finally admitted. "But you must admit that I had just cause. It is despicable what you and Jason are doing to Dominic's marriage." Growing incensed once more, she crossed her arms over her chest and muttered, "And I am not sorry for what I did either! No matter what you do to me!"

Morgan pulled the horse to a stop and turned to face his

wife. At the slightly apprehensive expression that crossed her face even as she raised her chin defiantly, Morgan burst out laughing. "I should beat you, you little witch! But since I adore you and would not harm one hair on your head, I suppose that I shall have to simply *love* you to death!"

The sea-green eyes suddenly dark with emotion, Leonie threw her arms around Morgan's neck and kissed him soundly. "Oh, Morgan, *mon amour*, it was so lonely without you last night . . . I very nearly came back after you."

Chuckling, one arm securely around his wife's waist, his chin resting on the honey-colored curls beneath his chin, Morgan slapped the reins on the horse. It was a *very* slow trip back to Oak Hollow.

While Morgan and Leonie might have resolved their differences, the same could not be said for Dominic and Melissa. And as the day passed and Melissa continued to treat him with all the cool courtesy of a hostess unexpectedly called upon to entertain a less-than-welcome guest, Dominic's sense of umbrage grew.

It didn't help his frame of mind that Melissa was in particularly glowing looks this day either. There was a faint flush to her cheeks and her eyes were unusually bright, and the gown that she had selected to wear just happened to be, of all the gowns he had ordered for her, the one he liked best. It was a frivolous confection of apple-green silk trimmed lavishly with laces and flounces, and even as unjustly treated as he felt, he couldn't help admiring how lovely she appeared. Nor could he help noticing the way her tawny hair curled about her shoulders, the glowing strands brushing across her cheeks and tumbling about her neck . . . precisely in the places he would have liked to put his mouth.

Annoyed with the train of his thoughts, he forced himself to dwell blackly on her unfair behavior to him. She wouldn't even listen to him—*if* he had been at liberty to explain things to her. That was a subject he and Morgan had touched on last night, and they had come to the conclusion that the less said the better, Morgan pointing out with a great deal of indignation Leonie's reaction to his explanation—and they had been married for almost ten years! Melissa's ability or inability to keep her mouth shut was an unknown factor to be considered also, and while Dominic didn't *think* that she was a loose-tongued gossip, they couldn't take any chances. All in all, Dominic was thoroughly disgusted with the entire situation, the prospect of ever sharing an even remotely normal marriage with Melissa fading with every passing moment.

That he wanted a normal marriage was quite an admission for him. And it wasn't just the normalcy of sharing his wife's bed that he wanted; to his growing dismay and horror, he very much feared that he wanted precisely what his brother Morgan had—a marriage filled with love and trust.

After Morgan and Leonie had departed, Dominic had moodily watched Melissa as she flitted about the small house, suddenly seeming to suffer an attack of housewifely zeal. She and Mrs. Meeks spent an inordinate amount of time discussing and reviewing the work of the new housemaids and making certain that all signs of last night's festivities were erased and the household back on a more normal schedule. Seeing that the house and grounds were in immaculate order appeared to absorb Melissa's complete interest, and Dominic idly considered tracking in a trail of horse manure just to get her attention.

But he soon gave up such petty thoughts and amused himself simply by staring at his wife, taking sardonic pleasure when she became aware of his unblinking gaze and lost her thread of conversation with Mrs. Meeks. With interest he watched the blush in her cheeks deepen and travel down her throat and chest, and he caught himself wondering how far the scarlet color went . . . to her breasts? Was their creamy hue now faintly pink? Did her berry-sweet nipples darken in color too? A decidedly sensuous smile played across his mobile mouth, and this time when his thoughts strayed into forbidden territory he made no attempt to stop them.

Melissa might have appeared indifferent to his presence, but that was far from the truth. To her chagrin, she was unbearably conscious of his tall, lean body sprawled so nonchalantly in one of the chairs in the salon. He was dressed today with an attractive casualness, his white shirt partially undone, his buff breeches, an old pair, fitting his long legs superbly. The black hair was carelessly tousled, curling rebelliously just near the collar of his open shirt, and Melissa was unhappily aware that she had never seen a man she found half as devastatingly handsome as she did her despicable husband.

Deciding that she could concentrate better without Dominic's disturbing presence, she suggested to Mrs. Meeks that they move into the breakfast room to continue their absorbing discussion of whether it was time to apply another coat of beeswax to the banister which led upstairs or if they should wait a week or two. Dominic, for some unfathomable reason, followed them, and Melissa was all too aware of him as he leaned negligently against the doorjamb, apparently avidly interested in their conversation. And so it went all day, no matter how she tried to ignore him or escape from him, he was always there watching her, listening to her, making her exceedingly nervous hour by hour. And if she could have known of the erotic images that chased themselves through his brain, he nervousness would have increased tenfold.

It didn't help matters either that as the day progressed, Dominic began to consume large quantities of fine French brandy, his speech becoming slightly slurred as darkness fell. Peeking a covert glance at him as they supped in the cozy dining room at the rear of the house, Melissa was amazed at how *un*intoxicated he looked, only that slight slur to his words and the extraordinarily precise manner in which he moved giving any indication that he was more than just a little foxed.

The meal was quiet, the only sounds the clink of silverware against china and the faint tinkle of crystal as Dominic refilled his snifter with brandy time and again. Suddenly their eyes met, and smiling mockingly, Dominic asked, "Would you care to join me in a snifter? I am told that brandy is an excellent sleeping draught."

Melissa sent him a haughty glance where he sat at the other end of the table, his chair turned sideways, his long legs stretched out in front of him. "I believe," she said stiffly, "that you might find a clear conscience a far more effective anodyne."

"A clear conscience?" he drawled, the gray eyes glittering brightly in his dark face. "Now why should you think *I* have a guilty conscience? I have done nothing to be ashamed of lately. As a matter of fact, I believe that most people would think that I have acted quite nobly considering the circumstances." His mouth twisted. "I did marry you, after all."

Thoroughly incensed, Melissa jumped to her feet, and throwing down her white linen napkin, swept around the table. "Well, thank you very much!" she said furiously, standing in front of him, her bosom heaving from the force of her anger. "It is a pity that your nobility didn't last longer than it took you to say your vows!"

Fascinated by the rise and fall of her chest, Dominic couldn't tear his eyes away from the soft flesh so temptingly near, and without conscious thought he reached up and pulled her urgently into his arms and onto his lap. Blindly he buried his face between her sweet-scented breasts, his mouth pressing hotly against the yielding flesh. "Is it a noble husband that you want, Lissa? A noble man, full of fine thoughts and virtuous works?" he muttered thickly.

Lifting his head, he stared into her stunned features and then, taking advantage of her momentary astonishment, he shifted her slightly until she lay in his arms, her head almost resting against his shoulder, her legs dangling from the floor. His mouth mere inches from hers, he demanded huskily, "If I were to seek to do worthy deeds in your name . . . would it soften your cold heart? Would noble works be the key that would unlock and release all that wild passion we shared on our wedding night? Would it?"

Breathless, her skin tingling from the touch of his mouth, her body all too aware of the warmth and hardness of his so close to hers, Melissa could think of nothing to say. Every instinct urged her to embrace him, to wind her arms around his neck, to hungrily kiss those firm, pleasure-giving lips so near to her own, but the memory of Deborah's smug smile last night floated nastily through her brain, and in one violent movement she disentangled herself and leaped to her feet. Unshed tears gleamed in her golden eyes, and more in sadness than in anger, she cried, "Stop it! Don't toy with me this way! I cannot bear it!" And with that she fled the room, her silken skirts flying behind her.

His expression utterly stupefied, Dominic stared in the direction in which she had disappeared. Toy with *her?* The woman was mad! She had done nothing but turn his world upside down and inside out; had calculatingly trapped him into marriage; had taken his poor, unsuspecting heart and torn it from his breast, trampled it cruelly beneath her feet—and she dared to accuse *him* of toying with her!

He sat there in brooding silence for some time, nursing his grievances, hardly aware of the advent of the butler into the room until that gentleman coughed delicately and asked, "May I begin to clear, sir?"

Absently Dominic stared at the man. "Oh, of course," he replied after a moment and stood up. The impact of all the brandy he had been drinking hit him, and feeling a bit fuzzy, he added, "Have a large pot of coffee sent out to the gallery. I believe that I shall sit there for a while before bed."

Several cups of strong black coffee and a few hours later, Dominic was more himself, although there were still enough brandy fumes swirling through his brain for his thoughts to be considerably less than rational. Actually, they were quite *ir*rational, an unrelenting desire to prove to his wife that he was *not* toying with her taking strong hold of his senses. *He* hadn't been the one to banish her from the bedroom; he hadn't been the one who had broken off their promising embrace last night, nor had he been the one who flaunted a nearly irresistible body in front of the other! Oh, no, it wasn't he who advanced so tantalizingly and then at the last moment retreated. And, by God, he wasn't going to put up with it any longer!

A stubborn set to his chin, he went inside and ran up the stairs two at a time. In his bedroom, he stripped and, more out of habit than anything else, swiftly sluiced his body with the tepid water waiting on the washstand.

He hesitated for just a moment in front of the door that connected their bedrooms, the faint light spilling beneath the door revealing that Melissa had not yet retired for the night. Was she in there longing for him? he wondered. Or was she thinking of some other man? Latimer?

Giving an angry shake to his dark head, he deliberately dispelled that ugly image. He would not consider the possibility that his wife really wanted another man—he didn't want another woman, so how could she want another man? That his logic was twisted did not occur to him, nor did it seem to dawn on him that with the situation between them the way it was, his wife was not likely to look kindly on his appearance in her room. But none of that bothered him. In the brief time that he and Melissa had been married, he had done nothing but rack his brains trying to understand what had happened between them, baffled by her incomprehensible decision to deny them both the pleasures of the marriage bed. But no longer. His reasons for doing what he intended to do weren't even clear to him. It wasn't just the need to relieve the hungry passion her mere presence aroused within him; it was something much deeper, more elemental. Perhaps it had something to do with the way Latimer had looked at her last night, the way she had seemed to respond to the other man's attention. Or it might have to do with the need to show her with his body what he had not yet fully admitted to himself—that he loved her and wanted her in all the ways that a man wants the woman he loves. Mayhap in his confused thinking he wanted to show her that by making love to her, no other woman held any allure to him; that while he might seem to flirt and encourage another woman, *she* was the one in whose arms he wished to lie; it was *her* kisses he wanted, her body he claimed. Only hers. And last of all, perhaps he wanted to prove once and for all that every time she spurned his advances, every time she scorned his touch, she lied. . . .

He dared not let himself dwell on what might happen if he were wrong, if all that sweet fire and desire were not really for him. And driven now by the dictates of his own body as well as by the demons in his brain, he opened the door and in naked splendor walked into her bedroom.

The room was bathed in the glow of soft candlelight, and unerringly he stalked over to her bed and pulled aside the gauzy curtains that draped the large bed.

Lost in her own unhappy musings, Melissa had not heard either the door opening or his approach, and the sudden movement of the bed-curtains startled her. Eyes wide, she stared at him, and then, as the fact that he was completely naked impinged upon her consciousness, her breath was caught in her throat.

Dominic was magnificent as he stood there before her, apparently not at all perturbed by his state of undress, his gray eyes fixed hungrily on the soft flesh that rose and fell beneath the filmy scrap of a garment that Melissa had worn to bed. The garment was of spun silk, ivory in color and trimmed abundantly with fine lace; it was both provocative and modest, the nearly translucent material revealing as much as it hid, the full, flowing sleeves and gently rounded neckline giving it a virginal appearance.

Melissa had been sitting on the lavender coverlet, a pile of silken pillows at her back, and Dominic thought he had never seen anything lovelier as she sat there, her legs tucked beneath her, her glorious hair tumbling unrestrainedly about her shoulders, her mouth half parted in surprise. Unable to help himself, he bent over and claimed those half-parted lips, his kiss oddly gentle.

Heart hammering in her chest, Melissa didn't know whether to be pleased or disappointed when he lifted his head a second later. Trying desperately to still the wild excitement that was clamoring in her veins, she kept her gaze averted from his naked body and asked breathlessly, "What are you doing here?"

It was a stupid question and they both knew it. Melissa could have bitten her tongue when she saw the mocking little smile that quirked at the corners of Dominic's mouth. Looking everywhere but at him, she muttered inanely, "It isn't . . . it isn't seemly to wander around naked."

"My body displeases you?" he asked.

"Oh, no! I think it is wonderful!" Melissa said in a rush; then, realizing what she had admitted, she clamped her lips together, a charming blush staining her cheeks.

Dominic smiled with all the understandable smugness of a man who knows his woman appreciates his physical attributes. His gaze roaming possessively over the soft curves of her body, he murmured, "And I find yours utterly delectable!"

For a moment her eyes clung to his as she tried to gauge the sincerity of his words. The warm expression in his gray eyes made Melissa's pulse jump, but then, recalling that he was a practiced womanizer, she said dully, "Mine and that of any other woman who catches your fancy!"

His hands clamped brutally around her upper arms and he dragged her less than gently up against him. "No," he said harshly. "No other woman but you." His mouth swooped and trapped hers in a demanding kiss, one hand sliding behind her head to hold her captive as he searched her mouth with frank pleasure. "Only you," he muttered finally when he lifted his lips from hers.

Wanting to believe him, so very weary of fighting him as well as the inexorable demands of her own body, Melissa made no attempt to escape from his grasp. Did it really matter that he didn't love her? she mused sadly. Once she had foolishly banished him from her bed and she had bitterly regretted it ever since, so why not take what he offered? She wanted him. He was her husband. She loved him; how could she *not* accept this second chance?

She wasn't the only one who was remembering that she had banished him from her room. His eyes darkening, Dominic suddenly swung her up in his arms. "Tonight," he growled softly, "you share *my* bed, sweet witch, and I doubt that even you would have the audacity to order me from my own bed."

For now, Melissa had pushed aside all the old reasons for her mistrust of him and, generous in her defeat, she reached up and pulled his dark head down to hers. Her mouth sliding with exquisite tenderness across his surprised lips, she murmured, "But why should I? It's where we both want to be."

Dominic was so stunned by her unexpected capitulation that he never remembered moving away from her bed, never remembered their entering his own room, never even remembered laying her down on his huge mahogany bed; and it was only when he noticed the striking contrast of her ivory gown against the midnight blue of his velvet coverlet that he became aware of their surroundings. And by then it didn't really matter to him where they were. . . .

Groaning his delight, he kissed her passionately, all the hunger and desire of these past days suddenly unleashed within him. With equal fervor Melissa returned his kisses, her tongue unashamedly seeking his, twining and teasing, driving him half mad with longing.

It was heaven to have her in his arms again, to feel again the warmth of her body pressing against his, to feel her long legs entwined around his as they lay side by side, their hands roaming feverishly over the other's body. The smoothness of her fine silk garment rubbed erotically against his naked flesh, but he could not bear even that frail barrier between them, and almost savagely he ripped it from her body, sighing with pleasure when his seeking fingers found her bare skin. He had wanted to be gentle with her, to make slow, tender love to her, but he could not; all the nights of denial, all the sleepless hours he had spent reliving their wedding night, had built within him such a passionate need that he was nearly shaking from the force of it. Leaving a trail of fiery kisses in its wake, his mouth slowly slid to her neck, his tongue and teeth gently biting and tasting as his hands hungrily cupped her breasts. Burying his mouth against her throat where the pulse beat frantically, he muttered, "I've missed you so . . . I've thought of nothing but this for days, wondering if I had imagined how soft your flesh is, how sweet your mouth, how easily you make me burn to have you . . ."

The nights of denial had taken their toll on Melissa also, and although the uncontrollable desires that drove Dominic were new to her, they were no less powerful. She was already boneless with wanting, the fierce passion that only Dominic aroused within her blotting out everything but the joy of being held in his arms, of knowing again the wonder of his kiss, of once more losing herself in the magic which Dominic wove so skillfully, so effortlessly, around them. His words were erotic, the naked hunger in his voice as arousing as his touch, and her arms wrapped around his shoulders, cradling his head nearer to her. Her lips gently caressing the dark hair of his head, she admitted shyly, "I've . . . I've missed you too. I—I never meant to drive you away. . . ." With so much unknown between them, it was as close to an apology for her actions on their wedding night as she could come, as close to admitting that she loved him.

"Oh, Jesus!" Dominic groaned against her throat. "What am I going to do with you? You've turned my world upside down, and just when I'm convinced that you're a heartless jade, you say something that completely alters my conception of you." His head still bent, in between sharp little kisses, he asked with an odd note of pleading in his voice, "Have you really missed me? Really wanted me in your bed again?"

It was a most promising conversation. Unfortunately, with Dominic's fingers insistently pulling on her throbbing nipples and his mouth slowly moving upward, Melissa couldn't think straight. She could only feel, feel the demanding ache that was spreading throughout her body, her skin tingling wherever Dominic touched her, and helplessly she groaned, "Oh, yes! I never wanted you to leave me!"

Her admission seemed to shatter the last of his control and he caught her lips with his, kissing her fiercely, almost savagely, and his hands sliding around her slim body to lock her in a powerful embrace. With a hunger that seemed endless he kissed her, his tongue filling her mouth, probing with devastating thoroughness the sweetness he found there.

Crushed next to him, her breasts nearly flattened against his hard chest, her mouth ardently accepting his ravenous invasion, Melissa reveled in the knowledge that, for tonight at least, it was her body that he wanted, her kisses that he demanded. Her arms tightened around him, her warm body moving with explicit need against his, wanting his possession with every fiber of her being.

The soft thrust of her body against his was an exquisite torment and he was almost painfully aware of everything about her, from the honeyed warmth of her mouth to the provocative thrashings of her hips and legs as she sought a closer intimacy. A growl of frankly carnal pleasure broke from his throat as he caught her slender hips in both his hands and held her firmly against his swollen and aching member, his own hips moving in a sensuously lazy rhythm that gave them both a hint of the ecstasy that would come.

Melissa writhed in his embrace, frantic for him to take her and equally frantic to touch him, to caress him, to let him know just how powerfully he affected her, just how deeply stirring she found his lovemaking. Her entire body seemed to be on fire, her breasts full and aching to feel his mouth upon them, her nipples hard and throbbing, her breath coming in soft little gasps when his head dropped and began to slide openmouthed down her chest.

Mindlessly she arched upward, offering herself to him, sighing gently when his lips at last closed over a coral nipple, sharp pleasure shooting through her body as he suckled hungrily on the rigid tip. Intensifying the sweet sensation, his teeth rubbed lightly against the sensitive nipple of first one breast, then the other, sending giddy waves of delight coursing through Melissa.

His hold on her hips had loosened, and freeing her arms, she began to caress him, her hands moving in ever-widening circles down his back until she reached his muscular buttocks. Almost wonderingly, she ran her hands over the smooth flesh, kneading and exploring the warm firmness.

Her tender ministrations only made Dominic more aware of how her slightest touch enthralled him, his already painfully erect manhood swelling to impressive proportions as her exploring fingers traveled languidly from his buttocks up his spine and around to his chest. When her searching hands finally found his own hard little nipples, he could—not suppress an excited groan, her movements copying his, her slim fingers gently tugging and pulling on the highly responsive nubs.

Blindly he caught her lips with his, kissing her urgently, revealing plainly the depth of his arousal, his tongue plunging hotly into her welcoming mouth. Wild with passion, he slid his fingers down her flat belly, lingering for a teasing moment in the tangle of tight, soft curls between her legs before he reached the area he sought.

The intimacy between them was still too fragile, too bewilderingly new for Melissa not to react to his probing fingers, and instinctively she stiffened. It was almost as if she feared the pleasure she knew he would bring her, and her thighs closed protestingly around his hand. Her action didn't seem to perturb Dominic; if anything, he found it strangely moving. His lips against hers, he commanded huskily, "Don't. Open your legs to me, let me give you pleasure . . . let me give us both pleasure."

The blood pounding dizzyingly in her brain, her body consumed by desire's fever, wordlessly she obeyed him, her pale thighs parting slackly. A muffled sigh of satisfaction broke from him and his fingers knowingly sought entrance to her body, sending pleasure spiraling wildly through her. He caressed her gently at first, slowly building the hungry need inside her, and then, as Melissa began to thrash even more violently, her hips rising up against his tormenting fingers, his movements became less controlled, more urgent, and she shivered with near ecstasy. Racked by the compelling need to have him give her the release she so desperately sought, she writhed with carnal abandonment beneath his touch, her fingers digging into his shoulders. "Oh, please!" she gasped. "Please, take me, let me feel you inside me. I want . . . I want you. . . ."

Shaking from the force of the powerful desire that was surging through his veins, his face hard and set with a passion too-long denied, Dominic gave them both what they yearned for, his bulging shaft thrusting into her with a nearly frenzied motion. Bodies fused together, they lay there oddly breathless, staring at each other, just savoring the delicious sensations that were rippling through each other's body.

Still not moving, his big body braced not to lie heavily on hers, Dominic kissed her slowly, with great tenderness, and then rhythmically he began to move within her, sharpening the keen edge of passion that pierced their bodies. Wanting desperately to prolong the sweetness of their mating, Dominic tried frantically to refuse the demands of his body, his features twisted by the effort it took not to seek that final pinnacle of pleasure.

Arms wrapped around him, her tongue hungrily exploring his mouth, Melissa could feel his restraint, could hear his labored breathing, and it heightened her own arousal, her hips heaving upward to eagerly meet the downward plunge of his. He felt huge as he lanced into her and she took a lover's pride in his size and strength, her hands sliding to his driving buttocks to clench that firm flesh and spur him onward. With every stroke he took, delving deeper within her, the fiery, demanding ache that raged in her loins became more intense, more ravenous, until she was wantonly twisting beneath him, soft moans of pleasure and entreaty mingling together as her own passion-maddened movements brought them closer to that longed-for peak of fulfillment. This exquisite torture could not last, and suddenly, like the rush of a storm-swollen river, ecstasy burst through her straining body, making her cry out with the joy she experienced.

Her cry shattered what little remained of his control, and groaning his own delight, Dominic shuddered as his body was racked by the fierce momentum of his own release. Passion fading slowly, they still clung tightly to each other as languid contentment replaced the elemental forces that had, such a short time before, driven them mercilessly.

For a long time they lay locked together, neither one wanting to break the intimate contact between them, neither one wanting to face the difficulties that still confronted them. Though desire had been sated, some need to touch and caress still remained. Lazily, Dominic kissed her, suddenly inordinately grateful for whatever fate had brought her into his life. And when she would have moved, would have displaced his weight, he captured her arms above her head, and nuzzling her neck, muttered, "No. I want you again. Can't you feel me stirring inside you, feel me responding to your satin warmth?"

Vibrantly aware of his hardening body, Melissa smiled languorously, her nipples suddenly tingling, her body instantly surging to life once more. Her eyes bright with mischief and rising passion, she murmured, "You mean you aren't going to send me from your bed?"

Already half lost in the conflagration that was flaming through his body, Dominic thrust possessively into her and swore thickly, "Oh, Jesus! *Never!*"

Chapter Twenty-two

THE SUN was high in the sky when Melissa awoke the next morning, and as she glanced bewilderedly around her bedchamber, she wondered miserably if she had imagined last night, if her fevered longings had taken the form of a particularly lifelike dream. Despairingly she buried her head in her pillow and instantly became aware of some things of vital interest: she was stark naked, and she was blushingly conscious of a faint soreness between her legs, of a tenderness in her breasts that could not have been brought on by a mere dream—no matter how real it might have seemed!

A slow, ecstatic smile spread across her face as she turned and stretched like a well-fed cat. For whatever reasons, Dominic had come to her last night and in the ensuing hours he had made it quite, *quite* clear that he was a man of astounding sensual appetite. Furthermore, during those long, exciting hours in his arms she had learned to her delight and a little embarrassment that she possessed a hunger as great as his own and that she was becoming more than slightly addicted to his passionate lovemaking.

Dreamily she considered last night, remembering how fiercely he had claimed her body time and again, remembering how he had looked when he had first come naked into her room, recalling the width of his muscled chest, the narrowness of his waist and the swollen, upthrusting size of his . . .

A hot blush burned in her cheeks, and deciding that she was turning into a most depraved, lascivious creature, she bounded from her bed, suddenly eager to see her husband.

Ringing for her maid, she dragged on a lace-trimmed robe and waited impatiently for Anna's appearance, wondering where Dominic was, wondering why he had put her back into her own bed.

Anna stuck her head inside the room and flashed Melissa a smile. "Good morning, madam. Your bath is almost ready; the master ordered it for you before he went for his ride. He said that he was quite certain that you would want one immediately upon waking."

There was a knowing gleam in Anna's dark eyes that flustered Melissa a bit, but nodding her tawny head, she replied, "Thank you, Anna. I do want a bath, and could you have some chocolate and a hot bun brought up?"

After last night, everything seemed mundane to Melissa, and though the bath was fragrant and refreshing, her thoughts kept straying to Dominic as she idly speculated on what it would be like to share a bath with him, to soap his wet body, to feel him come to life under her hands. . . .

If Anna noticed that her mistress seemed particularly distracted this morning, she made no comment, cheerfully helping her to dress and arranging the thick, shiny hair into artless curls. Having finished her chocolate and eaten the freshly baked bun, Melissa fiddled in her room for a few moments, suddenly attacked by a bout of paralyzing shyness.

She had been without shame last night, had eagerly acted the part of a wanton in her husband's arms, but she had awakened alone in her own bed and she wondered with growing dismay if she had dissatisfied Dominic in some way. Had she disgusted him by her abandoned ways? Was that the reason he had returned her to her bed?

Nibbling her lower lip, she nervously paced the confines of her room, all the old mistrust and uncertainties suddenly rising up to dim her happy spirits. But though Melissa was conscious of the troubles that lay between them, she was curiously no longer willing to blindly believe that Dominic was the philandering husband he appeared.

She had experienced no great insight during the night, but there was one particularly insistent notion in her brain that stubbornly refused to go away, no matter how silly it might seem to be. Dominic had been her only lover, and she had nothing else on which to base her belief, but she could not accept the idea that he could make such tender love to her, could hold her in his arms so tightly and kiss her so warmly, if he were having an affair with Deborah Bowden. If it was Deborah whom he wanted, why bother with her? Why seek her out and why deny that there was anything between Deborah and him? The law, Melissa acknowledged slowly, was all on his side—she was his wife, he legally had complete control of her life, was able to do as he pleased, so why the unnecessary pretense of wanting her?

It simply didn't make sense. She had told him that they would each seek their own pleasures, and he had been infuriated—was it because he was not guilty of the sins she had laid at his door?

Of course, there were Uncle Josh's comments . . . and there was Latimer's letter to her. . . . And she couldn't forget the morning she had found Dominic with his arms about Deborah. . . . And then, she admitted with a sinking feeling, there had been his actions just the other night at their dinner party. . . .

Melissa shook her head angrily. No. She was not going to believe that he could be so dastardly as to make love to her when it was really another woman he wanted. Especially since he seemed so very honorable and noble in all other aspects.

A frown creasing her forehead, she stared sightlessly off into space, common sense warring with the insistent dictates of her heart. Was his lovemaking last night really proof of anything? she finally asked herself listlessly. Wouldn't a practiced womanizer act just as he had? Wasn't it true that men felt things differently than women? That a man could make love to many women, driven by nothing more than common lust? While a woman . . . A woman would give herself only to the man she loved.

What a silly notion! Melissa thought irreverently. If a man can make love to many women without love, why should it be any different for a woman? It was an intriguing thought, but it didn't help resolve the conflict in her mind.

Despite the misgivings that raged in her breast, Melissa stubbornly refused to return to her old belief that Dominic was a blackguard and a cheat. Except when it came to women, he had always acted in a considerate and generous manner, and though there were certain incidents that gave Melissa pause, she began to carefully examine the evidence against him.

Josh. Her eyes narrowed, she thought about Uncle Josh's earlier statements about Dominic and dwelt quite a long time on the unsettling fact that Josh, who loved her and cared for her, had been perfectly happy, it seemed, to marry her off to a young man he had freely stigmatized as a rake. Somehow that idea didn't ring as true as it once had to Melissa. Could Josh have painted Dominic far darker than he was in the hopes that she would become interested in him? It was more than possible, Melissa thought with a snort, remembering how eager Josh had been to get her married.

Latimer. Melissa shrugged. Latimer's letter could be easily dismissed, and she had never placed much faith in his words anyway. He had proved himself everything that Dominic was not, and she was astute enough to realize that since he had failed in his objective to make her his mistress, spite alone might have motivated his ugly accusations. *Might* have.

And as for Lady Bowden . . . Melissa scowled fiercely. As for the brazen Lady Bowden, she had always been of the opinion that the older woman was a forward piece. Hadn't Deborah been fawning over first one eligible man and then another since she had first arrived in the neighborhood? Why, she had even cast eyes on Zachary and Zachary didn't seem to mind in the least if the besotted looks he sent her way were any indication! Granted, her overtures had not been as flagrant as they had been with Dominic, but still—!

Rather pleased at the direction of her deductions, Melissa smiled faintly. Of course, she hadn't proved anything conclusive; she had merely looked at things from a different perspective. And some things that should have occurred to her sooner slowly unraveled in her brain.

There had never been any question that Zachary had

been impressed and drawn immediately to Dominic, and that should have made her think a little more deeply about Dominic's supposedly flawed personality. Wouldn't Zachary have noticed something and warned her? Josh's ready acceptance of Dominic into the family was suspicious too, especially if he really believed that Dominic was just a blackguard. Wasn't it far more likely that he would have kept his new nephew-in-law at arm's length?

Melissa's lips pursed, and she decided that one of the very first things she was going to do this afternoon was ride over and have a rather pointed conversation with her uncle. Josh might bluster and shout, but in the end she knew he would confess, *if* he had concocted that story about Dominic.

Talking to Royce, too, might be a good idea. Royce would know if Dominic were indeed a callous womanizer. A wide, pleased smile suddenly spread across Melissa's face. Of course! She should have paid more attention to Royce's actions during this whole affair. Josh *might* have been willing to sanction a marriage to an unscrupulous rake to gain control of Sally's fortune, but Royce, who knew Dominic intimately, would never have allowed her to be married to a man he thought unworthy under any circumstances!

Extraordinarily pleased with the train of her thoughts, Melissa fairly danced out of her bedchamber. There was a great deal she intended to find out today. And if she was right . . . She shivered with something near to ecstasy as she considered what her future might be.

Melissa had not been the only one to do some serious thinking this morning, nor was she the only one to come to certain encouraging conclusions. Dominic had awakened at the first light of dawn and had spent an excessive amount of time staring idiotically down into Melissa's sleeping countenance.

With greedy satisfaction his eyes drank in each lovely feature, from the wildly tousled honey-brown curls to the pink sole of one slim foot that peeked out from the tangled linen sheets. He decided that he had never seen a more beautiful sight and that having Melissa in his bed was a habit he was definitely going to enjoy cultivating.

His eyes trapped by the sweet curve of her mouth, he couldn't control the impulse to taste that honeyed warmth once more, and his head dipped and he gently pressed his lips to hers. She stirred in her sleep, a little frown marring the serenity of her features. Seeing her reaction, he smiled faintly. After last night and the hours he had kept her awake, he wasn't at all surprised that she slept so deeply or that his kiss didn't bring her eagerly awake.

Knowing that he was not going to be able to simply lie there beside her and that if he didn't get away soon from the seductive warmth of her body, he was going to wake her and prove that he was an absolutely insatiable animal where she was concerned, Dominic reluctantly got out of bed. For a moment he toyed with having his bath in her room but decided against it and very gently lifted her from his bed and carried her into the other room, placing her once more in her own bed.

Back in his own room, despite the earliness of the hour, he rang for Bartholomew and wasn't in the least surprised when his bedroom door opened almost instantly.

Bartholomew's sallow features perfectly devoid of expression, he asked quietly, "Would you prefer your coffee before you bathe or afterward, master?"

His manner carefree and jaunty for the first time in several weeks, Dominic grinned at his manservant and demanded, "Does nothing I do catch you off guard? I would have thought that my summons would find you in bed at this hour of the morning."

Bartholomew sent him a reproving glance that was at variance with the twinkle in the knowing brown eyes. "I wouldn't be fulfilling my duties properly if I wasn't capable of anticipating your most likely wants, sir."

"Oh, God! You're beginning to sound depressingly like your Uncle Litchfield," Dominic said with a mock groan.

Bartholomew, with a disgustingly superior smile on his face, bowed and murmured, "That is high praise indeed, sir. You overwhelm me with your compliments."

Laughing at his valet, Dominic said lightly, "Enough! Now go see about my bath and bring the coffee back with you."

Having bathed and eaten, and fortified by several cups

of strong dark coffee, Dominic decided that an early morning ride would not come amiss. Whistling cheerfully, he wandered down the stairs and out of the house. His step as light as his spirits, he made his way to the stables and after rousing out a sleepy-eyed groom, a few minutes later he rode away, his destination unknown.

It was a fine morning, the blistering, debilitating heat of August having faded to the far more pleasant warmth of September. This early in the day, the humidity was not as powerful either, and Dominic's horse, a rather flashy dark brown gelding with three white socks and a large white star in the middle of his handsome face, tended to cavort and prance, as if signaling his pleasure in the morning.

Since he had no particular destination in mind, Dominic let the horse explore at will, his own thoughts dwelling blissfully on the events of last night. A silly little smile on his face, he finally admitted to himself that marriage— to the right woman, of course—had much to recommend it. And infuriating though she might be, as incomprehensible as her actions might appear to him, he conceded that Melissa was the right woman for him.

It wasn't, he mused slowly as his horse danced under his slack grip of the reins, just the rightness of having Melissa in his bed either. They had spent quite a lot of time together since they had married, and reviewing those past weeks, weeks when he had been denied any sort of intimate contact with her at all, he was amazed to discover that he had actually enjoyed that time with her. Naturally, he added hastily, it would have been *much* more enjoyable if he could have partaken of the delights he had known last night, but even without the pleasures of the flesh to cloud the issue, he had found the early days of his marriage most delightful. At least, he clarified with a scowl, it had been delightful when he hadn't been thinking of the underhanded way Melissa had trapped him into marriage or been considering her a greedy little hussy.

His scowl deepened and, almost irritably, he jerked the horse away from a particularly succulent clump of grass that grew near the narrow, winding path. Oblivious to the tangled undergrowth of the tall, slim beech trees, the fragrant yellow jasmine and trailing trumpet vines, as well as the deeply green magnolia trees and the towering oaks that grew in wild abandon, he continued on his way, his thoughts focusing on Melissa's seemingly contradictory behavior.

During the time that they had been married, he could not think of one instance when she had displayed any signs of avarice or taken a marked interest in his money. Granted, he had lavished expensive gifts and luxurious items on her, but he had always had the distinct impression that she had been slightly uncomfortable and uneasy with his generosity. Of course, that could all be an act on her part, he thought reluctantly, but . . .

A bit angry at the unwelcome direction of his musings but unable to stop their flow, he tried to view the past few weeks and the occurrences that had led to their marriage dispassionately. It was difficult for him to do because his emotions kept getting in the way, but finally, after a long struggle with himself, some interesting ideas began to emerge from his muddled thinking. Ideas that he should have considered long before now.

Dominic had always had the reputation of being a shrewd and perspicacious young man, and understandably, he had been quite proud of that fact. Even as a very young man he had been able to easily see beyond the charm and ingratiating manner of those who would trick and cheat him; able to spot at once insincerity cloaked by simulated artlessness, deceitfulness gowned by clever guilelessness. His ability to view the antics of others with a sometimes friendly, sometimes coolly detached interest had been a great boon to him, and he had grown used to thinking himself infallible when it came to understanding his fellow man. The only time his instincts had failed him had been during his brief infatuation with Deborah.

He hadn't been able to see beyond her pretty face and beguiling smiles then, so why did he think that he was reacting any differently with Melissa? Did he have a blind side when it came to his relationship with women? Royce had taken Deborah's measure at once, but he had not. Was he one of those poor fools always being duped by a woman whose conniving ways were perfectly obvious to everyone but himself?

His mouth twisted disgustedly. It was possible, but he did not believe that his instincts had let him down that badly—*twice!*

Look at Morgan. Stephanie had befuddled him, but then he'd had the good luck to find Leonie.

Perhaps, Dominic thought with a small smile, he would be as lucky. Perhaps he was being as blind about Melissa as Morgan had been about Leonie.

That novel idea brought him to an abrupt standstill, his hand jerking his wandering horse to a most unexpected stop. What if he had been wrong about Melissa? What if she hadn't married him simply for money? What if there had been a perfectly legitimate reason for her having been in his room that night?

At the moment, he could think of no excuse strong enough to put her at the inn that night other than the desire to trap a rich husband, but for the sake of argument, he would go on the assumption that she had been there for an innocent reason. And if that were the case, then she had been as trapped as he had been. . . . He frowned. But if she was innocent, why had she agreed to the marriage? Surely she could have explained everything to her uncle. And though the situation had been deplorable, if her reasons for being there were valid, surely Josh would not have insisted upon the marriage. And if she *really* had been opposed to the marriage, as she had pretended at first, why had she finally capitulated if it hadn't been an act in the first place?

Not at all satisfied with his speculations, Dominic turned his attention to the people around Melissa and their opinion of her. It was at that point that his theorizing became remarkably similar to Melissa's, if he had but known it. For Dominic, his conclusions were far easier to come by, as he wasn't laboring under the impression that his spouse was a creature of indiscriminate morals. He only had to wade through his own notions of why Melissa had acted as she had; there had been no Josh Manchester to fill his head with lies, no Latimer to add to the lies and no clinging former lover, à la Lady Bowden, to give proof to the lies.

Since he had known Royce the longest and trusted his opinion implicitly, it was only natural that Dominic consider his friend's estimation of Melissa. His gray eyes narrowed in concentration, he thought back over the various statements that Royce had made about Melissa, and something that should have been obvious to him before suddenly struck Dominic. Royce had *wanted* him to marry Melissa! Had in fact been quite pleased with the way things had turned out. A wry grin on his face, he realized that Royce had subtly abetted Josh when that gentleman had been singing Melissa's praises to the skies. And if Melissa were a conniving and unscrupulous little jade, would one of his best friends be in favor of his marriage to that same creature? Absolutely not! he thought with a widening smile. If Royce had the least suspicions about Melissa, had thought her anything less than a perfectly acceptable bride, Dominic had no doubt that his friend would have warned him. It had been apparent too, now that he thought of it, that Royce had a deep fondness for his cousin. Royce had spoken of her gallantry and beauty and, Dominic remembered, had had a dangerous expression on his face when he had first come upon Dominic and Melissa in bed. It became blindingly obvious to Dominic that Royce held her in the highest regard, ready to do battle even with a good friend to save her honor. It seemed extremely unlikely that the sort of woman he had envisioned Melissa to be would provoke that sort of reaction from cynical Royce.

Feeling very satisfied with himself, Dominic eventually turned his horse around and headed back to the cottage. He didn't possess one shred of proof to bolster his growing conviction that he had misjudged his young bride badly, but he was oddly pleased with his deductions and he had made an important decision.

There was only one person who could answer the questions that still troubled him, and that was Melissa herself. Before the day was very much older, he was going to have a fairly blunt conversation with his wife, and she was going to explain *exactly* why she had been at the inn then and why she had finally agreed to marry him! It suddenly dawned on him that he wanted to do nothing to disrupt the gentle feelings Melissa had aroused within him, and he came to the conclusion that although he was burning with impatience to hear her answers, today might be too soon. He would simply look over the lay of the land and choose the right time to demand his answers . . . but it would be soon. *Very* soon. A sensuous smile flitted across his face. And after she had prettily explained everything to his satisfaction, he was going to take her to bed and experience again all the joy he had felt last night in her arms.

Guiding his horse down the lane that led to the cottage, his brain filled with erotic images, Dominic was jolted from his pleasant pastime by the sight of a tall, long-legged black stallion tied to the hitching post near the side of the house. He would have known that particular horse anywhere, and he spurred his own horse forward, eager to greet this unexpected but most welcome guest.

Throwing his reins to the groom who appeared just as he pulled his horse to a stop, Dominic dismounted swiftly and raced up the broad steps two at a time. His foot had barely touched the floor of the gallery when a laughing voice rang out to his left. Spinning in that direction with a wide smile, he caught sight of the tall, broad-shouldered gentleman coming toward him. Hand outstretched, his voice full of warmth and affection, Dominic said, *"Adam St. Clair!* When you didn't come to the wedding, I assumed that you must have met your fate and that some irate husband had finally given you your just deserts!"

Adam St. Clair, his bright blue eyes full of mischief, murmured, "At least *I* am not the one caught in the parson's mousetrap! Good God! I could not believe my eyes when I returned home and read the invitation to your wedding." He looked suitably mournful for a moment. "You realize that now that you have been leg-shackled, Catherine will not give me a moment's peace? Whenever she becomes too insistent about my unmarried state, I have always been able to fob her off by telling her that she needn't worry—you weren't married yet either! Now what am I going to do?"

Dominic burst out laughing, his pleasure in seeing his

friend from Natchez very evident. The two companions shook hands enthusiastically, and after much pounding of each other's back and several ribald comments about the other's appearance and habits, they walked to the end of the gallery, where Adam had been sitting talking to Melissa.

As if it were something that he did every morning, Dominic strolled up to Melissa and, despite the interested onlooker, dropped a brief kiss on her surprised mouth. "Good morning, my dear," he drawled softly, his eyes intently studying her lovely features for a moment before he sat down in the chair next to her.

Somewhat flustered, Melissa busied herself by fussing with the items on the silver tray for a few minutes. Realizing that there was no cup for Dominic, she hastily rang for a servant, glad to occupy herself with housewifely details until she could regain her composure.

Sprawled comfortably in his chair, Dominic looked warmly at his glowing bride and said teasingly, "It seems that I cannot leave for a morning ride, madam, that I don't return home and find you entertaining guests! In this case a guest whose penchant for poaching other men's wives is well known to me." Sliding a caressing finger along Melissa's suddenly hot cheek, he added, "I think I shall have to shoot him before he even begins to think about trying any of his tricks with *my* wife!"

Her heart racing beneath the lacy insert of her attractive, high-waisted gown of cherry-pink muslin, Melissa said breathlessly, "He's already warned me of his reputation and has promised, since your skill on the dueling field is common knowledge, *not* to make any attempt to sway my emotions." Her own eyes brimming with mischief, she murmured, "I think that he is being most considerate and magnanimous, don't you? After all, he is nearly as handsome and charming as you!"

Adam St. Clair *was* a very handsome and charming young man, and there were those who would have been hard pressed to choose between him and Dominic. It didn't help matters that the two men in question were conspicuously similar in appearance and background. Like Dominic, Adam was tall, standing well above six feet; and like his friend's, his hair was thick and black, not as curly as Dominic's, but with an attractive wave to it. Their ages were the same too, Dominic being the older by just a few months, and until Dominic had purchased Thousand Oaks, they had both called the Natchez area home—Adam's plantation, Belle Vista, situated a scant three miles from Bonheur. But if there were many similarities between them, there was one marked difference: Adam had been born and raised in England, not coming to America until he was eighteen years old; instead of the drawling manner of speaking that Dominic had, his English accent was very apparent in his clipped speech, although the years in Natchez had softened it considerably. Adam was more intense also, possessing a more fiery, explosive personality, far more hotheaded than the cooler, calmer Dominic.

Even if the two young men had not taken a liking to each other at first meeting, their friendship probably still would have prospered—Adam's younger sister, Catherine, was married to Jason Savage, who just happened to be a close friend of Morgan's. There was a great deal of interaction between the Savages and the Slades, and so naturally Adam had always been included and he was as familiar with Dominic's family as Dominic was with his. Of late, the meetings between the two had been few, Dominic busy with his life and Adam equally busy with his own affairs, and so Dominic's delight in being with his longtime friend was not surprising.

The servant arrived with the other china cup as well as a freshly brewed pot of coffee, and it was only after everyone had been served that Dominic settled back in his chair and asked, "Now, what sort of excuse are you going to offer for not being here for my wedding?

Adam grimaced, his air of relaxation vanishing. "I'm afraid that Jason's business kept me away from Belle Vista until just recently. It was only when I stopped by the house on my way to New Orleans that I even knew of your wedding." His mood changed for a moment and he cast a languishing glance in Melissa's direction. "If only I had seen you first! Just think, madam, instead of that lump beside you, you could have been married to me!"

Melissa smiled at his teasing, and feeling very brave,

she put her hand on Dominic's sleeve and remarked, "You are too kind, sir!" She cast Dominic an uncertain look and added softly, "But I am . . ." She hesitated, then, encouraged by the warm expression in Dominic's eyes, said in a rush, "Content with the husband I have!"

Suddenly oblivious to Adam's presence, Dominic brought her hand up to his mouth and pressed a kiss on the back of her hand, his eyes locked intently on hers. "Are you, my dear? Are you really?" he murmured.

A lovely blush flooded her cheeks and, unable to sustain his probing stare, she glanced away and muttered helplessly, "I believe so."

Adam watched the scene with great interest, marveling at the change in the onetime avowed misogynist. Dominic might have protested loudly about the vices of marriage, but it appeared that he had radically changed his mind since they had last spoken. Deciding that he had called at the wrong time, Adam coughed delicately and said, "It seems that I have arrived at an inopportune time. Shall I leave?"

Recalled to their duties as host and hostess, Melissa and Dominic instantly uttered protests, and the conversation took a less personal turn as they began to hastily question Adam about the usual things—when had he arrived in the area? where was he staying? would he be here long?

Laughing, Adam held up a hand. "One question at a time, please! But those you've asked are easily answered. I arrived last night and went immediately to Oak Hollow, since I knew Royce would have word of your whereabouts." Adam smiled ruefully. "I had already taken a room at the tavern in town, but Royce insisted that I stay the night." He shot Dominic a teasing glance. "Since your abdication of the bachelor state, he is feeling rather bereft, and I believe he simply needed reassurance that he is not a vanishing species."

"And did you calm his fears on that point?" Dominic asked lightly. He had expected a glib answer from Adam and was slightly startled when an odd expression crossed Adam's face.

Almost frowning, as if he were confused about his own feelings, Adam said slowly, "Yes . . . yes, I did." His mood changing in a flash, he grinned and added, "He was quite relieved, I can tell you!"

The conversation continued in a lighthearted vein for several more minutes, and thinking that Dominic might like some time alone with his friend, Melissa eventually rose and took her leave of them. Since there were no pressing tasks that required her attention, she contented herself with wandering dreamily about the grounds, her gaze misty and a soft little smile on her lips.

Nothing had been settled between her and Dominic, and last night had proved nothing that she hadn't already known—Dominic wanted her body and he could arouse her to the heights of passion. But there was something different between them, and this difference wasn't just on her part. Dominic felt it too; it had been obvious in the way he looked at her, the way he spoke to her. Dared she hope that he had fallen in love with her? That even if all the lies she had heard about him proved to be true, miraculously he felt something deeper for her than he had for any other woman?

Even though he was listening interestedly to what Adam had to say, there was a part of Dominic's brain that was very busy mulling over the current, pleasant state of affairs that existed between him and Melissa; and while he was quite delighted with Adam's unexpected arrival, he was conscious of a strong desire within himself for Adam to leave . . . soon. Right now the most important thing on his mind was making certain that nothing would alter the growing rapport he sensed between him and his wife. He was on the point of politely suggesting that it might be better if Adam *did* call later when the other man said something that had his undivided attention.

"I've been biting my tongue since I arrived here, not wanting to say anything in front of Melissa, but the war news is bad, Dom. Very bad."

Seeing that he had Dominic's full concentration, Adam said bluntly, "The British attacked and burned the capital on the twenty-fourth of August!"

Part Four

To Trust My Love

The violet loves a sunny bank,
  The cowslip loves the lea;
The scarlet creeper loves the elm,
  But I love—thee.

Proposal
—Bayard Taylor

Chapter Twenty-three

THERE was a moment of stunned silence as Dominic took in all the disastrous implications of Adam's news. If Washington had fallen . . . He swallowed painfully, the horrifying vision of British Rule rising before his gaze. The war had never seemed real to him before; it had been too far-flung, too sporadic, too ill-defined to make itself felt beyond being an annoying nuisance. But this! This changed everything!

His voice was thick and rusty with emotion as he finally asked, "The President? His Cabinet?"

Quickly Adam reassured him. "The President escaped, although our forces were so mismanaged that at one point he and his party nearly plunged right into the middle of the British advance! And they would have done just that if a self-appointed scout, *self*-appointed, mind you, hadn't warned them at the last moment!"

Adam's face showed his disgust and contempt for what had been the disgraceful disarray of the American troops at the Battle of Bladensburg, which had taken place just outside the capital city. Shaking his head, he muttered, "Between them, General Winder, our disorganized commander of the army; Armstrong, our sulking and arrogant Secretary of War; James Monroe, supposedly our Secretary of State, but ever eager to try his hand at military tactics, and our ineffectual President, they practically *gave* the British a victory!"

Having vented at least some of the rage he felt for what had been shocking ineptitude, he went on dispiritedly. "It is hard for me to believe it even now, but with little more than twenty-six hundred men, the British were able to vanquish an American force of more than six thousand!" Shame evident in his words, Adam added dully, "We should have won, but almost from the first volley of rockets, the first thunder of the cannon, our lines broke, and in little more than half an hour our troops were in full retreat. It was a complete rout!"

Numbed by Adam's shocking account, Dominic could only stare at his friend, not quite able to believe that things had been as bad as stated. Giving himself a mental shake, he leaned forward and said hopefully, "But that was at Bladensburg. What happened at Washington? Surely we were better organized in the defense of our capital?"

Adam smiled bitterly. "There was no defense. The place was in utter chaos, people streaming out from the city in all directions, their belongings piled high on carts and wagons, rumors flying wildly through the streets, the military . . ." He gave a harsh laugh. "The military were as anxious as the civilians to put as much distance between themselves and the advancing British forces as possible. Oh, Winder tried to rally his men, but by then more than half his troops had taken to their heels and there was no stemming the tide—we ran like sheep chased by a pack of dogs."

Unwilling to dwell on the ignoble picture Adam presented, yet desperate to know the worst, Dominic questioned sharply, "You said that the capital had been burned. If there was no battle at the site itself, no one to offer resistance, how did the fire come about?"

Adam shrugged. "Major General Ross and Admiral Cockburn, the British commanders, merely wanted to teach us a lesson. And while I don't like to speak well of the enemy, they did show considerable restraint in their actions, even going so far as to not blow up the capitol building itself when several of our women begged them not to, fearful that the explosion would destroy their nearby homes. In the main, only public buildings were put to the torch, but Washington is still a sad sight . . . our capital is in ruins."

There was nothing Dominic could think of to say, the enormity of what had happened leaving him filled with a helpless rage. The shameful defeat at Bladensburg and the infamous burning of Washington were such devastating blows to the American government that he wondered bleakly if it could recover. His voice a mixture of anger and despair, he asked, "Do the British still hold the city?"

"No. After the most important buildings were aflame, they retreated. Before I left the area, there was speculation that their next target might be either Annapolis or Baltimore." Adam ran his hand tiredly over his face. "I didn't want to leave until I had definite word on where they might strike next, but I dared not tarry too long—Jason will want a factual account from me as soon as possible." He smiled faintly. "And since it was at his, er, request that I be in Washington, and since my entire purpose was to be his 'eyes,' it seemed logical that once the city had returned to something even only faintly resembling normality, I should be on my way."

"Jason sent you there?" Dominic inquired instantly, his surprise momentarily pushing aside the catastrophic events of the burning of Washington.

Adam nodded. "You know Jason—he believes firmly in keeping his finger on the pulse of the country. I believe he has even convinced some other poor fool to spy for him in England. He has tentacles everywhere, it seems." A grin broke across Adam's lean features. "He is more like his Uncle Roxbury than he would care to admit."

"Ah, speaking of Roxbury . . ." Dominic began and proceeded to explain, in a less-than-complimentary tone of voice, Jason's fine hand in his own affairs.

Having been enmeshed in Jason's machinations on more than one occasion, Adam listened with commiseration. He couldn't help being amused by the situation, though, and when Dominic finished speaking, Adam's blue eyes glinted with amusement. "And is your bride most understanding about your apparent flirtation with another woman?" he asked.

"Now what do you think?" Dominic retorted, the memory of the harsh words he and Melissa had exchanged a scant forty-eight hours ago still rankling and reminding him unpleasantly that things had not been completely settled between them. "I don't believe that Melissa is a chatterbox, but I cannot take the chance—and then there is the depressing possibility that even if I were to tell her the truth she might not believe me! Might even think I was lying to her!''

Adam could not help teasing him about the situation, but the topic of the war was too compelling to be ignored for long, and in just a few minutes they were deeply involved in a discussion about the repercussion of the burning of Washington. The conversation could have gone on indefinitely, but Adam was pressed for time and after a short while he said regretfully, ''I really must be on my way. I have lingered here much longer than I intended, but I did not want to be in the area, however briefly, without calling on you.''

They both rose to their feet and slowly began to walk down the length of the gallery toward Adam's horse. ''I can only hope that when next we meet, I have much better news for you. In the meantime, I must leave for Terre du Coeur. Jason will have my hide if I do not reach him without further delay.'' Swinging effortlessly up onto his restive horse, Adam said lightly, ''It is too bad that I cannot remain here and lift the burden of remaining, ah, *friendly* with Lady Bowden from your shoulders.''

Dominic smiled faintly. ''Yes, I'm sure that you would not find it a very arduous task.''

Adam laughed; then, his dark face suddenly serious, he murmured, ''Be careful, Dom. That brother of hers sounds like a nasty brute.''

Dominic needed no warning, well aware, after the beating he had taken in London, of Latimer's dangerousness. He merely commented, ''Royce will keep watch at my back, and knowing that Latimer is capable of anything will make me all the more cautious in my dealings with him.''

Adam nodded and then, kicking his horse, rode away. A slight frown between his eyes, Dominic watched Adam's tall form disappear down the driveway, the sensation that there were troubled days ahead for all of them very strong. The British strike at Washington had changed the whole tenor of the war for him, and he suspected that he would not be alone in this feeling. Mulling over the far-reaching implications of Adam's unwelcome news, he finally went in search of Melissa. Though he appreciated the niceties of Adam's restraint, he felt that there was no use in withholding the information from her; soon the entire countryside would be aflame with it.

Dominic was entirely correct in his assumption, and in those first black, disbelieving days, as word of the terrible destruction wrought on the nation's capital filtered slowly throughout the country, the opinion was against the President and his Cabinet. The Winchester, Virginia, *Gazette* blared: "Poor, contemptible, pitiful, dastardly wretches! Their heads would be but a poor price for the degradation into which they have plunged our bleeding country."

Eventually the tide of rage and indignation faded and there was a wave of sympathy for the embattled President. The change of attitude was best expressed by the influential Niles' *Weekly Register:* "War is a new business to us, but we must 'teach our fingers to fight'—and Wellington's *invincibles* shall be beaten by the sons of those who fought at *Saratoga* and *Yorktown.*"

The burning of Washington seemed to unite the country as a whole, help flooding in from all directions. The greatest outpourings of men, money and sympathy came from the big cities along the coast and the Northeast. Rufus King of New York, the darling of the Federalists, declared that he would "subscribe to the amount of my whole fortune." In Frederick, Maryland, a company of eighty-four men was raised within twenty-four hours and within another four hours was marching to Washington. As far away as the Richland District of South Carolina, the citizens raised a hundred men and three thousand dollars for supplies. Even New England, which had been hotly antiwar, rallied to the cause, Governor Martin Chittenden of Vermont declaring passionately, "The time has now arrived when all degrading party distinctions and animosities, however we may have differed respecting the policy of declaring or the mode of prosecuting the war, ought to be laid aside; that every heart may be stimulated and every arm nerved for the protection of our common country, our liberty, our altars, and our firesides." It was all very stirring, and up and down the Atlantic seaboard the country was galvanized into action.

In the interior, where the news was already several weeks old when it finally arrived, the reactions were not as obvious, although the anger was just as intense. As had occurred along the coastal reaches of the country, there was furious talk of raising men and money, but soon enough common sense prevailed. They were weeks, possibly months, away from being of any help, and the rumors of a possible British attack on Mobile, Alabama, or New Orleans had men thinking of protecting the territory closer to home. Everyone, however, seemed caught up in the events of the war, eager for news, less complacent and more ready to commit himself to the war effort.

As could be expected, the situation between Dominic and Melissa was momentarily eclipsed by the upheaval within the nation, and it was many days after Adam had departed before things began to return to something approaching normality. During that time Dominic had been totally preoccupied with considerations pertaining to the war, and there had been several meetings held by the various plantation owners and businessmen in Baton Rouge to discuss various strategies and methods to best use the men and arms available to them. This was not only to protect their own homes and families, but also to be ready to go wherever they were needed on a moment's notice.

Morgan and Leonie had left Baton Rouge immediately after Adam, Morgan feeling, not unnaturally, that his place was in New Orleans. There were times in the days that followed, when tempers frayed and angry words were exchanged as hot-blooded gentlemen argued over the *best* plan for the area, that Dominic wished for Morgan's cool practicality. He and Royce did their utmost to keep friends and neighbors from taking out their frustrations on one another, Dominic saying wryly to two rather flush-faced gentlemen that "It is the British we wish to kill—not ourselves!"

Latimer's presence at some of the town meetings made Dominic decidedly uneasy, but as everything discussed was of a most general nature, he did not think that Latimer would learn anything of great value . . . or anything that couldn't be discovered on any street corner, opinions being freely exchanged everywhere. He kept a careful eye on the Englishman, though, noting whom he talked with at length and with which gentlemen he seemed to be on the best of terms. It came as no surprise to him that Latimer concentrated his attention on those individuals, like Colonel Grayson, who either had once been British officers or were descendants of those who had been labeled "Tories" and had fled the Colonies for the sanctuary of the Louisiana Territory when the War for Independence had broken out. Latimer's actions only confirmed Jason's suspicions, and while the ridiculous story that Deborah had told Dominic had to be at least considered, it had been the opinion of Morgan, Royce and Dominic that the philanthropic organization was merely a rather flimsy ruse to cover the Englishman's true activities. Of course, there was no proof of anything, and Dominic supposed that was what grated on him the most, that and having to watch a man he clearly viewed as an enemy be accepted and apparently well liked by people who should have known better. He and Latimer politely avoided each other's company, and when they did meet, as happened occasionally in the small society in which they both moved, they would exchange only a cool nod of the head and then find some compelling reason to move on.

The constraint between them was not as noticeable during the many town meetings they attended immediately after the burning of Washington, but as the first anxious weeks passed and Dominic and Melissa began to accept more and more invitations to social functions in the neighborhood, two things became obvious to those who paid attention: that Zachary Seymour appeared to be Deborah Bowden's constant companion (except for those times when she was to be found fawning over Dominic Slade) and that Mr. Slade did not seem to care overmuch for the handsome Englishman. It was also apparent that Mr. Latimer was equally not fond of Mr. Slade's company.

Melissa, of course, noticed it at once, but then she had good reason to observe the two men closely. Their reaction to each other came as no great surprise to her, although she did wonder at the degree of dislike that existed between them. After all, she had only *suggested* that she might be interested in Latimer. She finally came to the lowering conclusion, especially when she remembered Latimer's letter, that the enmity between the two men had nothing to do with her—it was somehow tied up with what had happened in London in connection with Lady Bowden. A very lowering conclusion indeed.

Even though nothing had been settled between Dominic and Melissa and they slept chastely, each in his own bed, there did exist between them a tacit truce of sorts. It was as if, during this time of anxiety and upheaval within the nation, their problems had been put aside and all their energies were taken up with the more serious matter at hand—the war. The news of the burning of Washington had come as a terrible shock to Melissa, and she had experienced all the rage and fear of any normal American; and like women all across the nation, her next thoughts were of her menfolk and the dangers they might face.

She had felt both guilty and relieved when it had been decided *not* to send a contingent of volunteers to the Atlantic seaboard, but rather to keep them in readiness to be used in possible defense of the southern borders. Sending a beloved man, whether husband, lover, father or son, off to war would never be easy, but with things so unsettled between her and Dominic, Melissa dreaded the idea of waving him off to war, never knowing if the powerful feeling that seemed to be growing stronger day by day between them was real and true or simply a fantasy. . . . Just the mere notion of him facing a barrage of English gunfire filled her with terror, and the war suddenly became very real to her.

But as the days passed, as September slowly gave way to October, her first rush of fear gradually lessened, particularly when the news that came trickling down the Mississippi River from the towns and cities in the north was only good: Baltimore, under the generalship of Samuel Smith, had valiantly repulsed the British attack on that city during the first week of September. Even more satisfying to the Americans, Major General Robert Ross, one of the British officers who had ordered the burning of Washington, had been killed by a sharpshooter. Then on September 11, at Plattsburgh, New York, a large British invasion force, under the command of Sir George Prevost, had been defeated; and on Lake Champlain, the American naval captain Thomas Macdonough had displayed some brilliant tactics and annihilated the British squadron which had accompanied Prevost. The news might be weeks old by the time it reached the remote towns and villages of the country, but it was just as joyfully received as if the event had happened yesterday.

As things slowly settled back into some appearance of normalcy, Melissa's thoughts increasingly returned to the bewildering and dissatisfying situation that existed between Dominic and her. She saw him seldom these days; it seemed to her that he was always rushing out the door on his way to some important meeting, and though he was unfailingly polite to her those times they were together, attending this party or dinner or that one, it was not quite the relationship she had envisioned that morning Adam St. Clair had arrived with the news of the burning of Washington. They were still as chaste as if they were brother and sister. It was a situation which Melissa found completely mystifying, especially since Dominic had sought her out and, during the night which had followed, had left her in no doubt of his desire for her. Unfortunately, it was equally true that he had not expressed any undying love for her, nor had he declared that he would spend every night in her arms. But if she found the situation mystifying and unacceptable, she was not quite brave enough to change it. For many more nights than she cared to contemplate, she had lain awake in her own lonely bed, trying to gather enough nerve to fling open the doors that separated their bedchambers and march boldly into her husband's room and . . . seduce him! Some nights she would actually get as far as her hand on the doorknob before her courage would evaporate and she would scuttle miserably back to her own bed to spend the remainder of the night tossing and turning, afflicted by the most explicitly carnal dreams imaginable.

Melissa might have been able to do as she desperately wanted if there had not been the painful question of Dominic's involvement with Deborah Bowden. There were times she could have sworn that he cared nothing for the other woman, that he was actually annoyed by the way

Deborah attempted to monopolize his attention at the various social functions that they all attended, and yet he continually allowed Deborah to get away with the most outrageous conduct. Melissa was in a state of constant, angry bewilderment. Dominic's manner to her, the few moments they had alone, was warm and gallant, the expression in his gray eyes making her pulse quicken; and then the next, he appeared to be vitally absorbed in some silly antic of Deborah Bowden's.

Of course, Melissa admitted guiltily to herself, *she* hadn't helped matters either by letting Latimer attach himself to her side. But what else could I do? she thought mutinously. If my husband is going to be off dancing attendance on some other woman, shouldn't I be allowed to amuse myself with a handsome man? The problem was that Melissa was not at all amused by Latimer and that every moment she spent in his company was dreadful. Not that he forced himself on her—he always acted scrupulously polite—but whenever she was with him, she was always miserably conscious of the fact that it was because of his sister that she even tolerated his company and that if Dominic had not left her side to be led around by Deborah, she would have nothing to do with Julius Latimer!

Her irrational belief that Dominic might not be as black as Josh and Latimer had painted him had taken quite a beating these past few weeks, but she was still clinging stubbornly to the notion that she might have condemned him unfairly. This was rather hard to do when she saw him smiling with apparent besottedness into Deborah's animated features, and while her earlier confidence was somewhat eroded, she was still determined to talk to Josh about Dominic. She had made several attempts to do so recently, but Josh, like Dominic, had been taken up with affairs relevant to the war and had been absent from Oak Hollow those times that she had called to see him.

Royce, too, had proved to be singularly elusive, and her attempts to have any sort of private conversation with him were always brought to an abrupt end when he would hastily recall an appointment for which he was late. If she had not known better, she would have thought that Royce was avoiding her. But why would Royce suddenly become so . . . uneasy in her company? What did he have to hide?

Frustration made her blunter than she would normally have been, and one afternoon in early October, Royce called unexpectedly to find Dominic gone from the house, and was about to ride away when Melissa hastily stopped him. "Don't go! I wish to talk to you."

A decidedly wary expression flitted across Royce's handsome face, and edging toward the door, he said politely, "Another time, my dear. I really must be on my way."

But Melissa was not to be denied. Catching Royce's arm, she looked up at him and in a tone of voice halfway between pleading and demanding, she said, "Royce, your errand cannot be *that* urgent—I must talk to you."

He might have made good his escape, except her pale features and the faint bluish circles under her eyes that clearly spoke of sleepless nights gave him pause. He, more than any other outsider, knew of the difficulties Melissa was facing in her marriage. He suspected that, while the marriage might not have been a love match to begin with, neither Dominic nor Melissa was as indifferent to the other as either might pretend. In fact, he would have wagered a very large sum on the notion that they were helplessly in love with each other! Which he found rather amusing, especially with the added ingredient of Dominic's involvement with Deborah injected into the already tense situation. And though he had no qualms about watching Dominic wiggle and squirm in the prickly quagmire created by Jason's request, figuring that Dominic was quite capable of fending for himself, he was not immune to the suffering of a cousin for whom he had a great deal of fondness. Up until this moment, he had found the entire episode highly entertaining, especially observing Dominic trying to woo a wife and keep a grasping harpy like Deborah Bowden on convivial terms at the same time, but the unhappiness in Melissa's eyes lessened his enjoyment considerably and, his hard face softening, he capitulated to her request, saying gently, "If you insist, my dear."

Allowing Melissa to guide him to the salon, he seated himself next to her on the sofa, and taking one of her hands in his, dropped a fond kiss on the soft skin. Meeting her troubled gaze, he asked, "What is it that is causing you such distress?"

Her sweet mouth twisted slightly. "Is it so obvious? I thought that I was hiding it rather well."

"Not from me," he replied quietly, and not relishing his own predicament, he plunged right into the speech. "I suppose it is Dominic and his flirtation with Deborah Bowden? I told you the night of your dinner party that you had nothing to fear from that creature."

"Then why does Dominic let her fawn all over him?" Melissa fairly wailed, all her fears and uncertainties billowing up inside her.

"Because he must!" Royce replied bluntly, not liking his role at all.

Melissa's eyes widened, her confusion apparent. "Because he must," she repeated blankly. "Why? What sort of hold does she have over him?"

Royce sighed. "She doesn't have any hold at all over your husband, and if you weren't such an innocent, you would know that he would like nothing better than to throttle the clinging Lady Bowden and never stray from your side again."

Her eyes fixed on his with painful intensity. "How do you know that?" she asked huskily. "He d-d-didn't want to marry me—you know that your father forced us to wed." She swallowed with difficulty. "A-a-and L-L-Lady Deborah is very beautiful and sophisticated."

"And a more conniving, self-centered little bitch would be hard to find!" Royce growled roughly, his contempt and dislike of Lady Bowden more than obvious.

Since Royce had always acted in public as if he, too, found Deborah charming, Melissa was even more bewildered by his words. "I thought that you were as enamored as Zachary . . . and Dominic by her."

"Good God, no!" Royce burst out. "I've never liked her—not even in Dominic's salad days when he was foolish enough to think, at least for a little while, that he might be in love with her. To anyone with a normal amount of common sense and not blinded by her pretty face, it is glaringly apparent that she is as dangerous and unprincipled as her brother.''

"You don't like Julius either?" Melissa asked with astonishment. "Why, Royce, you are with him all the time! At every party I have been to lately, it seems that you and Julius are practically inseparable . . . except when Julius is with me.''

"And I've been meaning to talk to you about that, sweetheart,'' Royce began with an ominous glint in his golden-brown eyes. "What the hell are you playing at by encouraging that bounder's attentions?''

Her temper rising a little, Melissa glared at her cousin. Stiffly she said, "If Dominic feels it is perfectly acceptable to chase after another woman, I see no reason why I cannot have a, er, friendship with a gentleman!''

"Well, for God's sake, at least choose a gentleman,'' Royce said irascibly, "and not that cad!''

There were several glaring inconsistencies in Royce's statements. Her eyes narrowed in thought, Melissa asked slowly, "If he is such a bounder and a cad, why are you such good friends with him?''

It suddenly occurred to Royce that he was on the point of revealing far more than was necessary for Melissa to know. He had only meant to comfort her, *not* to divulge information that might put her in danger. Unlike Dominic, Royce knew very well that Melissa could keep her mouth shut, and under different circumstances he would not have hesitated to tell her everything. But Melissa was also quite reckless and adventuresome, and he shuddered to think of what might happen if she decided to help in the delicate situation. That she would want to help, would in fact try her own hand at spying, he had little doubt, memories of their childhood and certain dangerous pastimes that they had undertaken together in their youth flashing across his mind. No. He could say nothing more and must regain some of the ground that he had lost. Besides, he decided virtuously, it was up to Dominic to explain matters to Melissa—he would be infringing on a husband's rights if he were to take Melissa into his confidence. That he was acting just a bit cravenly, he was very well aware, but knowing Melissa's temper and guessing how she would react to the role in which they had cast her, Royce felt no compunction about his actions. Let Dominic handle his own wife, he concluded sardonically—far be it for a mere cousin to intrude.

Having come to that decision, he promptly carried their discussion back into Melissa's camp. Putting on his sternest face, he said in a righteous manner that would have done Josh proud, "It is not for you to question my acquaintances. And you are not such a goose that you don't know that a gentleman may have several, ah, friends whom he would never introduce to the females of his family."

"Stuff and nonsense!" Melissa retorted angrily, her eyes gleaming with indignation. "Latimer is not some back-alley rogue you just happened to meet one night when you were out carousing. He is accepted everywhere, and there are many perfectly respectable people in the community who find his company, and that of his sister, highly agreeable. So I ask you again—why do you call him a cad but act his friend?"

Irritably Royce wished that Melissa were not quite so observant, and he knew that he must divert her attention instantly or she was going to come perilously close to guessing what he and Dominic were doing. And if it weren't for his certainty that she would want to be included in the charade, he wouldn't have minded in the least, but thinking of Latimer and visualizing what the Englishman might do if Melissa started asking some pointed questions made Royce exceedingly uneasy.

His handsome features arranged in a most arrogant expression, Royce said coldly, "What I may or may not do is none of your business. I am simply warning you that Latimer is not quite the gentleman he appears to be and that you would be wise to find someone else on whom to practice your wiles."

It was at times like this that Melissa longed fiercely for the freedom of childhood. Her hands were clenched into two rather respectable little fists, and she would have enjoyed nothing better than blackening Royce's eyes as she had once done when they were children and he had enraged her in just this same manner. Reminding herself forcibly that she was a grown woman, a married lady now, she contented herself with glaring at him and saying in a stiff voice, "I see that we have nothing else to say to one another. I apologize for detaining you." Turning her back on him, trying to hide both the hurt and the rage that his words gave her, she added, "I'm sure that you can find your way out."

Royce hesitated a second, hating the situation and cursing his own ineptitude. He had accomplished nothing but to hurt Melissa even more and to create a breach between them. His features softening, he took a step in her direction, saying in a coaxing tone, "Lissa, I never meant to cause harsh words between us, nor did I mean to wound you. Please, let us be friends again."

It was very difficult for Melissa not to yield to the pleading note in Royce's voice, but she was not going to pretend that everything was normal between them when it was obviously not. He was hiding something from her, she could sense it. But what? she wondered with a frown. When he had first entered the room, he had been full of concern for her, but the moment she had mentioned Latimer's name his entire manner had changed. Latimer . . . Latimer and his sister seemed to arouse the strangest reactions in the men of her family of late. Even Zachary appeared to be besotted by Lady Bowden . . . but that was something else, and forcing her straying thoughts to the matter at hand, Melissa suddenly realized that Royce had become cold and forbidding only when she had homed in on the fact that he was saying one thing and acting another in connection with both Latimer and his sister. How very interesting. And aware that it would do her cause no good to remain estranged from Royce, reluctantly she decided to accept his offer of peace.

Facing him, she gave him a slight smile. "We shall always be friends, Royce—even when you infuriate me the most."

He chuckled and dropped a brief kiss on her forehead. "That's my Lissa! And now, sweetheart, I really must be off." His face sobered and he muttered, "Lissa, don't worry about things. All this will end soon."

With that he was gone, leaving Melissa staring blankly at the doorway through which he had disappeared, her thoughts traveling in precisely the direction he had not wanted. Royce did not like either of the Latimers, she thought slowly; didn't like them at all, but on the surface he pretended to find them very good company indeed. Why? Why did Royce keep saying that Dominic's flirtation meant nothing to Dominic and yet Dominic seemed unable to resist Deborah's blatant lures? Could Dominic be playing the same mysterious game that Royce was with Latimer? Seeming to find Deborah attractive when in fact he did not? And, most curious of all, why would they be doing this?

Melissa spent several hours puzzling over the contradictory behavior of both Royce and Dominic in connection with the English visitors, but she could come up with no satisfactory answers. And thinking about Lady Bowden brought to mind something that had been troubling her peripherally for some time: not only did Lady Bowden appear to have her claws in Dominic, but the older woman also seemed to have enamored Zachary.

Since her marriage to Dominic, Melissa and Zachary had naturally not seen as much of each other as they had when living in the same house together, but brother and sister still managed to get together quite a bit. Either Zachary came calling or Melissa rode over to Willowglen to see him, and then there were the various social functions which they both attended. Not until this moment had Melissa actually realized how many times Deborah had been at Willowglen when she had called, nor how often Deborah had accompanied Zachary when he had come to visit her. In public, too, Deborah always seemed to be in Zachary's vicinity—except, Melissa admitted darkly, when the Englishwoman was hanging onto *her* husband! She supposed that she had been aware of Deborah's presence in Zachary's life, but she hadn't ever stopped to consider what it might mean.

Pushing aside for a little while the dilemma of Dominic and Deborah, she began to speculate about that same lady's relationship with her brother, not liking some of the conclusions that flitted across her brain. Lady Bowden, she acknowledged uneasily, had never appeared to pay Zachary the least heed until the Seymour fortunes had changed and Zachary had come into his share of the trust. No, that wasn't true, she decided with a frown. It had been after her marriage to Dominic. . . . Perhaps, when Deborah had realized that one rich gentleman was beyond her grasp, she had set her sights on another? A younger, more malleable man? A mere boy to be mesmerized and dazzled by the ripe beauty of an older woman?

Greatly disturbed by her train of thought, Melissa restlessly paced the confines of the small salon, hoping that her own dislike of Deborah was at the root of these unpleasant speculations. But she could not shake the sensation that while she had been absorbed in her troubles with Dominic, she had been overlooking the danger Deborah might present to Zachary's young heart. Trying to tell herself that she was just looking for another reason to mistrust Deborah, Melissa attempted to push away the ugly thoughts that were circling through her mind, but though she halfheartedly convinced herself that she was merely being silly, there were two questions that would not go away. Was Deborah only amusing herself at Zachary's expense? Or did she have a deeper motive for displaying a predilection for his company?

Chapter Twenty-four

SEATED in the parlor of the handsome house he had recently leased on the outskirts of Baton Rouge, Julius Latimer was staring at his sister, wondering much the same thing. His eyes narrowed and watchful, he studied Deborah for several long moments as she fiddled with her cup of tea, pretending not to be aware of his scrutiny.

The siblings were alone at the moment. Julius was seated in a high-backed leather chair, and across the room Deborah was sitting near a small table which held a silver teapot and the remnants of a light meal. The conversation between the two had been sporadic and only mildly interesting to either of them, but Deborah had mentioned Zachary Seymour's name in passing, and that had brought something to mind for Latimer.

Unlike Melissa, who knew Deborah only slightly, Latimer harbored no doubts about what his sister was up to; after all, they had discussed her actions at length and had decided that Zachary Seymour, now that the trust which had crippled his finances and made him an ineligible party had ended, might prove a valuable source of some extra money. The fact that he also now had a very wealthy and generous new brother-in-law made him even more appealing to the brother and sister, and they had immediately put in motion a plan that had worked very well for them in the past: Deborah's sweet smiles and artful wiles completely enslaving their prey while she cleverly solicited expensive trifles and gifts from the thoroughly besotted gentleman. And to their gleeful satisfaction, everything appeared to be going as planned, Zachary apparently perfectly happy to bestow more than one costly gewgaw upon the woman who smiled so warmly and beguilingly at him, allowing him to believe that she found him utterly fascinating.

But of late, Latimer had begun to wonder if Deborah might be carrying this little charade farther than they had planned—a furious, heart-wounded, rejected suitor was *not* what Latimer had in mind when he had broached the plan to his sister. A light flirtation, a mild dalliance, had been what they had discussed; and steepling his long, narrow fingers before him, he now remarked casually, "Aren't you laying it a bit too thick and rare in regard to the Seymour cub? You've picked up some very nice trinkets from him. Those sapphire earrings he gave you last week are particularly lovely and should fetch a tidy sum once we reach London . . . but we certainly don't want any ugly scenes or complications along the way."

Deborah merely smiled. "Oh, pooh! You are just starting at shadows. Believe me, I know how to handle my men, and Zachary is a lamb."

Julius did not look convinced, well aware of his sister's great vanity. "He did not look so lamblike to me the other night when you waltzed off with Slade at the Hampton soiree."

"Hmm, I know," Deborah replied smugly. "He was quite angry with me, and it provoked a rather excitingly violent passion from him." A dreamy smile on her lips, she murmured, "Zachary is *such* a virile young man! I very nearly gave in to his demands to let him make love to me."

Latimer's face tightened. His voice dangerously soft, he said, "I thought we'd decided that you were not going to let things get out of hand. You were, if my memory serves me correctly, only to entice him, not seduce him!"

"You worry too much, brother mine," Deborah retorted with a hard note. "I know exactly what I am doing! Besides," she added petulantly, "I deserve some sort of reward for passing up the opportunity to be Dominic's wife and for suffering through that travesty of a marriage with old Bowden." Her lovely features twisted and she muttered, "You don't know what it was like forcing myself to kiss that randy old goat and then letting him touch me and make love to me. If you hadn't taken care of him when you did, I don't know how much longer I could have put up with him without murdering him myself!''

"Will you shut up about that!" Latimer growled. "Your loose tongue is going to send us both to the gallows. The incident with Bowden is behind us, and you needn't keep bringing it up."

Shrugging her slim shoulders, Deborah took a dainty sip of her rapidly cooling tea. "Very well, but stop harping to me about how I'm handling my end of things." A sly look entered her eyes. "You didn't do so well with the hoyden."

His blue eyes very cold, Latimer said icily, "I may not have bedded the wench yet, but I did get the twenty-five thousand dollars—which was what we were after in the first place. It was only when I thought there was little hope of gaining the money that I decided to get some sort of recompense from the situation, and taking that haughty little bitch to bed seemed appropriate." A faintly lascivious smile touched the corners of his thin lips. "Teaching her to obey me in *every* way might almost have been worth the money."

"Yes, and if you don't stop gambling the way you have been lately, you're going to lose every penny of it!"

"Oh, shut up! I know what I'm doing. Roxbury may have funded this trip and he may have promised us a small fortune when we return to England, but in the meantime, there are appearances to keep up if I am to maintain my standing among these men. The same men, don't forget, whom Roxbury wants me to cultivate and bring over to our side. Taking part in their pursuits is only one way of ingratiating myself with them . . . and there is something else, too, for you to remember the next time you chastise me for gambling. Many of these planters are incredibly reckless gamblers, and there are several fortunes to be made by a man clever with the cards—far more money than Roxbury has promised us. I intend to take full advantage of this unexpected opportunity, and if I seem to lose for a while, so much the better. When I start to win . . ." A crafty expression entered the cold blue eyes. "And I *will* start to win very soon—then you'll be quite happy with the results of my gambling, believe me.''

"Have you set your sights on anyone in particular?''

Latimer nodded. ''Hmm, yes. That Franklyn boy is just the sort of careless young fool who makes it almost sinful for me to pluck.''

Deborah snorted. ''I just hope he doesn't realize that he *has* been gulled and there is more of that same nasty business there was in London.''

Latimer brushed her comment aside, saying lightly, ''It doesn't matter. Even if he were to suspect that I had cheated him and was stupid enough to challenge me to a duel—what do we care what these provincials think? We'll be leaving here soon—the plan is for us to be in New Orleans before the first of the year, and shortly after that, if all goes well, we'll be back in London, *this* time with a respectable fortune to command.''

Looking unconvinced, Deborah asked, ''Must you lose so much money to him before recouping?''

"I don't intend to lose much more, but it was important to lull him into being overconfident about his abilities to best me. And by having lost the amount I have, there will be several gentlemen who will think that my luck merely changed and will not be as suspicious as they would have been if I had simply proceeded to strip the silly cub of his fortune.''

"Do you think that your antics will escape Dominic's notice?'' Deborah asked dryly.

An ugly look crossed Latimer's chiseled features. ''So much the better, my dear, if they don't! I wouldn't make the same mistake I did the last time I faced him on the dueling field. Only one of us would walk away this time, and you can be sure that it will *not* be me who lies bleeding in the dirt!''

Her petulant expression returning, she said moodily, ''I still don't know why you didn't want me to marry him when I had the chance. He is far more wealthy than that old goat Bowden, and I certainly would have enjoyed being in *his* bed a great deal more.''

"Is that why you are fawning all over him now? Hoping for a taste of what was denied you then?''

"Why not?" Deborah demanded hotly. "You have your women, and I don't see why I can't bed the man of my choice for once, instead of making myself agreeable only to those you choose for their generous pocketbooks!" A pout on her lovely mouth, she muttered, "I would have liked being married to Dominic."

His annoyance showing, Latimer stood up and walked across the room to stand near her. Pouring himself a cup of tea, he said half angrily, half ruefully, "If I had known precisely *how* wealthy he was, I would not have stood in your way. I thought he was simply an arrogant colonial on the lookout for a bride with whom to impress his yokel friends back home." Stirring his tea with a silver spoon, he mused aloud, "But even if I had known of his wealth, I still don't think your marriage to him would have been a good idea. He is too sharp by half, and I don't believe he would have stood still for us to bleed him—I would have had to finish him off a lot sooner than I did Bowden."

"Well, we certainly didn't gain very much from *that* plan of yours, I must say!" Deborah retorted waspishly. "And I don't know that I would have wanted you to kill Dominic—who knows, I might have wanted to *remain* his wife."

"Now, that I rather doubt! Can you picture yourself surrounded by a brood of brats? Living here at the edge of nothing? It is hardly the setting I would choose for you, my dear," Latimer drawled, and when his sister merely sniffed disdainfully, he added, "Since we arrived here you have done nothing but complain about how crude and boring you find the country and the people. Do you really expect me to believe that you would be content to be buried in this barbarian wilderness? Away from all the glitter and excitement of London? You delude yourself."

Deborah hunched a shoulder. "You're probably right. And I must say that Dominic is not quite as I remember him. Oh, as handsome, to be sure, but he seems—"

"Less infatuated? Less likely to overlook your flaws? Less inclined to indulge you?" Latimer asked sardonically. "You forget that he has a wife now—a very beautiful wife."

"And does it ever gall you!" Deborah retorted sweetly. "You may pretend that you don't care that she escaped you and married him, but I know you too well to believe that nonsense."

A hard edge to his voice, Latimer replied, "Keep any thoughts you may have about my intentions for Melissa Slade to yourself! I have worked too hard to regain a friendly footing with her for you to ruin it all by a loose tongue! All you have to do is keep Zachary sweet and, if you wish, amuse yourself with Dominic, but don't get any clever ideas about my relationship with Melissa in that pretty head of yours."

Deborah shot him a venomous look, but she made no comment. It was only at times like this that she felt the faintest stirring to escape from under Julius' thumb. For the most part she was perfectly happy to let him set the order of her life, even when it involved the disagreeable necessity of marrying a man old enough to be her grandfather. Julius had always dominated her, and since Deborah was essentially lazy, greedy and vain, she had always found it far easier to go along with whatever he planned than to strike out on her own. Dominic's offer had been tempting, but Deborah did not like the idea of being on her own, of being without a *man* to arrange everything for her; and though there was the odd occasion when she fleetingly considered taking up with someone other than her brother, she always dismissed it. Julius allowed her more freedom than either a husband or a lover would, and since she loved herself far too much to waste any real emotion on anyone else, it seemed just as well to let Julius see to everything. In her own fashion she was really quite fond of her brother, but that didn't mean that she was always pleased with his plans, or that she didn't chafe now and then at his arrogant disposal of *her* wants and desires.

Sulkily she regarded his handsome face. "It isn't fair," she finally said sullenly. "You're up to something with that silly little hoyden, but I'm not allowed to make love with her brother if I want."

"The lady's husband doesn't satisfy you?" Latimer asked mockingly.

If anything, her sulky expression increased. "He probably would if I could get him into bed, but we are always surrounded by other people."

"Since you seem to want him so badly, can't you arrange a rendezvous with him? In the right setting I'm sure that you'd have no trouble convincing him to sample your charms."

A cunning expression suddenly entered her clear blue eyes. "Of course!" she cried gaily. "Why hadn't I thought of that!" Her sour mood vanished as if it had never been, and now in perfect good humor, she sprang to her feet and fairly danced from the room.

But upstairs, as she sat behind a lovely little rosewood desk, her light mood vanished. A faint scowl on her lovely face, she stared at the empty sheet of paper. Composing the note to Dominic was not going to be a problem—she knew just what to write that would bring him on the run. Her problem was selecting a proper place for them to meet and naming a time that would ensure their privacy.

Nibbling distractedly on her quill, she sat there, lost in thought as she selected and then discarded several possible sites for the type of rendezvous she had in mind. It must be a private and secluded place; it must be romantic and it must be away from the immediate proximity of the house . . . yet not too far away. With an ill-tempered movement, she threw down her quill and crumpled the blank sheet of paper. There was no point in writing the note to Dominic until she had determined their meeting place. With a disgruntled droop to her Cupid's bow mouth, she wandered from her bedchamber, busily casting through her mind for any place that might be even remotely suitable for Dominic's seduction. . . .

Deborah was not the only one planning a seduction, but whether Latimer wanted to seduce Melissa simply for herself or because she was Dominic's wife was unclear to him. He had worked very hard these past months to undo the damage he had inflicted by miscalculating Melissa's pride and spirit earlier, and during the past few weeks he had begun to hope that he had managed to restore at least some of her trust in him. It had been most difficult for him to act the part of a truly repentant friend eager to make amends, always having to hide the hatred and envy he felt for Dominic, always having to be careful to conceal the rage and resentment he experienced at the knowledge that she had escaped his grasp and married the one man he detested above all others. A slow smile suddenly curved Latimer's mouth. But it seemed that at last his meek manner and solicitousness were going to reap him the prize that he wanted.

Latimer's smile deepened. His sister had unknowingly helped his cause. Her blatant pursuit of Dominic had driven Melissa closer to him, and that more than any other reason was why he was willing to let Deborah continue her less-than-proper antics. If Deborah did manage to seduce Melissa's husband, so much the better; he would take great pleasure in providing the mistreated wife with an obliging shoulder to weep on, Latimer thought cynically. And if Melissa felt mistreated enough . . . Latimer almost smirked. If he read the situation correctly, once Melissa learned that Dominic had actually bedded Deborah, he strongly hoped that she might be willing to pay her errant husband back in kind . . . and *he'd* be standing right there with his arms held wide open!

Melissa's unexpected and thoroughly unwelcome marriage to Dominic Slade had come as a nasty shock to Latimer. He'd been so sure that he had her trapped, so positive that she would prefer giving herself to his attractive self rather than seeking some other means to meet his demands, that the news of her impending marriage to Dominic had left him dumbfounded. It was weeks before he could finally accept the fact that she had truly escaped him and that his wicked little plan of sampling her charms before informing her, with a suitable amount of regret, of course, that he had decided he really must have the money after all, had failed. He had been furious, and even the receipt of the money owed him had not lessened his irrational feeling of having somehow been cheated.

Time in Baton Rouge was growing short for Latimer. In keeping with the schedule that he had agreed to with Roxbury in London well over a year ago, he was to leave for New Orleans in a matter of weeks. If he was to have his satisfaction, it must be soon. And before he left there were several little items he intended to bring to pleasant conclusions, Latimer thought with a faint smile. Planting a prominent pair of horns on the arrogant head of Dominic Slade was only one of the delightful occurrences he had to look forward to before he departed for New Orleans. There was also the matter of the Franklyn boy. . . .

Whistling softly to himself, Latimer rose from his chair and walked directly to his bedchamber. Selecting a rather fine white silk waistcoat decorated with tiny black polka dots, he began to dress for the evening's entertainment— a small, all-male dinner party at the home of a wealthy young bachelor, Thomas Norton, who lived just a mile from Baton Rouge. Royce Manchester was to meet him here, and together they would ride to the Norton house.

Thinking of that, Latimer frowned slightly. He was just a little suspicious of Royce's apparent affinity for his company, though he could find no fault with the other man's manner. In London, Royce had clearly been aligned with Dominic, and on a few occasions that Latimer could bring easily to mind, Royce had been exceedingly cool and disdainful to him.

Naturally, it had occurred to him that Royce could be and was very likely spying on him, trying to catch him in the midst of some nefarious deed, and Latimer almost laughed out loud at the thought. The beauty of Roxbury's plan, and the only reason he had consented to take part in it, aside from the very generous benefits, was that it held, at worst, only a nebulous risk. He wasn't about to put his head in a noose for the amount of money Roxbury was willing to pay him!

Besides, he mused smugly as he wandered down the curving staircase which led to the entry hall of the house, why should he risk his neck when there were so many easier ways to make a fortune? Especially when there was such a ripe pigeon for plucking, like the Franklyn heir so close at hand? A cruel little smile tugged at one corner of his chiseled mouth. Tonight's party might very well see the turning of Mr. Franklyn's luck at cards. . . .

Dominic was also attending the same dinner party this evening, but unlike Latimer, he was not looking forward to it. Of late, it seemed that he seldom had a moment alone with Melissa, and he had been planning on enjoying a quiet night at home with her. A quiet night alone together that might allow him to, at long last, solve the mystery that was his wife. Unfortunately, Royce had thrown a damper on Dominic's much-longed-for evening of domestic tranquility by insisting that he attend the Norton party.

The amber-gold eyes glittering with decided annoyance, Royce had said bluntly just three days ago, "You may have to endure Deborah's clinging embraces whenever you happen to attend the same function, but *I* am forced to be constantly in Latimer's company—and it is damned distasteful, I can tell you! The fellow's a nasty bit of goods that ordinarily I wouldn't pass the time of day with, and for the past six weeks or so, I've been acting as if he's my best friend—and so far all for naught, for what I've learned of his connection to Roxbury! I've wenched with him, gotten drunk with him, attended cockfights with him and generally made myself available to him, and it has not, believe me, been the most enjoyable time I have ever spent! The man's a black-hearted rogue! I do not find him either amusing or intellectually stimulating, and if I have to endure another evening dancing attendance on him, I may very well do him a violence!" Fixing a burning eye on Dominic, he had concluded, "The least you can do is attend the Norton party and share my misery."

Reluctantly, Dominic had allowed himself to be persuaded, and so it was that instead of the intimate evening he had hoped for, he found himself committed to several hours of male revelry. Zachary was also attending, and they had planned to ride together to the Norton house. Dominic had just reached for the starched white cravat which Bartholomew was holding when he heard the sound of Zachary's voice drifting up the staircase.

Zachary had arrived unfashionably early, but as he was used to running tame through the Slade cottage, it presented no problem. Handing his tall, curly-brimmed beaver hat to the waiting butler, he wandered into the small salon at the front of the house and was pleased to find his sister sitting comfortably on the sofa, a slim book of sonnets in her hand. From her position and dress, a delightful gown of jonquil muslin, it was obvious that she was remaining home this evening, and gently Zachary teased, "What is this? The most-sought-after young matron in the neighborhood content to sit alone by her own fire? Do my eyes deceive me?''

Laughing, Melissa put down her book and said affectionately, ''Oh, Zachary, you dolt! Don't be ridiculous. You make it sound as if I am a gadabout of the worst sort.''

Lowering his long, elegant length into a nearby chair, Zachary replied with a smile, ''Well, you must admit that we have been very gay these past months, even with all the war talk. It seems that since your marriage—and the disbursement of the trust—we have both become *very* popular! I do not think that I have spent two evenings home this month!''

Her heart swelling with love and pride, she surveyed her brother as he lounged in the chair. He looked very sophisticated this evening, the crisp white cravat intricately folded at his neck, the dark blue silk jacket fitting his broad shoulders admirably and the black kerseymere breeches lying snugly against his muscular thighs. He looked the very picture of a wealthy, indolent young aristocrat, and Melissa found it incredible to think that less than six months ago they had been frantic to keep a roof over their heads.

She smiled at him and said almost wistfully, ''Things are very different for us now, aren't they?''

Zachary caught the wistful note in her voice, and his own smile faded as he leaned forward, his young face intent. ''You don't regret the marriage, do you, Lissa?'' His eyes boring into her, he asked, ''You are happy? I know that at first things were strained between you and Dominic, but . . . that is all in the past now, isn't it?''

His questions came as a surprise to Melissa, and for a long moment she hesitated in answering him. Did she regret marrying Dominic? Oh, no! her heart cried; absolutely not! But she did wish most passionately that the circumstances had been different, wished that she could have had a normal courtship, that she could have known that when Dominic asked her to marry him, it had been because he had wanted it and not because he had been compelled by an unpleasant set of incidents. Was she happy? A smile flickered briefly on her full mouth. There were times when she was ecstatically happy. Times when her happiness was almost tangible, so strong and bonedeep that she was certain she could touch it. But then . . .

She sighed. Despite the odd affinity between them, despite all the thrilling glances they had exchanged lately, despite the warm smiles and sweet promises she thought she glimpsed in Dominic's eyes, she could not be certain that she was not deluding herself, that her powerful desire to believe Dominic was *not* a callous womanizer and that he *had* come to care for her was not simply clouding her judgment. As for there being any strain between them, it definitely was not in the past and would not be, she thought vehemently, until something was done about Deborah Bowden! For a brief second an alarmingly feral light glinted in the lovely topaz eyes, but with an effort she brought herself back to the present and her brother's waiting silence.

There had been few secrets between the siblings; they had always been completely honest with each other, and for those reasons, Melissa answered cautiously. "I'm not *un*happy, Zach. I just wish . . ."

Her lack of words was eloquent in itself. His young face hard, Zachary reached across to grasp one of her slim hands. "Lissa, if there is something, *any*thing I can do that would make things easier for you, you know you have only to ask."

A lump in her throat, she slowly shook her head. "There is nothing that you or anybody else can do—it is between Dominic and me."

Her words did not satisfy him and, his fingers tightening on hers, he said softly, "I've wondered often at the suddenness of your marriage—you went from disliking him one day to being his bride the next—and though I said nothing at the time, I was confused and troubled by it."

The two occupants in the little salon were so intent on each other that neither heard Dominic's steps as he descended the staircase, nor were they aware of his presence as he hesitated outside the doorway, reluctant to interrupt them. They were both so serious and absorbed in their conversation that he was on the point of turning away, of giving them a few moments more of privacy, when Zachary's next question stopped him cold.

"Lissa, did Josh force you to marry him? Was it because of that damned trust?"

A stout denial hovered on her lips, but she hesitated that split second too long and Zachary pounced on it. "It *was* because of the trust, wasn't it? What did Josh threaten you with that made you change your mind about marriage?" Zachary inquired sharply, his fine mouth taut.

Dismay obvious in her face, Melissa sat there staring at her brother, desperately trying to decide how much of what had happened that fateful night would be safe to tell him. Berating herself for not swiftly distracting him, knowing that he would not let up now until he had the entire truth from her, Melissa said carefully, "The trust did have some bearing on the marriage, but it wasn't the only reason that I consented to marry Dominic."

"Aha! I knew it!" Zachary crowed exultantly. "Not that I don't understand why he would make a good husband," he added fairly. "It was just that you'd turned down several other equally wealthy and"—a quick smile curved his lips—"equally handsome young men, and then, out of the blue, you agreed to marry a man you'd known only a few weeks."

Remembering those early meetings with Dominic, the way his presence could send her pulse racing and her heart pounding, she said dreamily, "Sometimes it happens like that . . . time doesn't always make any difference to your emotions."

"That may be," Zachary agreed, but with a definite cynical ring to his tone. "But you have to admit that there was something a bit suspicious about your sudden engagement and marriage to Slade. I want you to tell me the truth about it and not try to fob me off with all the little bits and pieces that you think it is safe for me to know."

Melissa started at his words, her eyes growing very wide. How did he . . . ?

As if reading her mind, Zachary smiled gently. "Lissa, I know you probably better than anyone in the world and I know precisely how your mind works. You and I have been through much together, and if there is one thing I have learned about you, it is that you have always tried to protect me from the worst.'' He grimaced ruefully. ''I am no longer a child, Lissa. I will always be your younger brother, but I hope that you will not continue to shield me from certain possibly unpleasant things that I should know.''

''Oh, Zack!'' she cried distressfully, ''I never meant to—''

''I know, sweetheart, but as you've told me often enough, the burden sometimes becomes lighter if it is carried by two instead of one. Now tell me the truth and quit trying to protect me.''

Anxiously her eyes searched his; she wanted terribly to tell the truth to someone but was afraid to do so. Huskily she asked, ''If I tell you the truth, do I have your solemn promise that you will do *nothing* rash? That no matter how ugly or sordid something is, you will not provoke a duel?''

Zachary drew back slightly, obviously not liking this trend of conversation. A frown between his heavy black brows, he asked half angrily, half wryly, ''And if I won't promise, you won't tell me what really happened?''

Her expression worried but determined, Melissa nodded. ''Either I have your promise or this conversation stops immediately.'' Tensely she waited for his answer, knowing that if he agreed to her terms, though he might rant and rave and plead to be given back his promise, he would keep it. But without that promise . . . She trembled slightly. Without his promise, he would storm out of this room in search of Latimer, murder in his heart.

Zachary eyed her suspiciously for a long moment and then slowly and with obvious reluctance he nodded his dark head. ''You have my promise.''

Wanting to make positively certain that he could not maneuver around those simple words, she said clearly, ''I have your promise that no matter what I tell you, you will neither take nor plan a revenge and that especially you will challenge *no one*, no matter how dastardly the deed, to a duel.''

His jaw clenched and the topaz eyes so like hers glittering angrily, Zachary gritted out, "I promise to everything that you have just said!" Resentment getting the better of him, he added in a grumbling tone, "But I think it's damned unfair what you have asked of me!"

In the doorway, Dominic still stood motionless, one part of him appalled at his blatant eavesdropping, the other too riveted by the conversation to move. His breath suspended in his chest, his heart pumping with quickening excitement, he waited, torn between dread and eagerness for Melissa's revelations.

As soon as Zachary had given her the answer she wanted, Melissa nearly went limp with relief. And now that the moment had come, she seemed unable to control her tongue, the words flooding out as she relived those awful days leading up to the night in Dominic's room. She gave only the barest details, but watching Zachary's face darken, watching the fury grow in his golden-brown eyes, she was inordinately thankful that she had extracted that promise from him.

"That bloody bastard!" he burst out wrathfully. "I'd like to get my hands on him!"

Alarmed, Melissa dug her fingers into his palms. "You promised! You said no matter what!"

He gave a bitter laugh. "You have my word, my dear—and even though it would give me great pleasure to rip out his liver, I will not. But how I am to be civil to the bastard is beyond me! Lissa, you little fool! You should have told me!"

"And have you go out and instantly challenge him to a duel? Possibly lose your life? What would that have accomplished?"

Sending her an impatient look, he muttered, "Will you stop trying to protect me? We could have faced his threats together—at least you wouldn't have been alone." When her expression did not change, he added heavily, "Oh, don't worry, I've given you my promise and I shall not challenge him. Now tell me the rest, although some of it I can guess myself. It was because of Latimer that you offered to sell Folly to Dominic, wasn't it?"

Melissa nodded and once again picked up her tale, telling of the note from Latimer demanding that she meet him at the inn, of her decision to do so and why. It was not an easy story to tell and it became even more difficult when she came to the part of the mistaken room and Dominic's entrance into the scenario. She faltered only slightly at the part of waking up and finding herself in bed with Dominic, but then hurried on past the embarrassing moment of being discovered by Royce and Josh. Bleakly she told Zachary of Josh's threats to remove him from her care if she did not agree to the marriage.

There was a dangerous silence when she finished speaking. Worn out from the telling of her tale, she leaned back against the sofa and wearily closed her eyes. "So now you know how it was that I came to marry Dominic Slade."

"Good God! Lissa, why didn't you say something? I would have understood. If you had told the truth, I'm positive that Royce and Uncle Josh would have been more understanding about the situation."

Melissa's eyes opened and she sent him a sardonic glance, saying dryly, "Do you really believe that? It was a ready-made opportunity for Josh to accomplish what he had been trying to do since I turned seventeen. Do you honestly think that Royce or Josh, for that matter, would *not* have gone in immediate search of Latimer? That one or both wouldn't have demanded the satisfaction of a duel . . . and possibly died as a result? Do you think I could bear to have that on my conscience?"

Zachary fairly bristled, his outraged pride very evident. "It is our duty to protect our women from vermin like Latimer! It would have been only right if they had challenged him!" His anger and his resentment of the promise she had extracted from him chafing him badly, he said stiffly, "I think it was unfair of you to demand such a promise from me. You must allow me to take care of the fellow!"

When Melissa shook her head angrily in the negative, Zachary bounded to his feet and moved agitatedly to stand in front of her. "Lissa, you *must* release me!" His hands clenching tightly at his sides, he pleaded, "You must give me the right to avenge you!"

"Avenge?" Dominic echoed softly from the doorway,

a most peculiar expression on his dark features. Walking indolently into the room as if he had just arrived on the scene, he inquired coolly, "What is this talk of vengeance?"

Chapter Twenty-five

LIKE TWO guilty schoolchildren, Zachary and Melissa swung around to face Dominic, both of them babbling the most absurd nonsense in their frantic desire to hide from him not only the subject but the seriousness of their conversation.

"Vengeance?" Zachary repeated with suspect innocence. "There is no talk of vengeance here—I was just trying to convince Lissa to allow me to, um, make amends for having neglected her of late."

"Oh, yes!" Melissa broke in quickly, as Dominic's eyebrow slanted skyward with open skepticism. "And I was just telling him that I didn't mind in the least that he has been so busy these past few weeks."

There was a moment fraught with tension as they waited anxiously for his reaction, and their relief was almost patent when Dominic said smoothly, "Your devotion to each other is to be complimented." Glancing across at Zachary, he drawled, "And while I am reluctant to tear you away from your sister, I do believe that it is time for us to be on our way. Don't you agree?"

"Oh, absolutely!" Zachary said hastily. Dropping a brief kiss on Melissa's cheek, he gave her hand a reassuring squeeze and fairly bolted from the room.

Sauntering over to where Melissa sat on the sofa, Dominic surveyed her in silence for a long, unnerving moment, an odd smile on his hard mouth. His eyes shuttered, their expression hidden from her as he reached down and picked up one of her limp hands. Pressing a warm kiss on her cold fingers, he muttered in a thickened voice, "I wish that we could be alone this evening, that I did not have other commitments . . . but perhaps it is just as well—there are things that I must do this night.''

His grip on her hand increased and, surprising her, in one powerful movement he jerked her upright and pulled her slim form next to him. His lips lightly brushing her cheek, he growled, ''That I have kept my hands off you these past weeks is nothing short of miraculous!''

Reveling in the pleasure both his words and his touch gave her, Melissa gathered up her courage and asked shyly, ''Why have you? I thought . . .'' A charming blush stained her face. ''I thought that after . . . after that night that you would . . .''

Embarrassment stopped her from saying more, but Dominic understood precisely which night she was referring to, and a decidedly tender expression appeared on his face. ''That I would care to repeat the process?'' he teased gently. His fingers suddenly tightened around her shoulders and his mouth had a distinctly sensuous curve to it. ''Oh, sweetheart, you can't know *how* much I have longed to have you share my bed again, the nights I have lain awake remembering what it felt like to have you in my arms, but until . . .'' His mouth twisted with distaste. ''There are certain . . . entanglements I must rid myself of before I dare allow myself to give in to temptation as far as you are concerned. When next we lie together, I want there to be no shadows or misunderstandings between us.'' His gaze intent, he stared into her eyes. ''Do you understand what I'm saying?''

Melissa nodded slowly, all her hopes and longings suddenly blazing in her beautiful eyes. ''I think so.'' Her voice was husky as she added, ''But please . . . let it be soon.''

Dominic groaned and his lips caught hers in a deeply passionate kiss, all the hunger and frustration of the past weeks explicit in the way his mouth moved almost savagely against her softly yielding flesh. As quickly as the kiss had begun, it was ended and, his breath coming in short, rapid bursts, he said roughly, ''This very moment would not be soon enough for me. I swear, sweetheart, that it will not be much longer.'' Pressing a brief, hard kiss on her mouth, he spun away and strode rapidly from the room.

With stars in her eyes, Melissa absently touched her fingers to her stinging lips, not quite able to believe the scene that had just passed. Dared she hope? A shiver of delight snaked up her spine, and wrapping her arms around herself, she danced joyously about the small salon, an idiotic smile on her lips.

The smile on Dominic's mouth was almost as foolish when he joined Zachary on the gallery of the cottage, but as they rode away, his smile faded and his eyes narrowed as he considered his own stupidity. How could he have been so blind? It had all been right there before his very eyes, but he had refused to see it, to believe it. Stubbornly refused, he thought angrily. Stubbornly and pigheadedly refused to trust his own instincts. But not any longer, he decided with a grim twist to his mouth. And never again. Melissa was exactly as she appeared—beautiful and brave and gallant and a darling! The idiotic smile spread across his face once more as Dominic stared blindly ahead, wondrous visions of the future that could be his dancing enticingly through his brain.

In the faint moonlight that shone over the countryside, Zachary noticed Dominic's silly grin and decided that it was safe to risk some conversation. "Er, am I to understand that things are well with you and Lissa now?" he asked lightly.

"Well enough," Dominic returned easily, "but I'm hoping that before much longer they will be even better. *Very* much better!"

Encouraged by these words, Zachary daringly chose to probe a bit deeper. Keeping his eyes on the twisting moonlit trail, he asked carefully, "Lady Bowden run her course with you?"

Dominic shot him a sardonic glance. "Lady Bowden never had a course to run with me—though it may have appeared to the contrary."

Frowning, Zachary pulled on the reins of his horse, halting the animal. "What the devil d'you mean by that?" he inquired sharply.

"Precisely what I said. The lady holds no appeal for

me whatsoever." A look of sudden comprehension creeping into his face, Dominic added slowly, "Whatever charm she might have held for me ended the instant I first laid eyes on your sister."

"You mean," Zachary demanded with angry incredulity, "that I have been throwing myself in the path of the brass-faced, light-skirted frigate all for nothing?"

"My dear Zachary, you unman me!" Dominic said, a thread of amusement obvious in his voice. "Have you been offering yourself as sacrifice?"

Looking slightly nettled, Zachary kicked his horse into motion and replied stiffly, "Well, it just seemed to me that you and that forward piece were a mite too thick for my liking, and I thought that I would—"

"Throw a bit of competition my way?" Dominic inquired dryly.

A belligerent expression in the tawny eyes, Zachary muttered, "Why not? Lissa's my sister and I didn't want you to make her unhappy."

Dominic's amusement fled and his voice was thick with emotion as he said, "I have no intention of ever making Melissa unhappy again, and if she will let me, I have every intention of spending my life showing her precisely how much she means to me—how empty my life would be without her."

Uncomfortable at the intensity of Dominic's tone, Zachary said with an attempt at lightness, "It's not *me* that you have to convince! I always knew you were a right one, but you have had me worried with your antics around that Bowden wench."

A harsh expression on his face, Dominic replied, "I think you can safely forget about Lady Bowden. She has served her purpose."

Zachary might have wanted to ask a few more questions about this most intriguing subject, but something in Dominic's manner made him decide to let the matter drop. Before another topic of conversation could be introduced, the lights of the Norton place came into view, and the next several moments were taken up with dismounting and being greeted by their host.

Tom Norton was a tall, blond stripling who had been

blessed with both a generous nature and a substantial fortune with which to indulge his every whim. It was to his credit, being the only surviving son of a widowed mother, that he was neither spoiled nor extravagant in his tastes. He had, however, upon reaching his majority just a few months previously, decided it was time that he had his own home and had purchased the snug little house where tonight's entertainment was being held.

Norton had invited approximately a dozen or so gentlemen to his home, most of them younger men like himself and Zachary, but there were four or five men in their early thirties also attending, so Dominic did not feel like a graybeard watching the antics of the young. And since it was at Royce's behest that he was attending this strictly masculine party, he wasn't surprised, when he was shown into a large, pleasantly elegant room, to find Royce leaning negligently against the mantel of a marble-fronted fireplace, a resigned expression glimmering in the topaz eyes. Nor did Latimer's presence at one of the many card tables which had been set up for gaming startle him in the least.

After having been introduced to several young men whose faces he recognized vaguely from other social functions he had attended, and a snifter of brandy had been thrust into his hand, Dominic unobtrusively made his way over to Royce's side. Dominic sipped his brandy and murmured, "I see that our friend still prefers to practice his expertise on the downy ones."

"Hmm, yes. That's the Franklyn cub, and Latimer has been cultivating him for several weeks now. He's lost an impressive sum to the young fool and I believe that he's decided it's time for his luck to change. I shouldn't be at all surprised if Franklyn leaves the table tonight a loser," Royce remarked dryly, his eyes on the fresh-faced young man who was the object of Latimer's attentions.

Latimer and Franklyn were playing cards at a table at the far side of the room, and as Latimer's back was to the two men near the fireplace, Royce and Dominic were able to watch the game closely without alerting Latimer to their interest in the proceedings. And both were aware the instant Latimer's luck changed, the moment the needed card was slipped from the sleeve of his coat.

"Ah, he is very good at it, isn't he?" Dominic commented languidly. "So good, in fact, that even watching for the move, I nearly missed it."

Royce muttered something obscene under his breath. "And this," he added harshly, "is the fellow I have had to associate *intimately* with these past weeks! You have had the easier task, believe me!"

"Perhaps," Dominic replied coolly. "But I'm beginning to believe, for all our efforts, that Latimer and his sister have been playing us for fools. I've been thinking about them and I've come to several conclusions." At Royce's cocked eyebrow, he went on smoothly. "Latimer's no spy. A gambler and a cheat and a bully, yes, but not a spy—he hasn't the brains for it. I think what little information we've gleaned from Deborah is almost all the information there is to learn. She's not the most intelligent woman I know, but she never would have divulged Roxbury's connection, or Roxbury's request to contact certain former British citizens, if she had thought it would put her brother in danger."

"What if she doesn't know the whole story? What if there is a great deal more that Latimer has *not* told her?"

Dominic shook his dark head decisively. "Think, Royce! They work together. I realize now that they always have, and they are far too concerned with feathering their own nest and saving their own necks to be involved with something as dangerous as spying—we *hang* spies, or have you forgotten?"

His eyes resting speculatively on Latimer's back, Royce drawled, "They also hang murderers . . . and we're damn sure that he killed old Bowden and with Deborah's connivance."

"I know that! But there was little risk for them. An old man, alone at night, the servants gone . . . what chance would Bowden have had against them? They chose their target wisely. But a spy . . ." Dominic frowned. "A spy, especially one who intends to remain alive, cannot always choose the people who must be dealt with . . . and spying involves many people scattered throughout the countryside, not just one old man." When Royce remained silent, Dominic said impatiently, "My God! Look at the trail they've blazed from the east to here! They've made no attempt to cover their tracks; there are no plans to return to any of the places they have been, and whatever military information they may have learned along the way is months old by now. They have moved openly and leisurely across the country, stopping for an indefinite time whenever it strikes their fancy. They've not hidden the fact that they are British or that they are here in this country only for the duration of the war. Granted they may exclaim that it is their strong sympathy for our cause that made them take such a drastic step, but have they done anything to *help* our cause? I mean,'' Dominic went on seriously, ''have they joined any organizations for the war effort? Aligned themselves with any political figures? Has Latimer ever mentioned joining the army to fight?''

''That doesn't prove anything,'' Royce returned sourly. ''If he is a spy, he would not want to be hampered by military duties. And they couldn't very well hide the fact that they were British citizens.''

Dominic sighed wearily. ''No, they couldn't, but while I would enjoy watching Latimer swing for spying, I cannot believe that he is a spy.'' His expression thoughtful, he continued. ''Now, an advance guard for a *real* spy, that I could believe.''

Royce looked startled. ''Of course, that's it precisely!'' His low voice did not hide his excitement.

His own thoughts running along the same path, Dominic muttered, ''Why didn't we think of that before? He is not the spy, but merely a drudge to do some initial cultivating, someone to make social contact and to select those men who *might* be open to a treasonous offer. An offer the man who will come *behind* Latimer will make.''

Slowly Royce said, ''It is the only solution that makes any sense. Especially knowing what we do about Latimer and what is likely or not likely to appeal to him.''

Dominic took another sip of his brandy, his eyes once more on Latimer, his thoughts for the moment leaving the puzzle of the Englishman's reasons for being in the United States and traveling along a far different path. A path that considered various methods of extracting a suitable revenge. Dominic's mouth twisted. Actually, Latimer had unknowingly done him a favor . . . after a fashion, for if Latimer hadn't . . . then Melissa wouldn't have . . . A wave of black rage suddenly swept through him when he speculated on what might have been her fate if she had not mistaken the rooms that night at the inn. His gray eyes narrowed dangerously. It was time, he thought coldly, for Latimer to learn a lesson. A rather costly lesson, he decided with a savage smile.

Very deliberately, Dominic set down his snifter and drawled grimly, "I think I shall go and pay my respects to friend Latimer. I might even give him a more worthy opponent than that young cub."

Royce stiffened at Dominic's words, shooting him an uneasy glance. What he saw didn't quell the sudden suspicion that his friend had a deeper motive for seeking out the Englishman. There was about Dominic the air of a deadly predator just having sighted prey. Royce grabbed his arm and said in a low, urgent undertone, "Don't be a fool! I'll not act your second and watch you risk your life needlessly."

Giving him a disdainful glare, Dominic shook off his hand. "I have no intention of doing anything so foolhardy. Besides," he added softly, "killing the bastard isn't good enough. I wish to harm him where it will hurt him the most—his money bags!"

Helplessly Royce watched as Dominic walked over in the direction of Latimer's table. Too well did Royce recognize the menacing set to that dark head and broad shoulders and he sighed, knowing that whatever course Dominic had chosen, he would be there at his back to watch and protect. Cursing under his breath, Royce pushed himself away from the mantel and slowly made his way to Latimer's vicinity.

As if sensing danger, Latimer glanced up from his cards, his expression of lazy confidence disappearing, replaced by a carefully bland countenance. Betraying nothing but polite interest, he said casually, "Young Franklyn is having trouble finding his pace. He is not quite up to my mettle this evening . . . would you care to take his place at the table?"

Dominic smiled wolfishly, a cold glitter in the hard gray

eyes. "My thought exactly!" His smile now holding a great deal of warmth and charm, he turned to look at the slightly affronted, fresh-faced young man who sat across the felt-covered table from Latimer. "Do you mind?" he asked courteously. "Latimer and I are old . . . ah, adversaries, and since he appears to be having the devil's own luck at the moment, it seems an appropriate time to renew our . . . rivalry. That is, if you have no objections?"

After Latimer's insulting dismissal of his talents, Franklyn was flattered by Dominic's solicitous attitude. "Of course not, sir!" he replied quickly. A wry smile curved his delicate mouth. "I *have* been playing rather badly this evening."

Dominic sat down at the place Franklyn vacated and said cryptically, "Perhaps it is the *cards* and not your skill."

Latimer froze, his eyes flat as he asked in a dangerous tone of voice, "And what do you mean by *that?*"

"Why, nothing," Dominic replied easily, that wolf's smile once again appearing. "Shall we begin?"

On the other side of the room where he had been talking with Daniel Manchester, Zachary had idly noticed Dominic's passage. It was only when he saw *where* Dominic had been headed that his interest quickened. He felt distinctly uneasy when George Franklyn rose from the table and Dominic took his place. His unease increased when he noticed that Royce was determinedly making his way to where Dominic sat, the expression on that handsome face not at all encouraging.

He glanced again at his brother-in-law, and from what he saw, he was conscious of a shiver of apprehension. Dominic might be smiling and acting politely, but Zachary was reminded vividly of that first night he had dined with Dominic and Latimer's name had been mentioned. Something about Dominic's smile and the waiting stillness of his body made Zachary extremely nervous.

Making no attempt at politeness, Zachary broke into Daniel's rhapsodies about a diamond-patterned entryway for his new home and said curtly, "I want to watch the game between Dominic and Latimer. Come with me, if you like."

Before Daniel's astonished gaze, he strode quickly away, making for Royce's side. Daniel, possessing a rather sharp intellect behind his genial manner, was instantly conscious that something was in the wind and wasted not a moment before following in Dominic's wake. And as was often the case, when one or two other young gentlemen noticed the cluster around the table where Latimer and Dominic were playing piquet, they also wandered over to see what held everyone's rapt attention.

If Latimer was dismayed at suddenly finding his table the focal point of so many interested pairs of eyes, he gave no sign of it, merely smiling and nodding at each new arrival. The presence of so many gentlemen did hamper him, though, and not daring to run the risk of exposure, he decided that he would have to play a completely honest game. With this many onlookers and this early in the evening, before the liquor had really begun to flow, it was far too dangerous to practice a little sleight of hand.

Dominic was well aware of his adversary's predicament, and cold amusement flickered in the depths of his eyes as he said softly, "Since we seem to have gathered an audience, we should make it worth their while. What were you and Franklyn paying a point?"

Latimer hesitated and then replied, "It was a friendly game—merely ten dollars."

Dominic's eyebrow cocked. "A thousand dollars a game is rather a high price to pay for friendship, I think, but since you and I are such old *friends,* let us make it more interesting . . . say fifty dollars a point?"

It was not an outrageously high amount, but it was a bit steep, especially since over the weeks Latimer had lost more than he had intended in order to woo George Franklyn into complacency, and he was quite bitterly aware of Dominic's skill and expertise in all games of chance. Not happy with the circumstances that had come about so unexpectedly, Latimer paused, his brain busily seeking a way to turn events to his advantage. Speculatively, he considered the dark face across the table from him. To his experienced eye, it was apparent that Slade was spoiling for a fight, and Latimer almost smirked with satisfaction. A man letting temper ride him was always an easy mark.

Thinking that he might very well come away the winner and recoup some of the losses he had allowed Franklyn to inflict, he drawled lightly, "Fifty? I thought you stated we would make it interesting. Now, a hundred dollars a point I find far more interesting than a paltry fifty."

Dominic smiled widely and Latimer had the queasy sensation that he had somehow fallen into a trap. Before he could think more about it, Dominic said cheerfully, "Excellent! Would you care to deal or shall I?"

Latimer shrugged, his blue eyes watchful. "Please, go ahead."

Adroitly Dominic shuffled the deck of thirty-two cards and with a skill that bespoke long practice, expertly dealt out twelve cards to each of them. Both men were exceptional players and the game moved swiftly, neither one seeming to hesitate as discards were made and points called. The play progressed to the taking of tricks, and it soon became apparent that the two men were well matched, the scores remaining nearly even as the hands continued.

In the end Latimer won the game and he did nothing to hide his satisfaction as he said smugly, "I believe that you owe me ten thousand dollars, Slade."

"But surely you are going to give me a chance to gain revenge, aren't you?" Dominic asked dulcetly, a faintly quizzical smile curving his handsome mouth.

There were murmurs of assent from all around the table, and although Latimer would have enjoyed nothing better than to stroll away with Dominic's money resting snugly in his purse, he was uncomfortably mindful that not to give Dominic a rematch would be a black mark against him and might hamper his chances to begin plucking the Franklyn boy. Beating Dominic had given him a great deal of pleasure; it had also increased his arrogance, and the lure of winning more money was simply too powerful for someone like Latimer to resist.

The next game was very close, but Dominic won it, his expression enigmatic at the outcome of the final tally. Leaning back in his chair, he took a sip from the snifter of brandy that had been brought to him during the game. His eyes on Latimer, he drawled, "Well, now we are even . . . how boring! Shall we play another?"

Annoyed at the loss but convinced that it had been a mere fluke, certain that his own skill at the cards far outweighed his opponent's, Latimer consented eagerly and they began to play again. And in the hours that followed, Latimer's self-confidence grew, even though the wins and losses between them remained relatively even.

As the evening slid by, the group of men around the table ebbed and flowed, some gentlemen wandering off to seek new amusements or to join other friends, new onlookers taking their places. Royce and Zachary, however, apparently remained enthralled by the game being played, neither one of them moving as much as a foot away from the table. Aware that something was going on, yet not quite certain what, Daniel chose to stay fairly close to the other two, but he was guilty of straying from time to time, although he kept a watchful eye on what was transpiring.

Midnight came and went. One o'clock, two o'clock passed. The candles sank lower in their sockets and some of the gentlemen began to bid their host adieu, but still Dominic and Latimer continued to play. Somewhere around half-past three, just as the last game ended and the two men were once again even, no clear-cut winner having emerged from the many hands they had played, Dominic said slowly, "It seems we are very well matched. Shall we call it a night?"

Giving no sign of any interest in Latimer's answer, Dominic idly shuffled the cards he held in his lean hands. But there was a peculiar stillness about him that made Royce, who now sprawled comfortably nearby in a chair to Dominic's left, instantly very alert. Dominic's actions had puzzled him all evening, not only his choosing to gamble with Latimer but also the way he had played his cards, and it suddenly, blindingly, dawned on Royce that Dominic had been deliberately misplaying his cards, that he had *allowed* Latimer to win and then only when *he* chose. Sitting up straighter in his chair, Royce looked across at Dominic, the suspicion that he had engineered this precise sequence of events taking strong hold of him. While Dominic feigned indifference, he really wanted to play one more game with Latimer. And if Royce read the clues right, *that* game would be for very high stakes indeed! Everything else that had transpired so far had been mere dust thrown in Latimer's eyes to conceal the trap which Dominic was now ready to spring.

Latimer coolly appraised Dominic's offer, the desire to win resoundingly against a man he clearly considered an enemy warring with a faint premonition of danger. And yet, on the surface, all seemed well. He felt confident that it had been mere chance that they had arrived at this present state of affairs, simply bad luck that he had not been able to keep and even increase his winnings. Besides, it was important that he *win;* he had been quite conscious of George Franklyn watching from the sidelines and he did not want that young man to think he was not a worthy opponent—that kind of opinion would be fatal to his plans. Speculatively, he eyed the man across the table from him, noting the heavy-lidded eyes and the empty brandy snifter at Dominic's elbow. He lifted his own brandy snifter and took a sip. "Do you not wish to continue?" Latimer finally asked as he set down the snifter very carefully.

As if to confirm that the lateness of the hour was telling on him, Dominic stifled a small yawn. "That all depends upon you," he returned politely, and indicated to a hovering servant that he wished his snifter refilled.

Encouraged by these signs, Latimer said carelessly, "Why not? This will not be the first time that I have gambled until dawn."

Dominic's lids lowered and, his eyes on the cards in his hands, he murmured, "Whatever you like . . . but since the hour grows late and we have had time to take each other's measure, why don't we increase the stakes a trifle?"

"What did you have in mind?" Latimer asked in a bored tone. "One hundred and fifty dollars a point?"

"Paltry, my dear fellow! Paltry indeed!" A slight smile curved Dominic's mouth. "I was thinking more of . . . say . . . five hundred dollars a point?"

There was a concerted gasp from the remaining onlookers, even Royce's eyebrows rising in surprise at the amount. This was deep gambling indeed! What the devil was Dominic after?

Latimer hesitated, greed warring with caution. Fifty

thousand dollars was a fortune! But if he lost, his finances would be in an extremely precarious position. The loss would wipe out nearly everything he had accumulated at present; would, in fact, leave him in desperate straits. But if he won . . . The inveterate gambler in Latimer refused to think about the future if he lost, the temptation of winning such a rich sum from Dominic Slade overriding all other considerations.. His blue eyes glistening with avarice, Latimer replied recklessly, "Fine!"

"For one game only," Dominic said silkily. "Whatever the outcome of this game, we will both abide by it. Agreed?"

Latimer clearly did not like this provision, his body stiffening slightly. That little niggle of danger he had kept at bay all evening returned full-blown, but just as the close-watching audience had kept him honest so far, that same audience and the unfavorable effect there would be on their perception of him if he were to refuse, impelled him to say curtly, "Agreed."

Latimer lost the cut to deal and in the time that followed, it appeared, also his luck. He went down badly, Dominic playing with a ruthless aggression that robbed him time and again of a major hand he had been certain would score. The first orange-and-gold streaks of dawn were spilling into the room as the final hand was being played.

Dominic leaned back lazily in his chair, his expression one of sleepy indifference as Latimer eyed the cards held so carelessly in Dominic's hand.

Testily, Latimer said, "Your point is good, sir."

"And my quint?"

His mouth tight, Latimer nodded and muttered, "That also."

The game continued, but it was obvious that Dominic was the far better player. The end came swiftly. After glaring at the array of face cards Dominic displayed before him, Latimer stared at the one card still held in his opponent's hand. Knowing everything hinged on this one call, he considered his own cards, before saying baldly, "A heart!" and slapping the rest of his cards on the table.

Dominic smiled. "My win, I think," he drawled softly,

showing a nine of spades. Glancing at the score pad, Dominic murmured dulcetly, "Not a bad night's work. I do believe that you owe me something in the vicinity of fifty thousand dollars."

Concealing with an effort his rage and desperation, Latimer merely shrugged. "I have lost that much and more in an hour's gambling at White's in London." Rising from the table and brushing aside an imaginary bit of lint from his coat, he added, "Perhaps we can meet at my banker's this afternoon—I do not as a rule carry that sort of money upon my person."

Smiling that wolf's grin, Dominic replied with every evidence of amiability, "Whatever is convenient for you. Shall we say two o'clock this afternoon?"

Maintaining his air of nonchalance, Latimer answered easily, "Of course."

It was not to be expected that Royce and Zachary would keep their questions to themselves, and despite Daniel's interested presence, they had no sooner bidden their yawning, droopy-eyed host good-bye and ridden but a few yards away from Norton's house than Royce pounced. "Would you mind," he asked with excessive civility, "telling me what the purpose of *that* was? God knows, unless you have suffered a sudden and catastrophic reversal of fortune, you don't need the money."

"You don't even like Latimer," Zachary chimed in. "Yet you spent the entire evening with him!"

Dominic smiled serenely at his two questioners. "Let us just say that I had a debt to settle . . . with interest."

Royce's eyes narrowed. "And have you settled the debt?"

A twinkle in his gray eyes, Dominic grinned. "In spades, sir. In spades."

Chapter Twenty-six

IT WAS only after he had left his horse with the groom and was slowly walking toward his own house that it occurred to Dominic that it might be a bit awkward coming home after a night spent gambling. Gone were the days when he had only his own wishes to consider, and he realized that however noble his motives might have been, Melissa still might not take kindly to his return at this hour of the morning.

His position was further complicated by all that had not yet been said between them, and he was uneasily aware that now she would suspect her husband was not only a womanizer but an unregenerate gamester too! It didn't help matters any that he wanted to keep tonight's doings a secret from her until after he had met with Latimer and actually taken possession of the money.

Dominic quietly walked up the steps of the house, hoping that he might be lucky enough to reach his own rooms before anyone in the house saw him. Feeling uncomfortably like a man with a nefarious deed in mind, he stealthily opened the front door and peeked inside.

The entryway was empty and with relief he crept across the hall and made his way to the stairs. His relief, however, was short-lived. One foot was already on the stairs when the butler suddenly appeared out of the breakfast room, giving a great start when he spied the master of the house.

"Master Slade!" he exclaimed with astonishment. "I did not know that you were up and about. You startled me."

Smiling wryly, Dominic tried to pass the incident off

nonchalantly. "I'm sorry. I was, er, out for a morning ride."

If the butler thought it strange that Dominic had chosen to wear the same clothes from the previous evening, he did not make a comment. He merely nodded his head and said politely, "It is a very good morning for it. I hope you enjoyed your ride?"

"Oh, I did. But I am in much need of a wash before joining my wife," Dominic explained needlessly and began to hurry up the stairs, desperate to gain the safety of his rooms.

Unfortunately, Melissa was an early riser and Dominic had made it only halfway up the stairs when, vibrant and glowing from a night of blissful dreams, she materialized at the top of the staircase. To say which of them was the more surprised would have been impossible.

Her carefree smile fading a trifle, Melissa took in Dominic's slightly dissolute air, her eyes lingering on the faint blue circles beneath his eyes before traveling to the limp cravat and wrinkled breeches. She had no trouble recognizing his clothing as that which he had worn when he had left the previous evening. A faint frown appeared on her forehead as she asked incredulously, "You are not *just* returning from Tom Norton's?"

His cravat suddenly feeling as if it were choking him, Dominic slowly ascended the few stairs that separated them. "Ah, as a matter of fact, yes," he admitted sheepishly. A rueful smile tugged at the corners of his mouth. "I had not envisioned our next meeting this way, but if you will bear with me just a few hours longer, I hope that you will find my reasons for being out all night more than satisfactory."

It was a difficult moment for Melissa for several reasons. To remain out all night, no doubt gambling, did not bespeak a man of steady character, and she was more than a little daunted by this further display of his cavalier attitude toward her. For weeks now, with nothing but intuition to go on, she had been telling herself that she had mistaken his nature, that there was some logical explanation for his actions in connection with Deborah Bowden. She had desperately wanted to believe that things were not as they seemed, but noting the attractively haggard air that hung about him and the faint whiff of brandy that drifted to her, she was sickly aware that she might have been living in a fool's paradise. There were only so many excuses one could make for his behavior, and now, in addition to telling herself that he was *not* the callous womanizer he appeared, she was also being asked to overlook the distasteful implications in his actions this past night.

It was an especially bitter stretch of her credulity—too often Melissa had seen her father return home in just this condition, albeit her father had usually been drunk, but her heart sank nonetheless. It was all too painfully true, also, that her father had lost enormous amounts of money in "friendly" card games with neighbors and old acquaintances, and she wondered dully if, having watched helplessly as her father had gambled away a fortune, she was now fated to watch her husband do the same thing. Something rebelled within her at that thought, but her voice was neutral as she asked, "Do you do this sort of thing often?"

Dominic's eyes searched hers, and with a sinking sensation he saw that she was withdrawing from him, the expression in her beautiful eyes shuttered and unrevealing. Gone was the soft light that had given him so much hope and pleasure these past weeks. Not wanting to have another barrier between them, he grasped her hand and said urgently, "I swear I never will again. And you must believe me when I say that I do not usually make a habit of remaining out all night. There was something that I had to do . . . something I trust that you will approve of when I explain it to you." The gray eyes warm and compelling, Dominic pulled her unyielding body closer to him. His lips against her cheek, he said softly, "If you insist, I shall tell you this moment what I have been about, but I would prefer not to go into explanations right now, not until I have tangible proof of my activities these past hours."

Melissa hesitated. Her heart was willing to give him whatever he asked of her, but common sense cautioned her not to be taken in by his charm. It could be that he merely needed time to concoct an excuse that he thought might be acceptable to her . . . or he could be telling the truth.

Mistrust evident in her tone, she demanded, "If not now, when did you have in mind to make these explanations?"

Dominic gave her a bone-melting smile. "Would four o'clock this afternoon suit you?"

Melissa nodded curtly, certain that her brains had been addled, but hoping desperately that her blind trust in Dominic was not misplaced.

Pressing a brief kiss to her forehead, he said gaily, "Good! Wear one of your prettiest gowns and meet me at the hammock at four this afternoon."

Uncertain whether to laugh or scream with frustration, Melissa watched him disappear into his set of rooms. Then she shrugged her shoulders and began to walk down the stairs. Soon enough she would know if she was the most trusting wife in the world—or the greatest fool in nature!

At precisely two o'clock Dominic presented himself at the only bank in town. The intervening hours had been spent pleasantly; he had gone to bed and had slept soundlessly, awakening in time to enjoy a leisurely meal in his rooms and a revitalizing bath before dressing and riding into town. He wasn't surprised in the least to find Royce and Zachary, both showing signs of having passed the time in much the same manner, waiting for him when he arrived. Tying his horse to the hitching post, he dismounted, and casting them a sardonic glance, inquired, "Come to make positive that he pays his debts, have you?"

Royce merely grunted and replied, "And to make certain that you don't do anything foolish—like challenge him to a duel."

Dominic smiled. "Oddly enough, I find that it has given me greater delight to wound him this way than any other that I could think of."

Royce looked skeptical but said nothing more, and the three of them entered the building. They were shown immediately into Mr. Smithfield's office. Latimer, looking tired and rather grim, was already there, seated in a leather chair near Mr. Smithfield's big oak desk.

Mr. Smithfield, his plump features showing disapproval, indicated three more high-backed leather chairs similar to the one in which Latimer was sitting. Clearing his throat portentously, Mr. Smithfield said carefully, "Mr. Latimer has explained the situation to me and has enabled me to pay you the majority of what he owes to you this afternoon."

"Majority?" Dominic asked with a cynical twist to his lips. "It is my recollection that we played for the full amount last night, not the *majority*."

Latimer went rigid in his seat and a nasty gleam came into the cold blue eyes. "Without leaving my sister and me absolutely penniless," he growled, "I have the ability to pay you thirty-five thousand dollars this afternoon."

Dominic looked abstracted. "Forgive me," he murmured, "but am I wrong in recalling that the debt is for fifty thousand dollars?"

"Goddammit! You know that you are not wrong!" Latimer burst out furiously, all the chagrin and rage he felt at his current predicament suddenly boiling to the surface. Gallingly aware that it was imperative that he not disgrace himself, he fought to bring his temper under control. Trying to quell the murderous thoughts that raced through his brain, Latimer glared at Dominic, hating him with every fiber of his being. His voice stiff, he finally got out, "I have every intention of paying you." Intent upon impressing the others of his honorable intentions, he added mendaciously, "I do not make wagers that I cannot meet, but it will take me a short while to lay my hands on the remainder. I had hoped that you would be a gentleman about this and allow me the extra time."

There was a deceptively sleepy expression in Dominic's eyes. "Ah, yes, a gentleman. It would be most *un*gentlemanly of me to strip you of everything, wouldn't it? To rip the roof from over your head? To cast you and your lovely sister into the street with only the clothes on your backs? Who knows, that might leave you at the mercy of anyone . . . you could even find yourselves compelled to do things utterly abhorrent to you, things that are repugnant and degrading. No real gentleman would put you at such risk.'' Dominic looked squarely at Latimer, the gray eyes hard and merciless. His voice very soft, he added, ''No, only a bounder, a cad, a scoundrel of the blackest kind, would do such a thing.''

Suspicion sharpening in Latimer's brain, he stiffened, his body braced as if for a blow, but Dominic turned away, saying indifferently, ''Of course you may have more time to meet the remainder of your debt. Unlike others, I am not a monster. How much time would you like? A week? Two, perhaps?''

Latimer might have hoped that Dominic would prove to be generous in allotting him more time, but it appeared those hopes were groundless. Even if he had intended to pay Dominic the amount owed, which he had not, unless something miraculous occurred it would be impossible to meet Dominic's terms in less than six months. Latimer's hand clenched into a fist. Someday, he thought viciously, Mr. Slade was going to pay for this humiliation. Pay and pay dearly. . . .

Wrenching his thoughts away from various methods of extracting revenge, Latimer angrily considered his situation. Time was what he needed most at the moment; last night's doings had very nearly brought him to a standstill, but he still had one or two tricks up his gambler's sleeve. There was the Franklyn cub for one thing, and though he would now be forced to pluck the stripling for more than he had originally planned, those winnings would almost completely replenish his depleted funds. And then there was the ship that would be taking him to England sometime after the first of the year. If he could delay the final payment of the debt for just a few months, he and Deborah would be on their way to England and out of the reach of Dominic Slade—at least for a while—and he could consider at a later date what to do if Slade appeared in London demanding payment. There were all sorts of tragic accidents that could be arranged in London. . . .

Latimer found himself in an extremely delicate position. He must maintain his reputation within the small community of Baton Rouge if his plans to plunder the Franklyn boy's fortune were to come to fruition, yet he did not have the funds to pay Dominic. It would be fatal for his schemes if it became common knowledge that he made wagers he could not cover. No one would be willing to gamble with him, and that reputation would no doubt follow him to New Orleans, making it difficult, if not impossible, for him to gull any other pigeons like Franklyn. Latimer had great hopes for New Orleans and he didn't want to jeopardize the opportunities that wicked city offered to someone like him.

Stalling Dominic was Latimer's most immediate problem. If he could convince Dominic to wait until, say, the first of the year, which was less than three months away, it would give him time to get his hands on the Franklyn money and leave for New Orleans. Roxbury had promised to have more funds waiting for him there, so no matter how much or how little he won from Franklyn, his most pressing monetary problems would be over once he was in New Orleans. But Latimer had no intention of leaving the country with little more than the money that Roxbury had advanced him, even though a small fortune would be waiting for him in London. Nor did he plan on only dipping lightly into the Franklyn fortune, or paying Dominic one cent more than was necessary.

Having turned over several different ideas in his mind, Latimer suddenly smiled faintly and murmured, "I'm afraid that you find me in a most embarrassing situation." At Dominic's sharp look, he spread his hands deprecatingly and said glibly, "As you know, I am not permanently domiciled in this country, and since I planned to travel extensively during my stay here, before I left England I had made previous arrangements for funds to be divided amongst the various banks in the various cities which I intended to visit. It seemed easier than carrying large sums of money on my person. I'm afraid that the remainder of my monies is currently waiting for me at a bank in New Orleans." Leaning back in his chair as if he had not a care in the world, he said casually, "Delightful though my visit here has been, I plan to leave for New Orleans within the next few weeks or so, and it would be more convenient for me if you would allow me to pay you once I have arrived there." His features betraying only polite interest, he added, "Unless, of course, that is not satisfactory to you. If you have some pressing need for the money, I shall naturally write to the bank in New Orleans and see that the necessary funds are sent up here immediately."

Dominic had not the slightest doubt that once Latimer reached New Orleans any hope of receiving the remainder of the debt would vanish. He didn't know of the ship that would be waiting in January, but he did know his man, and almost as if he had been privy to Latimer's most private thoughts, he knew that Latimer would find a way to avoid paying one penny more than he had already. For a long moment, he deliberated, undecided whether to demand full payment or to let Latimer dangle a while. . . .

Deciding that it wouldn't hurt to punish Latimer a bit more, Dominic said slowly, "I have no objection to waiting for my money until you reach New Orleans." A smile spreading across his handsome features, he added softly, "It is rather a coincidence, you know. I, too, am planning to leave for New Orleans during the next few weeks—a belated honeymoon, you might say."

Latimer had just started to relax, but at the news that Dominic would be in New Orleans, he felt his nerves stretch, the sensation of being a very small mouse trapped in the claws of a very dangerous cat almost overpowering. And his uneasiness was not quelled in the least when Zachary said with great astonishment, "Lissa never said anything about going to New Orleans!"

His eyes never leaving Latimer's face, Dominic said easily, "I just now thought of it—it will be a surprise for her."

Latimer did not misunderstand him and, his voice tight, he asked, "It is decided, then? I shall pay you in New Orleans?"

Having grown bored with the game, Dominic sat up alertly in his chair and said briskly, "Yes, of course, but I suggest we name a date for the payment. It is not wise to let these things drag on."

"Very well," Latimer replied politely. "Shall we say the first of December, in New Orleans?"

"Splendid," Dominic said heartily.

Longing to throttle him, Latimer sent Dominic a false smile and rose to his feet. He hesitated a moment before saying diffidently, "I would appreciate it if no word of what was discussed here this afternoon was bandied about."

"Naturally. It would be most ungentlemanly of us to discuss your private affairs," Dominic agreed dryly.

Mr. Smithfield cleared his throat. "Mr. Slade, do you wish these funds deposited in your current account?"

His part in the proceedings done with, Latimer was on the point of departing when Dominic said, "Stay, Latimer—don't you want to know where your money is going?"

Hardly able to conceal the rage that twisted within him, Latimer swung back to glare at Dominic. "I hardly think it matters to me anymore, now that the money is no longer mine."

Dominic smiled at him. "Listen and see if you don't change your mind."

His eyes never leaving Latimer's face, Dominic said harshly, "I want you to open a new account, Mr. Smithfield, and put all of the money from Mr. Latimer in it. The account will be in my wife's name *alone* . . . . all of this money will be hers. A *re*payment of sorts."

A muscle twitched violently in Latimer's hard cheek as enlightenment dawned, and the blue eyes ablaze with rage, he took an angry step forward. "You *know!*" he hissed, all the hatred he felt for Dominic plain to see.

Dominic smiled like a satisfied tiger. "Precisely," he replied coldly.

Unable to maintain even a semblance of a polite facade, Latimer snarled, "You may have won this hand, Slade, but there will be another time, and then, by God, you'll pay for this!"

Spinning on his heels, Latimer strode from the room, the door swinging shut behind him with an explosive bang. There was a moment of silence; then Mr. Smithfield exclaimed with amazement, "Upon my soul! I would never have thought that Mr. Latimer would behave in such a fashion. He always seemed such a gentleman."

None of the other three men in the room made any comment and Mr. Smithfield returned promptly to the business at hand. "If you wouldn't mind waiting a few minutes, I shall have all the papers drawn up for you."

Dominic inclined his head politely and shortly thereafter he and the others took their amiable leave from the banker. There was little conversation among the three men as they mounted their horses and began to ride away from town, but the last small wooden building had barely been passed before Royce demanded bluntly, "Would you mind telling me what the thunder that was all about? Ever since you arrived at the Norton place last night, I have had the most curious sensation of having walked into a play that had already gone two acts before I arrived!"

Dominic grinned at him. "It is a private matter. One that involves a lady very dear to me, and it would be most cavalier of me to discuss it with you." The gray eyes dancing with amusement, he added, "It is sufficient to say that I used the cards rather than the sword to extract my satisfaction . . . something I think will please the lady in question."

Before Royce could utter the scathing comment that hovered on his lips, Zachary blurted out, "You overheard our conversation last night!"

Dominic nodded his dark head and admitted brazenly, "Exactly! But you would do well to keep that information to yourself; in fact, forget the conversation ever took place."

A note of long suffering obvious in his voice, Royce remarked, "Has no one ever told you that it is not polite to discuss secrets in front of someone else?" At the two broad grins that met his words, Royce muttered, "Oh, very well, *don't* tell me—I can figure out most of it myself! Keep your bloody secrets!"

Royce was looking so offended that the other two burst out laughing and a moment later, somewhat sheepishly, Royce joined them. Good humor restored among them, they soon took their leave of one another.

Upon reaching the cottage, Dominic left his horse at the stable and with the new account book tucked securely in his waistcoat pocket, his step was light and eager as he bounded up the stairs to the gallery. Stopping at the house just long enough to warn the servants that he and Melissa were not to be disturbed, he went in search of his wife.

The hammock, strung between two oak saplings, was situated in a quiet, shady nook some distance behind the cottage. Live oak trees draped with Spanish moss, and beech and elm trees festooned with red trumpet vines and sweetbrier, pressed close to the small clearing which contained the low-slung hammock. A faint breeze wafted the mingled scent of magnolia blossoms and yellow jasmine through the air as Dominic silently walked up to the brilliant blue hammock and glanced down at its occupant.

Melissa was sound asleep, a small, leather-bound volume of love sonnets lying on her breast. His face tender, Dominic stared at her sleeping features for several long moments, finally noting with pleasure that she had followed his request and had chosen to wear a new gown, a frothy confection of willow-green sarsenet trimmed with yards and yards of delicate, ecru-colored Mechlin lace. A smile of almost idiotic delight was on his face as his eyes traveled over her long, dark lashes, down the straight little nose to consider the soft, sweet mouth and stubborn chin. His wife, he thought with a mixture of astonishment and great exultation. His dear, darling, gallant wife.

Staring at her sleep-serene features, he wondered how he could ever have suspected that she was merely a scheming, greedy little jade out to trap a rich husband. The truth was so obvious once he put aside his outrage and wounded pride at finding himself drawn to her that he wondered how he could have avoided it for so long. A rueful smile curved his mouth. Pure, blind stubbornness, he admitted to himself. That and perhaps resentment at the way she had tangled his emotions from the moment he had seen her. He had not wanted to fall in love, had never planned to marry, and yet the instant Melissa had come into his life, something deep within him had changed, but he had been too obstinate to recognize it for what it was. No longer, he vowed silently. She had become the most precious thing in the world to him and he would do nothing to jeopardize the powerful bond that existed between them, despite all the silly misunderstandings and foolish mistrust.

In one easy movement, Dominic knelt down beside the hammock, the gray eyes ardent and warm as they rested on Melissa's face, but the faint crackle of paper reminded him of how near he had come to never knowing the joy of loving her, and he frowned. If she had not made a mistake about the rooms that night at the inn, how very different their future might have been and how empty his life would be without her in it. He could almost thank Latimer for being instrumental in driving Melissa into his arms. Almost. The rage he had experienced when he had learned of Latimer's perfidious bargain suddenly gusted through him, and his expression turned grim and forbidding. Unconsciously the fingers of one hand tightened about the curls that lay so near her cheek.

Dominic's grip on her hair was unknowingly painful and Melissa stirred restlessly, her eyes opening as she became aware of her surroundings. Seeing Dominic's dark, angry face so close to hers, still only half awake, Melissa recoiled from him, giving a soft, startled gasp as she did so.

Instantly remorseful at having frightened her, Dominic loosened his grip on her hair and his expression became endearingly contrite. "Forgive me. I did not mean to frighten you."

Warily Melissa regarded him, not quite having made up her mind how to deal with him when they were finally alone. She was still angry and distressed by the knowledge that he had thought nothing of remaining out all night gaming, especially since she had spent that same night weaving wildly romantic dreams about him. She had whiled away the hours since they had last met dithering between treating him with cool indifference or demanding furiously to know what he meant by treating her in such a disgraceful manner. A womanizer was bad enough, but did he have to add gaming to his sins?

Calling herself all kinds of a fool, Melissa had reluctantly dressed with care for their meeting this afternoon and had dutifully, if truculently, arrived at the spot he had indicated with time to spare. The afternoon had been unusually warm, and despite the turmoil in her mind, lulled by the droning sound of bees, she had dropped off to sleep.

She had been enjoying a very pleasant dream in which Dominic swore undying love for her, begging abjectly for her to forgive him, when she had awakened to find the object of her dreams, instead of gazing besottedly at her, wearing a very unfriendly expression indeed!

Before she could speak, Dominic smiled at her, his demeanor changing in a moment, becoming gratifyingly similar to her dream. Thinking that she had never looked lovelier with her hair attractively tousled about her face and her cheeks flushed from sleep, he murmured, "Have you been waiting very long for me?"

His eyes moved caressingly over her face and traitorously, Melissa felt her heart quicken its pace. Feeling at a distinct disadvantage lying in the hammock, she started to sit up, but Dominic gently pushed her back. "Stay," he said softly. "You present a charming picture just as you are . . . the only thing that could be improved upon would be me lying by your side."

She wanted to be very angry with him, or at the very least, aloof and disdainful, but as she looked at him, seeing the dark circles under his eyes and the faint lines of weariness that still marred his handsome face, something melted inside her. Hating herself for being a spineless goose where he was concerned, she muttered with less heat than she had planned, "If you would stay home nights instead of gallivanting all over the place . . ."

"Are you very angry with me, Lissa?" he asked quietly, one hand reaching for hers. His warm fingers closed around her hand. "You have every right to be, but there was something that I had to do and it took me much longer than I had planned. As I told you this morning, I do not make it a habit to be out at all hours of the night." He grinned wryly. "There was a time in my salad days when such conduct was common, but no longer . . ."

Not wanting to let him off too easily, yet unable to sustain any real fury, she managed to say indignantly, "Well, you certainly have a peculiar way of revealing it!"

"I certainly do, don't I?" he replied with equanimity. Reaching into his waistcoat pocket, he dropped the small book onto her chest. Smiling at her, he murmured, "I hope that this will help redeem me in your eyes."

Her puzzlement obvious, Melissa struggled to sit up, the hammock swinging wildly until Dominic steadied it. Sitting rather awkwardly in the middle of the hammock, a frown between her eyebrows, she stared at the book. It made no sense at first, being simply an acknowledgment that an account in her name alone had been opened and that the sum of thirty-five thousand dollars had been deposited in it. Having no idea where the money had come from, Melissa, not unnaturally, assumed that it was Dominic's money and that he was attempting to placate her by giving her money.

Thoroughly insulted, the topaz eyes glittering with fury, she glared at him and spat, ''How dare you treat me in this manner! Do you think that mere money can buy you anything you wish? That every time you treat me in an insulting and callous manner, you have only to bestow a gift upon me for me to turn a blind eye to your scandalous conduct? How *dare* you!'' Her voice was shaking with rage as she finished speaking the last words, and looking very much like a wrathful Amazon, the tawny hair fairly bristling with anger and the golden-brown eyes spitting fire, she threw the bankbook in Dominic's face. ''Keep your damned money! I never wanted your *money*, you stupid jackass!''

Realizing instantly where he had gone astray, Dominic caught her shoulders in his hands. When she tried to throw off his hold, his grip tightened and he shook her gently. ''Lissa, the money isn't mine,'' he said softly. ''It's Latimer's. I spent last night, coldly and calculatingly, winning it from him—for you. It seemed simpler than killing him, and since you seemed so determined to keep all of us males from the dueling field, it was the only solution. *That* is why I was out all night.''

Astonishment held her motionless. ''Latimer's?'' she repeated stupidly. ''Why would you . . . ?'' Comprehension struck her and her face changed ludicrously, her eyes widening and her mouth falling open. For a long moment, she looked into his dark, smiling face, almost unable to believe the warm light she saw shining in the gray eyes. ''You overheard me talking to Zachary last night,'' she finally said slowly.

Dominic nodded. "Yes, I admit that I eavesdropped shamelessly on your conversation, and while I would normally condemn such practice, I cannot say that I am the least bit remorseful over my actions." His voice dropped to a low, intimate drawl. "How else would I have learned that my bride, who I thought had neatly trapped me into marriage for what it would bring her, had been the innocent victim of a totally unscrupulous villain? That it was an accident that you were in my rooms that night. That it was a frantic attempt to save your home and honor which compelled you to make me that ridiculous offer for Folly. That instead of being a scheming, greedy, little harpy, you were in fact a gallant, stubborn, virtuous, wayward, maddening *darling!*"

Suddenly shy, but quite eager for this most interesting conversation to continue, Melissa fastened her eyes on his neatly arranged cravat, her hands playing with the lapel of his jacket as she inquired diffidently, "Did you *really* think that I had married you solely for your money?"

"Hmm," he muttered as his lips caressed the curls near her temple. "Perhaps at first." Feeling her stiffen slightly, he added hastily, "But only for a *very* short time." A wry note came into his voice as he added, "It soon became apparent to me that while you liked the clothing and gifts I gave you, you would have been perfectly content without them. It puzzled me for quite some time. I couldn't understand why, having gone to such lengths to trap me into marriage, you showed no inclination to enjoy the fruits of your efforts."

Her arms crept around his neck. "It wasn't because of your money that I married you," Melissa whispered.

"I'm aware of that now . . . and while it is regrettable that Josh used Zachary as a means to compel you to marry me, again I cannot say that I feel the least shred of remorse that he did so." Feathering soft little kisses along her jawline, he muttered, "I am quite a reprehensible fellow where you are concerned."

Thinking foggily that he should not take all the blame for their misunderstandings and remembering certain incidents that showed her in a less-than-complimentary light, she snuggled even closer to him and confessed eagerly, "I am at fault too! There have been times when I have used you shamefully." Shyly she admitted, "I did not mean to send you from my bed so cruelly on our wedding night. I have regretted it terribly, but I was so confused and I feared that—"

She stopped abruptly, realizing unhappily that she had been on the point of declaring how desperately she longed for him to love her. She wasn't quite confident enough of his feelings to take such a bold step. Even though it was gratifyingly apparent that he felt very strongly about her and that he no longer seemed to mind the fact that he had been forced to marry her, it did not mean that he loved her. Nor, during all of this delightful conversation, had the vexing, painful question of his involvement with Deborah Bowden been resolved or even mentioned.

Since Deborah Bowden was the last person on Dominic's mind, he didn't connect Melissa's sudden silence with that lady. He had been held too spellbound by Melissa's fascinating disclosures to think of anything but how much he adored her and, utterly enchanted by her words, he had all he could do to keep himself from sweeping her into his arms and fervently proclaiming his love for her. But he was intensely curious about what she had not said, and so, pressing tiny, ravishingly sweet kisses at the corners of her mouth, he coaxed, "You feared that . . . ?"

Melissa was melting into his arms, her cheek against his, and Dominic was positive that his heart had stopped beating while he waited breathlessly for her next words. Unfortunately, it was not Melissa's soft voice that broke the silence, but Josh's hearty tones as he entered the clearing and boomed out, "Ah, here you are! Been looking all over for you. Servants said you weren't to be interrupted, but I knew you wouldn't mind seeing me! Especially since I have such good news!"

Chapter Twenty-seven

DOMINIC *did* mind. Quite a lot, as a matter of fact. Suppressing a murderous urge to throttle Josh, he gently put Melissa from him, stood up and turned around. Forcing himself to act civilly, he inquired with far less interest than he might have shown at another time, "What good news, Josh?"

His genial features fairly beaming, his hands rubbing together with childlike glee, Josh said jubilantly, "Ships, my good man! Ships! Two of 'em, in fact!"

While Dominic looked confused, Melissa rose gracefully from the hammock, knowing exactly what her uncle was referring to, and sent him a delighted smile. "They got through the blockade?" At Josh's pleased nod, she rushed up to him and flung her arms impulsively around his neck, still clutching the bankbook Dominic had given back to her. "Oh, Uncle Josh! I am so happy for you! I know how very much you have wanted this to happen."

"Can't deny that, m'dear!" Josh agreed exuberantly, nodding his head several times. "Got word this afternoon from New Orleans. My agent says that with the British blockade keeping so many ships from port, these two cargoes will fetch a fortune!"

Smiling fondly at him, Melissa patted his arm. "I *told* you not to worry, that if you would just be patient all your worries would be resolved." And though she was very happy for Josh, she could not help but recall how determined he had been to gain the money from the trust left by her grandfather . . . at her expense. She no longer resented the fact that he had forced her to marry Dominic, but Josh's news only clearly illustrated what she had known all along—sooner or later his fortunes

404

would right themselves, and if she had married any of the many suitors he had pushed her way simply to ease his momentary crisis, in the end her sacrifice would have been for naught. It was a sobering thought, but she did not dwell on it. She was married to the man she loved, and if Josh had managed to engineer it for all the wrong reasons, it no longer mattered. She could not help teasing him just a little, though. With a twinkle in her lovely eyes, she murmured, "You see, you didn't need the money from the trust after all! Just think, you might have sacrificed my happiness unnecessarily."

Josh shot Dominic a nervous glance. "Er, we don't need to go into that right now, m'dear," he said a little sheepishly. "Just wanted to tell you the good news and to invite you both to the party we are having the evening after next. Want to share our good news with the neighborhood."

Melissa bit back a giggle, thinking privately that Josh was as transparent as just-washed windows. He might say he wanted to share the good news, which he did, but he also wanted to crow a little and to make certain that everyone knew that Josh Manchester was once more plump in the pocket, make no mistake about that!

"Sally and I thought we'd put on a dinner and then the gentlemen could play cards while you ladies discuss everyone who isn't at the house!" Josh said mischievously. "Will you both be there?"

Dominic draped a possessive arm about his wife's shoulders. "Certainly," he said easily, suddenly exceedingly grateful that Josh's ships had not managed to slip through the blockade any earlier. Who knew, if Josh hadn't felt so desperate for funds, he might not have been so quick to see Melissa married. Reaching out, Dominic surprised everyone by shaking Josh's hand with unwarranted satisfaction. "Splendid news, sir! I am very happy for you!"

Slightly taken aback by Dominic's enthusiasm, Josh said, "Well, yes, it is. Must be off now. Have to see several more people this afternoon."

Josh had just started to walk away when Melissa quickly decided to take advantage of his unexpected visit. She had been longing to speak to him about the things he had once said about Dominic, and in view of the past few weeks, *especially* in view of what had transpired last night, she did not want to waste this opportunity. "Uncle, wait!" she cried. "I wish to speak with you a moment."

Throwing Dominic an uncertain glance, she said, "Do you mind? I shall not be long, but I need to talk privately with my uncle."

Dominic clearly did mind, but since their intimate mood had been shattered and it seemed unlikely that they would be able to rekindle it immediately, he reluctantly nodded. "Of course. I shall see you at the house in a few moments."

When Josh and Melissa were alone in the small clearing, Josh eyed his niece with some misgivings. Surely she wasn't going to berate him for having arranged things so he could get his hands on Sally's share of the trust. He couldn't have known that the two ships would make port, could he?

Testily, he muttered, "Now, Lissa, if it's about that damned trust, I don't want to hear it! I did what I thought was best and things worked out, didn't they?"

"It isn't about the trust," she said with a smile. "It's about Dominic."

"Eh?" he grumbled uneasily. "What about him? Think he's a fine man. A good man. As a matter of fact, he's a much better man than any of those other fellows I tried to push your way."

"Then why," she asked levelly, "did you tell me all those awful things about him?"

Having long forgotten his original plan, Josh grew quite outraged. "Awful things!" he repeated with angry incredulity. "I never said one disparaging word about him! Why, from the moment I first clapped eyes on him, I thought . . ." What he had thought and what he had done during those first early weeks suddenly burst unpleasantly across his brain, and a decidedly guilty expression filled his face. "Ah . . . well . . . you see . . ." he began helplessly.

Hands on her hips, one foot tapping ominously, Melissa demanded, "Are you telling me that you don't remember warning me against him? You don't remember warning me that he was rather fond of a certain type of woman and that he was a gambler?" Josh's expression of guilt increased and Melissa was hard pressed not to laugh. The wretched dear *had* tried to make her think ill of Dominic. Hoping what was forbidden would prove attractive? Struggling to maintain her outwardly angry posture, Melissa narrowed her eyes. "I seem to remember clearly you telling me that he wasn't the type of man you wanted me to marry."

Running a nervous finger around the inside of his cravat, Josh mumbled, "Well, um . . . I just thought . . . that since you hadn't seemed to like any *proper* suitors . . . that maybe . . . if I made Dominic *appear*, um . . ."

Josh had *lied* to her! Melissa thought blissfully. Dominic was none of the things he had implied! Controlling a strong desire to rain delighted kisses over her uncle's increasingly discomforted features, Melissa still couldn't help teasing him. "You *lied* to me!" she exclaimed in horrified tones. "All these months I have been thinking that I have been married to a womanizer and a gambler!"

"Oh, Lissa, no!" Josh expostulated feebly, obviously greatly upset at this news. "I never meant for you to think such a thing. I only meant to arouse your interest in him!"

Melissa dropped her head to hide her laughter-filled eyes. "Uncle!" she moaned sadly. "How could you mislead me this way! I *trusted* you! Your lies have *ruined* my marriage!"

Utterly dismayed by these dramatic revelations, Josh said, "Oh, my dear child! It was never my intention to cause you one moment's distress. I shall speak to your husband immediately and explain matters to him." Suddenly aware that the gentleman in question might not take too kindly to his slanderous statements, Josh added dismally, "No doubt he will call me out when he learns the truth."

Josh glanced uncertainly at Melissa, racking his brain to think of some further words of comfort to offer her, but something about the way she was hiding her face from him, something about the way she was holding her hand over her mouth . . . Suspicion sharpening his gaze, he reached over and jerked her hand away from her mouth.

"Lissa, you little minx!" he declared half angrily, half laughingly when he saw the merry features lifted up to his. "You have been playing a May game with me!"

Smiling warmly at him, his unrepentant niece freely admitted it. "It's true! But I think you will agree that you deserved such a trick after what you did to me."

Somewhat shamefacedly, Josh nodded his head. "I should

not have meddled as I did, but," he continued hopefully, "you must admit that it all worked out for the best."

Melissa's smile became very soft and tender. "Perhaps," she said dreamily. "Perhaps it has after all."

After waving her uncle a fond good-bye, Melissa walked slowly toward the house, a sensation of delightful exhilaration building within her with each step she took. Dominic had not said that he loved her, but his actions were certainly those of a man in love. Why else would he have sought out Latimer and not only recovered what Latimer had received from her but added a tidy profit to it as well? Bemusedly she looked at the bankbook clutched in her hand. He was her husband, there had been no need for him to set up the money in a private account for her, but he had done so. Surely that indicated something more than just simple generosity. Oh, dear God, please don't let me be wrong! she thought fervently.

She had been a little insulted when she had learned that he had assumed she had married him for his money, but looking back over the events that had led to their marriage, she admitted fairly that her actions *had* appeared in a less-than-complimentary light. He had known hardly anything at all about her, and considering the circumstances, it would have been strange if he *hadn't* thought her a mercenary piece of goods, she finally concluded. A warm glow entered the topaz eyes. Even believing that she was a greedy schemer, he had treated her honorably and been generous to a flattering degree. Thinking of all the gifts he had lavished on her—the cottage itself, the beautiful clothes and costly feminine fripperies that cluttered her wardrobe and dressing table—Melissa was suddenly ashamed of the seemingly capricious way she had treated him on more occasions than she cared to think about.

As she walked up the steps to the house, a troubling thought occurred to her, causing the light to fade from her eyes. Even though he now knew that she had not trapped him, that it was by accident she had been in his room that night and that Uncle Josh had compelled her to marry him, Dominic had still been forced into a marriage he hadn't wanted—he had told her so himself. A small chill slid down her spine. Perhaps he was just a noble man who was determined to make the best of a bad situation.

That first heady rush of elation was ebbing, and with doubt beginning to slowly creep into her happy thoughts, Melissa entered the house and went in search of her husband. She found him in the salon, idly flicking through the pages of a newspaper.

They had been poised on the brink of a precious moment when Josh had interrupted them, and although there was no impediment to their taking up where they had left off, it was exceedingly difficult to instantly recapture the mood that had prevailed such a short time ago. For no rational reason, there suddenly existed an odd constraint between them, each one eager to continue that most interesting conversation, but neither one quite certain how to begin.

When Melissa hesitated in the doorway, Dominic smiled at her as he got up and went to her. "Your uncle gone?"

"Yes. He said to tell you good-bye," she replied primly. Unconsciously her fingers tightened around the bankbook, and flushing slightly, she crossed the room to stand in front of Dominic.

"I want to thank you for what you did . . . and apologize for misjudging your motives," she said earnestly.

Mutely they stared at each other, the sweetness and promise of their earlier meeting suddenly swirling around them.

His dark face intent, Dominic fastened his hands around Melissa's shoulders and pulled her gently to him. "It isn't your gratitude or apology that I want," he murmured huskily.

Breathlessly, a quiver of renewed hope surging through her, Melissa swayed closer to him. In a voice barely above a whisper, her soft mouth just tempting inches from his, she asked, "If not my gratitude or my apology, what do you want from me?"

Absorbed in each other, they did not hear the sound of footsteps crossing the gallery, but the sudden, thunderous knocking on the front door made Melissa jump and Dominic curse vehemently beneath his breath.

A menacing expression in the gray eyes, he gently put Melissa from him and snarled, "If that is your blasted uncle again, I vow I shall . . ."

Striding out into the entryhall, he reached the door and

angrily flung it open. His unwelcoming countenance did
not change in the least when he discovered Royce on the
other side of the door. "What the blazes do *you* want? I'm
beginning to think that you damned Manchesters are deliberately trying to keep me from finding any marital harmony at all!"

"Come at an awkward time, did I?" Royce asked with
interest, apparently not the least perturbed by either Dominic's black expression or his unfriendly greeting. Ignoring
his host's decidedly unwelcoming air, Royce smiled
slightly and said, "It is not me you should vent your spleen
on, but your brother's friend Jason Savage—he is the reason I am here."

"Jason?" Dominic repeated darkly. "When did you
hear from him?"

"If you will invite me in," Royce said sweetly, "I shall
be most happy to tell you."

Ungraciously Dominic did so, wondering viciously why
he had ever envied Morgan his friendship with Jason, or
why he had ever thought that it would be exciting to be
involved in some of the adventures he had heard Morgan
and Jason discuss over the years. Right now, if he never
heard Jason's name again it would be far too soon!

Knowing that Royce would not have come to see him
if the matter were not important and having the uneasy
premonition that it would be some time before he would
be able to renew the tantalizing mood with Melissa, Dominic grudgingly resigned himself to the present. Stopping
at the doorway of the salon, he stuck his head inside and
said to Melissa, "Royce has arrived and wishes to speak
with me. I have no idea how long I shall be with him."

Melissa nodded, having recognized her cousin's voice.
Walking up to Dominic, her eyes glowing with promise,
she smiled reassuringly at him and, her hand gently stroking his cheek, murmured, "Go with him. We'll have time
to talk later tonight . . . when we're alone."

At the implication in both her look and her voice, Dominic was struck by an overpowering wave of love for her,
and heedless of Royce's inquisitive presence behind him,
his eyes dark with emotion, he jerked her to him and
crushed her lips to his. Lifting his mouth from hers, he

muttered, "Believe, madam, I shall be waiting most impatiently for us to *finally* be alone with each other."

And then, leaving Melissa standing there with a dazzled expression on her lovely face, he spun on his heels and disappeared with Royce. Fingers on the lips Dominic had kissed, she stared at the empty doorway, willing him to reappear, willing him to continue kissing her in that same deliciously ferocious manner. Thinking of the sweet promise of the night to come, she felt a flutter of anticipation stir throughout her entire body. Wrapped in a rosy haze, she fairly floated from the salon and up the stairs to her room.

There was no rosy haze to cloud Dominic's thoughts as he showed Royce into the tiny study at the rear of the house. Flinging himself down into one of the three chairs the room contained, he snapped, "Now what brought you here in such a hurry? I would have thought that after our late night last night you would have decided on a better way to spend your afternoon than badgering me!"

"But you know how much pleasure it gives me to annoy you," Royce returned serenely. "And, of course, we both know that I have nothing else to do with my time than to think up ways in which to irritate my friends."

A reluctant laugh was dragged from Dominic and he said more politely, "Oh, have done and tell me what Jason wants now."

Extracting an envelope from his coat pocket, Royce handed it to him, saying, "I believe I know what your letter from Jason contains. In addition to yours, there was one waiting for me when I returned home from town this afternoon. I suspect that your letter will reveal the same information as mine."

It did. The letter was brief, but the news substantial.

Dominic,

A spy for the British, a fellow named Anthony Davis, has been captured here in New Orleans. He was reluctant to talk at first, but after a while with some persuasive gentlemen I know, he was induced to do so. Roxbury, he told us, had sent him here and he was to meet with Julius Latimer on the fifth of December. Apparently, during his travels Latimer has been preparing a list of various men who would be *inclined* to deal with our spy. I want those names! But you must obtain them without alerting Latimer. Do nothing about him yourself—we will be waiting for him when he arrives in New Orleans. In the meantime, find that list and copy it. Either you or Royce are to bring the copy to me here in New Orleans, as soon as possible.

It would seem that you were right—Latimer is not our spy. His task for Roxbury was merely to observe and to select those men he judged the most likely to turn traitor. Armed with the list of names, our spy would do the rest.

In light of what we have discovered, once you have your hands on Latimer's list, you may cease your agreeableness to the fair Deborah—which I am certain will delight you!

I have sent this letter to Royce's address, as I was not certain if you would still be domiciled in Baton Rouge or if you had left for Thousand Oaks. I have written Royce a letter that duplicates this one almost exactly. I hope that you and he will be able to strike quickly and that you have no difficulty in finding that most important list of names.

My best to you and your bride.

Jason

In silence Dominic handed the letter back to Royce, and Royce quickly scanned the contents. "Hmm, there is nothing in this that is any different from mine," Royce said when he was done reading.

Dominic remained silent for a long moment; then, running his hand tiredly over his face, he said, "I suppose the first place to search for that list would be among Latimer's personal possessions. I can't say that I relish going through his things, but for my own sanity and to comply with Jason's request, the sooner we do it the better."

"I agree," Royce said as he settled his long length in a chair across from Dominic. "From my regrettably close association with him, I happen to know that Latimer and his sister are to dine this evening with the Richardsons out at Rose Mount. It should be quite late before they return home. Richardson is an avid gambler but an unlucky one, and after last night, I'm sure that Latimer will be trying to recoup some of his losses."

Dominic threw back his head and stared gloomily at the ceiling, his delectable visions of recapturing those enthralling moments with his wife vanishing. Ruefully he murmured, "It *would* have to be tonight!" Not yet willing to relinquish all hope, he glanced across at Royce. "I don't suppose that we could do it tomorrow evening. A day or two shouldn't make that much difference."

"What if we don't find it tonight? It's conceivable that it may take us several days to discover where he has hidden it. Besides," Royce added in a reasonable tone, "he may have plans to remain at home tomorrow night, and Friday night is my father's little celebration, which we *both* must attend. If we strike tonight and luck is with us, I will be able to leave for New Orleans on Saturday morning."

Sending him a sardonic look, Dominic drawled, "You're not planning on having me deliver the list to Jason?"

"Oh, no!" Royce replied angelically. "You are newly married and your time is far too valuable to be taken up with having to traipse down the river to that wicked city."

"Hungering for a little excitement and some new vices, are we?" Dominic asked with a grin.

The two men began to seriously consider the distasteful task that lay ahead of them. Since it was already gone six o'clock, Dominic invited Royce to stay and dine. The meal that followed was not *un*pleasant, Melissa fulfilling her duties as hostess admirably, Dominic being the friendly host and Royce acting the part of the polite guest, but it cannot be said that it was the most enjoyable repast that the three had ever shared—especially since two of the trio were violently wishing the third member in perdition!

Leaving the gentlemen to their port and cigars when the meal was over, Melissa wandered into the salon, her warm, rosy thoughts dwelling bemusedly on the evening which was surely to follow Royce's departure. It was only when the gentlemen, having hastily finished their liquor, joined her that she received the decidedly unwelcome news that Dominic would be going out . . . again. Looking at her husband with bewildered disbelief, she repeated stiltedly,

"Leaving? You're going out with Royce this evening? But I thought that . . ."

Royce glanced from one unhappy face to the other, and quickly plumbing the situation, said instantly, "I believe that I shall step outside and enjoy a cheroot. Join me when you are ready to leave, Dominic."

The other two hardly noticed his passage from the room, Dominic swiftly striding over to where Melissa was sitting. Grasping her hands tightly in his, he pulled her upright and, his eyes pleading for understanding, said urgently, "Melissa, I must go with him! But I swear to you that this will be the last time that I leave you like this."

Bitter and mistrustful, her dreams blackened and fading, she stared stonily at him. "It seems to me that we have played out this scene before. There is always someplace that you *must* go, some incident, such as your shocking behavior with Lady Bowden, that I *must* overlook." Her eyes full of pain and anger, she spat, "Well, it has gone against my nature, and I have tried very hard to be a meek and biddable wife, but I am afraid that you have tried my patience for the last time. Go tonight, if you wish, but do not expect me here when you decide to come home!"

Dominic's face went white and he said tightly, "Don't be a little fool! I want to be here with you more than anything else in the world, but there is a pressing circumstance that requires my immediate attention—and I don't like it any more than you do!"

Her eyes burning with golden fire, Melissa said jealously, "Lady Bowden, I presume? She has suffered *another* crisis of some sort that requires your instant presence?"

Thoroughly enchanted by this satisfying display of jealousy, Dominic grinned, his teeth flashing whitely against his dark face. "No, my green-eyed darling, it is *not* Lady Bowden! There is *nothing* that she could do or say that would ever take me from your side!"

Melissa regarded him suspiciously, one part of her wanting very much to believe him, another part full of distrust. She could not help but be charmed by his words, but she was not willing to let matters end there. "If it is not Lady Bowden, then who or what is it that is so important?" she demanded sharply.

Dominic hesitated. In the beginning he had been un-willing to tell Melissa of Jason's request because he had not really known her, had been uncertain if she could be trusted. It occurred to him rather forcefully now that his love for her would be a paltry thing if it did not also entail trust. By refusing, for whatever reasons, to tell her what he had been about these past months and why he was so intent upon leaving with Royce this evening, he was both insulting Melissa's intelligence and tarnishing his love for her. Love, he realized, was a powerful emotion able to withstand incredible adversities, but without trust it would neither grow nor endure; instead, the golden future he en-visioned for them could very well turn to common dross. Profoundly aware that he had come unexpectedly upon a fundamental crossroad in his relationship with his wife, Dominic did not hesitate any longer. Almost with relief, he bluntly and succinctly told her of the suspicion sur-rounding Latimer and of the reasons behind his apparently indulgent manner toward Deborah.

Oddly enough, Melissa believed him without question. What he was saying explained so many of his seemingly contradictory actions. And perhaps simply because she loved him and wanted to believe, she did. Her eyes grew very round, her mouth opening and shutting several times as the implications of his measured words sank into her brain. It was indescribably gratifying to learn that, far from being entranced by Lady Bowden, Dominic had only tolerated the other woman's demands in order to learn of Latimer's activ-ities. It was also exceedingly fascinating to discover that in addition to being a thoroughgoing scoundrel, Latimer was also involved in spying! Melissa was as patriotic as the next person, but it must be said that the part of the conversation she found the most riveting was Dominic's explanation for his apparent absorption in the other woman. Pushing aside Latimer's part in the situation for the moment, she lifted shining eyes to Dominic and asked wonderingly, "It was only to find out what she knew about Latimer's objectives that made you act so mesmerized around her?"

The gray eyes smiling, he nodded. "Can you really be-lieve that having you as my wife, I would *willingly* endure her company longer than necessary?"

Melissa's gaze dropped, and assailed by the shyness that could overtake her at the most inopportune times, she muttered, "You didn't really want to marry me . . . Josh forced you to do it."

"Oh, Lissa, you little goose!" Dominic said half impatiently, half laughingly. "The situation that Josh found us in was unfortunate, but *no one* could have made me marry you if I hadn't been willing to do so in the first place. The incident in my room at the inn was shocking and regrettable, but there was no irreversible harm done. If I had held firm, Josh would have had no choice but to hustle you down the back stairs and think me the worst sort of blackguard. I would not have been happy or pleased with that reputation, but there is no way in hell he could have forced me to marry you if I hadn't wanted to!"

Her heart thumping wildly in her breast, she glanced up at his lean, intent features. "You wanted to marry me?" she got out breathlessly.

Honesty made Dominic admit, "I don't know that I wanted to marry you exactly. I just knew, at first, that I wanted you in my arms and bed and that I didn't find the idea of being your husband at all objectionable." He smiled crookedly. "It was only as time went on that I knew I most desperately wanted and *needed* you and that whatever the reasons behind our hasty marriage, I could not imagine life without you."

Demurely Melissa confessed, "I didn't mind being married to you either."

"Mind?" Dominic questioned teasingly, one heavy brow flicking upward. "Is that the best you can do when I have just laid my heart at your feet?"

Her eyes wide and questioning, she asked softly, "Have you really laid your heart at my feet?"

Mindful of Royce waiting, no doubt with increasing restlessness, Dominic exclaimed almost despairingly, "Jesus, Lissa! I adore you! You have to know that! Why else would I buy Folly from you at that utterly ridiculous price? Why else would I bestow this cottage and land, the gifts and everything else I have, on you if it wasn't because I was mad about you and wanted you to have anything you wanted?"

Smiling dreamily at him, Melissa drew his face close to

hers. "I never wanted anything," she murmured tantalizingly against his lips, "except *you!*"

Dominic's response was swift and ecstatically satisfying to both of them. His arms tightened fiercely around her and his mouth sought and hungrily found hers. With ardent eagerness Melissa met his powerful embrace, her body arching seductively against him as his tongue darted ravenously into the warm recesses of her mouth. Arms locked around each other, they swayed together in a passionate embrace, the emotions they had both fought so hard to hide and control suddenly bursting forth.

The blood thudding in his brain, his arms full of warm and yielding flesh, Dominic forgot everything but the sweetness of holding his wife. He kissed her with increasing urgency, the desire to lose himself in the silken heat he knew awaited him relentlessly driving him as his arms dropped and his hands cupped her buttocks and he pressed her even closer to his swollen, aching manhood. He had wanted her in the past, but never like this, never knowing fully that it was love that drove him, love that made the wanting and hunger so sweet, so intoxicating.

Drowning in the honied warmth of his kisses, her body on fire to know his touch once more, Melissa was helplessly caught in the same elemental maelstrom of emotion, her body straining frantically against his, her hands running feverishly over his broad back as Dominic's kisses grew wilder and more passionate. Her breasts were full and heavy, her body boneless with wanting, the pressure of Dominic's thrusting, rigid flesh rubbing against her, exciting and arousing.

It was only the sound of Royce's voice that brought them, instantly and jarringly, back to their surroundings. "Ahem," Royce said politely from the doorway. "I hate to interrupt, but we *do* have an appointment, old friend."

Melissa sagged against Dominic, her thoughts of her cousin not at all kind. Dominic's were perhaps even less kind than Melissa's as his lips buried in her soft curls. "Royce, remind me to call you out when this is all over. I shall take great pleasure in putting a hole through you!"

"Whatever you say," Royce returned imperturbably. A

slight smile on his handsome mouth, he added, "I take it you and Melissa have settled your differences?"

Resolutely putting Melissa from him, Dominic smiled down at her and murmured, "Yes, I think you can safely say that—but not because of any help from you!"

"Well, you know that I make it a rule to never interfere in domestic affairs," Royce teased.

Melissa and Dominic both sent him a look that spoke volumes, and Royce, feeling that he would be no match against the two of them, shrugged his shoulders. "I shall await you outside."

Dominic grimaced and turned back to Melissa once Royce had disappeared. "I excessively dislike leaving you tonight, particularly *now*, but . . ." he murmured.

Melissa sighed. "I know. The sooner you find that list, the sooner we can put Latimer and . . ." A militant sparkle lit the golden-brown eyes ". . . his *sister* from our lives." With great feeling she added, "And it cannot happen soon enough for me!"

Laughing, Dominic hugged her to him. "Sweetheart, you never had anything to fear from that quarter. I resented every moment I had to spend in her presence mainly because it kept me from you!"

Immensely comforted by this knowledge, Melissa rubbed her cheek against his. "Oh, I do hope that I am not dreaming, that you really are saying these delightful things."

Dominic smiled, and dropping a kiss on the top of her head, he promised, "It is not a dream and I have many more delightful things to say to you later, but I really must go now."

She looked at him and asked anxiously, "You will be careful? There is no real danger to you?"

Dominic shook his dark head confidently. "No. Latimer is away from the house and Royce will be with me. If all goes well I should be home within a few hours—hopefully having successfully found that list of names." Gathering her close to him, he kissed her eager lips deeply and then, pushing her away slightly, said huskily, "And now I must go or Royce will come in and interrupt us again."

A soft, warm glow surrounding the region of her heart, with only faint misgivings Melissa waved the two men on their way a short moment later. She did not watch them entirely out of sight, superstitiously fearing bad luck if she did so. Deliberately she turned away and, a half smile on her lips, dreamily made her way inside.

Chapter Twenty-eight

DOMINIC did not fear bad luck, but he certainly could have wished that the timing to search Latimer's rooms had come at a less inconvenient moment—and *that,* he thought sardonically, was putting it very mildly indeed! Still, it was a task that had to be done, and determinedly he put away thoughts of Melissa and concentrated on the hours ahead.

It did not take them more than an hour to reach the house that Latimer had leased just beyond town, and as darkness had fallen nearly two hours earlier, they were able to conceal their presence by simply remaining in the rambling, untamed forest that surrounded the house and grounds. Dismounting from their horses, they tied the animals securely to some sturdy oak branches and then turned to consider the house.

The house was not overly large, but it was two-storied and, as was usual for houses in Louisiana, the bottom story was completely encompassed by a wide gallery. The kitchen was set a little distance from the main house and beyond that, Royce knew, the stables and servants' quarters were situated. From the faint glow of candlelight in one or two rooms of the main house, it was apparent that someone was still stirring; whether it was Latimer and Deborah or a busy servant remained to be seen.

The hour was shortly after nine o'clock, and as the moon was waxing full, silvery light clearly outlined the house and grounds. Leaning back against the trunk of a tall beech tree, Dominic said softly, "I could wish that there was a little *less* moonlight, but hopefully there will be no one around to see us." Motioning toward the house, he asked,

"What do you make of those lights . . . a change of plans or servants?"

Royce rubbed a hand thoughtfully across his chin. "I don't know. I suppose we shall have to go to the stable and see which horses, if any, are missing."

It took them but a few moments to gain the stable, and after slipping past the nodding stableboy, Royce gave a quick check around in the murky darkness and was able to say lowly, "The buggy and pair are missing, so I would assume Latimer and his sister kept to their original plans. It must be servants still moving around in the house."

They carefully made their way back to their horses and settled themselves comfortably to wait for all signs of activity to cease. Lying on the ground, propped against the smooth trunk of a tree, Dominic yawned hugely after several moments and then muttered, "I don't know about you, but after last night, I am not as alert as I would like to be."

Royce grunted in agreement and suggested, "Why don't you try to sleep and I'll keep watch for a while? Hopefully, whoever is in the house will seek out their own quarters before much longer. If not, and I grow sleepy myself, I shall wake you."

Dominic needed no urging and within moments was sound asleep. Unfortunately, the light within the house continued to shine and Royce, having underestimated his own stamina, nodded off a short time later.

The snapping of a twig nearby as some night animal moved through the forest brought Dominic instantly awake several hours later, and sitting upright, he glanced across at Royce. Grinning, he saw that Royce had succumbed and was deeply asleep. He looked quickly to the house and seeing that it was in darkness, he examined the black sky; judging from the moon's position, it was past midnight. They had no time to waste and hurriedly he prodded Royce awake.

"Oh, Jesus!" Royce groaned. "I had no idea that I was *that* tired! It is a good thing that our lives did not depend on my keeping watch!"

Dominic made some light reply and then they both began to concentrate on the matter at hand. Deciding that the sound of Latimer's return would have awakened them, it was agreed to go ahead and gain entrance to the house despite the lateness of the hour and the possibility that Latimer could appear at any moment.

"We'll hear his approach and should be able to escape the house without notice," Dominic said quietly.

Conscious of the passing minutes and using the cover of the forest, they quickly made their way to the far side of the house and with agile swiftness silently scaled the gallery roof. It took but a second to gain entrance to the house via a window that had been left unlocked. Inside, Dominic struck a flint and lit the candle he carried for tonight's foray. Lifting the candle high, he surveyed their surroundings, discovering that they must have entered the house through Deborah's bedroom window.

Wasting no time, they crept out into the wide hallway, and seeing but one door across the hall, they entered it, both sighing with nervous relief as the dancing golden light revealed a man's bedchamber. Methodically and efficiently, they began to search through Latimer's effects. It was a distasteful, nerve-racking business. With one ear cocked for the sound of an approaching carriage, they moved as silently as possible about the room, poking and prying into every conceivable hiding place, even searching through Latimer's clothing. Nowhere did they find anything that resembled a list of possible traitors, and Dominic's heart sank. Were they going to have to come back again? And again?

Moodily replacing the garment he had just checked, Dominic happened to glance at the floor of the wardrobe and Latimer's boots and shoes. Almost idly he picked up a pair of boots and in the dim, flickering light of the candle examined them. Finding nothing within the boots, he was on the point of dropping them onto the floor and reaching for another pair when something about the heels caught his attention. Frowning, he stared and then he called to Royce. Royce immediately left off his unenthusiastic search through Latimer's supply of neatly starched cravats and hurried over to Dominic's side.

Pointing to the cleverly built-up heel, Dominic murmured, "I didn't know that our friend needed any extra height, did you?"

"By God, no!" Royce muttered, his topaz eyes glittering with suppressed excitement.

Carefully they scrutinized the boots, comparing the heels with another pair in the wardrobe and discovering that the ones Dominic had first examined were considerably taller and bulkier than the others. It took them a few minutes to find the tiny secret compartment concealed in the hollowed-out heel of the left boot, but find it they did, and reaching inside, Dominic drew out a many-folded piece of paper. Holding the candle close, both men eagerly scanned the list of names revealed, Dominic giving a small exclamation of surprise when he recognized a few of them.

"There are some powerfully connected people on this list," he whispered to Royce. "And most of them are near the capital. It is a good thing that Jason caught his spy and we knew what to look for."

Royce agreed, but they wasted no more time in speculation. Bringing out the quill, paper and ink he had brought with him from home, Royce sat down and quickly copied the names. It took but a second to return the original list to its hiding place, and Dominic had just blown out the candle as they prepared to leave, when he lifted his head and said urgently, "Listen! I think I hear horses."

He did, the creak and jangle of harness as well as the sound of hoofbeats carrying clearly through the night air. As one, Dominic and Royce moved toward the door and drifted silently across the hall to Deborah's room. Nimbly both men slid out the window and down the gallery roof, the noise of the nearing vehicle becoming louder and more distinct with every passing second. Fortunately, the vehicle was approaching on the opposite side of the house, and Royce and Dominic rushed for the concealing forest the moment their feet hit the ground. Mounting their horses, they spun them about and without a backward look urged the animals deeper into the moonlit forest. It was only when they had put some distance between themselves and the Latimer place that Dominic allowed himself to comment on their successful venture.

A laugh in his voice, he said lightly, "We may not be

professional spies, but I do believe that we deserve congratulations for this night's work!''

Royce gave a satisfied chuckle. "Indeed, I agree with you, although I must admit that we escaped with not a moment to spare. But I have to confess that I found the entire episode quite exhilarating!" He grinned. "I wonder if friend Latimer's night was as successful as ours.''

Latimer's evening was not one that he cared to dwell on, even though he had managed to walk away from Richardson's card table a winner. Compared with what he had lost to Dominic, the amount won, however, had been trifling, being a mere thousand dollars; and even telling himself that tonight had been a good portent did nothing to soothe the hatred and fury that roiled in his breast whenever he thought of Dominic Slade.

Nothing, he thought sourly, had gone right for him since Dominic had come onto the Baton Rouge scene. If it had not been for Slade, Melissa would have given in to his demands, and if it hadn't been for Slade he would not now be in the precarious position of not being able to keep up appearances for very much longer—appearances he desperately needed if he was to retain any chance of recouping his disastrous loss by gulling the nearest ripe pigeon. His sights had been set on Franklyn for some time, but now he was reduced to even plucking someone like his host tonight.

Reaching the stable, he rousted out the sleeping stable-boy, and after tossing the reins to him, turned to help his sister down from the rig. As they walked slowly toward the house, Deborah said sullenly, "What a dreadful evening! I have never been so bored in my life!" Casting him a resentful glance as he opened the door and ushered her inside, she added peevishly, "It was all very well for you to spend the evening gambling with that old roué, but I was forced to listen to boring story after boring story about that frumpish old cow's one trip to London! The next invitation you accept, make certain it will be a lively party, or I will not go!''

Not in the best of tempers, Latimer snarled, "Shut up! I told you why it was so necessary to dine with them this evening. At least we have a thousand dollars more than we did when we started out.''

Her lovely face spiteful, Deborah snapped, ''And whose fault is it that we have been brought to such straits? Fifty thousand dollars! I told you not to keep gambling! It is all your fault!'' Working herself into a self-pitying rage, she flounced into a nearby chair and stated viciously, ''I *hate* this place! I detest America! I wish we had never come here! I hate it, do you hear me?''

The blue eyes cold and furious, in two long strides Latimer was towering over her. The sound of his hand striking her cheek as he brutally slapped her echoed in the room. Icily ignoring her cry of pain, he said harshly, ''I hear you, and I'm sure that anyone else within a mile of this place can hear you too! Now cease your whining and listen to me!''

Cradling her stinging cheek with one hand, Deborah sent him a hostile stare, all the helpless anger and resentment she felt at his actions clear to see in her eyes. ''Don't I always listen? Am I not always a dutiful little sister? Have you forgotten that I married that wretched old man because you insisted he was a better bargain than Dominic Slade?'' She gave a bitter laugh. ''A better bargain! By Heaven, that's amusing!''

His own face contorted with rage and bitterness, Latimer said vehemently, ''If you will stop feeling sorry for yourself, it is about Slade that I wish to talk.''

As if her anger had never been, Deborah's eyes suddenly glistened avidly, and forgetting her scarlet cheek, she dropped her hand and leaned forward eagerly. ''Yes? Are you going to help me?''

From the instant he had risen from the table at Tom Norton's house last night, Latimer had thought of little else than a way to extract a suitable revenge against Dominic. And now, twenty-four hours later, knowing *why* Dominic had set out to ruin him, knowing that Melissa had told her husband *everything*, he wanted savagely to punish them both. It was his most fervent desire to make them *both* pay for what had transpired last night. To hurt Dominic, to humble him by cold-bloodedly seducing his wife and making sure that Dominic *knew*, seemed a fitting revenge. It would *almost* be worth having lost a fortune, he thought cruelly, to plant a pair of prominent horns on Slade's head *and* to have Melissa in his own bed. He smiled nastily. It might be only for one time, while she was still stunned and angry enough to pay Dominic back in kind, that he possessed Melissa, but that one incident would haunt man and wife for the rest of their lives!

Looking at his sister, he said slowly, "Yes, I *am* going to help you get him into your bed—and just as soon as possible!"

"Oh, darling, *darling* brother, I knew you would not fail me!" Deborah exclaimed delightedly as she leaped gracefully to her feet and brushed a light kiss on his cheek. Standing close to him, her hand resting on his shoulder, she looked up at him hopefully. "What do you plan for me to do?"

Some of his own good humor restored, Latimer gave her an affectionate pat on the cheek he had slapped so heartlessly only moments before and said lightly, "I'm sorry that I hit you, puss, but you do annoy me terribly sometimes."

Now that he was going to help her, Deborah was ready to forgive him anything, and with harmony existing between them once more, she smiled sunnily up at him and declared grandly, "You can hit me anytime, provided you get Dominic Slade into my bed!"

Latimer chuckled and turned aside to pour them both a glass of port. "Have you found the spot for your seduction of him?" he asked.

Some of her good mood fled and, a bit petulantly, she confessed, "No! I've looked everywhere, but there is no place private and yet close enough to the house for me to use."

Frowning slightly, he inquired, "Must it be close to the house? Couldn't you arrange something in town?"

Sending him a disgusted look, she replied, "That would be too obvious. Besides, if he is coming to see me, because I'm afraid of you and want him to take me away, I can't already *be* away, can I?"

"Hmm, I see your point. This, er, love nest is to be the place you escape to when you wish to avoid my terrible rages—your sanctuary, the only place you feel safe from me?"

"Exactly!" Deborah said gleefully. "I considered the little summerhouse out back, but it is too open and within sight of the house. But I want the place to be nearby so that the servants don't have to cart all the necessary furnishings all over the countryside."

Latimer paced up and down, occasionally sipping his port as he considered and discarded several places. Stopping suddenly directly in front of Deborah, he asked slowly, "What about the gazebo on the docks?"

"That rickety old building?" she shrieked with dismay. "Near that smelly swamp?"

Nodding his blond head, Latimer said calmly, "Hear me out before you dismiss the idea out of hand." And at Deborah's reluctant agreement, he continued. "First of all, the building is on the land that comes with the house, so we can do what we want with it. Second, it is out of sight and earshot of the house. The building is very secluded, even if it is old and, as you say, rickety. As for the swamp . . ." He smiled at her. "It isn't my understanding that it is the *swamp* which will command Slade's attention."

Thoughtfully, Deborah turned the idea over in her mind. Other than the proximity of the swampy pond, the gazebo did have several things to recommend it, she finally conceded. It would take a lot of work to prepare the place as she envisioned the finished product in her head, but . . .

"I'll look it over tomorrow morning, and perhaps by the end of the week we can set events in motion," she said finally.

Latimer shook his head. "No. I want to waste no more time. Just as soon as I can get my hands on the Franklyn money, we are leaving for New Orleans. I find that this place has lost its charm for me too, and if I had my way, we would both be on that packet which arrived this afternoon from New Orleans and which will be returning there on Friday morning." Taking another sip of his port, he stared blindly at the far wall, all his thoughts and energies on getting revenge—and money.

"Josh Manchester's party is also on Friday," he murmured reflectively. "And I already know that young Franklyn will be attending. I would have preferred another location and time for my sudden run of luck, but since last night, I no longer have the luxury of waiting for the most opportune moment. I shall have to make my move that evening. It is unfortunate that the packet is leaving a day too soon for us, or we would be on it."

"Well, then, there is no hurry about Dominic, is there?" Deborah asked reasonably.

Latimer smiled tightly. "I have plans of my own, but in order for my plans to be effective, *yours* must take place first. By this time tomorrow night, I want you to have enjoyed the pleasures you think you have missed."

Having fantasized for many years about Dominic's lovemaking, Deborah was not loath to go along with her brother's ideas. And her vanity was such that she was quite positive that, once having lain in her arms, Dominic would want to repeat the process several more times. . . . Visualizing a rosy future in which Dominic was so enamored of her charms that he deserted his wife and followed her to England, Deborah said dreamily, "Whatever you say, dear brother."

She was not quite so sanguine the next morning when he roused her out of bed at the unheard-of hour of seven o'clock, nor were her doubts about the suitability of the gazebo laid to rest as they walked out onto the narrow, half-rotted dock to view the building. Clinging tightly to her brother's arm, Deborah gingerly approached the formerly attractive but now timeworn and neglected structure.

Originally this particular spot had been lovely, the sprawling, irregularly shaped pond kept fresh and clear by a small creek that had emptied into it, the creek re-forming at the opposite end of the pond where a wide, shallow overflow area had been created by tightly interlaced logs. In the spring, wildflowers abounded on the banks of the pond, willow trees and birch growing right down to the water's edge in some places. The delicately latticed gazebo jutted off to one side about halfway out on the narrow dock, and it took little imagination to visualize the past with children fishing or swimming in the shallow pond while their mothers sat in the small gazebo and enjoyed a cozy gossip, sipping tall glasses of lemonade.

But that had been many years ago, and now the pond was choked with duckweed and algae, the creek having changed its course, leaving the pond without a constant influx of fresh water. While the seasonal rains helped some, by autumn the remaining water was a murky green soup of rotting vegetation. Holding a perfume-scented lace handkerchief to her nose, Deborah exclaimed, "Oh, this will *never* do—such a noxious odor!"

"That can be taken care of," Latimer returned carelessly as he stepped cautiously into the gazebo. Finding the floor solid, he glanced around, noting the cobwebs and the occasional broken lattice. The place was filthy and had obviously been unused for many, many years, but he saw nothing that would preclude it from being the site of Dominic's seduction.

Deborah, however, was of another mind. "You cannot be serious!" she shrieked, giving a shudder as her gaze took in the ramshackle interior. But it was the slightly sinister pond that disturbed her the most, and gazing at its unmoving vegetation-clouded surface, she shuddered again, thinking of all the hidden horrors she was positive lurked just underneath.

But Latimer was not to be swayed, and despite Deborah's vociferous protestations to the contrary, he immediately set the servants to work on the building. When she viewed it several hours later, Deborah resentfully had to admit that he had been right. No longer did the interior appear ramshackle and unused, for after a thorough sweeping and scrubbing, several costly items from the house had been installed, and the look was quite different.

Upon the floor now lay a small green-and-cream Oriental rug, and to ensure privacy as well as to hide any unsightliness, several bolts of startling pink muslin material swathed the walls, the ends all caught together and attached to the roof to form a tentlike canopy.

A gold damask-covered chaise had been installed, and mounds of blue satin pillows were placed strategically nearby. Next to the chaise stood a small mahogany table, its gleaming surface nearly hidden by a silver tray which held a decanter of brandy and a pair of snifters. Near the entrance had been placed a candlestand with a crystal candelabrum upon it. The scent of lilacs and roses perfumed the air, the rug and pillows having been liberally sprinkled with scented water before their installation.

Grudgingly Deborah congratulated her brother. "This was exactly what I had in mind . . . except for the proximity of the water," she said as she walked around the small room, her hand idly touching the fine muslin which seemed to flow everywhere. Her eyes on the chaise, imagining herself and Dominic locked there in a torrid embrace, she smiled. "It is perfect, Julius! I shall go up to my room to write the note to Dominic and have it delivered immediately!"

A short while later, her pitiful note begging for Dominic's *instant* help on its way, Deborah merrily ordered a bath prepared for herself and then browsed happily through her overflowing wardrobe trying to decide which of her many gowns would be the most seductive . . . and easy to remove. Unaware of Dominic's clandestine activities last night, she could not have guessed that when her servant arrived with the message at the cottage, it would be to discover that the master of the house was still abed and that it was the mistress of the house who received her calculatingly worded little note. Nor would she have recalled that in her haste to get the message sent, she had neglected to address the envelope, merely ordering the servant to deliver the note to the Slade house.

Long after the servant had ridden away from the cottage, Melissa stared at the blank front of the envelope, the scent Deborah always wore wafting up to her nostrils. Even if she had not recognized Deborah's perfume, the servant had politely identified himself as being from Lady Bowden, so she was without a doubt about who had sent the letter to her husband and, despite its lack of address, that it *was* for her husband!

Seating herself on the gallery, she carefully laid the envelope down on a nearby table, her expression pensive. Should she waken Dominic? she wondered somberly. The note *could* be important. But then again . . . Her soft mouth tightened. Then again, it could be Lady Bowden angling for an intimate tête-à-tête with *her* husband! As she thought of Dominic, of the way he had been sleeping so deeply when she had left him this morning, Melissa's features were suddenly tender, all thought of Deborah's motives for writing Dominic vanishing as she lost herself in the sweet memory of last night.

Melissa had been able to occupy her time doing various feminine tasks for a few hours after Dominic and Royce had ridden away for the Latimer place, but all the while her thoughts had been on them and what they were doing. She told herself time and again that they would be safe, that there was nothing to worry about, but she still could not help being concerned and anxious for them to return. Sternly she had kept all her fears at bay, reminding herself that Dominic and Royce were quite capable of taking care of themselves, but it was difficult for her to be entirely at ease. Fighting her fears became even worse once she had retired for the evening, and lying alone in her bed, she berated herself for not having demanded that they take her with them. Why, she could have acted as lookout, if nothing else! she thought belatedly. Giving up all pretense of sleep, she wandered into Dominic's room. Seated in the middle of his big bed, she settled down to wait for his return, ridiculously comforted by clutching the pillow that still bore his scent. Fears abated for the moment as she recalled the look on Dominic's face when he had said, "I adore you!" Dreamily she stared into space, the knowledge that Dominic loved her filling her with a warm glow.

Melissa curled up in the middle of the blue satin coverlet, Dominic's pillow clasped reassuringly against her slender body, and the sleep which had eluded her so far gradually crept over her. And it was thus that Dominic, exhausted but elated, found her when he returned home sometime after four o'clock in the morning.

Hardly daring to believe his eyes, he called softly, "Melissa?"

Melissa heard his low voice, and waking with a start, she sat bolt upright in bed, her hair tousled and her cheeks rosy from sleep. Looking like a blinking-eyed kitten, she spied Dominic's tall form approaching and exclaimed happily, "Oh, you are home! I was worried and waited up for you. I could not sleep."

Absently unbuttoning his shirt, his smile very tender, he sat down on the edge of the bed. "Oh? And what was it you were doing just now?" he teased gently, the gray eyes moving caressingly over her face.

The knowledge that he loved her emboldened her, and she threw herself into his arms, laughing. "I wasn't sleeping," she murmured softly. "I was dreaming . . . about you."

"Were you, now?" Dominic replied huskily. Melissa's warm body pressed ardently against him, making him forget all sorts of things, such as how late it was . . . how little sleep he'd had in the past forty-eight hours . . . how tired he was. . . . Gathering her closer, his teeth nibbling gently on the lobe of her ear, he asked thickly, "And what was I doing in this dream of yours?"

A shiver of desire snaked down Melissa's spine, and marveling at her brazenness, she rained teasingly sweet kisses across his face and throat, her fingers sliding under his half-opened shirt, sensuously exploring the warm, taut flesh that she found. "Oh, you were doing this . . ." she muttered as her hand rubbed his flat nipples. "And this. . . ."

Dominic groaned as her hands continued to move intimately over him, and the hungry ache that had struck him the moment he had laid eyes on her suddenly exploded in his belly. Capturing her mouth with his, he kissed her fiercely, his tongue thrusting demandingly into hers, his hands urgently running up and down her body as the rigid control he had placed on himself all these weeks was violently wrenched away, leaving only a powerful, elemental passion in its wake. Together they sank slowly backward onto the bed, mouths, arms and legs entwined. . . .

With a start Melissa brought herself back to the present, a faint blush on her cheeks as she became aware of her swollen nipples rubbing against the fabric of her gown. This would never do! she told herself severely, and looking at the letter from Deborah, she frowned. Though it was late afternoon, she knew that Dominic would not awaken for at least another hour or two. It had been dawn before they had fallen asleep in each other's arms, their bodies sated, their love for each other fully acknowledged, and although it had been nearly noon when Melissa had awakened, Dominic had not even stirred when she slipped from the bed—and she certainly was not going to wake him now to give him a message from Deborah Bowden!

For several minutes she considered opening the envelope herself. Her conscience troubling her, but arguing that the envelope was *un*addressed and so *could* have been meant for either of them, she took a deep breath and, not giving herself time to change her mind, quickly opened it. Swiftly reading Deborah's pitiful little plea, Melissa was struck by doubt.

She didn't believe for one moment that Deborah's need was as desperate as claimed; on the other hand, Melissa remembered the look in Latimer's cold blue eyes, the violence she sensed within him that day in the tack room when he had first broached his ugly plan, and she wondered if there wasn't an element of truth in what Deborah had written. Perhaps Latimer *had* beaten her savagely. It was possible that she *did* fear for her life. And, knowing Dominic, she thought it was entirely possible that he *had* offered Deborah sanctuary. But then . . .

Her eyes narrowed. It was also, she thought reflectively, quite possible that everything in the note was a sham and that Deborah's only purpose in writing it was to bring Dominic on the run. And *that,* she decided firmly, was intolerable!

Glancing again at the dainty script and deciding that if Deborah's plight was as wretched as claimed, the other woman would welcome help from any quarter, Melissa stood up resolutely. *She* would come to Deborah's rescue. *If* Deborah needed rescuing, she concluded cynically as she left the gallery and headed for the stables.

Fortunately, she was still in her riding habit, not that it would have made much difference to her, and within minutes she was on her way, the powerful black gelding she had chosen to ride hitting a distance-eating stride that rapidly brought Melissa near her destination. She was familiar with the house that Latimer had leased and equally familiar with the gazebo, where Deborah had written she would be waiting for Dominic. Not totally convinced of the truth of Deborah's letter, Melissa took no chances, guiding her horse off the main trail some distance from the house and approaching the gazebo from the opposite side of the pond.

A careful scrutiny of the area revealed nothing out of the ordinary and cautiously she edged the big horse around the pond, keeping herself well concealed in the forest until she had reached a point not far from the beginning of the docks. Dismounting lithely, she tied her horse securely to a slim birch tree. She hesitated a moment, her gaze moving once more over the area. Beset with thoughts of spies and the dangers associated with such people, she continued to stand there hidden by the forest, wondering uncertainly if what she was doing was wise. It probably wasn't, but then Dominic had said that Latimer was not a *real* spy. Annoyed with herself for letting her imagination overpower her common sense, Melissa stepped forward boldly, her leather riding crop gripped tightly in one hand. The crop wouldn't prove to be much of a weapon, should she have to use it, but its solid weight in her hand comforted her.

Warily she approached the dock and just as warily stole across its narrow width, getting closer to the gazebo. It was only when she was but a few feet from the building that she became aware of the faint odor of lilac in the air and noticed for the first time the pink material which concealed the interior of the gazebo. A woman's soft humming emanated from inside the muslin-swathed structure, and with a narrowing of her eyes, she realized that it was a happy sound. Not at all the sound of terrified sobbing!

Growing more positive by the second of the wisdom of her decision to come here, Melissa intrepidly marched to the opening of the gazebo, the scent of lilacs and roses forcibly assaulting her nostrils. The sight that met her gaze made her extremely thankful that she had not awakened her husband! It was glaringly obvious, after one swift, all-encompassing glance around, that it was not a rescue that had prompted Deborah's letter, but blatant seduction!

The sheer lurid *pinkness* of the interior nearly made Melissa blink, and despite the gravity of the situation, she had to suppress a giggle as she tried to imagine Dominic's face if he had ridden posthaste to answer Deborah's plea for help and had found *this!* And as her gaze fell upon the supposed damsel in distress, she had to fight to keep a stern expression on her face—to find any damsel looking *less* distressful would have been difficult!

Unaware that she now had an audience, Deborah lolled about in what she no doubt assumed was an alluring pose, half reclining, half sitting on the gold chaise, a snifter of brandy in one hand. She was wearing the most indecent garment Melissa had ever seen, a nearly transparent lilac gown which opened down the front, the only thing holding it together a small bow which fastened under Deborah's full breasts. It took Melissa a moment before she recognized the garment as the gauzy overdress of a ball gown, and she had to admire Deborah's ingenuity and audacity in wearing such a provocative piece of clothing. Humming happily to herself, Deborah took a healthy gulp of the brandy just then and from her awkward, jerky movements it was apparent that this was not the first brandy she had consumed this afternoon.

Melissa had not infrequently dwelt on the scathing setdown, the fitting revenge she would bestow upon Deborah Bowden one day. Under different circumstances, today would have provided a perfect opportunity, but secure in the knowledge that Dominic loved *her,* she didn't fear Deborah any longer or feel the need for taking vengeance. As she stood there at the entrance to Deborah's ridiculous little love bower, Melissa was conscious of a stab of pity for the other woman, not unmixed with contempt at her unscrupulous methods of obtaining male company, especially the company of a *married* male.

Abruptly it occurred to Melissa that she no longer had any reason to confront Deborah. Dominic loved *her;* Deborah had long ago thrown away whatever chance she might have possessed to gain his affection. Suddenly yearning to have her husband's arms about her and feeling just a trifle foolish at her melodramatic ideas of extracting revenge, Melissa cautiously started to edge away.

Whether her foot scraped on the rough wooden planking

or if it was the movement of her body that caught Deborah's attention, Melissa didn't know, but unexpectedly Deborah turned her head and was staring straight at her. Wishing intensely that she were anywhere but right here, Melissa could feel an embarrassed flush burning up over her face as she stared helplessly back at Deborah.

The effect upon Deborah, however, at the utterly startling sight of Dominic's wife standing at the opening of the gazebo was quite dramatic. She paled; she shrieked and gave such a violent jerk of surprise that the brandy went flying all over her as she promptly fell off the chaise. Lying on the floor in an inelegant heap, she stared with alarm at the tall, commanding figure in the doorway, her gaze fastening with horrified fascination on the menacing leather quirt held in Melissa's hand.

A guilty conscience is a most peculiar thing, and instead of realizing that Melissa was at least as mortified as she was, Deborah could see only a tawny-haired, vengeance-seeking Amazon come to horsewhip her through the countryside. All her sins flashed before her; every time that she had clung to Dominic, every incident when she had tried to seduce him away from his wife, passed clearly and vividly through her brain, and Deborah was frantic to avoid the just punishment she was convinced Melissa had come to wreak upon her.

Concerned that Deborah might have hurt herself, Melissa started forward to offer help, but she had barely taken one step when Deborah scrambled to her feet and, hands outstretched protectively in front of her, screeched, "Stay there! Don't come any closer or I'll scream!"

Thoroughly nonplussed, Melissa stared at her, wondering if she were confronting a madwoman—Deborah certainly resembled one with her wild, staring eyes and hysterical actions. Her voice very soft and calm, Melissa said reasonably, "There is no need to scream—besides, no one could hear you."

Reading a sinister intent in Melissa's innocent remark, Deborah thought only to put as much distance as possible between herself and this female instrument of revenge. Keeping her eyes on Melissa for any sign of aggression, she warily inched backward, muttering, "It's not my fault!

This was all Julius' idea—he planned it. He made me do it!''

"Oh, that's ridiculous!" Melissa burst out contemptuously, her temper rising at the despicable way Deborah tried to throw all blame onto Latimer. Shaking her quirt for emphasis, she added, "You're lying! And even if he did plan it, *you're* the one who is waiting here half naked!"

The sight of the raised quirt was Deborah's undoing, and Melissa had barely finished speaking when Deborah squealed, *"Don't touch me!"* Desperate to escape, forgetting where she was, how very small the gazebo was, Deborah edged farther backward, falling against the lightly fastened muslin material. One minute she was standing there and then the next she was slipping through the gaping hole hidden behind the excruciatingly pink fabric. Frantically she tried to prevent her fall, her hands wildly clutching at the material, and for one second she hung half out of the building. Then, with a great ripping sound, the fabric gave way and Deborah, shrieking with terror, plunged into the rank green water.

Openmouthed with astonishment and faintly conscious of a flicker of anxiety for a fellow human being in distress, Melissa swiftly crossed the room to stare out of the hole left in the rotten latticework. Below Melissa, encumbered by yards of clinging, wet material, her beautifully coiffured blond hair having a distinct green hue from algae and duckweed, was Deborah . . . a wet, spluttering, thoroughly furious Deborah!

Because she was no longer in imminent danger from Melissa, Deborah's nerve had returned along with her temper, and she proceeded to curse with a fluency and vulgarity that made Melissa's eyes go round. Stopping long enough to breathe, she glared at Melissa and spat, "Look at me! This is all your bloody fault! I hate you! I hate this country and everyone in it! I wish I had never come here!"

Since it was obvious that Deborah had suffered no harm, Melissa smiled saucily and said over her shoulder as she walked out of the building, "You no more than I, dear lady!"

Chapter Twenty-nine

REACHING her horse, Melissa mounted and, wheeling the animal about, watched as Deborah, the muslin material coiling around her body like a slimy pink snake, grappled to make the edge of the shallow pond. It was quite a struggle, the heavy waterlogged fabric slowing her progress, and the slippery, uneven bottom of the pond making it difficult to maintain her balance. Melissa had to choke back a laugh as Deborah stumbled and fell face forward in the swampy water not a yard from the shore. Unwilling to leave without seeing Deborah firmly on land, Melissa kept her restive horse steady until at last Deborah gained dry land. Taking one final look at the bedraggled and thoroughly infuriated Deborah as she staggered a few more feet from the pond, yards of algae-stained material trailing wetly behind her, Melissa could no longer prevent a small chuckle from escaping. There was now no reason to remain, and she kicked her horse into motion and galloped away.

Too intent on her own progress as she lurched in the direction of the house, Deborah was not even aware that Melissa had left. Her only thought at the moment was to gain the sanctuary of the house and, once she had rid herself of the clinging, wet fabric and the noxious odor which clung to her skin, to personally oversee the burning down of the gazebo! When it was a smoking ruin, *then* she intended to put as much distance as possible between herself and the site of the most humiliating moment in her life. She was leaving Baton Rouge! And *no one* was going to talk her out of it!

And so it was that when Latimer returned home some three hours later, having prudently absented himself for the afternoon, he found his entryway filled with trunks and boxes piled haphazardly. "Good God! What is going on?" he demanded of the harassed butler.

"Your sister, sir, she is leaving," the man said without any emotion. "She is in the main salon waiting to talk with you before she boards the packet this evening. It is leaving in the morning for New Orleans."

Latimer hurried down the hallway, all sorts of wild ideas shooting through his brain as he tried to guess what terrible calamity was forcing Deborah to take such rash action. Had Slade suffered a fatal accident when the two of them were alone in the gazebo? Had she *murdered* Slade in a fit of temper? What in hell had gone wrong?

Smelling of roses and gowned impeccably in a lovely frock of blue satin, Deborah was pacing impatiently up and down the long room when he entered it and rushed up to her. "Are you all right?" Latimer demanded. "What is this nonsense that you are leaving? What the devil happened this afternoon?"

Her voice bitter and sullen, she proceeded to tell him exactly what had transpired, although Melissa would not have recognized the story that Deborah told. "She attacked me, Julius! I feared for my very life! And then if it was not enough to assault me with a horse whip, she tried to drown me in that awful pond!" The blue eyes were kindling with remembered rage. "She is a savage, brutal person—just like this country—and I am not remaining here one moment longer than it takes me to reach New Orleans. As for the ship that we are to meet in January—it cannot appear too soon for me!"

Latimer tried to reason with her, and though he did have some difficulty believing her story without question, he recognized the obstinate jut of her chin and realized that there was no swaying her. Whatever had really happened, it was obvious that their plan had gone dreadfully awry and that any hope he had entertained of using Deborah's seduction of Dominic as a means of bringing Melissa into his arms had been smashed.

"Very well," he said finally. "I will take you to the packet tonight."

As if realizing for the first time that she would be on her own, Deborah asked nervously, "Won't you come with me? There is nothing here for either of us. It is time we moved on."

"It may be time for us to move on," Latimer said with an ugly twist to his mouth, "but before we do I have a score to settle with Dominic Slade and his wife."

Her eyes fearful, Deborah demanded, "What are you going to do?"

"I don't know," Latimer admitted coolly, "but I don't intend to leave Baton Rouge without making both of the Slades very sorry that they ever crossed me." He smiled at Deborah and said in a lighter tone, "Don't worry, puss—I shall join you in New Orleans before the end of the month. You have the name of the hotel where we are to stay and you know the banker we are to see there. I shall write you a letter to present to him, explaining that I have been unavoidably delayed and that you are to have complete access to my account there." Pinching her gently on the chin, he added, "Don't spend it all on new gowns—when we meet that ship in January, we cannot take very much with us. It will be a military ship, so most of your trunks and baggage will have to be left behind."

Deborah pouted. "I don't see why!" Then, struck by another thought, she suddenly smiled. "But it won't matter. With all the money we are to get from Roxbury, I shall simply buy myself an entirely new wardrobe."

"And do not forget that one of the reasons I am remaining behind is to pilfer the Franklyn cub's fortune," Latimer drawled, a calculating gleam in the blue eyes. "Think of me tomorrow night at the Manchester place, winning all that lovely money for us."

Escorting Deborah on board the packet an hour later, Latimer remarked, "Now, do not forget that a gentleman by the name of Anthony Davis will, no doubt, come to call on you. You may speak freely with him—he is one of Roxbury's men. Also, a gentleman named Samuel Drayton might attract your attention. It is Drayton who will lead us to the rendezvous site in January. Both men know that we are expected in New Orleans soon and will be watching for our arrival.''

''Will you be all right alone here?'' she asked anxiously.

Latimer smiled confidently down at her as he ushered her into the cramped, unpleasant little room that would be her quarters until the packet docked in New Orleans. ''Nothing is going to happen to me,'' he said smoothly. ''This will be the first time we have been separated and, in this less-than-civilized country, one can never tell what may happen, but I'm sure nothing will.''

Her worries easily allayed, Deborah turned her attention to her new quarters, her complaints loud and unending. Several moments later, when Latimer bade her a brief farewell, she was still criticizing her accommodations, and he walked away with her long list of grievances ringing in his ears.

But Latimer had his own grievances to consider, and during the short ride back to the house he brooded on the various methods with which he could strike back at Dominic and Melissa. Everything that had gone wrong with the trip to America he now blamed on Dominic's unwarranted interference, and as for Melissa's part in all of his troubles . . . His mouth thinned. Melissa had gravely wounded his pride and he hungered to punish her for having chosen to marry Slade instead of submitting to *his* demands! He had almost convinced himself that *he* would have married her! But had it mattered to her? No! She had cruelly spurned him, had teased him and led him on, until she had found a wealthier suitor! Like his sister, Latimer could easily twist facts to satisfy his own purposes . . . and his purpose was revenge. . . .

Revenge was the last thing on Melissa's mind when she had ridden home some hours earlier. Even the ridiculous scene with Deborah had faded from her mind, and her thoughts were solely on her husband. A dazzling smile on her lips, she left her lathered horse at the stables and hurried to the house.

Crossing the hallway, she met Bartholomew on his way upstairs with a steaming bucket of hot water. Running up the steps ahead of him, she asked, "Is that for my husband? Is he awake now?"

"Yes, madam," Bartholomew returned in measured accents. "The master woke up some time ago . . . he seemed a trifle annoyed when he learned that you had gone riding and that no one knew when you would be back, nor where you had gone."

Melissa flushed guiltily, never having given Dominic's reaction to waking and finding her gone a moment's thought. Speculatively she eyed Bartholomew as they reached the top of the stairs. It was not proper to gossip with one's servants, but Melissa could not help inquiring, "And now? Is he still a 'trifle annoyed'?"

A twinkle in the brown eyes, Bartholomew replied, "I believe, madam, that his, er, annoyance will vanish the moment you walk in."

Melissa sent him a blinding smile. "Oh, I hope so!" she breathed fervently.

Motioning him to go ahead of her into Dominic's room, she whispered, "Don't tell him I am back yet—I want to surprise him."

Nodding wisely, Bartholomew did as instructed, answering Dominic's barked "Has she returned yet?" with a sedate "I do not know, sir. Shall I check at the stables?"

Dominic's back was to the door as he sat in the huge claw-footed copper bathtub, wisps of steam rising slowly in the air, and consequently he did not see Melissa slip inside his room. Her gaze rested lovingly on the portion of his broad back that was exposed above the rim of the tub, and her heart gave a little jump when he answered Bartholomew's question with an explosive "Goddammit, yes! It isn't like her to just ride off, especially not after last—" He stopped speaking abruptly and said in a more normal tone of voice, "Let me know the instant she returns."

"Very well, sir," Bartholomew replied, winking slyly at Melissa as he walked past her and out the door. For several moments after Bartholomew had departed, Melissa just stood there leaning against the doorjamb, her eyes on Dominic, a warm feeling of anticipation curling lazily within her.

Then, smiling to herself, she felt for the key behind her and, finding it, with a quick twist locked the door. Dominic had been grumbling to himself and did not hear the soft click of the key when it turned in the lock. Stealthily, Melissa removed her boots, then began to undo the buttons of her riding habit as she walked slowly across the room toward Dominic.

Some sixth instinct must have warned him that he was no longer alone, because he suddenly slewed around in the tub, staring in her direction. A lazy smile curved his lips and a frankly carnal gleam came into the gray eyes as he murmured, "Coming to join me, I hope?"

Melissa bit back a gurgle of laughter and with great care unhurriedly removed the top of her riding habit to reveal the fine linen chemise beneath it. An answering gleam in her own eyes, she asked with suspect doubtfulness, "Do you think I should? Would it be proper?"

With interest he watched as she came nearer, sweet, hot desire building in his veins with every step she took. "Oh, I'm quite sure that it would be perfectly proper," he returned huskily, his gaze mesmerized by the slow, sinuous slide of her riding skirt to the floor.

Standing before him in her chemise, she toyed with the dainty little strap on one shoulder. Then she walked to the edge of the tub and with exaggerated fastidiousness commenced to remove her remaining piece of clothing. Avidly his eyes feasted on the beauty slowly revealing itself to him: the high, coral-tipped breasts, the nipples already puckered and stiff; the narrow waist; the alabaster sheen of the flaring hips and the long, slender legs.

Through passion-narrowed eyes Dominic stared at her, the knowledge that this was his wife, the woman he adored, filling him with a fierce delight. Gliding to his knees in the water, he reached for her. His arms went firmly about her waist as he pulled her to him. His cheek resting against her soft, warm midriff, he closed his eyes in sheer pleasure at her nearness and muttered gruffly, "The next time I wake and you are not in my arms, I shall beat you!"

Not the least disturbed by this apparent threat, Melissa nodded her head in perfect agreement and flexed her fingers with sensuous enjoyment in his thick dark hair. "Of course," she murmured docilely, "and after you have beaten me . . . ?"

"After I have beaten you," Dominic fairly purred, "I shall have to kiss all your hurts . . . like this. . . ." Deliberately his lips closed over her nipple, pulling it hungrily into the wet warmth of his mouth, his tongue flicking tautly against the sensitive tip.

Melissa moaned softly, her hands cradling his head nearer to her sweetly aching breast. Languor creeping through her limbs, she swayed gently against him, the muted throb of rekindling passion increasing its tempo.

There was nothing hurried about their movements; it was as if last night they had momentarily dulled that first razor's edge of passion and could now simply savor the joy they found in each other's arms. Last night had been the greedy feasting of a starving lover, but now . . . now was a banquet of erotic delights to be relished slowly.

Nuzzling her tingling nipple, Dominic slid his hands to her hips, gently exploring the smooth flesh of her buttocks as he said thickly, "I'm on fire for you already, sweetheart . . . all I have to do is touch you and my body burns for you." Sliding without haste backward into the water, he gently dragged Melissa with him, deftly guiding her pliant body where he wanted.

The water was warm, and, filled with a strange inertia, Melissa rested against Dominic's hard length, distinctly aware of every muscle and sinew of his tall form beneath her. A ripple of intense pleasure surged up through her as she felt his bulging shaft nudging hotly between her thighs, and her arms twined around his neck, pulling his head down to hers, her lips eagerly seeking his.

They kissed with easy intimacy, their tongues lazily stroking against each other in unhurried, teasing movements, both of them conscious of the obsessive, all-consuming passion that welled up more powerfully with every languid motion they made. It was exquisite torture to deliberately deny themselves deeper caresses, but by an unspoken consent they contented themselves with increasingly more passionate kisses, the hungry fire within them blazing brighter and brighter.

Lifting his lips from hers, his eyes smoky with desire, Dominic said roughly, "You're driving me mad!" His gaze dropped to her breast, the swollen nipple half out of the water. Lifting her slightly, he bent his head, hungrily sucking the coral tip deep into his mouth. *"Quite* mad!" he said in a muffled tone as his lips traveled up her chest to find her mouth once more.

With growing urgency their bodies moved against each other, the silken feel of Melissa's slender form rubbing next to his sending a bolt of naked longing through Dominic. Her body touched his everywhere and he groaned with delight when her hand began to travel with a tormenting lack of haste over his chest, down across his flat belly to tangle in the thick curly hair at the junction of his thighs. She seemed to hesitate there and he nipped her ear, saying huskily, "Oh, Jesus, Lissa! Touch me!" and ungently dragged her hand where he wanted it most.

Wonderingly, Melissa touched him, excited and fascinated by his shape and size, her fingers gliding teasingly up and down the rigid length. There was much pleasure, she discovered, in giving pleasure and, enthralled by her own power, she caressed him more passionately, her own arousal deepening.

His fingers suddenly bit into her waist and insistently he pulled her up over him, her knees fitting snugly on either side of his lean hips in the narrow confines of the tub. One hand behind her head, he caught her lips with his, his mouth moving demandingly over hers, all restraint gone. Blind to everything but his great need, Dominic sought the eagerly yielding flesh between her legs, caressing her urgently until Melissa was writhing uncontrollably against his fingers.

Trembling from the force of the passion that raged within her, Melissa said against his mouth, "Take me, darling. Let me feel you inside me."

Dominic needed no further urging, his body surging upward as he guided her onto him. The silken warmth as she sheathed him was nearly more than he could bear and he twisted wildly beneath her, his fingers digging into her hips while he fought against quick release.

Her eyes glistening with passion, Melissa watched him

fight for control and then, a siren's smile on her kiss-swollen mouth, she began to move up and down slowly, reveling in the sweet sensations that swept through her body. But the fire that drove Dominic drove her too, and fiercely she pushed down on him, eager to share again the joy she knew awaited them.

Dominic could bear the exquisite agony of Melissa's movements no longer and he held her captive as he thrust urgently up into her. Racked by desire, Dominic drove into her again and again, every deep stroke of his body bringing them nearer to the brink of ecstasy.

Impaled by Dominic, his hard body driving frantically into hers, Melissa was mindless with pleasure when that first sharp jolt of rapture hit her body, and with a soft sigh of fulfillment she collapsed against him, tingling pleasurably from the force of her release.

Feeling the tremors that shook Melissa, Dominic lost his battle to prolong their pleasure, and groaning his own delight, he let that same rapture crash over him. Replete and sated, he drew Melissa nearer to him and kissed her tenderly, murmuring his love for her even as their lips met.

Sweetly she returned his kiss and together they lay there in the cooling bathwater, whispering all the vows that lovers do, and when the chill of the water brought them back from their rosy world, they laughed and proceeded to give each other a hasty wash. The hasty wash, however, led to other things.

Consequently, it was not until they were seated in the dining room enjoying a plump stuffed chicken that the subject of Deborah Bowden came up. A bit uneasily, Melissa mentioned the note that had arrived and her subsequent reading of it. Dominic merely looked interested and did not appear to be the least perturbed at what she had done. He was not precisely pleased when he learned the contents of the letter, nor was he completely thrilled with the news that Melissa had gone to meet Deborah in his place.

"Good God, Lissa! You took a terrible chance!" he exclaimed, his only concern being for her safety. "It could have been a trap! And I'm not talking about seduction either. Latimer has good reason to dislike us and he could very well have meant to do me a mischief.''

Melissa smiled at him saucily. ''Well, it all turned out rather well, if I do say so myself.''

''Oh?'' he said warily, not quite certain that he trusted that gleam in his wife's eye.

Struggling to keep a straight face, Melissa gave him an unvarnished account of her meeting with Lady Bowden, and if she had harbored any lingering doubts that he might have nurtured a spark of feeling for the other woman, they were utterly vanquished with his shout of genuine laughter ringing through the room.

''In the pond?'' he asked with delight. And at Melissa's nod, he added, ''Good! Serves the scheming little hussy right!''

And that, Melissa thought with satisfaction, is *that!* Something occurred to her suddenly, and she said, ''Oh, dear! There is Uncle Josh's party tomorrow night—I wonder how she will act when we meet.''

Dominic had been admiring the curve of his wife's bosom where it swelled above the low-cut bodice of her green satin gown, so he replied indifferently, ''Does it matter? I would far rather talk about us than the sodden Lady Bowden, wouldn't you?''

Melissa instantly agreed and they spent the remainder of the evening in complete harmony with each other. Not surprisingly, they retired early.

On Friday evening, however, as they were ushered into the handsomely furnished salon in the Manchester home, Melissa could not help but unobtrusively glance around to see if Deborah was present. There was no sign of the Englishwoman, although Latimer was there, deep in conversation with young Franklyn.

Dinner was a pleasant affair, and it was not until the ladies were comfortably situated in the salon again and the gentlemen had disappeared into Josh's study to play cards and follow masculine pursuits that Melissa learned of Deborah's hasty departure. She was sitting on a lovely Sheraton-style sofa upholstered in an elegant tapestry print of blue and gold, her aunt at her side, when Sally said softly, ''You know that Lady Bowden has left us?''

"Left us?" Melissa repeated casually. "What do you mean? I'm sure that I saw Mr. Latimer here tonight."

"Oh, yes," Sally said, "*he* is here, but his sister left for New Orleans . . . our sultry weather upset her delicate constitution and it was felt an immediate departure was necessary for her health. He explained everything to me when he arrived." A wistful look entered Sally's pale blue eyes. "I had hoped that Royce might find Lady Bowden attractive . . . it would have been so thrilling to have an actual member of the English aristocracy in the family. Of course," she murmured uncertainly, "there is the problem of our weather for her. . . ."

Melissa nearly choked on the cup of tea she had been sipping. Royce and Deborah! Oh, wait until I see him, she thought with unholy glee; how I shall tease him on his narrow escape!

Royce and Dominic, too, for that matter, would have appreciated being able to escape from tonight's gathering, each for his own reasons. Royce was eager to be on his way to New Orleans; upstairs in his room, his valise stood all packed and ready, the list for Jason even now burning a hole through the sole of his left silk stocking, where he had placed it for safekeeping. Until he turned those names over to Jason, Royce was determined to know precisely where that list was at all times, even if it meant wearing the damned thing! As for Dominic, his desire to be elsewhere this evening had nothing to do with the list. His love for Melissa and hers for him was so newly acknowledged and discovered that he objected strongly to anything that took her from his arms and prevented, even momentarily, their absorbing discovery of each other's thoughts and emotions. That he thoroughly enjoyed discovering all the sweet charms of her lovely body also had a great deal to do with his reluctant presence at the Manchester home.

But both men had resigned themselves to the evening ahead and had been visiting and talking with various friends and acquaintances when they became aware of the fact that Latimer and George Franklyn were playing for disturbingly high stakes at one of the small tables Josh had ordered set up for cards and gambling. It was Zachary who alerted them to the situation when he wandered over and joined them as they stood conversing amiably with a group of friends. Sipping his glass of Madeira, Zachary gave Dominic a speaking look and murmured, "It would appear that Latimer's luck has changed. He and Franklyn have been playing piquet for just a few *parties,* and already George has lost nearly seventeen thousand dollars to Latimer."

Royce and Dominic exchanged glances and, as inconspicuously as possible, gradually drifted over to the table. If Latimer was aware that he now had two pairs of suspicious eyes watching his every move, he gave no sign, but continued to play with ruthless intensity against the younger man.

Oddly enough, it was Franklyn himself who caught Latimer in the act of cheating. They had just begun to play a new round when Franklyn's hand suddenly shot across the small table, and gripping Latimer's right wrist, he cried triumphantly, "I thought so! I was not certain after the last *partie,* but this time I was watching very carefully." He gave Latimer's wrist a violent shake, and there was a shocked, angry gasp from the others in the room when a card fluttered to the table from Latimer's coat sleeve. Dominic found it rather fitting that it just happened to be a spade . . . the queen.

"No wonder you were able to claim carte blanche last hand!" Franklyn stated grimly, his young face set and dangerous. "How many more cards do you have hidden up your sleeve, you damned cheating bastard?"

An appalled silence fell over the room, every eye trained on Latimer. There was little that these hard-drinking, hot-tempered, neck-or-nothing gentlemen would not overlook in the character of one they admitted to their ranks, but to cheat at cards was tantamount to social suicide. Latimer was utterly ruined! He was finished here in Baton Rouge, and from the furious expressions of the gentlemen in the room, he would be lucky to escape without a sound thrashing. Only Dominic and Royce seemed unmoved by what had happened, both of them alert and waiting for Latimer's next move.

Completely disgraced, any chance of regaining the fortune he had lost to Dominic gone, Latimer was confronted by a bleak future in his remaining months in America. It was not just tonight's lamentable end that caused his face to whiten with rage and chagrin, but the certain knowledge that all up and down the Mississippi River word would travel that Julius Latimer was a cheat, a man not to be tolerated in polite circles, a man to be despised and shunned. He would no longer be of any use to Roxbury, and the unpleasant thought crossed his mind that Roxbury might not be willing to pay him the full price agreed upon. Latimer had no doubt that eventually his reputation would follow him to England, and instead of being eagerly welcomed into the homes of the wealthy and powerful, he would be treated like an outcast.

As the seconds passed and Franklyn and Latimer stayed frozen in their original positions, the threat of violence hung in the air. There were few things more despicable and abhorred than a man who cheated at cards, and there wasn't a gentleman staring at Latimer who didn't itch to lay his hands on him.

Clearly guilty, Latimer knew he was in a dangerous position, and glancing from one outraged, menacing face to another, he was aware of a trickle of fear coursing down his back. This was not sophisticated London, where gentlemen handled their differences with a rigid and prescribed set of rules, but the wilds of Louisiana, where men had been known to settle their disputes in a swift and brutal manner.

It took but a moment for these thoughts to flash through Latimer's mind and, fueled by a desperate wrath, he exploded into action, his free hand smashing into Franklyn's surprised face as he jerked his wrist out of the young man's slack grasp. In one blinding second he had reached into his jacket and pulled forth the small, deadly pistol he carried at all times.

His face contorted by fury, he snarled, "Stay back! The first man who takes a step forward will die!"

There had been a concerted surge forward by the gentlemen in the room when he had struck Franklyn, but at his words, everyone froze. Latimer smiled thinly, a feeling of power sweeping over him. "Not so brave now, are you?" he said sneeringly.

No one answered him, everyone sensing his dangerousness. And Latimer was dangerous. Very dangerous. He was a man who had nothing to lose. He was a ruined man, but more than that, he was a cruel, cowardly man; and as he stood there, his brain racing at a furious speed while he craftily considered a way to snatch victory out of defeat, his eyes landed on Dominic.

Maddened by sudden, blinding rage as he gazed upon the one man he blamed for his downfall, Latimer violently swung the pistol in Dominic's direction and fired. The sound of the pistol firing was thunderous and the smell of gunpowder filled the study.

Dominic had no chance to defend himself. There was a searing pain along his temple and then blackness descended as he crashed senseless to the floor.

Murder in his eyes, Royce leaped toward Latimer, but Latimer was ready for him, the pistol aimed squarely at Royce's chest. "I wouldn't if I were you," Latimer said coldly. "Now stand back, all of you!"

In impotent rage, Royce remained where he was, his gaze going apprehensively to Dominic's still body, a small pool of blood forming near the dark head. Pain and grief ripping through his heart, Royce fiercely willed his friend to move. His breath stopped when he saw the slight movement of one hand. Hope springing in his breast, he glanced quickly back at Latimer and snapped, "Well, what are you waiting for? Aren't you going to make good your escape—before we decide to rush you? After all," Royce said in a deadly tone, "you have only one more round left . . . and while you might kill one more of us, the others would be upon you."

This thought had already occurred to Latimer and, his eyes full of hatred, he slowly backed toward the door. He could not see Dominic's body from his position, but he was satisfied that if he had not killed him, he had at least gravely wounded him. Taking immense satisfaction in the knowledge that if Dominic were not dead, he would remember this night for a long time, Latimer bolted from the study.

Royce was in motion the moment Latimer disappeared, and rushing to Dominic's side, he knelt and had just put out a hand to touch him when Dominic rolled over and groaned, "Jesus Christ! I'm glad the bastard hasn't improved any since the last time he shot at me."

A few smiles and grins of relief met Dominic's words, but others, Royce and Zachary among them, still looked grim. Josh, his bluff features pale with anxiety, said, "Good God! He tried to shoot you down in cold blood! An unarmed man! He shot an unarmed man!" Then, struck by another thought, he added incredulously, "In my house! He shot an unarmed man in my *house!*"

There were murmurs of concern for Dominic as Royce helped him to his feet. Blood matted his dark head and ran down one cheek, but a swift examination by Royce revealed that the bullet had only creased Dominic along the side of his head.

Touching his wound gingerly, Dominic winced and asked with suspect mildness, "What happened after I hit the floor? All I remember is Latimer firing at me and then nothing until I heard a door slam."

"You didn't miss a great deal," Royce said dryly. "The slamming door was Latimer's departure not quite two minutes ago."

Dominic sent him a sharp glance. One eyebrow lifted, he drawled, "And no one has left to go after him yet?" An ugly notion suddenly bursting in his brain, he started forward, saying harshly, "Or made certain that the ladies are safe?"

"Good heavens!" Josh blurted out. "You don't think . . . ?"

A ripple of alarm traveled around the room and almost as one the gentlemen surged toward the door. Dominic's hand was on the knob when unexpectedly the door flew open, nearly knocking him down.

Her eyes round with horror, her usually serene features revealing strong agitation, Sally Manchester threw herself onto Josh's massive chest, sobbing, "Oh, Josh! It is terrible! That man! He has Melissa!"

Dominic needed no explanation about the identity of "that man," and heedless of his weakened state, he spun around to face Royce. "Pistols?"

Wordlessly Royce strode to his father's desk, pulled

open a bottom drawer and lifted out a fine mahogany case. The raised lid revealed two elegantly slim, exquisitely crafted dueling pistols.

The silence broken only by Sally's soft crying and Josh's rumbling murmurs of comfort, Royce and Dominic coolly and methodically loaded and primed the pistols. Royce glanced at Dominic's pale, bloodstained face and asked, "Are you up to this?"

Dominic flung him a vicious look. "She's my wife! What the hell do you think?"

His young face as pale as Dominic's, Zachary said half angrily, half pleadingly, "She's my sister! Let me go!"

Sighing, Dominic said dully, "I cannot. If anything were to happen to her . . ." His throat closed up and he could not go on.

Fighting to keep his fears from overpowering him, Dominic walked over to Sally and Josh. Very gently he said, "What happened? Where did they go?"

Dabbing at her tear-filled eyes, Sally replied in a quavering voice, "He just burst into the room, looking like a madman! I was so surprised—he always seemed like such a *nice* man!"

Resisting the urge to shake her, Dominic prodded, "What happened after he came into the room?"

"He took Melissa! He just marched right up to her and grabbed her arm. Said that he would hold her hostage. That he would kill her if anyone followed them. He put the awful pistol to her head and said that if we made a sound, he would shoot her dead in front of us! Then he started dragging her out of the room."

"How soon after they left did you come in search of us?" Royce asked intensely. "Did you see in which direction they went?"

"Oh, I didn't wait!" Sally said rather proudly. "Melissa was squirming and making things so difficult for him that I was able to slip out of the side door and come here instantly!"

Wild hope surged through Dominic and he demanded urgently, "Are you saying that they haven't left the house yet?"

"I shouldn't think so," Sally answered doubtfully.

"Melissa was fighting him every step of the way, so he is not able to move with any swiftness."

Dominic raced for the French doors that opened to the gallery which surrounded the house. "Royce, you take the hallway—I'll circle around the house and try to cut them off at the front. The rest of you stay here!"

Ignoring his pounding head, fear mingling with hope in his heart, Dominic sped out the French doors and ran desperately along the gallery at the side of the house to the front. He was dizzy with pain from his wound as he reached the corner of the building, but pain was forgotten when he spied Latimer and Melissa struggling at the top of the broad steps.

The heavy white columns which supported the gallery interfered with a clear shot, and clutching the dueling pistol more firmly in his hand, Dominic leaped from the gallery to the ground. Moving swiftly, he stepped away from the building, placing himself off to the side of Latimer, but in a position that gave him an unobstructed view of the man and woman at the top of the stairs.

"Latimer!" he called harshly. "Wouldn't you rather have another shot at *me?*"

Latimer froze, hardly able to believe his eyes and ears. Forgetting Melissa for a moment, he glared in Dominic's direction. It was almost inconceivable to him that it was truly Dominic standing on the ground below him, but as his gaze took in the blood which trickled slowly down Dominic's cheek, he realized that he had only wounded him.

In horror, Melissa stared at Dominic, fear for him momentarily driving every other thought from her mind. This was a nightmare! It did not seem real. Could it have been only minutes ago that she had been sitting comfortably in the salon, conversing with the young lady who was to become Daniel's bride? Mere moments ago that she had first heard the shocking sound of a shot reverberating through the house? Only minutes ago that Latimer had burst into the salon and, his face twisted in rage, had seized her brutally and attempted to take her away with him?

She had been so astonished that in those first moments she had not realized her danger, but when she had, she had instantly resolved not to go meekly and had struggled as stubbornly as she dared to escape from him. With a pistol pressed terrifyingly into her temple, she had been frightened to do much beyond dragging her feet and trying to throw off his hold on her arm. Once she had kicked him, but he had struck her savagely across the cheek and she had not known if she dared to anger him further.

And now, worse than any nightmare, was Dominic, his poor wounded face making her heart weep as he stood there risking his life for her. Latimer would kill him! She sensed this in the sudden coiling of his body. Could feel him loosening his grip on her arm. Felt the pistol leave her temple as he began to swing the weapon in Dominic's direction. . . .

Screaming a warning, Melissa viciously jabbed her elbow into Latimer's midriff. Her mind moving at blinding speed, she had known instinctively that Dominic would never risk a shot as long as there was a chance that she might be hit; and almost simultaneous with her jab at Latimer, she dropped to the ground, her bronze silken gown billowing around her, leaving Latimer standing there with no shield.

Dominic did not hesitate. His aim true and sure, he killed Latimer where he stood, a clean shot between the eyes. And then he was flinging aside the smoking pistol to leap up the steps, to gather his love close to his breast. . . .

That night, as they lay together in the quiet and privacy of their bedroom, Melissa said softly, "I wasn't really frightened until I saw you standing out there—then I was terrified!"

Dominic's arm tightened around her as he too remembered his awful fear for her, and he pulled her slender length nearer to him. "Don't dwell on it, sweetheart. It is over and done with and Latimer will bother us no more."

"What will happen to Deborah?" she asked.

Dominic shrugged. "Nothing. The Deborahs of the world can take care of themselves, and while I am sure that she will miss him, I am equally sure that it will be only a matter of time before she finds another man who will take care of her."

"I couldn't," Melissa said quietly, one hand trailing gently down the side of his face.

"Couldn't what?" he asked, surprised.

"Couldn't find someone else."

"I should hope not—at least not until a decent interval had passed," Dominic said with a laugh. Then he loomed up over her, his laughter gone, and muttered in a shaken voice, "I love you so, Lissa. If Latimer had—"

Her eyes soft and glowing, Melissa pressed a silencing finger to his lips. "Shh. We will not talk of it. We will talk only of our love for each other and our new home." In the darkness, she shot him a mischievous glance. "You are going to take me to Thousand Oaks someday, aren't you?"

"Yes!" Dominic said with mock fierceness, and kissing her teasingly at the corner of her mouth, he added, "But only after you have told me how much you love me. . . ."

Sighing blissfully, she put her arms around his neck. "Well, I love you more than Uncle Josh and Aunt Sally," she said innocently. "And I love you more than Zachary and Royce. And I think I love you even more than Folly."

"*Think* you love me more than a damned horse?" he asked dryly, his fingers moving caressingly through her tawny curls.

Melissa kissed him soundly. "I know I love you much more than Folly!"

"How much more?" he demanded huskily.

Her arms tightened around his neck. "Oh, so very much more," she breathed fervently. "So very, very, *very* much more. . . ."

Shirlee Busbee

million-copy bestselling author